MURDER BACKSTAGE

A JOSEPH HAYDN MYSTERY

NUPUR TUSTIN

Foiled Plots Press

Murder Backstage
A Joseph Haydn Mystery
Foiled Plots Press

ISBN 979-8-9863995-0-8

Typesetting services by BOOKOW.COM

Acknowledgments

A book about murder behind the scenes of an opera stage would be impossible to write without some knowledge of what goes on backstage. I'm especially grateful to Dr. Jeremy Gray of the Bampton Classical Opera in Oxfordshire for generously sharing many details of what goes on behind the scenes.

Dr. Gray also very kindly directed me to a copy of Haydn's *Le pescatrici*, the opera under production in this book. Thanks also to Dr. Gray's colleague, Gilly French.

This book was an especial delight to write—since much of the research involved watching Haydn, Gluck, and Mozart operas on DVD! Many thanks to my wonderful husband, Matt, whose gracious support of my passion makes these books possible.

Thanks also to my readers—in particular, the wonderful members of my ARC team. Your enthusiasm for my books keeps me going! God bless you all.

And last but not least, thank you to my Heavenly Father. You make all things possible; You grant us our dreams; and through You we fulfill our destiny!

Chapter One

A soft breeze wafted in through the open Music Room window. The only pleasant thing on this excessively trying day, Kapellmeister Joseph Haydn thought as he felt its gentle caress against his feverish brow.

The rehearsal was going just as badly as the Emperor must secretly have hoped it would when he had grudgingly agreed to the staging of Haydn's *Le pescatrici* in Vienna—the consent wrested from lips so unwilling, it would surely have been easier to wring water from a rock.

But the Empress had willed the performance, and Emperor Joseph—still merely a co-regent—had no power to thwart his mother's wishes. Nevertheless, His Majesty had managed to wedge in his oar with a stricture so absurd, Haydn was certain it was intended to mar the performance.

How could it not, he thought, listening with half an ear as the young soprano at his side blundered through her part. She was wholly inadequate, a woman with all the mannerisms of a prima donna and none of the skill. But Haydn was saddled with her, thanks to the Emperor.

"It would hardly be fair to our Viennese singers," His Majesty had observed, cold blue eyes resting on Haydn's employer, "were all the roles to go to your Hungarian troupe, Esterházy."

As though Prince Nikolaus Esterházy employed only Hungarian singers rather than the very finest Italian and German performers at his command. Although why their nationality should matter, Haydn failed to understand.

That, in all truth, it did not was evident from the virtuous smirk that had accompanied the Emperor's words.

"It is surely bad enough," the Emperor had continued, "that our instrumentalists will be deprived thanks to Haydn here"—His Majesty had indicated the Kapellmeister with a slight, stiff movement of his long fingers—"insisting on his motley group playing the music."

"But, Your Majesty, how could it be otherwise?" The Prince had ignored the aspersion cast on his orchestra—as superb a group as could be found anywhere in the vast empire the Habsburgs controlled. "It is, after all, Haydn's setting of the opera that we are to enjoy."

But in the interests of tact and much against his Kapellmeister's opinion on the subject, His Serene Highness had agreed to the Emperor's stipulation. The *dramma giocoso* would only feature singers from the Burgtheater where the opera was to be performed.

The last phrase of the aria sounded, and the singer's voice faded to a fortunate close.

Could the impresario of the Burgtheater who had furnished the wretched woman be persuaded to replace her? Haydn's mind busily turned over first one strategy, then another as his fingers moved with practiced ease over the keyboard.

But Giuseppe Affligio—relying upon the Emperor's word about the performers—had proven a remarkably hard nut to crack.

Had he not spent good money to hire the singer, Affligio, ever the businessman, had asked. Why then should he part with her?

"Herr Kapellmeister?" A sharply rising soprano intruded upon Haydn's wandering thoughts.

Haydn glanced up, suddenly aware that the orchestra had ceased to play. The singer standing on his left, by the fortepiano, pouted her displeasure at him. Her companion's shapely eyebrows were raised as well. And farther beyond, his Konzertmeister looked over his shoulder in mild surprise, bow poised expectantly over his violin.

What had he done to earn their disapprobation? Haydn swiveled to his right, seeking his brother's eyes. But even Johann stared at him.

Had his distracted state been quite so evident, the Kapellmeister wondered.

"Lesbina requires a response, brother," Johann reminded him.

Haydn stared at him blankly. Had he not sung the response?

"You played through Frisellino's part but omitted to sing it," his brother explained. He stood by the fortepiano, a blessedly calm albeit slight figure in the storm of what appeared to be a doomed production.

"*Ach so*," Haydn said, not recalling the omission at all. "If that is the case"—he offered a weary smile around the room—"I must apologize, ladies and gentlemen."

He listlessly turned the pages of the score back to the section that began Frisellino's response to his beloved, Lesbina. It was an opera he was proud of—the finest he had written thus far.

So well received in Eszterháza, Empress Maria Theresa herself had requested a second performance of it in the imperial capital. Yet, with singers such as these, who in Vienna would know it?

"It is no matter," Johann responded to the Kapellmeister's apology with a nod of encouragement at the waiting singers and musicians. "We can play through it again."

He turned once more to Haydn, a sympathetic smile on his face.

There was a difference of eleven years between them, yet Johann, with a wisdom far beyond his years, had no doubt divined the true state of Haydn's mind.

The Kapellmeister returned his brother's smile gratefully. The grace Johann never failed to demonstrate in troublesome situations helped to bolster his sagging spirits.

He dutifully sang the response, forcing himself to muster the necessary enthusiasm for the part. They were rehearsing the finale that concluded the second act of the opera—a quartetto sung by the fisher-women, Lesbina and Nerina, and their respective lovers, Frisellino and Burlotto.

Johann had taken the part of Burlotto to Matilda Bologna's Nerina, a singer so versatile she could easily have sung all three female roles in the *dramma giocoso*.

Would that she could, Haydn thought, his spirits flagging again as Fräulein's Bologna's colleague joined her voice to his own.

Loretta Renier had a weak voice, shaky in the upper ranges. Squeaky too, Haydn thought, wincing as Fräulein Renier struggled to reach a high note, sounding as pleasant as a door swinging on a rusty hinge.

God have mercy! What was a man to do with a singer such as this? He stopped playing.

"The part may be too high for you, Fräulein," he suggested.

"Much too high," Johann readily agreed. He turned to Haydn. "May she not be better suited to Eurilda, brother?"

Or the chorus, Haydn thought wistfully, where Loretta Renier's awful voice might be drowned amongst louder and more tuneful ones. But the Emperor had insisted that Loretta be given one of the principal parts. There was no consigning the woman to a minor role.

"Eurilda might be a better choice," Haydn conceded unhappily. The melodic lines for the role were simple with few leaps and the entire part could be brought down an octave to accommodate Fräulein Renier's limited range. Yet the part required a richness of tone and depth that Loretta Renier clearly lacked.

He turned the pages of the score, glancing at Fraulein Renier as he did so. "Shall we try Eurilda's *Questa Mano*, Fräulein, to see if it would better suit your voice?"

Loretta Renier pouted her pretty pink lips.

"I would rather be Lesbina, Herr Kapellmeister," she announced. "Eurilda has no coloratura at all. And her arias might just as well be recitatives for all the melody they receive."

"It is precisely the role's lack of coloratura that is a blessing, Fräulein," Haydn uttered through clenched teeth. It was only when he heard Matilda Bologna's quickly suppressed gasp of amusement, and saw out of the corner of his eyes the way her hand flew to her mouth to contain her mirth, that he realized he may have gone too far.

Loretta Renier was not a woman to brook criticism of any kind.

Her blue eyes flashed dangerously. "I can perform coloratura as well as any singer in the Empire, Herr Kapellmeister. The Emperor will tell you so."

Haydn had no doubt that he would. Rumor had it, Fräulein Renier was the latest in a long line of mistresses. Nevertheless, he wished he had stayed his temper. It would not bode well for him were the woman to take her complaints to the Emperor.

"Your coloratura, madam," he began only to be interrupted by his brother.

"Is too good, I am afraid." Johann smiled regretfully. "As a rustic character with pretensions to nobility, Lesbina's coloratura must be convincingly unconvincing, madam. Who would believe that of your performance?"

Loretta Renier gaped. Then the uncertain smile on her lips stretched into a delighted simper. She tossed her head, brushing one small hand carelessly against her dark locks. "It is true. I can only give of my best —even when the role requires poor singing. I simply cannot do it."

"Precisely, Fräulein." Haydn valiantly ignored Matilda Bologna's choked sputter of amusement and smiled gratefully at his brother. Johann's tact had yet again saved them from a contentious situation.

But how many more such moments would he be forced to endure?

⸺◆◆◆⸺

Rosalie—Principal Maid to the Esterházy Musicians—gazed at the letters. The mailbag had brought her two that morning. One from her mother in Rohrau. The other from—

"Begging your pardon, Frau Heindl?"

Rosalie heard the voice behind her, but the words didn't immediately register.

She was standing within a sheltered alcove in the vast entrance hallway of the Esterházy Palace, sorting through the stack of letters the mail coach had just delivered for the musicians and the maids who attended to them.

There was a thick stack, as always, for Herr Haydn, a few for Master Luigi, the Konzertmeister, and a pile of envelopes for the musicians.

From their wives, no doubt, who weren't allowed to accompany their spouses—a hardship Rosalie, now a married woman, could sympathize with. She and Gerhard had been married for barely six months, but here she was in Vienna without him.

Still, Gerhard, a wine merchant who supplied the Esterházy wine cellars, had occasion to make the half-day trip from Eisenstadt at least once every ten days. And if Rosalie wasn't mistaken, one of the two letters the mailbag had brought her that morning was from her husband. It was postmarked from Eisenstadt.

She gazed at the letter, running a loving finger over her new name. Rosalie Heindl.

Frau Heindl. Dear God! Someone had been calling *her.*

"Frau Heindl?" The voice behind her grew a little louder, and she felt a sharp tug on her arm. "Frau Heindl?"

Hastily tucking the letters into her apron pocket, she spun around.

"I'm sorry, Frida," she said to the wide-eyed young maid staring at her. "I didn't mean to ignore you."

She had been Rosalie Szabó for so long, thinking of herself as Rosalie Heindl—much less Frau Heindl—would take some getting used to.

"Is something wrong?" Rosalie smiled encouragingly at the maid. The poor thing—a palace maid for no more than a month—looked positively panic-stricken.

"I'm truly sorry to disturb you, Frau Heindl. But the Officer's Mess isn't clean yet, and the footmen want to carry the tables and benches back to their place. I don't know what to do."

"*Ach so.*" Scrubbing the floor in the Officer's Mess had always been a notoriously difficult job and the footmen, eager to be done with the task of hauling the furniture back into position, were always trying to rush the maids.

It was the one chore Rosalie was thankful to be relieved of in her new position as Principal Maid to the Musicians—a title Herr Haydn had persuaded His Serene Highness to create so that she could continue working.

The greater responsibility and respect the position accorded her—not to mention the significant rise in pay—had gone a long way toward overcoming Gerhard's objections to her continuing to work for the wealthy Hungarian magnate.

But Rosalie had been reluctant to accept the position at first. Her closest friend Greta had worked at the palace far longer than she had. Any promotion rightfully belonged to Greta. Herr Haydn had found a solution for this problem as well. He'd discreetly suggested that the responsibilities of the new title might be great enough to require the appointment of two women—herself and Greta.

"Did you scrub the floor with bile soap as I suggested?" Rosalie asked Frida as they walked down the hallway toward the Officer's Mess.

"Yes." Frida bobbed her head eagerly. "And the grease stains are gone. But the smell of stale food still remains. Even though I've thrown open all the windows."

Rosalie wrinkled her nose as they crossed the threshold into the Mess. Frida was right. The smell of food was heavy and overpowering.

"What should I do?" Frida asked again.

"Rub some fragrant green herbs into the floor," Rosalie replied. "That should do the trick." It was a remedy her mother-in-law had shared with her. A mixture of mint, fennel, and tansy spread onto a clean floor and rubbed into it with a broom would quickly rid any room of its stale, musty odors.

Leaving Frida to her task, Rosalie returned to the hallway. It had been a good half hour since the mail coach had arrived and Herr Haydn was no doubt eagerly awaiting his mail—especially his copy of the *Wienerisches Diarium,* the court newspaper.

Letters neatly arranged, she was about to pick up the silver salver when the loud rumble of carriage wheels and thundering hooves assailed her ears.

Moments later, the double doors at the entrance swung open and her employer, Prince Nikolaus Esterházy, swept into the hallway, coattails flying behind him and silver-topped cane swinging as he strode past her.

His Serene Highness had just reached the staircase when he spun around, his sharp eyes searching the empty hallway before alighting upon her.

The stormy expression on the Prince's features struck Rosalie like a blow from a heavy hammer. Unable to help herself, she pressed her salver to her midriff and shrank back against the wall.

Chapter Two

Bᴜᴛ the Prince's displeasure was fortunately not directed at her.
"Haydn!" The Kapellemeister's name burst out of His Serene Highness's mouth like a single staccato shot from a hunting rifle. "Is he within?"

"I-in the Music Room," Rosalie said, so startled, her heart still pounded within her breast. "Rehearsing with Fräuleins Bologna and Renier."

Rosalie lifted her salver with its stack of letters, about to offer to take up a message since she was destined for the Music Room, but the Prince had already whipped around. His bulky frame ascended the staircase with a speed unbecoming to both his girth and his status.

Whatever was the matter, Rosalie wondered. She had never seen the Prince so agitated.

The question was still ringing in her head when a softly voiced enquiry near her ear caused her to jump yet again.

"Is Herr Haydn in trouble, do you suppose?"

"Dear God, Greta!" Rosalie clutched her chest as she turned toward her friend. "Must you creep up on one like a ghost?"

Greta waved the complaint aside, the empty basket she carried nearly sliding off her plump wrist. "What could have put His Serene Highness in such a tizzy?" she wondered, tilting her head to one side and tapping a plump forefinger against the corner of her mouth. "I saw him jump out of his carriage before his coachman could even climb down to open the carriage door for him."

Rosalie nodded, unsurprised.

His Serene Highness had also been in too much of a hurry to allow a footman to let him in and take his coat, hat, and cane.

"The matter, whatever it is, must be urgent," she said. "He didn't even bother to call for a footman to fetch Herr Haydn." She twisted around to look at Greta. "His Serene Highness bolted up himself."

The behavior was quite out of character for their employer. In all the years they'd worked at the palace, neither she nor Greta had ever seen the Prince—or the Princess, for that matter—so overcome as to forget there were servants to do their bidding.

"They'd better not make a habit of it," Greta remarked ominously. "At this rate, they won't need any servants to fetch and carry for them."

"But you have letters to deliver, I see." She grinned, tipping her chin at the salver. "Shall I come up with you? The wine for the musicians' afternoon meal"—she swung her basket up as she spoke—"can wait."

Rosalie suppressed a smile. She knew what her friend was getting at. Taking the letters up would serve as a convenient excuse to see and hear what the fuss was all about. Curious to the point of being nosy, Greta had no compunctions about standing outside doors and listening in on conversations that piqued her interest.

"How else would we know what's going on?" she often said in her own defense. "It's not like anyone tells us anything. For all that we have new titles, we're still a couple of obscure palace maids who serve the musicians."

"Well?" Greta now demanded. She poked eagerly through the letters on the salver. "Here is the court newspaper, too, and we all know how anxiously Herr Haydn awaits his copy."

Rosalie was about to concede the point when the headline on the *Wienerisches Diarium* caught her eye.

"*Tragedy at the Burgtheater*?" She read the headline out loud. "Good heavens, what could've happened? Did Karl say anything about it?"

Her startled violet eyes sought out her friend's bright blue ones. Surely, if anything untoward had happened at the theater, Greta would be the first to know. Her young man worked there after all.

"Why, Greta, whatever is the matter?"

To Rosalie's shock, Greta's face had turned pale and her plump lips were pursed.

"We should read that before you take it up to Herr Haydn, Rosalie. Karl didn't meet me yesterday. I thought he might be busy. But what if . . ."

Greta pressed her lips together, clearly unwilling to voice any unwelcome thoughts.

———◆◆◆———

Prince Nikolaus settled himself against the gold-upholstered backrest of his armchair, his fingers interlaced over his richly embroidered waistcoat. He had omitted to take off his coat. And his hat—a three-cornered affair the same shade of blue as his coat—still sat perched upon his head.

"I bear ill news, I fear, Haydn. Giuseppe Affligio has been struck down."

"Struck down?" Haydn repeated, at a loss to understand His Serene Highness's words.

The Prince's interruption of their rehearsal had come at a most opportune time. At the exact moment, in fact, that Loretta Renier had been laboring through *Questa Mano*—blithely murdering its rich melody, if one were being honest. And Haydn had been on the verge of bluntly uttering the fact.

He had just finished explaining for the third time how to vary the tone on repeated notes—"Yes, but you have your fingers to strike the keys," Loretta Renier had argued. "With what am I to strike my vocal cords?" —when a brusque knock had startled the entire room.

Before Haydn could respond, the door had been thrust open and Prince Nikolaus had swept in, barely acknowledging either the orchestra or the two singers.

"Haydn! A moment of your time. In my chamber, immediately, if you will."

Struck down! Haydn was still trying to grasp the Prince's words. How had the impresario of the Burgtheater been struck down? With what? An image flashed through his mind of a bolt from the heavens smiting Giuseppe Affligio. But, of course, lightning could not have been responsible.

"Dead," The Prince clarified, brushing the air impatiently with his hand as though that particular fact carried little significance.

"Dead?" Haydn's eyebrows shot up. "He was in perfect health but a few days ago."

Haydn had rushed to the Burgtheater two afternoons ago in search of Herr Affligio. There he had asked for—and been refused—a singer to replace the impossible Loretta Renier.

"My dear Herr Haydn"—Affligio, a portly, middle-aged man, had smiled indulgently at him, looking like a father chiding a recalcitrant toddler— "in such cases, it is the music that must be changed. Not the singer."

Now the man was dead! An untimely death, given the sudden nature of it. Most likely not from natural causes given the excellent state of his health.

That meant it would have to be investigated. But surely the Prince couldn't expect him to drop everything in order to do so!

"I am afraid I cannot—" Haydn began.

"But you must, Haydn," Prince Nikolaus interrupted him.

A patch of bright sunlight brightened the green door of the Esterházy wine cellar on the Haarhof. Wanting to read the newspaper article in private, Rosalie had accompanied Greta out to the narrow alley that ran alongside the palace—between Wallnerstrasse and Naglergasse.

"God forbid, it should be some awful accident backstage!" Greta set her basket on the raised step in front of the cellar door. "If the ropes were to fail—which they've been known to do—and one of those heavy sandbags landed on someone's head . . ." She shuddered.

"I know," Rosalie said. "Karl would lose his job. Let us hope it's nothing as bad as that." She leaned against the door and held the newspaper aloft. A cool breeze ruffled her hair, playfully batting against the sheets and pushing them into her chest. Impatiently, she thrust the sheets out again and located the article.

"What does it say?" Greta peered over her shoulder.

We are greatly grieved to inform the public, the article began in a ponderous manner, *of a terrible tragedy that has befallen the Burgtheater.*

"A fire, do you suppose?" Greta asked as she silently moved her lips, reading the words.

"I doubt it." Rosalie pointed to the next line. "No fire, however fierce, could reach as far as the city gates."

Greta read the words.

The effects of the unfortunate incident are far-reaching and affect the Theater am Kärntnertor as well.

"No, I suppose not," she agreed. "That's a relief."

The Kärntnertortheater, situated near the Carinthian Gate, one of the four gates leading into Vienna, was a full two-and-a-half miles from the Burgtheater on the Michaelerplatz. A fire raging in the city center would hardly spread to the outskirts of the city.

"Besides, Karl can scarcely be held responsible for any incident that involves both theaters," Greta continued. Her natural curiosity seemed to have returned, for she went on: "Although I can't think of anything that could affect both places, can you?"

"It seems to be a death," Rosalie replied, reading the next line. "*The public will be saddened to learn that a most honorable personage associated with both theaters is no more.*"

"Must be one of the singers," Greta remarked. "God knows, some of them are old enough to be halfway to their grave." Her features brightened. "Well, they can hardly blame Karl for that."

As a stagehand, Greta's sweetheart, Karl Schulze, could be faulted for accidents with the ropes and sandbags used for the theater's rigging or a fire caused by the candles that illuminated the stage. But if an aging singer had met their Maker, that was surely nothing to do with Karl.

Rosalie was about to agree when her gaze fell on the next section.

We regret to report the death was neither due to natural causes nor due to any sudden or prolonged illness. It was—dear reader, we pray you are seated —nothing less than murder!

"Dear God," Rosalie breathed out the words in a hushed whisper. "The poor soul was murdered."

"Murder!" Greta squealed, tugging the newspaper toward her. "Where does it say that? Why would anyone murder a singer? Whoever it is must be quite important. I've rarely seen the Prince in such a pother. Do you think they want Herr Haydn to look into the matter?"

"They must." There was seldom a crime in their vicinity that the Kapellmeister wasn't called upon to investigate. "But it wasn't a singer who was murdered," Rosalie added quietly. "It was the impresario himself. Look!"

Giuseppe Affligio, the gentleman in question, was found stabbed to death in the small private chambers he occupied beneath the stage of the Burgtheater.

"No one knew about Herr Affligio's chambers down there, Rosalie." Greta's face had turned pale and her plump fingers closed tightly around Rosalie's wrist. "No one save those who worked with him."

Rosalie nodded. "That's exactly what the article says." She read the passage out loud.

"The location of Herr Affligio's quarters below stage was known to few people beyond the employees of the Burgtheater. Members of the general public could meet the great impresario only by appointment in a small office adjoining the ticket booth outside the auditorium.

"Therefore, it is speculated the killer was someone known to the unfortunate gentleman."

"Oh, Rosalie!" Greta wailed. "They will blame Karl for it. For all we know, they already have. He must be in jail by now. I should've known something was wrong when he didn't keep our appointment yesterday."

Chapter Three

Rosalie put an affectionate arm around her friend's shoulders and drew her closer.

"Now, why would they do that, silly? He isn't the only person who knows where Herr Affligio's private chambers are. It could be any of the singers. Or the stagehands. Or anyone who ever took a message to the man. Good heavens, they could just as easily suspect one of us."

She and Greta had often had occasion to carry messages to the impresario. Why, that was how Greta had made Karl's acquaintance. Rosalie was about to point this out when Greta shook her head.

"You don't understand, Rosalie." The color had drained completely out of Greta's cheeks, leaving her unnaturally white and deflated. "When it's a question of murder, the police guards look no further than the person closest to the poor soul who's lost his life."

"Nonsense!" Rosalie scolded. "Wherever did you get a notion like that?"

There'd be few murder cases solved if the police guards held to such ridiculous ideas.

"From Karl's cousin, who is a police guard," Greta said, her head jerking up defiantly. "Franz says when it's murder, you can be sure it's the person closest to the victim who's responsible. Men kill their wives, the son his parents, and the servant sets upon his master.

"And Karl was very close to Herr Affligio, Rosalie. His right-hand man, a fact everyone was aware of."

That was because Karl was invariably involved in any dealings one had with the impresario. He was indispensable to the running of the theater, although Herr Affligio received most of the credit for his hard work.

It was hard to imagine anyone content to remain in that situation. Not that Karl had ever seemed bitter. Still, every worm turns. Karl, goaded beyond measure, might have as well. But Rosalie kept that opinion to herself.

"All the more reason not to suspect him of murder, then," she assured her friend instead. "An assistant the impresario trusted so greatly—how could anyone think him guilty of such an awful crime?"

"An assistant well aware of Herr Affligio's every move," Greta replied gloomily. "And with the knowledge to catch him by surprise. That's what the Police Inspector will say." She looked at Rosalie, a determined glint in her eye. "We shall have to let Herr Haydn know—"

"Greta!"

The deep voice calling out her name startled them both.

———◦◦◦———

"The incident, Haydn, is tragic," Prince Nikolaus said, his voice firm, "but, at the end of the day, a mere trifle. The opera must continue."

"I-I could not agree more," Haydn stammered, astonished and relieved at the same time. The worst appeared to be over. No one expected him to look into Affligio's demise. In fact, the Prince's nonchalant reaction suggested a natural death.

There would be some slight inconvenience, the Kapellmeister had no doubt. It would mean meeting and coordinating with a new impresario. But the new man could hardly be more difficult to deal with than Affligio.

"Has His Majesty given any thought as to who will replace Herr Affligio?" he asked.

The Prince's lips tightened. "That is just it, Haydn. There will be no replacement."

"No replacement? How, then, does His Majesty expect the opera to continue?"

In addition to providing a suitable libretto and singers, the impresario was expected to arrange for costumes and scenery and to take charge of illuminating the theater. It was a vast undertaking, and for all that he had been a difficult person, Affligio had handled the technical details immensely well.

It was the one aspect of the performance that had caused Haydn no concern. The stage machinery, lighting, and scenery would be as spectacular as that in Eszterháza.

The Prince's eyes narrowed. "Continue it will, Haydn. It must. I have offered to take care of it myself."

"Yourself?" Haydn repeated, feeling like an echo. His mind boggled at the thought of the Prince taking himself backstage to direct stagehands and crew.

"We have staged many an opera, Haydn. And what impresario have we had to help us?"

That was true enough, although Eszterháza had both an opera director and a stage and costume designer to bring their productions to life.

"Your Serene Highness means to send for Herr Porta?" Haydn's hopes began to rise. With Nunziato Porta at his side and Pietro Travaglio and, who knew, a soprano or two that might also be smuggled in. Why, the opera could be an astounding success!

"Porta is on a leave of absence. As is Travaglio. I cannot send for either of them."

"On leave? But why?" Haydn blurted out the question, the impropriety of it escaping him until the words had already fallen off his tongue.

But the Prince fortunately took no offense. "There was no reason not to. It will be a month or more before we return to Eszterháza."

"Then"—Haydn passed a handkerchief over his forehead, mystified —"who is to take on Herr Affligio's job?" They could do without a stage and costume designer. But a director—in particular one as well-versed in the technical aspects of opera production as Porta—was a necessity.

"Why, you are, Haydn. Who else is there to do the job?

"Besides"—the Prince placed his palms flat on his thighs and smiled genially—"much of the work has already been done. The singers have been engaged. We have a libretto, the music is composed. You have merely to ensure the scenic flats are appropriately painted and provide for the costumes."

⚬

Haydn staggered into the Music Room, his mind reeling. He had protested his ignorance of matters pertaining to the stage, only to have

His Serene Highness immediately send for a leather-bound volume from his library, which he had thrust at the Kapellmeister.

"I trust this will suffice, Haydn. It is as thorough a manual on the subject as you could wish. There is nothing Motta does not cover."

With that airy remark—and a copy of *The Theatrical Writings of Fabrizzio Carini Motta*— the Kapellmeister had been sent on his way.

Haydn had leafed through the book, peering at page after page of diagrams, none of which matched their descriptions in Motta's text. Motta had discussed at great length the placement of boxes on either side of the stage, the depth of the stage itself, the width of the proscenium, and the relation of both to other lengths and widths in the theater.

But the Burgtheater's dimensions were already set, its horseshoe shape unable to be changed. Was he expected to modify the stage to compensate for the differences? And how would one do it? With the placement of the wings and backdrops?

Good God, what composer had ever been expected to manage such things?

There were lengthy discourses on the use of pulleys and winches and hoists—not a word of which had made much sense to the poor Kapellmeister.

Drawing a clean linen handkerchief out of his livery pocket, he passed the soft fabric over his brow.

"It would take a veritable genius," he muttered to himself, oblivious to the musicians and the singers in the Music Room, "to comprehend Motta's plans, much less execute them."

"What is the matter, brother?" Johann's slight figure drew closer, his gray eyes wide with concern.

The music had stopped. The two singers, the entire orchestra, and his Konzertmeister, Luigi Tomasini, gazed upon Haydn expectantly.

"It is Affligio, I suppose," Luigi guessed.

Haydn nodded, too overwhelmed to speak.

"He refuses to hire another soprano, does he not?" The Konzertmeister lowered his violin and bow and turned to face Haydn. "And rather than settle the dispute himself like a man, seeks like a coward to involve the Prince in the matter?"

It was a reasonable surmise. The impresario had been a source of constant trouble in the matter of singers. Three good sopranos were needed for the opera, but only two—one of them barely passable—had been made available to Haydn. As for the third, Affligio had been adamant that Haydn should content himself with a contralto.

"No, that is not the trouble," Haydn corrected his Konzertmeister.

"Not Affligio, brother?" Johann looked confused. "I thought you indicated that it was."

"It is Affligio," Haydn said, passing the handkerchief over his brow again. "He seems to have chosen this precise moment to meet his Maker."

Luigi's jaw dropped open and even Johann—normally imperturbable —gaped at Haydn in stunned disbelief.

"You cannot mean the man is dead?" Johann's eyes widened as Haydn nodded.

"Dead!" Fräulein Bologna gasped at the same time, her voice ascending to its highest range. "How can that be?"

Even Loretta Renier glanced up from the small mirror in which she had been admiring her features. The color, Haydn noticed, had fled from her cheeks.

"You must be mistaken, Herr Kapellmeister." A small frown marked her forehead.

Haydn shook his head. "I wish that were the case. But I am afraid he is gone."

"And His Serene Highness wishes you to examine the matter, no doubt," Luigi said.

The crease in Loretta Renier's smooth, white brow deepened.

"Why should His Serene Highness wish any such thing?" she demanded, looking, if anything, paler than before.

Her beautiful blue eyes moved sharply from Luigi's handsome features to Haydn's more homely, pockmarked face.

"If Herr Affligio has taken ill and unfortunately met his demise—"

"Nonsense!" Fräulein Bologna was quick to dismiss her colleague's assumption. "How could the poor man have taken ill all of a sudden? He was in good spirits but two nights ago."

"Perhaps he ingested something that disagreed with him, then," Fräulein Renier persisted. "An unfortunate incident, a mischance. Why should anyone be expected to look into it? And why, of all people, should it be Herr Haydn?"

Luigi grinned. "Because Haydn is cursed with an unusual perspicacity when it comes to such matters. The Empress herself is aware of it. If Affligio's killer is to be caught, then our Joseph is the man to do it."

Loretta Renier's lips pressed into a thin line. "Well, I don't believe anyone killed Herr Affligio." She drew her shoulders back and met Haydn's gaze squarely.

"You'll find we were all too dependent upon him to want him dead."

The singer's uncalled-for belligerence took Haydn aback. Loretta Renier could not have acted more put out if he had openly accused her of being a murderess.

Luigi opened his mouth to respond to the singer; but the altercation was making Haydn's head throb, and he determined to put a stop to it.

"I am inclined to agree with you, Fräulein," he addressed his remarks to the soprano before turning to his brother and Luigi. "Nothing His Serene Highness said induces me to believe the gentleman was killed. It must have been a natural death, however untimely. Or an unfortunate accident."

"Then why did the Prince ask to see you, Joseph?" Luigi pressed him.

For the third time, Haydn passed his handkerchief over his face. "Because he wishes me to take over Herr Affligio's job. Temporarily," he hastened to add. It was the only saving grace in the entire situation.

Even so, it was hard not to be bitter about his fate.

"I am to see to costumes and scenery, and God alone knows what else."

Chapter Four

"GRETA!" A burly young man with brownish-red hair and a short beard entered the alley and hurried toward the maids. "I was just coming to see you, and to apologize—"

"Oh, Karl!" Greta rushed to the newcomer and threw her arms around him. "Thank heavens, you're safe!"

Rosalie held back, uncertain whether to stay or leave. Greta would want to be alone with her Karl, no doubt. Was there any point standing around like a third boot?

She was on the point of leaving when Karl drew back, holding Greta at arm's length. He looked from the plump, blonde girl to Rosalie and then back again, clearly mystified by their concern.

"Of course, I'm safe. Why wouldn't I be?"

"But how could you be?" Greta twisted around to face Rosalie, her plump face wreathed in confusion. She beckoned her friend forward. "We've just heard the news."

"About poor Herr Affligio," Rosalie explained, holding the newspaper up.

"And you thought"—an indulgent smile spread over Karl's broad features as he gazed fondly down at Greta—"that there was a killer on the loose, murdering everyone in sight? Silly Greta, how you let your imagination run away with you! It should be you writing librettos, not I."

He enfolded Greta into his arms again, still smiling.

"But Franz said," Greta protested, "that when someone is killed—"

Karl pulled back before she could finish the sentence and frowned down at her. "And you thought I might have killed Herr Affligio?"

His astonishment was understandable. Truth to tell, there was no one less likely to harm the impresario than his assistant and stagehand, Karl Elias Schulze. Karl had aspirations of becoming a librettist. And for all his faults, Herr Affligio had not hesitated to encourage Karl in his ambitions—even to the point of promising to bring his most recent libretto to the stage.

No, Karl was unlikely to have murdered the impresario.

"I didn't think you'd killed him," Greta faltered as Karl's frown deepened. "But . . ."

"But your cousin's words convinced Greta that you might be under suspicion," Rosalie interjected. "Naturally, she was worried. Greta must have misunderstood Franz," she added hastily. "It seems such a foolish notion for a police guard to hold to, doesn't it?"

Karl shook his head, although the frown still creased his forehead.

"No. It is what Franz always says. When a man is murdered, look to his closest friends. But"—he looked down at Greta again, his chocolate-brown eyes softening—"it's not like the police guards disregard a man's enemies either. And in Herr Affligio's case, there was certainly one who wanted him dead."

"Who?" Greta wanted to know. "One of the singers?"

"No, a musician—a visitor to Vienna from Salzburg. He's been haunting the Burgtheater for months. I'll be glad to see the last of him." Karl's mild features wore a look of extreme aggravation. "A more annoying, abrasive character, you'll never find."

"Have the guards taken him prisoner?" Rosalie asked. If the man had been apprehended, it would save the Kapellmeister the trouble of looking into the matter. Better still, she wouldn't have to reassure Gerhard that she was safe in Vienna.

There was no keeping the news from her husband. And once he heard there'd been a murder, Rosalie wouldn't put it past Gerhard to insist she return to Eisenstadt—contract or no contract.

"That they have," Karl assured her. "Franz says they hauled him away just this morning."

Rosalie caught the sidelong, knowing look Greta was giving her. Her friend clearly wanted to spend time alone with Karl.

"I should take the news to Herr Haydn—along with his letters," she told Karl. "He'll be relieved to hear the killer has been caught."

Greta beamed gratefully at her. "That he will—now that he can carry on with his rehearsals without having to worry about catching a killer."

She turned to Karl. "The opera opens in a few weeks, but just this morning I heard Master Johann complaining to Master Luigi that the singing roles have yet to be assigned." Greta rolled her eyes. "Can you imagine?"

Rosalie was about to leave, but Karl's grave features and his words stayed her steps.

"I wouldn't be too sure of the fate of that opera. With Herr Affligio dead and no one to replace him, there's no telling how long the Burgtheater will remain open. Without an impresario to oversee the production, how can any work be brought to the stage?"

Rosalie swiveled around to face him. "But surely the Emperor will appoint a new impresario to take Herr Affligio's place? How could he not?"

But Karl just shook his head, hugging Greta closer to himself. "His Majesty will avoid replacing Herr Affligio for as long as he can. He detests the idea of anything that concerns spending money."

Greta clutched his arm. "But what of your libretto, then? Who will bring it to the stage?"

Herr Affligio had gone so far as to say a suitable composer had been found to set the words to music.

Karl smiled ruefully. "That, my dumpling, is the least of my concerns. I may soon be out of a job. We all might—the stagehands, the carpenters, the painters. Even the singers. Without Herr Affligio, who will see to it that we get paid? God knows, it won't be the Emperor. He does his best to avoid seeing to such things."

Rosalie saw Greta wince as Karl gripped her harder. "I know not what I will do, little dumpling. Or how long I can remain in Vienna." His features darkened. "Dear God, I wish the Salzburger had found a better way to settle his dispute."

There was nothing for it but to set out for the Burgtheater. Haydn stuffed a copy of the libretto—meticulously marked with the sets and props needed for each scene—into his leather case.

"I know not whether Affligio has already arranged for the fabrication and painting of the sets," he said to Luigi and Johann, who waited with him. The singers had already left and the orchestra had been dismissed for the day. "It never occurred to me to speak to him of such matters."

And now the man was dead. How fickle life was! So liable to change at a moment's notice. It was but two days ago that the impresario had been alive and well.

"It is not your fault, brother," Johann attempted to console him. "Who could have known we would find ourselves in this predicament?"

Who indeed? Haydn thought unhappily, turning around to see his Konzertmeister stroking the short tuft of beard on his chin.

"The impresario is also responsible for engaging singers, is he not, Joseph?"

Haydn nodded. He was about to say it was the one task that did not require his attention when the import of Luigi's words sank in. *Ach so!* His eyes widened in delighted surprise and his lips stretched into a pleased smile.

"If a third soprano is needed"—the Kapellmeister looked eagerly from Luigi to his younger brother—"who is to say I may not hire one? There may be a silver lining in this cloud of trouble after all."

Johann smiled back. "Let us pray there is enough money left in Affligio's budget for that purpose, then. If there is, I shall set about looking for a suitable singer immediately. Or we may send for one of our sopranos from Eszterháza."

It occurred to the Kapellmeister that the Emperor—parsimonious to a fault—might have some objection to make on the subject, but he did not let the thought trouble him.

The smile was still on his lips as he tucked the leather case under his arm when a sharp rat-a-tat on the Music Room door startled them. He had barely responded when Greta pushed her way in followed by Rosalie, carrying a silver tray laden with envelopes.

"That will have to wait, I am afraid," the Kapellmeister informed the maids with a rueful smile. "Is the carriage available? I must set out immediately."

"To the Burgtheater," Johann explained when the maids made no attempt to leave. Greta stood rooted to the carpet with her mouth hanging open and Rosalie still clung to her salver instead of setting it upon the fortepiano.

***

"The opera is to go on, then?" Greta finally found her tongue. Rosalie was equally at a loss. From what Karl had said, it was only a matter of time before the Burgtheater closed down. Who was there to run it without the impresario?

"Why would it not?" Master Luigi's eyebrows rose.

But who was to take Herr Affligio's place? Rosalie placed her silver salver on the fortepiano, although she retained her hold on it.

"But Herr Affligio—" she began only to be interrupted.

"Has met his Maker," Master Luigi said. "Yes—"

"Has been murdered," Greta put in, her voice intertwining with the Konzertmeister's.

"—we know—" Master Luigi's voice cut off, lurching to a halt as abruptly as a carriage hitting a rut in the road. His eyes narrowed. "What did you say?"

Rosalie exchanged a glance with Greta. Was the Konzertmeister really unaware of the manner of the impresario's death? Her puzzled eyes moved toward the Kapellmeister, whose cheerful smile had faded.

"Murdered?" Master Johann murmured in a low voice. "I thought the Prince indicated the death was entirely of natural causes, brother?

***

"As did I." Haydn searched the maids' features for an explanation. How had two maids, restricted to the confines of the palace, come by the awful news?

"He was discovered in his chambers at dawn yesterday," Rosalie volunteered. "Stabbed to death."

"How could you possibly know that to be the case?" It was unlike Rosalie, Haydn knew, to concoct sensational stories. But if Affligio had gotten himself killed, surely His Serene Highness would've been aware of the fact.

The Kapellmeister's unease intensified as the disturbing image of Loretta Renier's reception of the news surfaced from his memory. In hindsight, the singer's behavior had been most suspicious. A matter Haydn could hardly ignore. Not if Affligio had been murdered.

He stared at the two maids, waiting for some explanation that could ease his concern.

But Rosalie bit her lip. She tipped her head at the salver on the fortepiano. "It is in the court newspaper." She chewed on her lip again. "The headline caught our eye and—"

Haydn glanced over at the folded newspaper. *Tragedy at the Burgtheater. Ach so.*

"And we took a quick look." Greta's blue eyes blazed, defying the Kapellmeister to object to their perusal of his newspaper. But Haydn was well aware the maids enjoyed reading the newspaper as much as he and did not mind in the least.

"So it was the *Wienerisches Diarium* that informed you of the fact?" He breathed a sigh of relief. He turned to his brother and Konzertmeister. "I doubt the reporters would deliberately concoct a lie—not when the matter is so grave. But surely they must have been mistaken."

"No!" Greta shook her head vehemently. "Karl—Herr Affligio's assistant—confirmed the fact as well."

Haydn's hopes sank. No one had asked him to look into the matter. But if he had information regarding the situation, surely—

"This Karl"—Luigi's voice broke into the Kapellmeister's troubled thoughts—"what sort of assistance does he provide Affligio?"

"Oh, he does all sorts of things, Master Luigi."—To Haydn's amusement, Greta had grown quite animated. She liked the fellow, did she?— "Herr Affligio relied upon him for the rigging, to see to the carpenters and the painters. Mostly, though, Karl sees to the rigging and all the special effects. There's nothing he can't do."

"Nothing he can't do, eh?" Luigi stroked his beard thoughtfully as he looked back at Haydn. "I believe we may have found an answer to our situation, Joseph."

Despite his suspicions about Loretta Renier, the Kapellmeister was quick to recognize the solution the fates were offering him with regard to the more pressing problem at hand. He grasped eagerly at it.

"And is Karl willing to stay on at the Burgtheater—despite the loss of his impresario?" he enquired.

Greta nodded eagerly. "If there is a job still to be had, yes." Her gaze turned expectantly to Haydn. "All the stagehands there are worried they will lose their positions. Karl says the Emperor doesn't intend to appoint another impresario in Herr Affligio's place." She wrung her hands.

"And no one knows," Rosalie added, "what will become of them."

"Then I must assure them all will continue as before," Haydn said.

And as for Loretta Renier, the police station was on his way to the Burgtheater.

He would have a quick word with the Police Inspector and—content with having done his duty—let the matter rest with the men in charge of the investigation.

Chapter Five

Haydn was glad to see the carriage provided for his use in Vienna —a smart red-and-black equipage with the Esterházy griffin embossed in gold on the sides—standing ready for him in the inner courtyard.

The horses—sturdy white animals with gleaming coats and thick tails —waited patiently beside the uniformed coachman, who held the coach door open for Haydn and the burly young man who was to accompany him.

The Kapellmeister, his leather case tucked under his arm, hurried down the palace steps two at a time, eager to get going. Beside him, Greta's young man took the steps just as quickly, thick wooden clogs clattering on the stone stairs.

"I have business at the police station on Habsburgergasse," Haydn explained to him as he climbed into the carriage after giving the coachman his instructions. Karl Schulze, following him into the coach, asked no questions nor did he display any signs of surprise, merely nodding.

The young man's energetic nature had already endeared him to Haydn. His lack of curiosity on matters of no concern to him recommended him even further to the Kapellmeister. He was hesitant to voice his suspicions openly—to a man he barely knew at that.

Besides, he reminded himself, there might well be a reasonable explanation for Loretta Renier's behavior. And it would only set tongues unfairly wagging if he spoke of his conjectures too freely.

As the carriage trundled out of the courtyard—and onto the Haarhof, from where it would turn onto Naglergasse—Haydn turned to the man seated across from him in his leather apron.

Karl had assured him that the sightlines and dimensions Motta spoke of in his treatise were nothing to worry about. The architects who had designed the Burgtheater had ensured these considerations had been kept in mind.

But there was still the matter of the setting. He asked about it now.

"The sea beach for the first act has been painted," Karl replied. "The painters are working on a nighttime scene for the third act. Herr Affligio was most reluctant to go to all that trouble," he confessed with an apologetic smile. "Until he saw the lights couldn't be effectively dimmed to suggest a scene at night."

Haydn suppressed a shudder at the awful thought of a daytime scene being reused for the night. The brilliant colors would either ruin the effect or the lights—dimmed all the way down—would ensure that nothing could be seen.

Why the impresario cared about either the trouble or the expense, he found himself at a loss to understand. Surely, it was the Emperor's purse strings—managed by Affligio, no doubt—that bore the brunt of the cost.

He wondered—as he often had before—whether Affligio had been dipping his hand in the till. It would not be the first time a man left in charge of his master's affairs had cheated his employer.

"As for the grassy enclosure," Karl interrupted Haydn's musings, "my master meant to reuse some of the forests and glades we already have." He grinned. "After all, what opera does not include a forest scene?"

Haydn's eyes widened. *Dear God, whatever next!*

"Ah, but that will not do, I am afraid," he protested immediately. He drew forth the libretto from the case beside him. "It is a fishing village in Taranto. The audience must not be allowed to forget that the beach and the sea are close by."

The production in Eszterháza had included realistic settings. Haydn was determined they should be reproduced for the Viennese performance. The Empress would expect no less.

He opened his libretto to the tenth scene of the first act.

"And, look!" He leaned forward to show Karl the description of the scene. "The scene includes grassy seats scattered about the enclosure. Some sand strewn on the ground would not be amiss."

Karl craned his neck out obediently and peered at the page. "The seats—those are to be practical?"

Haydn nodded. "They must be able to bear weight. The same with the hill in the second act." He flipped the pages of the libretto until he found the sixth scene in the second act. "Lesbina descends it, you see, with an entourage and later, Nerina climbs up to the top of it."

Karl pursed his lips. Haydn's heart sank. That these were details foreign to the young man was obvious.

Clearly Affligio—the godforsaken scoundrel!—had not bothered to acquaint himself with the props and scenes required for the opera. If Karl was to be believed, Affligio had been content to merely have a beach scene painted, while the rest of the opera took place in settings reused from other performances.

The impresario was a menace, Haydn thought, too irate to consider that his ill-will was borne toward a man unfortunately dead.

"A platform with stairs, appropriately painted, will suffice, I am sure." Karl continued to stare at the page open in Haydn's hands, stroking the rough, curly hairs of his beard.

"Stairs at the back, I hope," Haydn corrected hastily. What kind of hill had stairs with which to ascend it? It was bad enough that some would be required. But to have them in the front would completely destroy the illusion for the audience.

Karl glanced up, an amused twinkle in his eye. "Of course, at the back, Herr Kapellmeister. I've worked in the finest opera houses in Naples. I know how to produce a good effect, never fear!"

"Naples?" Haydn was astounded. The city boasted some of the most exceptional opera houses and singers in Europe. Why should anyone fortunate enough to be employed there leave? "What brought you to Vienna, then?"

Karl shrugged his thick shoulders. "No one in Naples was interested in producing my librettos."

"And Affligio was?" Haydn asked. That would explain Karl's loyalty to the man.

"He said he had discovered a composer who could work with me." The eager look on Karl's features faded. "I suppose nothing will come of that now."

Haydn regarded the young man. He had been moved to make a rash promise but had fortunately stayed himself. But there was something about this eager, hardworking young man that he liked. Surely, it would do no harm to extend a helping hand.

"I make no promises, but if the story is any good, I will endeavor to set it myself," he said. At Karl's look of astonishment, he went on: "His Serene Highness enjoys a good *buffa*, and the season at Eszterháza is several months long. A fresh, new opera would be an excellent thing."

As would a librettist attached to the Esterházy court, but that was a matter for a later date.

<hr>

"I will be but a moment," Haydn assured Karl as the carriage rolled to a stop outside the police station on Habsburgergasse.

There were about a hundred such stations under Count Pergen, each manned by police guards—of somewhat doubtful integrity—and under the authority of a police inspector who reported to the Director of Police in Vienna.

The one on Habsburgergasse was closest to the Burgtheater, and Haydn assumed it was the one handling the impresario's death.

He jumped out of the carriage. The building—an imposing edifice painted in the pale ochre characteristic of most buildings in the city center—stood across from him. But a line of carriages, waiting to pass by on the narrow street, held him back.

The coaches rolled by, stirring up dust from the freshly washed street. A group of women in light summer dresses and parasols sauntered past as well. But when Haydn saw a covered wagon lurch heavily around the corner, he took his chance and dashed across the street.

Beyond the entrance—adorned on either side with columns in the shape of Themis, Greek goddess of justice and wisdom—a solitary police guard sat behind a desk in a spacious hallway, a voluminous notebook open before him.

"Business?" he asked brusquely as Haydn entered. The Kapellmeister stated it as succinctly as he could and with as much authority as he could muster. It was the only way with men as churlish and as wanting in manners as police guards tended to be.

"I come at the specific instructions of His Serene Highness, Prince Nikolaus Esterházy of Galantha," Haydn added, hoping to impress the guard further into doing his bidding. The Prince having done no such thing, Haydn could only hope the Police Inspector would not go so far as to raise the matter with his employer.

The guard's eyes widened and he hastily got out of his chair and rushed off down the hallway. He was back in a few moments, gesturing toward Haydn to follow him.

"Herr von Beer is able to grant you a few minutes of his time," the police guard informed Haydn loftily, apparently having recovered from his earlier awe.

"Then I am greatly in his debt," Haydn replied equably as the guard led him toward a massive door and knocked on it.

"Herr Haydn!" A slim gentleman elegantly dressed in a coat as richly embroidered as his waistcoat—rather than the blue-and-white uniform Count Pergen required of his men—rose to greet the Kapellmeister.

Dismissing the police guard with an airy wave, he leaned across his massive desk and stretched out a languid hand. "Albert von Beer at your service."

Haydn shook the proffered hand and took the blue-upholstered seat von Beer invited him to take.

"It is because you come from a highly respected nobleman, Herr Haydn," the Police Inspector continued as he resumed his seat, carefully spreading his coat out before he sat down, "that I have agreed to meet you. Although in a case like this, I see no reason to consider any further opinions. Unless, of course"—his lips stretched into an amused smile—"you bring some information that can miraculously exculpate the man responsible for the crime."

"You have determined it is a man?" How could von Beer be so sure of the matter, Haydn wondered. Poison could be administered by a woman as well as a man, could it not?

More likely to be a woman than not, his wife, Maria Anna, had once declared. And the barber-surgeon in Eisenstadt had agreed with that opinion.

"We hold him in the cells yonder." Von Beer gestured to his right. Haydn found his gaze following the man's hand. He had seen a corridor leading down that way when he had entered the Police Inspector's chambers. It led, no doubt, to the row of cells provided to detain those accused of a crime.

"A man has been apprehended?" he asked, his eyes returning to face the Police Inspector. "Already?" The swiftness with which the crime had been dealt with astounded the Kapellmeister. The police guards tended to shrug off as impossible any task more arduous than apprehending a man caught in the very act of committing his crime.

But they had already discovered Affligio's murderer?

Von Beer nodded, a self-satisfied smirk on his smooth features. "Just this morning, Herr Haydn. Just this morning. The police are not quite as incompetent as every Viennese has been taught by the infernal newspapers to believe." He leant back in his chair. "At least, not within this station."

"And this man you hold—he has confessed to the crime?" Haydn continued, not knowing what pushed him to ask the question. It was curiosity, he supposed, and force of habit.

Von Beer threw his head back and laughed. "Ah, the refreshing innocence of a musician wholly unacquainted with the world's vices! My dear sir, what criminal willingly confesses to his crime? Of course, he has not!"

"Then how can you be so sure you have your man?" Haydn persisted. And why had Loretta Renier looked so very guilty?

Chapter Six

Von Beer rapped his elegant fingers on the desk. "May I remind you that this is a question that does not concern you? Although out of respect for your employer I will entertain it.

"How do we know?" He placed his elbows on his desk and steepled his fingers. "Why, Herr Affligio's appointment book told us the entire tale. Our man was the last to see the good impresario alive. It is as clear as day."

"Is that all?" Haydn asked. It seemed an altogether flimsy reason to incarcerate the poor fellow.

Von Beer's blue eyes penetrated Haydn's features.

"There is more," he said coolly, "not that it is any of your concern."

Was there, indeed? Haydn raised his eyebrows expectantly, still reluctant to believe Loretta Renier was entirely innocent.

Von Beer looked exasperated. "A pair of very reliable eyes saw the man emerge from the Burgtheater at about the time we suppose Herr Affligio to have met his Maker. I merely await the autopsy report from the coroner to confirm the fact. And"—he leaned threateningly forward—"do not ask who this witness is. That information is for the Emperor's ears only."

"Indeed." Haydn was still grappling with the information he had received. How did it fit in with Loretta Renier's odd behavior? Had she witnessed the impresario's death? But in that case, why deny it?

No, in all likelihood, the woman had been in league with the poor fellow in von Beer's jail cell.

"The impresario was poisoned, I suppose?" he asked the Police Inspector. What else could it be with the soprano insisting Affligio must have ingested something that killed him?

"Poisoned?" von Beer repeated, astonished. "Whatever gave you that idea? The poor man was mortally stabbed—with his own dagger."

"Stabbed!" Haydn vaguely recalled one of the maids mentioning it, but he had not thought much of it. In light of the fact, the soprano's protestations made even less sense.

Von Beer glanced at his timepiece. "Herr Haydn, you will appreciate I am a busy man. You came to me with information. But so far"—the Police Inspector spread his hands out—"I have heard nothing and have been required to share more than I ordinarily would with an ordinary citizen."

Haydn swallowed. His suspicions didn't seem worth sharing. But he had come all this way. . . He took a deep breath and braced himself for the inevitable ridicule.

"One of Affligio's sopranos exhibited the most suspicious behavior when we learned of the impresario's murder not above an hour ago," he began. He recounted Fräulein Renier's words. "Her behavior was so suspicious, I can only wonder if she had some hand in Affligio's demise."

Von Beer shrugged. "It is hardly a crime to refuse to believe someone has died. Or to reject the manner of death. Am I to arrest the woman for her opinions?"

"But surely the matter should be looked into?"

"On the basis of a reason as insubstantial as the one you have given me, Herr Haydn?" Von Beer regarded him as though he had lost his wits. "I believe the lady in question enjoys the friendship of the Emperor. I see no reason to disturb her peace.

"I suggest you do the same, Herr Haydn. Leave well enough alone. Your meddling will do no good, I assure you."

<hr>

Outside the police station, a wagon rumbled heavily across the cobblestones. The strong aroma of meat and onions assailed Haydn's nostrils, reminding him he had missed the midday meal.

He hailed the aged street vendor, sprinting down the stone steps as he did so.

"Three of your *Leberkäse*, if you please." Karl and his coachman were no doubt famished as well, the Kapellmeister thought. "And give me the thickest slices you have."

He watched the vendor's gnarled hands deftly pack three slices of the onion-flavored meatloaf into sheets of brown paper, his mouth watering. As a young choirboy in Vienna, he had frequently looked longingly after vendors such as the one before him, too poor to enjoy their wares.

Now as Kapellmeister to the most powerful family in the Empire, such fare was regrettably too humble to be served at either his wife's table or his employer's.

"Here you go, good sir. Five kreutzers apiece."

Haydn took the packets, paid the man his money, and quickly crossed the street to where his carriage stood waiting for him.

The Burgtheater was but a short ride from the police station. Once the carriage was underway and Karl had chewed and swallowed nearly half of his *Leberkäse* and the thick slice of brown bread that accompanied it, Haydn posed the question that had been bothering him.

"Were the singers informed of Herr Affligio's murder?" Why not, he wondered, when Karl had known the fact?

Karl shook his head. He hastily chewed the bite he had just taken and swallowed before responding. "The Emperor insisted we breathe not a word of the subject to anyone. Some of the stagehands might know. But it was too early in the morning for any of the singers to have been about."

So neither Loretta Renier nor Matilda Bologna had known of the impresario's death. Small wonder the news had come as such a shock. Although Haydn had received the distinct impression that Fräulein Renier's astonishment stemmed less from the fact of Affligio's demise than that its manner—murder—had been so quickly recognized.

"The Emperor was out and about at that early hour, I take it," Haydn said. He must have been, the Kapellmeister thought, to have been aware of the murder and to issue instructions to those present at the scene.

Karl looked at him, bits of ground beef stuck in his beard. "It was His Majesty who discovered Herr Affligio, stabbed in his chambers."

"*Ach so!*" Haydn frowned. He gestured toward his chin to let Karl know he had crumbs to brush off as he mulled over the tidbit Affligio's assistant had provided.

How had His Majesty known a dead body was to be found? Had the discovery been innocent—mere happenstance? It was possible, he supposed, that the His Majesty might have had some business to conduct with the impresario.

But it was so unlike the Emperor to go in search of those he wished to meet. In such a case, a messenger would be sent with an urgent summons for the individual in question to bring themselves to court posthaste.

It was only when the Emperor wished to catch a person unawares that he took himself out.

The only other reason for a man to stumble upon a corpse—as Haydn had learned to his detriment in Prussia a year or so ago—was that he himself was the cause of the dead person's condition.

But that was a suspicion too awful—and far too dangerous—to contemplate.

"And so no one associated with the Burgtheater was aware of Affligio's death—or his murder?" Haydn asked again.

"I believe so. Although now that a man has been arrested, I expect it does no harm to inform them of the fact."

"You were aware that an arrest has been made?" Haydn froze in the act of brushing crumbs off his lap and turned to stare at his companion.

"Yes, a Salzburger." Karl nodded, seeming surprised at both the question and the Kapellmeister's reaction. "I heard it from a cousin of mine. He is a police guard."

"Indeed." Despite himself, Haydn found the disclosure displeasing. His encounters with the police guards had left him less than enamored of their probity. Honest and diligent, they were most certainly not.

It was not Karl's fault, Haydn realized, that his cousin had chosen to be a police guard. Yet, what did that say of a man that he was intimately associated with those reprehensible individuals?

He would have to be circumspect around the man—pump him for information as the need may arise, but be wary of sharing any of his suspicions with him. But Karl was speaking, and Haydn, preoccupied with his thoughts, had failed to hear much of what he'd said. He returned his attention to the young man.

"I cannot say I am surprised," Karl was saying. "The man was most quarrelsome, forever finding fault with one thing or another."

"Herr Affligio must have been a man of remarkably even temperament to have no enemies other than this fellow," Haydn remarked acerbically. "I take it none of the singers found any fault with him—or he with them."

"They seemed to get along well enough, as far as I could tell." Karl peered out the window. "Ah, here we are."

The carriage, traveling down Reitschulgasse, had come to the place where the street flared out into the broad circle that was Michaerplatz. The Burgtheater was on the left, dwarfed by the Imperial Riding School.

"The painters are in, but many of the stagehands are not." Karl turned to Haydn with an apologetic smile. "I will send out a message letting everyone know that the Burgtheater is to remain open and that their jobs are secure."

The kitchen was humming with activity when Frida burst in through the door and headed toward Rosalie. Frau Schwann, the Princess's lady's maid, bustled about next to Rosalie, preparing a tray for Her Serene Highness.

"The Princess has decided to take her midday meal in her parlor today," Frau Schwann leaned over to confide in her. "She can't abide the Duke of Württemberg or the Prince-bishop of Augsburg. They come unaccompanied by their wives, so it matters not that Her Serene Highness won't be there to receive them."

Rosalie stood beside the lady's maid, listening to the older woman and nodding, while carefully ladling out the partridge braised in wine and the butter-fried chestnuts that had been prepared for the musicians into a chafing dish.

"I've set the plates, the cutlery, and the wine glasses, Frau Heindl." Frida came up to stand beside her. The young girl's cheeks were flushed and her breath came in soft gasps.

"That is good, Frida." Rosalie smiled at the young maid and glanced up at the clock. They were right on time. It would be another twenty minutes before the musicians started filing into the Officers' Mess for their meal.

The kitchen door swung open and three footmen rushed in, hefted platters of venison, mutton, and duck, and hurried out again to the dining room where His Serene Highness would be joining his guests.

Frida tipped her chin at the silver chafing dish. "Is it time to take the food in?"

"Have the warmers been lit?" Rosalie asked. There was no point taking the food in if the water pans weren't steaming hot. Out of the corner of her eye she saw Greta barge in through the kitchen door with another maid in tow.

"Better give it another five minutes," Greta said. "Katya and I just got the burners started. It'll take a few minutes for the water to be hot enough."

But the crepes filled with apricot preserves didn't need to be served hot.

"You and Katya can take those—" Rosalie began when the bell summoning the musicians' maids jangled shrilly, making her bite her tongue.

Beside her, Frau Schwann gave a violent start. "Good Lord, what is the meaning of that infernal noise?" She looked over her shoulder at the bell that was still vibrating. "It's for one of you. What can those musicians of yours possibly want?"

Rosalie exchanged a glance with Greta, who shook her head. "It's not the musicians, mark my words. It's that old stick-in-the-mud, Herr Rahier. He was in the entrance hall talking with someone when Katya and I came in."

Rosalie glanced at the door. "I'd better go see who it is. It must be someone from the Burgtheater with a message from the Kapellmeister, and Herr Rahier probably has his knickers in a twist because the man deigned to use the front door."

She smoothed down her apron and headed for the door. The Estates Director, a tall elegantly dressed man who disdained wigs, was standing in the hallway, just as Greta had described, his forefinger pressed determinedly into the buzzer on the wall.

"There's no need to keep ringing that bell, Herr Rahier," she informed him firmly. "The entire kitchen can hear it."

There'd been a time when she'd quaked in her shoes in his presence. Not anymore. For one thing, she didn't need this job. Gerhard made enough money for them both to live comfortably. For another, over the years she and Greta had proven themselves valuable enough and discreet enough to earn His Serene Highness's appreciation.

Rahier frowned down at her, but he took his finger off the buzzer.

"Where are all the musicians' maids?" he demanded. "Shouldn't one be keeping watch at the door? I was summoned from my meal to attend to their visitors."

Rosalie peeked a glance beyond the Estates Director's tall, broad frame. A portly figure stood behind the director, wiping his face with a large square of linen. There was something familiar about the man, but Rosalie couldn't put her finger on what it was. A middle-aged woman with a long, white face waited next to him.

"The maids are preparing to serve the midday meal," she informed Rahier. "But I can attend to the gentleman and lady myself."

"They want the Kapellmeister. You had better fetch him." Rahier swept a gloved hand through the gleaming strands of his blond hair and strode away.

It was only when the portly visitor put away his handkerchief that Rosalie recognized him.

"Master Michael?" Whatever was Herr Haydn's middle brother doing here? In Vienna, instead of in Salzburg where he lived and worked?

Chapter Seven

"THE painters and carpenters will be below," Karl said, leading the way to a small door hidden from view in an out-of-the-way corner of the building—the very door the killer had apparently used to leave the building.

To enter it as well, no doubt, Herr von Beer at the police station had surmised.

It opened onto a flight of narrow wooden steps, dimly lit by the small quantity of sunlight able to penetrate the dingy panes of a tiny window.

Haydn stepped gingerly in, following Karl's stocky figure down the stairs.

The width of each step was such that he found himself standing sideways to accommodate the entire length of his feet. The stairs were rickety as well. Haydn was about to grip the metal railing on the side when he noticed cobwebs and dust and quickly pulled his hand away.

"Does no one ever clean this place?" the Kapellmeister complained, wrinkling his nose in disgust. Even as a child, he had borne an aversion to dust and grime. It was a habit encouraged by his mother, who had been unable to bear any traces of filth herself.

He whipped a kerchief out of his pocket, although the square piece of linen stood not a chance of withstanding the dirt that prevailed in this part of the building.

"Herr Affligio did employ a maid," Karl explained, looking over his shoulder, a rueful grimace on his face. "But she has always come and gone as she pleases. And now with the impresario dead . . ." He shrugged.

She was certainly not worth the money she was paid, Haydn thought, taking in his surroundings. It was but yesterday that Affligio had been found dead. Yet, Haydn was willing to wager there was at least a week's worth of dust in here.

Had the Salzburger accused of killing Affligio really made his way down these stairs—or up them? Through the grime? Haydn found himself beginning to feel sorry for the fellow. His suspicions of her notwithstanding, he doubted anything would have persuaded Loretta Renier to descend them. The grime would make short work of her expensive garments.

Karl's voice, evidently still speaking of the maid, intruded upon the Kapellmeister's thoughts. It was just as well she had not made an appearance, he was saying.

"Besides"—Karl looked over his shoulder—"with carpenters and painters going up and down all day, who could hope to keep the place clean?"

Anyone with a mind to do the job well, Haydn thought privately, although he remained quiet. He had never seen such haphazard cleaning.

The side of the handrail had been wiped clean, albeit in a slovenly fashion. The maid must have used her fingertip to lift the dust, Haydn thought as he gazed at the circular spots of clean metal punctuating the dirt. But the layer of dust on top remained undisturbed.

The cobwebs had been removed only from a certain height above the handrail to the top of the metal rail itself. No higher and no lower, as though the maid were loath to either stretch up or bend down to do her job. The upper edges of the clean area formed an uneven wavy line. Clearly, the woman had done no more than swirl her dust-cloth at eye level.

The small shape of the cleaning woman's flat-soled shoes was ground into the dirt on the tread—the only light area in the grime-darkened wood. How had Affligio tolerated such shoddy work?

They emerged onto a brightly lit—and oddly cleaner—area. "Herr Affligio's chambers are through there. Although few knew there was an entrance at the rear of the apartment." Karl pointed to a door so closely fitted in with the surrounding wall it was scarcely visible.

"And Herr Affligio was disinclined to invite anyone into the inner chamber. How the Salzburger found his way there, I cannot tell."

"There is more than one chamber?" Haydn peered at the wall, barely making out the outline of a door panel.

Karl nodded. "An outer chamber where he received visitors, singers, anyone whom he had business with. And an inner chamber, where few were invited to go in."

"Were you?" Haydn asked, hoping his question would not sound too blunt. It was none of his concern, after all.

Karl shrugged. "Sometimes. When the occasion demanded it."

Next to the concealed door was a partially open wooden cabinet door.

"Our sheaves and pulleys are in there," Karl informed the Kapellmeister. "Along with spare rope and sandbags."

They rounded a corner. Karl pointed to a door on the right. "That area stands directly beneath the stage. The chariots that pull the wings, the winch that with a single crank changes all the scenery simultaneously, and the machinery to hoist devils and evil spirits from the underworld are all in there."

Straight ahead were two doors. "The workshops for the painters and carpenters are on the left. The changing rooms for the singers on the right."

Karl looked over his shoulder.

"There is another staircase next to the changing room. It is the one the singers and musicians use—and anyone else who had need to see Herr Affligio." He smiled. "And that at least is kept clean."

"I am glad to hear it," Haydn replied, wondering why he had been made to suffer the grimy route downstairs, then.

———◆◆◆———

"Is Joseph upstairs?" Master Michael asked, showing no signs of having recognized Rosalie. That wasn't surprising. It had been two years or more that Master Michael had shown up, unannounced, in Eisenstadt in search of a violinist who had abandoned his family in Salzburg. "The matter is of the utmost urgency."

"I'm afraid not. He had to leave this morning—for the Burgtheater. But Master Johann is here."

Master Michael pshawed rudely. "What can that dreamer do to help? It is Joseph we need. But he, you say, is at the Burgtheater? Already?"

"Yes, when we heard the impresario had—"

"Excellent! Most excellent!" He looked at the woman with him. "There, what did I tell you? Didn't I say Joseph would come to our aid? And, look, he is already on the case."

He turned on his heels. "My brother has a good nose, one must grant him that. He must have sniffed out a problem with the entire situation the moment he heard of it."

What problem, Rosalie wondered. And what case? Surely, not that of the impresario's murder? There was, from what Karl had told them, no case there. An arrest had been made.

She hurried after the visitors. "He is not. . . That is to say, Herr Haydn is not—"

But Michael brushed her aside. "Yes, yes, girl, we know." He waved his hand dismissively as though shooing away a pesky fly and strode out of the hallway. The long-featured woman with him looked around her bewildered, and hurried after him.

Before Rosalie could ask if he wanted to leave a message Master Michael was gone.

⸺◦◦◦⸺

"I don't understand it," Rosalie told Greta after the musicians had been served. "What could've brought Master Michael to the city?"

"I hear His Grace is here," Greta said, helping herself to a slice of roasted venison. She pushed the platter toward Rosalie. Usually, they would've joined the other servants in the servants' hall. But there was too much work today, and they'd decided to take a quick bite in the kitchen while the musicians were eating.

"How did you hear that?" Rosalie nibbled at the venison. It was good enough, but she would've preferred a hearty stew or a bit of boiled beef. The Archbishop of Salzburg—judging by his infrequent visits to the city —had as little use for Vienna as did their employer.

"From Steffi," Greta said between mouthfuls of bread. Her childhood friend was a temporary maid in the Archbishop's household, sent for only when His Grace was in town. "Apparently His Grace gave one of their musicians a month's leave of absence. The month has turned into nearly a year, and His Grace is quite fed up."

"I don't blame him," Rosalie said. "Can you imagine if Herr Haydn were to take himself off to foreign parts for several months?"

"I don't see the Prince standing for that kind of behavior, I'll tell you that much. But that's not the worst of it. This man—imagine his cheek! —has been insisting he get paid as well."

"For traveling abroad and staying away from his duties!" Rosalie was astounded.

His Serene Highness esteemed the Kapellmeister so greatly, there was likely very little Herr Haydn could do to earn himself a serious rebuke. But Rosalie doubted that even Herr Haydn would be permitted to go traipsing off for an indefinite period.

"He's been to Mannheim and Paris and God alone knows where," Greta said. "And now here he is in Vienna, but still showing no inclination of returning to Salzburg. Anyway, when His Grace heard, he immediately hotfooted it to the city.

"Steffi says"—Greta giggled at the memory—"the musician had the gall to say the Gospel urged him to nurture his talents." She giggled some more. "And so the Archbishop was heard to say he could either return to Salzburg or be fired by the Gospel!"

Rosalie grinned. But that still didn't explain Master Michael's presence at the palace.

"I tried to tell him," she said to Greta, "that a man had been arrested for the impresario's murder, and that Herr Haydn wasn't on any case. But he wouldn't listen." She suppressed the indignation that she'd felt at Master Michael's rude dismissal of her.

They had grown up in the same village. Their mothers had worked together at the Harrach castle in Rohrau. There was really no need to treat her as though she were no better than a beggar. She might be a mere maid, but she earned an honest living.

Greta's sudden gasp startled her out of her outrage. "Didn't Karl say it was a musician from Salzburg who was arrested for the crime?"

Rosalie nodded. "So he did. You don't think it's one of Master Michael's acquaintances, do you?"

Greta helped herself to a crepe. "It's got to be. Why else would he be here—talking about Herr Haydn being on a case, no less."

"You don't suppose it's that musician Steffi was talking about, do you?" Rosalie asked her friend. "The one who's flown the Archbishop's coop?"

"It could be," Greta agreed. "It's the sort of thing you'd expect from a no-good person like that." She tossed her head. "I hope Herr Haydn refuses to help."

Chapter Eight

THE painted flats for the sea beach were exquisitely done. Haydn said as much to both the painter's foreman, who held them up for his inspection, and Karl. He had seen the four sets that would form the wings on either side of the front of the stage.

Now he stood beside the tall foreman in his paint-splattered leather apron and admired the flats that would form the rear wings. The Burgtheater stage, Karl had informed him, was equipped with seven grooves on either side. Quite enough to create a suitably magnificent scene.

Karl had also demonstrated how the flats slid through slots in the stage and were then fitted onto carriages under the stage floor. With a single crank of a winch, the carriages could then be rolled seamlessly on and off the stage.

"One might almost imagine oneself in the fishing village," the Kapell-meister said wonderingly, taking in the work.

"The men are good workers—and most diligent," the foreman, a man by the name of Rudolph, replied somewhat gruffly to Haydn's praise.

"I see that they are, Rudolph." Haydn cast another glance around the room. The evidence of the foreman's words was clearly visible in the workshop.

Groups of men stood around worktables in the center of the room applying finishing touches to flats. Other apron-clad men stood on ladders, painting the large canvas-wrapped wooden frames that leaned against the side wall of the room. After an initial glance at Haydn when he had entered the workshop with Karl, they had been too intent on their work to pay him any mind.

Nodding appreciatively, Haydn turned back to the flats he had been admiring.

The rear flats were irregularly shaped—showing the large prows of fishing boats with strips of sand extending outward. Karl came up to stand beside the painter's foreman and Haydn.

"They will be draped with fishing nets and hooks to complete the illusion," he said.

"And here"—Rudolph moved along the back wall—"is the backdrop. Sand in the foreground. The waves in the distance and a small boat."

"Would it not be better to have more?" Haydn asked.

"More?" Rudolph and Karl both stared at the Kapellmeister. "More what, Herr Kapellmeister?" Rudolph asked.

Haydn's gaze moved to the backdrop. "More boats, of course." He raised his head, looking from Rudolph to Karl. "It is a fishing village. There must be fishing boats."

"Having more would ruin the perspective when Lindoro enters the scene on his boat," Karl informed him.

Rudolph nodded. "One tiny boat on the left is quite enough. Lindoro enters from the right—"

"In a movable carriage shaped like a boat," Karl explained. "And his size contrasting with any boats painted directly behind him would spoil the illusion."

"Very well." Haydn nodded, well satisfied with the progress that was being made. Karl had assured the painters the theater would remain open and a message had been sent to the carpenters and stagehands as well.

He was about to take out his purse to give Rudolph and his men a reward when the foreman brought out a few more flats for him to inspect.

"Will these do?" he asked. "Or are there any changes required? If there are, it would be best to tell the men now."

Haydn gazed at the flats representing dark woods, the columns of a palace, and a temple of Apollo.

"B-but"—his eyes sought Karl's, mystified—"my opera calls for none of those scenes."

Karl's lips twitched. "Two other works besides yours are to be performed, Herr Kapellmeister. All open in the same week."

Haydn's jaw nearly dropped. Was he expected to put on operas besides his own? His Serene Highness had made no mention of any such thing. He caught the amused glance Karl sent to the painter's foreman. It would not do to have these men see him as a fool and play him for one.

Recovering his composure, he smiled at both men. "I will need to see the librettos for the works in question and consult with the composer and poet before I can determine whether any changes need to be made. Which are the two operas?"

"A revival of Herr Gluck's *Alceste*," Rudolph said. "These are the flats for that opera."

"If it's a revival," Haydn said, "then I expect we can re-use the same scenery used for the initial performance. Unless, of course, any changes have been made."

He turned toward Karl. "And the other opera?"

"Another revival," Karl said. "Very few new operas are written for the summer months."

"Then, gentlemen, I see no reason to re-examine Herr Affligio's decisions on the matter." He turned to leave, but Rudolph stopped him with a loud clearing of his throat.

Haydn spun around. "Is there anything else?"

"There is, indeed, Herr Kapellmeister." Rudolph stood with his legs apart, his muscular arms bulging as his large hands gripped his hips. "The small matter of our payment."

Haydn frowned. "How much are you owed?" Affligio had died but the night before yesterday. Had he not kept current with his payments?

"Two weeks' worth of wages. We were to be paid yesterday. Herr Affligio assured us he would have the money in our hands by the end of the day, but . . ." Rudolph shrugged.

But the impresario had not lived to see the beginning of the day, much less its end.

"Two weeks?" Haydn turned to Karl. How was it possible the men had been left unpaid for two weeks?

"It is true," Karl confirmed. He took a small notebook out of the large pocket of his leather apron and pulled out the pencil tucked behind his ear. It was a bit of charcoal, Haydn noticed, not graphite that was encased in the wooden holder.

"I have made a note of the details here," Karl said, pointing the tip of his charcoal at the page.

Haydn sighed. Two other operas in production; unpaid painters; what next—unpaid singers? Affligio's death was causing him more trouble than he'd anticipated.

"I suppose the singers must be paid as well," he said, not relishing the thought of dealing with an irate Loretta Renier. At least, Fräulein Bologna could be counted on to act with good grace.

"I know not," Karl replied. "Herr Affligio dealt with them himself."

"Oh, the singers have been paid, never fear," Rudolph said.

"Most likely they have," Karl agreed.

"*Gott sei Dank*," Haydn muttered. "No doubt, Herr Affligio wasn't keen to see a singer of Fräulein Bologna's caliber leave his employ for some other theater."

Rudolph rolled his eyes. "It was not her Herr Affligio was reluctant to see go. The only singer he had eyes for was Fräulein Renier."

Because of her intimate relationship with the Emperor, no doubt. But when Haydn hinted at that aspect of the matter, Rudolph merely sniffed.

"Oh, it was not only for the Emperor's sake. Herr Affligio—"

"Held Fräulein Renier in high esteem," Karl interrupted, his florid cheeks turning redder still. "She was a woman of many parts."

Rudolph sputtered, covered his mouth, and turned aside. When he turned back to face them, his face flushed, Karl continued:

"I will see to it that your men are paid, Rudolph." He glanced at Haydn. "I suppose His Serene Highness will not object—?"

"I see no reason why he should," Haydn said, not understanding Karl's reason for thinking the Prince might. It was not His Serene Highness's purse that would be burdened with the cost.

⋯⋯⋯

"Was your master frequently delinquent in his payments?" Haydn asked Karl as they stepped out of the painters' workshop. He turned to face the burly young man.

Karl looked unhappy. "I fear it was becoming a habit of late," he conceded. "Although, it was only the painters, carpenters, and stagehands who were affected."

Those least able to tolerate the hardship, Haydn noted with disapproval. It was bad enough when a man failed to deal with his own debts, but to play fast and loose with another's purse strings was surely unconscionable. Had Affligio been gambling with the Emperor's money?

"The singers, you say, were unaffected?" Haydn pressed the young man. They were better able to bear the burden, he supposed.

"What singer, of any caliber, would stay on under such circumstances?" Karl asked. "No, the singers had to be paid promptly. Herr Affligio knew they would not hesitate to leave if they were not."

Haydn bent his head, lips pursed, as they slowly walked down the hallway. He had thought the impresario a difficult man, stingy in the extreme—lazy, too, perhaps, in his propensity to re-use stock scenery for every opera he produced. But he had not considered him to be so little a man of his word as seemed to be the case.

Karl must have divined his thoughts, for he turned earnestly to Haydn. "It is not my master's fault. He was perpetually short of money of late. The theater is not as easy to run as most people suppose. The expenses are many, and they pile up quicker than the snow in winter."

"I suppose he had come into money recently."

"I—" Karl stopped short, clearly at a loss.

"He must have," Haydn insisted, "to have assured the painters they would have their money on the morning after they raised the issue."

Karl tugged at his beard. "He was a man of his word, true. And if he said he would pay them, then there's no doubt he would've. Yes, yes, I suppose he must've found his way to some gold." He raised his eyes. "It will be in his money box. It is kept in the inner chamber."

The chamber, Haydn reflected, where the man had been killed. That few knew about—save the man walking briskly before him. Had Affligio been killed for his gold?

"Did the police guards find any signs of theft?" he asked as he followed Karl to the impresario's chambers.

Karl looked over his shoulder. "None that I'm aware of." He shrugged. "Nothing seemed to be missing."

But who else other than Karl could've sworn to that? Was anyone else as familiar with the impresario's private chambers as his ever-helpful assistant?

Haydn brushed the thoughts aside. Dwelling on them would serve no purpose. And taking them to Herr von Beer would most likely be fruitless. The Police Inspector was satisfied he had got his man and would brook no opposition.

"Herr Haydn!" A deep bass voice brought him short.

Turning, he saw two men—one wigless, the other with a wig, the ringlets of which framed the sides of his broad face—bearing down upon him.

"Herr Haydn," the bewigged gentleman called again. "His Majesty assured us we would find you here. He said you were the man to approach on such matters."

Chapter Nine

"IT is Herr Gluck," Karl whispered into his ears, but Haydn was aware of that, being long familiar with the composer. "And the other is Herr Coltellini, the librettist."

"What may I do for you, gentlemen?" Haydn forced himself to smile, although he feared the composer's presence might have something to do with the revival of his *opera seria*. A change in scenes and settings that would require more backstage work.

He was beginning to understand how Affligio must've felt.

"It is La Renier," Gluck said in his loud, bass voice. "The woman must be taken off the opera. His Majesty has washed his hands off the matter. He says it is all in the impresario's hands now."

"If she has signed a contract, she cannot be taken off the opera," Karl informed Haydn.

"And has she?" Haydn turned to Gluck.

Gluck gave an exaggerated shrug. "How should I know, my dear Haydn? These are matters that belong under the purview of the impresario."

"The contracts will be in Herr Affligio's chambers," Karl said.

"Then I shall look them over as soon as I am able and determine what needs to be done," Haydn said. Would to God, the woman had failed to sign a contract for his opera as well. It would give him just the excuse he needed to rid himself of her.

"It had best be done quickly. The woman can neither sing nor act."

The composer's sensitive, mobile mouth contrasted with the determined glint in his intelligent gray eyes. Not a man to be contended with—unlike Marco Coltellini who, despite the firmness of his mouth, was the more malleable of the two men. Why had Coltellini, who wrote *buffa*, accompanied Gluck?

Gluck must have noticed the direction of Haydn's glance, for he continued: "And that brings me to the second matter. Marco here has made some changes to *Alceste*. Nothing major. The choruses have been cut out, a character added, an aria here or there deleted. Calzabigi, the stubborn fool,"—the man who had written the original libretto—"would not do it."

Haydn turned to Karl, who was shaking his head vehemently.

"That will not do. It will not do at all," he cried. He turned to Haydn. "The choruses divert the audience's eye from the scene changes. To cut them—all of them!—would make more work for the stagehands.

"And adding a new character will mean sewing new costumes!"

Gluck frowned. "Surely, that is hardly a consideration. Why—"

"If Karl here says it cannot be done, then I am afraid I cannot approve the changes," Haydn said firmly. He had no experience with technical matters, and only a fool would go against the advice of an experienced hand.

Gluck's frown deepened. "And the other matter?"

"I will have an answer for you by tomorrow," Haydn assured him.

⚬

Hours later, Haydn had still to find the money Affligio must have had expectations of receiving. Frustrated, he allowed his eyes to roam once more around the impresario's private chamber. The candles in the wall sconces and in the candelabra on the desk cast a warm glow over the room, but there was a distinct chill in the air.

It occurred to him that a fire would not be amiss, yet he was too preoccupied to light the porcelain stove.

His puzzled gaze lingered on the bureaus that lined the walls. A leather-covered money box—with two rows of drawers—stood atop the bureau nearest the paper-strewn desk. He had spent hours searching them all—every nook and cranny. But if Affligio had possessed any money, it was not here. A meager sum had been found in the ceramic, bear-shaped bank in the ticket booth upstairs.

"Herr Affligio keeps the proceeds from the ticket sales up there," Karl had said. "When the bank is full, it is brought down here and emptied into his money box."

There had been a small amount in the money box as well—but not enough to pay the painters or the carpenters, who would arrive on the morrow and expected to be paid in full before resuming work.

"They say they have mouths to feed," Karl had relayed the message he had received from the carpenters to Haydn, "and cannot afford to labor with no reward in sight."

Haydn had ended up using the bag of gold His Serene Highness had presented him with that morning—recompense for taking on the impresario's duties—to pay the painters. Karl, however, had insisted he had already been paid and refused to take a single gulden.

Haydn could not help wondering why. Had Affligio truly paid his loyal assistant? Or had the impresario expected the poor man to be satisfied with the promise that his libretto would be brought to the stage?

Karl would've been as easily fobbed off as the painters. From what Haydn had seen, the painters' foreman did not have it in him to sit idle. A fact Affligio would've been aware of and would not have hesitated to profit from.

"And that must mean," the Kapellmeister said to himself, "that Affligio had recently come into some money." Why concoct a lie and say he would pay them when the men could so easily be put off?

"But where, then, is the money now?" His gaze searched the room again. Had someone grown impatient, killed the impresario, and scoured his rooms for the money?

But the only man who had steadfastly refused to accept anything was Karl. Everyone else's eyes had lit up eagerly at the prospect of being paid. Moreover, Karl seemed to be the only person aware of the impresario's financial affairs and the details of where he kept his documents and gold.

Was Karl a man to be entirely trusted? Doubts about the young man snaked uneasily into his mind, refusing to be dismissed.

What had happened here? Who was responsible? The questions swirled through Haydn's brain as he surveyed the room. Where in God's name could the money be?

But staring where he had already looked before would not illuminate the problem. Haydn shook his head, forcing himself to drive the issue out of his mind. He had at least found the singers' contracts. He had better start perusing those if he meant to keep his word to Herr Gluck.

Exhaling heavily, he sank into the upholstered chair at Affligio's cluttered desk and prepared to cast his eye over the papers.

He had barely settled himself in when a strident bellow nearly unseated him.

"Joseph!" The portly figure of his middle brother, Michael, barged in through the doorway. "Have you gone deaf? I have been knocking on the door—pounding on it fit to wake the dead—these past ten minutes or more. Did you not hear me?"

Haydn had not. The walls of Affligio's private chamber were so solidly built, few sounds penetrated it from outside.

"Michael!" He stared at his brother in dismay. "What brings you here?"

It was nothing good, of that Haydn was sure. It never was with Michael. And his irate manner did not bode well either. The thought that his middle brother might have imbibed more than he should have flitted briefly across Haydn's mind.

But there was no stench of alcohol in the air, and Michael, crashing across the room like a mid-sized elephant, seemed to be in control of his senses.

"What brings me here?" he demanded, red-faced and puffing heavily. He pulled out one of the two chairs on the other side of the desk and sat down. "I would not have had to come had you but thought to bestir yourself enough to return to the police station, Joseph."

"Return to the police station?" Haydn replied, mystified. "I was there just this morning."

"I know. That pompous ass von Beer mentioned it. He said you did not ask to see the prisoner." Michael puffed breathlessly. "When I heard that, I was sure you would return. We waited as long as we could, Joseph."

A vague, unwelcome suspicion was beginning to stir in Haydn's mind.

"The Salzburger arrested for Affligio's murder, you know him, I suppose?"

How could he not have suspected that to be the case? Michael had lived in Salzburg for the better part of his life, an employee at the Archbishop's court. There were likely few musicians in the city his brother did not know.

"Know him?" Michael cried. "Of course, I know him! I have known him all these years." He leaned forward, his bloated features agitated. "He is no murderer, Joseph. I thought you were aware of that. Is that not the reason you went to see him?"

"This man," Haydn began cautiously—it took very little to ignite his middle brother's temper, and he had no wish to arouse Michael's ire any further. "Who is he?"

"*Who is he?*" Michael demanded, outraged. "Are you in your dotage as well as being deaf? Who is he, the man asks," Michael addressed the ceiling. "It is Leopold Mozart. Who else would it be? I thought you knew."

"I did not."

Chapter Ten

Haydn struggled to take in the news. Why should as reputed a violinist and composer as Leopold Mozart be suspected of murdering the impresario? What dealings could the two men have had?

Leopold had no ambitions of writing an opera, did he? Had never written one as far as Haydn knew.

"You were truly unaware of this?" Michael looked at him, eyes narrowed in suspicion.

"Until you informed me of it, yes," Haydn said. "Why did the police arrest him?"

Michael's exasperation expressed itself in a roll of the eyes. "They insist Leopold must have killed Affligio, being the last person to see him alive."

Ach so! Haydn nodded. He remembered von Beer saying something to that effect.

"Had he any reason to?" He scrutinized his brother's face, recalling some of what Karl had said about the Salzburger.

His brother opened his mouth, but Haydn interrupted before he could say anything. "They will not have taken him in without good reason, as you well know."

"There was some dispute about the staging of an opera," Michael conceded reluctantly. "Affligio said things no man should have said. It was unforgivable. Leopold was incensed, of course. What man wouldn't be?"

"Who heard the dispute?"

"The whole world, apparently. From Gluck and Coltellini to all the stagehands and even some of the singers. There seems to be no dearth of people who will testify to the argument."

Michael clasped his hands over his round stomach. "Leopold will go to the gallows if the matter is not thoroughly examined, Joseph. An innocent man will hang for a crime he did not commit."

The thought did not sit well with Haydn's conscience. But he could hardly take on the task of defending Leopold. Was he not already burdened—overburdened, if one were being honest—with as much as any man could shoulder?

"Speak with von Beer," he began to say when Michael interrupted tetchily.

"What good will that do? He is convinced he has his man and will look no further. By the by"—Michael's eyes narrowed again as he searched Haydn's features—"what took you to him this morning, if not to protest Leopold's innocence?"

"I—" Haydn hesitated, loath to admit the suspicions he had entertained all morning—suspicions that pointed everywhere other than the Salzburger. Michael's eyes continued to bore into his very soul.

"Can the Archbishop not help?" he asked helplessly. How could any man of honor stand by while the police hauled a man in his service off to prison?

Michael shook his head. "The Archbishop has long been in search of an excuse to rid himself of Leopold. Now that he has it, His Grace will not give up this opportunity so very easily."

Haydn leaned back wearily, thrusting his fingers into his wig and nearly pulling the thing off his head. Dear God, what had he gotten himself into?

"There must be some other way, Michael." He cast a desperate glance at the contracts strewn upon the desk. When would he have time to peruse them? "I cannot—"

"Frau Mozart and her children stand to lose everything if Leopold is not restored, Joseph. His reputation is destroyed, his sole source of income gone—"

"His pension?"

"The Archbishop refuses to grant it to the poor woman. He says by virtue of his criminal act, Leopold has forfeited any claims he or his family may have to it!"

If it were just a matter of defending Leopold's honor, Haydn might have successfully fought the urge to help. But how could he stand by and do nothing when there was a woman involved—a helpless mother with her young children?

"Very well," he said, cursing himself for the softness of his heart.

A half hour later, having made the necessary arrangements, the brothers were ready to leave. Haydn snuffed out the candles sputtering in the candelabra and gathered up the contracts on the desk. He pushed his chair back, about to snuff out the candles in the wall sconces as well, when Michael's horrified cry made him bite his tongue.

"What is it now?" he demanded, addressing his brother's wide, overcoat-wrapped back.

Michael, on his way to the door, had stopped in the middle of the room and stood staring at the carpet.

"Is this where he died?" he asked, looking over his shoulder, his usually red features blanched as white as an almond.

Haydn's gaze followed his brother's rigidly pointing forefinger to the large bloodstain on the carpet. Under the weight of his recent responsibilities, he had all but forgotten its existence.

"Yes, yes, that must be where it happened."

"And you still have the carpet here?" Michael could not have looked more horrified had the bloodstain been Affligio's dead body instead.

"Unfortunately, there was no time—and no one—to replace it," Haydn informed him wryly. "The maid Affligio hired has not made an appearance in days. And the other men have been left dangling so long for their money, it was as much as anyone could do to persuade them to resume their duties."

That was not entirely the truth. Other than the carpenters, no one had made a fuss. And Karl would gladly have removed the carpet, had Haydn allowed him to.

But the dark crimson stain—large and deeply soaked into the nap of the carpet—had intrigued Haydn no end. He had been told Affligio had been stabbed.

"In the chest," Karl had confirmed when Haydn had quizzed him on the matter.

Yet the bloodstain appeared to be where Affligio's head would have lain—judging by the deep indentation his large frame had made in the carpet. By the light of day, it had been easy to see the form of his body —legs spread wide apart, arms thrown to the sides—on the carpet.

And the stain rather than being between the arms was—mysteriously enough—above it. How had a knife wound to the chest caused the impresario to bleed profusely out of the back of his head?

"You had better get rid of it, Joseph," Michael now said, his coarse features contorted into a grimace. "Who knows but his restless spirit might infest the room if you let it remain."

He gingerly skirted around the stain and made his way to the door.

"Give sister-in-law and Johann my regards, if you will. I was at the palace today—with Frau Mozart. But we were in too much of a hurry and too desperate to meet you for me to recall myself to Johann."

Haydn nodded. "Of course. *Bis Morgen*—until tomorrow," he added as his brother left the room. He would have to put off going to the palace —to request a reimbursement of his expenses and to issue instructions to Luigi—until later in the afternoon.

The situation was far from ideal, but Haydn had decided it would be best to meet the Mozarts in the morning and get the affair over with as quickly as possible. There was little he could offer them in the way of succor other than to assure them he would investigate the incident and Leopold's role in it as thoroughly as he was able.

⁂

The stars were out and a damp chill had descended upon the air by the time the coachman Haydn had hired to drive him home drew up in front of Landstraße 51, the property his father-in-law owned on Raabengasse.

He let himself in as quietly as he could. A light burned in the kitchen.

His footfall lightly echoing on the cobblestones of the inner courtyard brought Maria Anna to the door.

"Where have you been all this time, husband?" she grumbled, her hands on her slender hips. "Your food grows cold. Would you have me stay up all night waiting for you?"

"What was to prevent you from retiring?" he retorted, too irritated to attempt to mollify her. "Could you not have kept the fire burning and gone to bed?"

He had been hard at work, as Maria Anna well knew. But to hear her talk, one might think he had stayed away on purpose—drinking and carousing the entire night!

"Go to bed!" His wife's voice rose. "And leave the fire untended? How could I do that? Would you have me burn down the house? Or your meat?

It would've been preferable to her recriminations, Haydn thought as he approached the door.

"And who would wash the dishes after you were done eating?" Maria Anna stepped aside to let him in.

"I am sure I could have managed the task," he muttered, relieved to see Johann sitting at the table as well. He was too exhausted to endure his wife's chafing.

Her frown of displeasure had deepened at his words, and she opened her mouth to speak when Johann's hastily voiced question stayed her.

"How goes it at the Burgtheater, brother? You found everything in order, I trust."

Haydn nodded. "The fabrication of the sets progresses apace." He took off his wig and coat. "Karl fortunately persuaded Affligio to create a separate set of flats for the nighttime scenes."

"He seems a capable young man," Johann remarked approvingly. "Intelligent, too. Only a fool would think the daytime scenes would serve just as well for one at night."

"He does have the technical aspects of the matter well in hand," Haydn agreed, but the suspicions that had haunted him through the day remained at the back of his mind.

Chapter Eleven

HE joined his brother at the table, suddenly aware of how empty his stomach was. Maria Anna had left a plate of buttered bread at his place. He took a large hunk and bit into it. The savory aroma of beef, onions, and vegetables wafted to his nose from the pot hanging over the fire. He was glad to see his wife had forgotten her anger enough to ladle out a large portion of it for him.

She brought the bowl to the table. "The impresario was ever the skinflint," she remarked, setting Haydn's meal before him. "Although one can hardly blame the poor man."

Not blame the man! Haydn nearly choked on his food. And even Johann raised his eyebrows. Maria Anna reserved her compassion for the most unlikely people, he thought.

"I hear you have taken on his duties, husband," she continued before either of them could ask her to explain herself. "But for God's sake, do not be fool enough to take on his expenses as well."

"Why would I do that?" Haydn barely refrained from rolling his eyes. "It is not as though I've agreed to assume his debts?"

But Maria Anna, lowering herself into her chair, merely pursed her lips. "You are too soft-hearted, husband, and too inclined to give your money away to the least deserving person. I suppose you took it upon yourself to pay all his unpaid workers."

How had she heard about that? God forbid, Johann should have mentioned the bag of gold he had received from the Prince that morning. It would be hard to explain why it had not accompanied him home that night.

"It is only a temporary situation," Johann was trying to assure Maria Anna. "His Serene Highness is determined that nothing will prevent a Viennese performance of brother's opera."

"And I am merely charged with overseeing the production of the operas." He turned to Johann. "There are two others besides my own. I was not happy to hear that, as you can imagine."

He had wished the conversation to take a less perilous turn, but the attempt was futile. Maria Ann was not to be swayed. "I still say, have a care for your pocketbook, husband."

And the remark unfortunately caught Johann's attention, who turned to her, a bewildered expression on his thin features.

"But why should brother's pocketbook be affected, sister-in-law? Are the men who work there not known to be honest?"

"It is not the men, brother-in-law," Maria Anna said. "It is the position itself. For one thing, the imperial household expects to view performances without ever paying a pfennig for the privilege. Who knows, but every other member of the nobility might have the same expectation. How the impresario ever made a profit, I am sure I don't know."

Haydn considered his wife's words. How she had come by her facts was a mystery. But he could not deny their merit. Dealings with many a count frequently involved much bowing and scraping before a person could hope to be paid. The Emperor was not the only one who made a note of expenses in his black notebook only to forget all about both the money and the man to whom it was owed.

Haydn should have thought of all this himself. He had been so certain Affligio was mismanaging the theater's funds, he had omitted to go through the impresario's account books.

He would get to it on the morrow, he decided, and determine whether any of the Burgtheater's patrons had been in arrears to the impresario. A polite note would suffice to recall the money.

If that did not work, the Kapellmeister would approach his employer. There was no reason why either he or His Serene Highness should be made to bear the imperial palace theater's costs out of their own pockets.

But surely in the Emperor's case there was some excuse. He said as much between mouthfuls of his dinner.

"How could anyone expect the imperial household to pay for a box when it is the Emperor's purse that bears the entire cost of the production? One might as well as ask His Serene Highness to rent a box at his own opera house in Eszterháza."

"The imperial purse may be supposed to bear the cost, husband, but it does not." Maria Anna's curls slapped her face as she vehemently shook her head.

Haydn frowned, his food forgotten. As always, his wife spoke with a certainty she could not possibly have. And it irritated him no end.

"How can you know that?" he demanded. How in the name of God did his wife—confined to her kitchen—manage to dig up such odd nuggets of information? It was inconceivable that she could have any knowledge of the impresario's arrangement with the Emperor.

"It is what Papa says. Do you never listen when he talks?" his wife scolded him. "That is why it takes him months to recover his expenses for any of Affligio's commissions. Because at the end of the day, it is inevitably the impresario—poor man—who finds himself saddled with all the bills, and then he must scramble to pay his workers. Not that he is above making them wait."

Haydn could not recall his father-in-law making any such comment, although he had listened to many a rambling story about delayed payments for the wigs Papa Keller provided both the court and the Burgtheater's performers.

"I was not aware. . ." The Kapellmeister glanced at his brother, wondering if Johann recollected the old gentleman's comments.

"I thought he greatly exaggerated the matter," Johann confided in a low voice to him when Maria Anna rose to get Haydn a second serving of stew. Aloud, Johann continued to Maria Anna: "But surely Affligio is reimbursed for any expenses he may have to bear."

"I wouldn't be too sure of that," she said darkly approaching the table again.

Haydn sighed. His wife's conviction did not bode well for him. Johann must have divined his mood, for he adroitly changed the subject.

"Is your presence required at the Burgtheater again tomorrow, brother?" he asked. "Michael—"

"He was at the palace?" Haydn raised his head sharply. That must have been how his middle brother had known exactly where to find him.

Johann nodded. "He was in too much of a hurry to stay or to leave a message."

"He came by Affligio's chambers this evening," Haydn explained as his wife rose again to portion out a slice of her almond torte with cherries for him. "That was what delayed me."

"What does he want with you?" Maria Anna looked over her shoulder at him. "Has he taken to writing operas?"

Haydn smiled. Michael was known for his religious music. He may have written an oratorio or two, but it would be unlike his middle brother to turn his talents to opera.

"No, he wishes me to—"

"Prove the Salzburger arrested for Affligio's murder innocent of the crime, I suppose," Johann said much to Haydn's surprise.

"However did you know?"

"It was merely a surmise"—Johann lifted his shoulders ruefully— "The maids said a man from Salzburg had been apprehended. What else would spur Michael to come in search of you?"

"He does not wish you to travel all the way to Salzburg, does he?" Maria Anna, about to slide the dessert plate before Haydn, abruptly pulled her hand back. "We have barely unpacked our bags and settled down. You cannot expect us to set out again. I will not do it, husband."

Haydn eyed the torte with its filling of cream and cherries; his wife still held the plate tantalizingly out of reach.

He raised his eyes to her. "I am not required to go anywhere, Maria Anna. The man is imprisoned here in Vienna. His family is in the city as well."

"And Michael knows him, I suppose," Johann guessed as Maria Anna finally relented, allowing Haydn his dessert.

"Only too well, I fear," Haydn said grimly. "It is Leopold Mozart."

<hr>

The next morning after he had paid the Burgtheater carpenters, Haydn set off with Michael to meet Frau Mozart.

"It will set the poor woman's mind at ease, Joseph," Michael said, easing himself into the carriage, "to have you confirm what the world —and her heart—already knows. That her husband has been unjustly accused."

The remark set Haydn's teeth on edge, but he restrained the acerbic response that threatened to burst from his lips. He knew only that

Leopold Mozart had been accused of murder. Whether justly or not remained to be seen.

"You must assure her of the fact," Michael persisted.

This time Haydn did not remain silent. "I can do no such thing, Michael, until I know more of the matter," he retorted in a tone that brooked no argument. "And I refuse to hold out false hope. I will look into the affair—it is all I promise."

Michael harrumphed. "Any fool can see Leopold is innocent. But have it your own way. You were always stubborn." He set his face toward the window, visibly annoyed.

The remainder of the journey passed in silence. The Mozarts had taken lodgings at the Red Sable, a narrow three-story house on the Hohe Brücke above Tiefer Graben. The house was tucked into a corner at the western end of the bridge.

A shallow brook gurgled below them, the sound reminding Haydn of the rush of the river Leitha through his hometown of Rohrau in the summer.

The woman who answered their knock on the door was tall and plump, garbed in a russet-colored, silk-lined gown with her blond hair neatly styled under a fine black lace cap.

"Herr Haydn!" The woman's dark eyes widened as she took a step back to let her visitors in. "You will help us, then? God have mercy on your soul!"

A short, blue-eyed boy, as fair-skinned and blond as the woman, stepped up. "I knew you would realize Papa is innocent. Now it's just a matter of convincing that dour ass of an Archbishop to do his duty and get Papa out of prison."

"Wolferl, your manners!" Frau Mozart gasped at the same time as Michael patted the boy on his head, saying: "There, there, my boy. Dis-respecting one's elders and betters never did one any good."

The boy—no more than an adolescent, Haydn realized—snorted. "If only His Buffoonship were worthy of respect."

"That's enough, Wolfgang," his mother chided. "Insulting His Grace won't do your father any good." She pointed toward the stairs. "Tell Katherl we have guests. Ask her to bring up a fresh pot of coffee and some of the *Apfelstrudel* we had last night."

"Why not send Nannerl down?" the boy complained. "It is a woman's job after all." But he tripped down the stairs, nonetheless.

Haydn smiled indulgently after the boy and then turned to his mother. "You have your hands full, I see."

The walls of his own house were doomed to be devoid of the eager voices of children. The Mozarts, despite their trouble, were blessed with a treasure far greater than any gold a man could earn. His remark had been intended as much to distract the good woman as to remind her of what she had.

Frau Mozart smiled wearily back at him. "He's a good enough boy, our Wolferl, and he means well, for all that he's impulsive." There were tired lines and shadows under her eyes, Haydn noticed, and she seemed to will herself to stand erect rather than let her shoulders sag under the weight of their present burden.

She led the way into a cheerful parlor and offered them a seat. The furniture was scratched, the curtains clean but faded, and the paint on the walls had been bleached by the sun.

Nevertheless, Frau Mozart's deft hand was apparent in the little touches that brightened up the family's rented lodgings. Fresh flowers filled the vases scattered about the room; knick-knacks were artfully arranged on the mantelpiece and side tables; and colorful landscapes and still lifes gave the parlor a convivial air.

Chapter Twelve

A competent housewife, Haydn thought appreciatively, as he lowered himself into an armchair.

Frau Mozart glanced at Michael before turning to Haydn. "Your brother assures me there is hope for my husband, Herr Haydn." She gazed expectantly at him.

Silently cursing his brother for fanning the woman's expectations too high, the Kapellmeister clasped his hands together, picking his words with care.

"How came your husband to have any dealings with the impresario?" he asked. "There was an opera, I understand."

She nodded, but before she could speak, Wolferl's young voice interrupted.

"The Emperor commissioned an opera, and Papa was supposed to see Affligio about it."

"Commissioned an opera? From your father?" Haydn twisted around to look at the young boy who stood in the doorway, his chin jutting out defiantly. That the elder Mozart had any interest in opera—much less the *buffa* variety—struck him as unexpectedly as a well-done false reprise.

"Of course not, Joseph," Michael replied, beaming proudly at the boy. "It was Wolferl who was to compose the opera. And he has done it! An entire opera. A boy not yet fourteen. Can you imagine it?"

"The Emperor asked if I wanted to compose an opera." Wolfgang sauntered into the parlor. "Naturally, I said I did. Who doesn't? It's the only way to build one's reputation. I said I wished to conduct it as well."

He smiled—a self-satisfied, insolent smirk of a smile that the Kapellmeister imagined must have raised many a man's hackles.

"Indeed." Haydn turned around, wondering if the boy was up to the task. He seemed to have supreme confidence in his own abilities. But there was a world of difference between understanding the rules of counterpoint and furnishing music for a drama.

"The Emperor asked for an opera?" he repeated, wishing to clarify the matter. "A *buffa*, I take it?"

"His Majesty did not ask for an opera," Frau Mozart corrected him. "He merely wished to know if our Wolferl wanted to compose one. It was nothing more than that," she continued hastily as her son made to interrupt her. "A casual remark thrown in politeness to a visitor at court."

"Oh, Mama!" Wolfgang blew out his breath in a huff of exasperation. His mother ignored him.

"But Leopold—" She shook her head and spread her hands wide in a gesture of helplessness. "Leopold insisted upon taking it as a commission. He got hold of a libretto from Signor Coltellini, and Wolferl set to work as though his life depended upon it."

"But my dear lady," Michael interrupted, "there was a contract, was there not?" He turned to Haydn, pushing himself to the edge of his seat in his excitement. "I could swear Leopold mentioned it to me."

Frau Mozart pressed her lips together, clearly not relishing having her interpretation of the matter questioned. "If there was, my husband did not show me the papers. And I cannot begin to know where they—if indeed they exist—might be. You will have to ascertain the facts from him."

Haydn noticed Wolfgang rolling his eyes impatiently. "Oh, Mama, must you take the dimmest view of the situation?" He turned his attention to Haydn. "Papa met the impresario and the man promised— upon his honor as a gentleman—to pay me a hundred ducats for the work. It's been a month at least since I completed the manuscript, and I have yet to see a single kreutzer.

"That any man would call himself a gentleman and yet have no scruples about cheating honest folk out of their hard-earned money. It's a shame, I tell you."

Haydn sighed. He would need to draw out the details of the arrangement from Leopold. Frau Mozart's pursed lips indicated she disagreed with her son. And where the truth lay, God alone knew. He rubbed his forehead wearily.

"So you gave the music to Affligio. What happened after?"

"Oh, there was one excuse after another. This had to be changed. That singer had complained about some trivial note or other. It could not be performed now. It could certainly not happen then. Papa was quite fed up, I can tell you that."

As well he might be, if he indeed had expectations, Haydn thought. But Michael openly—and foolishly in Haydn's opinion—sided with Wolferl. "Of course, he was, my boy. Of course, he was."

"One need not belabor the point too much," he reminded them wryly. "The police will unfortunately see it as furnishing a very plausible motive for murder."

"But it is not!" Frau Mozart cried in a rare flash of anger. Her cheeks were flaming and she nearly rose from her chair.

At Haydn's look of surprise, she quieted down.

"We have been traveling a year or more, Herr Haydn," she explained more calmly. "Money was short—and the situation made worse still by the Archbishop withholding my husband's salary. Then, not to earn any money at all, to have no opportunity to sell any of Wolferl's works, or earn a commission, however small. You can imagine how it affected our prospects."

"And your husband's temper, no doubt," Haydn said sympathetically. It was a genuinely felt emotion, but the words had also been put out as a trap to gauge the truth. Had Leopold been enraged enough to commit a heinous act?

It was Wolferl, white-faced, nostrils flaring, who took the bait. "Oh, Papa was livid!"

His mother shot him a warning look. "He took it as well as might be expected."

"He was determined the opera should be performed," Haydn suggested again in a sympathetic manner. A clash of wills could certainly have caused a terrible and entirely unintended outcome.

"On the contrary"—Frau Mozart met his gaze squarely—"he was resigned to the fact that Wolferl's work and our efforts had come to naught."

* * *

Steffi, the Archbishop of Salzburg's temporary maid in Vienna, shrugged out of her cape and shook her blond curls. "I wish His Grace would make up his mind whether he means to go or stay," she complained.

She gave Rosalie her cape to hang up and seated herself at the capacious table in the Esterházy servants' hall. "Count Kohary's establishment is in need of a permanent kitchen maid, and the position would be mine if only I can confirm I can start in the next few days."

"I thought His Grace meant to stay until he'd brought his musician to heel." Greta placed a chilled glass of lemonade and a plate of *Zitronenkeks*—lemon cookies—before her friend. Their morning chores were done, and it had been a pleasant, if unexpected surprise, to see Steffi at the door.

"Has the man been found?" Rosalie carefully draped Steffi's cape on one of the hooks by the door and returned to the table.

"Found and lost," Steffi sighed, biting hungrily into a buttery cookie.

"You're speaking in riddles, Steffi," Greta admonished her. She helped herself to a cookie—the sweet treats with a thin layer of icing were her favorite. But fond as she was of Steffi, Greta couldn't help reflecting that her friend had always been one to make much ado over nothing. "What exactly has happened?"

Most likely nothing much, she thought to herself.

"Well," Steffi began, wiping the crumbs from her mouth, "he came on Saturday morning, his tail between his legs, begging to be taken back. Said he'd return to Salzburg as soon as His Grace ordered it."

"And what did His Grace say?" Rosalie leaned forward, resting her elbows on the vast table. "That he wouldn't?"

"Oh no, His Grace was quite willing to take him back." Steffi took a sip of her chilled lemonade. "But the man—can you believe his temerity?—demanded His Grace pay him for all those months for which his salary had been withheld."

"Good heavens!" Greta gasped. "I hope His Grace tossed him out with a flea in his ear."

"Oh, he put his foot down, of course. Even so, we all thought the matter settled. That Herr Mozart—that is his name—would return to Salzburg and that His Grace would follow suit. If I'd known that wasn't to be the case, I wouldn't have applied for the position at Count Kohary's." Steffi pushed out her pretty red lips into a pout.

"And now he has gotten himself arrested." Steffi's emerald-green eyes flashed with anger. "And His Grace—well, I have no notion what His Grace means to do."

"Arrested!" Rosalie's violet eyes widened and collided with Greta's.

"Didn't I say it was him?" Greta folded her arms and jutted her chin out. She turned to Steffi. "He's been arrested for murder, has he not? This—what did you say his name was?"

"Mozart," Steffi replied. "Leopold Mozart." She frowned. "But how did you two find out about that?"

"Karl told us a Salzburger had been arrested for Herr Affligio's murder," Greta told her.

"And Herr Haydn's brother was here, demanding to see him just yesterday," Rosalie added. "He was with a plump, long-faced woman."

"That'll be Herr Mozart's wife," Steffi said glumly. "She sent a message this morning—wanting her husband's pension. That put His Grace in a foul mood, I can tell you. And now how am I to tell him I must leave next week? His Grace was ever a stickler for the letter of his contracts. And mine says I'm to be on duty until the day he leaves the city."

"Her husband's pension?" Rosalie's voice and eyebrows both rose. "When he has been arrested for murder? Do these people know no shame?"

"Evidently not." Steffi idly fingered her glass. "And they seem to have Master Michael twisted around their little fingers. He will hear no ill word said of them. I'm not surprised he hotfooted it here the moment he heard."

She raised her head, gazing hopefully at the other two maids. "How long will it take your Herr Haydn to get to the bottom of the affair? If the matter can be settled by the end of the week . . ."

Greta shrugged. "Who knows? He has enough to do as it stands. The Burgtheater needs a new impresario and His Serene Highness saddled the poor man with the job."

A determined glint appeared in Steffi's eyes. "There's no doubt in my mind, Herr Mozart did commit the crime. Be sure to tell Herr Haydn that. There's no need for him to waste his time trying to prove anything else."

Rosalie exchanged another glance with Greta. "Herr Haydn will need more than just your word, Steffi. How can you be so sure Herr Mozart is guilty?"

Steffi met her gaze squarely. "On the night that Herr Affligio was murdered—Sunday night that would've been—there was a violent pounding on our door." She turned to Greta. "It would've been your Karl, I suppose. Anyway, he asked for His Grace to come immediately because Herr Mozart had gone berserk and was threatening the impresario.

"I'm telling you I'm not surprised the man was arrested. His Grace must've felt the same. He went out at once that night, but I don't suppose he was able to meet Herr Affligio. He returned home, his face grave and his lips pursed. And the next morning he set out at dawn —to alert the Emperor, no doubt. His Grace always wears his crimson cape when he goes to the Hofburg."

Chapter Thirteen

"KARL did say it was the Emperor who found the body," Rosalie remembered. "But"—her violet eyes narrowed—"although Karl mentioned the loud disputes between the two men, he never said your Herr Mozart was violent."

"I don't suppose he was until that night," Steffi said. "Why, Herr Affligio came to visit on Saturday evening, and even he commented on it. 'The man's not an impulsive hothead, I'll have to give him that,' he told His Grace.

"Then he said"—Steffi giggled—"'the man's too shrewd and calculating to be diverted from his Christian ways.' His Grace didn't like hearing that, I can tell you. Oh don't speak to me of his faith, he says."

"I don't blame His Grace. Herr Mozart sounds like a holier-than-thou piece of work," Greta sniffed. She looked at Rosalie, but her friend's eyes were shrouded in thought.

"What I don't understand," Rosalie said, "is that if he wasn't the type of man to come so easily to blows, what set him off that night?"

"Who knows? But something must have. It is all the more reason to believe that he is guilty." Steffi swallowed the last of her lemonade.

"You can't believe he's not, can you?" Greta stared accusingly at Rosalie, who was still looking doubtful. But before Rosalie could respond the jangling of the bell startled them. "What now?" Greta cursed, barely able to hear her own voice over the din. It was the Estates Director, no doubt.

Who else was there in this household who rang a bell quite like that —with his finger pressed insistently over the button?

Motioning to Michael, Haydn rose, about to take his leave, when young Wolferl piped up: "Is it true you are to take over the impresario's duties, Herr Haydn?"

Haydn lowered himself back into his seat, wondering as he did so if his features reflected his astonishment. "I see it takes as little time for news to spread in Vienna as it does in the small town of Eisenstadt."

"It is true, then?" Wolferl persisted. At Haydn's nod, he breathed, "God be praised!

"Mama sent a message to the Burgtheater. That is how we found out. Affligio's assistant, much to our surprise, directed us to you."

Whatever for, Haydn wondered. He turned to Frau Mozart, whose acute discomfort showed itself in the bright crimson that suffused her pale cheeks. She twisted her fingers together. "I wished to know whether Herr Affligio had left any instructions about the money due to Wolferl," she said, her voice low and indistinct.

"There is money due to your son?" Haydn was stunned. What services had the boy provided to need payment? Before he could say anything more, however, Michael shoved his oar into the conversation. "You need have no worries on that account, dear lady. Whatever is due, Joseph will pay it, will you not?"

Haydn gritted his teeth, reining his temper in with difficulty. "I will need to ascertain the precise amount and the arrangement Affligio had with your son." He surveyed mother and son. "What was the payment for?"

"For the opera score, of course." Wolferl's blue eyes widened, as though astounded the matter required any explanation. "Affligio promised my father a hundred ducats."

Simply for writing an opera? Haydn wondered if the boy had understood the matter correctly. It seemed unlikely.

Wolferl crossed his legs and met the Kapellmeister's gaze squarely. "The music was well worth it, I can assure you."

"A hundred ducats *if* the opera was brought to the stage." Haydn stretched out the words, punctuating his remark with rests to betray a confusion he wasn't far from feeling. "Is that not right?" Unless, of course, he had misunderstood the reason for the dispute.

But if Leopold had reconciled himself to the opera being consigned to oblivion, surely he had also made peace with the fact that his son's work had been for naught.

No impresario would pay for music that would not be used.

"He said he had reconsidered the matter," Frau Mozart clarified. "That he had a proposition to make."

"When?" Haydn demanded, startled to hear the news.

Michael grunted impatiently. "Surely Frau Mozart and her children don't need to be troubled with these small details in their time of affliction, Joseph. How in the name of God does it matter where or when? Affligio said he had reconsidered." The armchair creaked as he shifted his bulk. "That is all we need to know."

Haydn ignored his brother and looked earnestly at mother and son. "Far be it from me to add to your troubles, Frau Mozart. But it is a temporary position I occupy, and I have little to no authority on the Burgtheater's purse strings. You will appreciate that I cannot make payments willy-nilly with no regard for contracts or agreements.

"If I am to help, I must know more. Are you aware of any of the details of Herr Affligio's offer?"

Wolferl shrugged and turned to his mother, who shook her plump head. "No. How could we be? It was only on Saturday evening that he sent word he was willing to reconsider."

"Saturday evening?" Haydn repeated. Four days ago, then. Barely a day after Affligio had categorically refused Leopold's demands, and Leopold had reluctantly resigned himself to leaving Vienna. What had caused the impresario to change his mind in such short order?

"Your husband agreed to meet Herr Affligio on Saturday, then?"

It must have been then that Leopold had been sighted outside the Burgtheater. His spirits soared. If the witness had simply been mistaken about the day on which he'd seen Leopold, it would be a simple matter to get him out of prison.

"No." Frau Mozart's flat voice punctured the Kapellmeister's rising optimism. "It was on Sunday that they were supposed to meet."

"On Sunday?" Haydn's voice rose so high he might have still been a soprano in St. Stephen's choir. "On Sunday?" he said again.

Dear God, how was anyone to believe the man had not committed the crime when he had been seen outside the Burgtheater on the day—possibly at the very time—of the impresario's murder?

"And they met, I take it?" he asked. Had Leopold left the impresario alive?

Frau Mozart shook her head. "It was a journey made in vain, I fear. Leopold said the impresario would not even answer his door."

⚬⚬⚬

"The truth could not be plainer," Michael declared as he and Haydn left the Mozarts' lodgings and made their way to their waiting carriage. "Clearly Leopold is innocent."

The Kapellmeister, clutching a thick manuscript Wolferl had insisted he take, held his peace. From what he had heard, the truth was not quite so cut and dried as Michael supposed. But to argue the point with his brother would be futile.

But Michael was not to be so easily dismissed. Haydn felt his brother's gaze upon him.

"Surely that must be evident, even to you, Joseph."

Ach so, he was a thickheaded dimwit, was he? A man with a thinner skin might have been offended. But Haydn was accustomed to his middle brother's scarcely veiled barbs and the gruff voice with which he habitually hurled them.

"My conviction—or lack thereof—will not get Leopold out of prison," he reminded Michael. "You forget he was seen in the vicinity of the Burgtheater at the time Affligio was murdered—and doesn't deny it. That does not bode well for him, I fear."

"Yes, he was at the Burgtheater. What of it? So were many other people. That fellow you were hobnobbing with this morning"—as though Karl, Haydn thought, were some scoundrel far beneath them—"and that brute of a man you were deep in conversation with."

The coachman opened the door.

"The carpenters' foreman," Haydn said, climbing into the carriage. "He needed instructions on the sets I require. I could hardly expect him to read my mind."

Michael waved an impatient hand, dismissing the explanation. "Yes, yes, it matters not who he is." He climbed in after Haydn. "The point is, they were all at the Burgtheater, too, and could have stabbed Affligio just as easily as Leopold."

Haydn waited until the coachman had closed the door behind them to return to his perch.

"Yes, but only Leopold had any quarrel with Affligio." Although that wasn't entirely true. The habitually delayed payments could have put any of the stagehands or painters or carpenters at the end of their tether.

Then again, Leopold's disputes had been the most vociferous.

"What quarrel?" Michael harrumphed impatiently as he settled himself in his seat. "Leopold had reconciled himself to returning to Salzburg. Was your mind wandering when Frau Mozart told us that?"

"On the contrary, I recall her words quite well." Haydn stared out the window. The carriage rolled forward and the clip-clop of the horses' hooves supplied a staccato rhythm to his thoughts.

Leopold may have resigned himself to leaving Vienna. But had Wolferl?

His gaze fell on the thick opera score sitting on his lap. Wolferl had pressed the manuscript into his arms—hoping, no doubt, that Haydn would reverse the dead impresario's decision.

"The work is flawless, I am confident of it," Wolferl had declared in his self-assured manner. "No archangel—I dare say, not even God himself—could find so much as a note out of place."

Taken aback by this cocksure assertion, the Kapellmeister had stared flabbergasted at the young boy. Frau Mozart's mouth pulled back into a rueful grimace. "For shame, Wolferl!" she chided the lad, placing a restraining hand on his shoulder.

"Mama is right," Wolferl continued undeterred. "I waste my breath stating the obvious. A man of taste such as yourself, Herr Haydn, is sure to recognize the work's merits."

Haydn's eyebrow rose quizzically. "Is the matter of my taste—such as it is—to be determined by my opinion of your work?"

Wolferl had the grace to blush. "Of course not. All I meant was that any objective listener can tell the work is pleasing."

Now as he sat in the carriage, Haydn fingered the score. The arias were certainly beautiful. A cursory glance had revealed that much.

What had caused Affligio's aversion to the opera? It could not have been malice alone.

A new *opera buffa*—one composed and conducted by a boy, no less —would've been a novel enough occurrence to draw the entire Viennese public into the theater, thus making the endeavor well worth the impresario's while.

Why, then, had Affligio been so opposed to it? Could it have been more profitable to stymie the production?

Chapter Fourteen

He turned to Michael. "Had Leopold any enemies?"

"Enemies?" Michael's brows came together in a displeased frown.

"Anyone who might wish to see him fail?"

"I know what the word means, Joseph," Michael snapped. "But your question makes no sense. Are you suggesting his enemies—whoever they might be—killed the impresario, hoping to put Leopold in prison for the deed?"

God grant him patience, Haydn thought. "I was merely wondering why Affligio was so set against bringing the opera to the stage," he explained. "Surely something could've been worked out."

When it came to staging an opera, nothing was set in stone.

Not the libretto, which frequently had to be changed several times. A story meant for the stage needed more action than one intended to be read. Not the music, which might need to be changed, edited out, or have numbers added, depending upon the circumstances. An aria might need to be cut here, a chorus or a march added there.

But all the changes and revisions served the final spectacle, and librettist, composer, impresario, and singers worked together—if not entirely in harmony—to make it possible.

Michael threw his hands up in a gesture of frustration. "Who can tell what Affligio's reasons were? The man was bullheaded and unaccommodating, according to Leopold. Still, he must have been brought to see reason. Why else would he have sent for Leopold?"

"Frau Mozart mentioned something about an offer." Haydn chewed his lip. What could that offer have been about?

"Precisely." Michael shifted his girth to face Haydn. "And that should tell the story plainly enough, Joseph. Why would Leopold kill the man when he might have been about to make good on the money he owed Wolferl?"

Why indeed, Haydn thought. Unless the offer had been so offensive, Leopold had lost his last ounce of patience.

Peter von Rahier, Estates Director to the Esterházy family, was seething. Where was the Kapellmeister? The Estates Director had noted Haydn's absence from the breakfast table that morning. It had been especially galling given that the Kapellmeister had also missed the midday meal the previous day.

True, there was nothing in Haydn's contract that obliged him to take his meals at the palace. But surely it was understood that as an Officer of the Court, he was expected to bring himself to the Officers' Mess and partake of the meals served to them all.

"He treats the palace like a common *Heuriger*," Rahier fumed, "coming and going as he chooses. How are any of the men under him to learn discipline if their betters behave in such an irresponsible fashion?"

He had cornered his nephew Albert, a violinist in the orchestra, as he sought to creep out of the Mess, unnoticed, only to learn from the lad's reluctant lips that the Kapellmeister had not bothered to show his face at all that morning.

"And when were you planning to bring the news to me?" Rahier demanded, irritated that the boy had allowed his preference for the Kapellmeister to override his duty to his uncle.

"I thought you knew," Albert said, his eyes wide with astonishment. "Does His Serene Highness not take you into his confidence anymore?"

Rahier frowned, more displeased than ever. "Why should he not take me into his confidence? Besides, what has that to do with anything?"

But the boy's comment suggested the Kapellmeister had somehow wormed his way into receiving the Prince's permission to traipse about town and do as he pleased. That His Serene Highness had not seen fit to entrust the matter—whatever it was—into his hands irked Rahier no end.

His blood churning, he strode down the hallway to his office when he heard a voice calling.

"I beg your pardon, sir."

Rahier ignored the voice. Let one of the footmen or the maids deal with the visitor, whoever he may be. He had more significant concerns to deal with.

The voice grew louder and more insistent. Rahier was still inclined to ignore it when it uttered the same words in French. Dear God, it was a member of the nobility. Clearly not someone who could be ignored.

He swung around, plastering an unctuous smile upon his face. The man who stood uncertainly in the circular entrance hallway was be-wigged, dressed in a sumptuously embroidered powder blue silk coat and pale cream breeches.

"How may I serve you?" Rahier asked in his best French as he came forward to greet the gentleman.

But to his annoyance, the visitor reverted to German. "I am looking for Herr Haydn. Is he here?"

"He is not," Rahier answered shortly. He jabbed his finger on a button in the wall to summon one of the musicians' maids. God alone knew why the Kapellmeister and his orchestra needed so many! But there was always a bunch of them scurrying around underfoot, and not one of them seemed to do much work.

"You may leave a message with one of the maids," he went on, satis-fied to see Rosalie Heindl bustling out of the kitchen. "See to it that the Kapellmeister receives this gentleman's message," he informed her.

Rahier turned on his heels, about to leave, when the newcomer intro-duced himself.

"Jakob Fugger, at your service. I wish to—"

Rahier wheeled around. "Fugger? You are the banker?" he asked.

What need did the Kapellmeister have of a banker? Such an influen-tial one, at that!

"I—er—Yes," the visitor replied, apparently startled by the question.

Rahier was equally astounded. The Fuggers, a merchant family from Augsburg, had been in the banking business for a century or more. They had long funded the marriage arrangements of the imperial family and even financed many an Archduke's election to Emperor of the Holy Roman Empire.

And this gentleman had come in person to meet the Kapellmeister! Rahier bristled. What had the man done to deserve such an honor?

"And you wish to see the Kapellmeister about—?" Rahier resumed his interrogation.

"A small matter of money." The banker—he seemed too young in Rahier's estimation to be at the helm of a well-known financial institution—seemed hesitant to say more. But Rahier pounced upon the admission.

"Money? The Kapellmeister is in debt?" Wasn't there something in the man's contract that indicated he could be dismissed for incurring unreasonable debts? And where there were debts, would there not also be evidence of gambling and other reprehensible behavior?

Aha! The sainted Kapellmeister was not quite so godly as he made himself out to be.

But before the banker could respond, Rosalie butted her meddlesome nose into the matter. "Herr Haydn is not at the palace this morning. But his brother, Master Johann, is. Would you like to speak with him?"

"If the Kapellmeister is in debt, the matter concerns the palace as well," Rahier interjected quickly. "How much money, precisely, is at stake?"

The banker hesitated, then turned to Rosalie. "Is Herr Haydn's brother authorized to act on his behalf?" He turned back to Rahier. "These are confidential matters, you see."

"Ring for Master Johann," Rahier instructed Rosalie with a dismissive wave of his elegant fingers. He was determined not to be gotten rid of quite so easily.

"I am afraid, Herr Fugger," he continued, turning to the banker, "that no matter concerning an officer of the Esterházy court can be kept entirely private. His Serene Highness, Prince Nikolaus Esterházy, will need to be informed of any debts. As will I, as the Prince's representative."

Fugger sighed. "Very well, then. It is a matter of seventy thousand gulden."

"Seventy thousand gulden!" Rahier nearly staggered back in shock. The Kapellmeister received a generous annual salary, as did he. But the sum Fugger had mentioned was one only princes could toy with.

"That is the principal," Fugger explained apologetically.

"And the interest?" God have mercy, Rahier thought. How much would that be?

"A mere trifle." Fugger smiled. "Eight thousand four hundred sixty gulden, no more."

God in heaven, what had the Kapellmeister gotten himself into? Out of the corner of his eyes, he saw Rosalie hovering by them. Nosy as always, he thought, annoyed.

"Have you sent for Master Johann?" he demanded. Turning to Fugger, he continued. "We will discuss the matter in my office, if you please."

<hr>

"There must be some mistake, Herr Fugger," Johann began, gazing earnestly into the bland features of the young gentleman who sat before them in the Estates Director's chambers.

How could there not be, he thought. Rosalie's message—that a banker insistent upon seeing brother over a matter of several thousand gulden—had been unnerving enough. Rahier's interpretation of the affair, typically, had been far worse.

"Your brother appears to have dug himself into a hole of monumental proportions, Master Johann." The Estates Director had openly smirked when Johann entered the room. Now, he gestured toward the banker. "The facts speak for themselves."

"Nonsense! The facts are utterly ridiculous," Luigi, who had insisted upon accompanying Johann, burst out. "Joseph is generous to a fault, but he is hardly profligate."

He stared at the banker who sat across from them at Rahier's enormous desk.

"And seventy thousand gulden is an enormous sum of money," Johann pointed out, as he crossed his legs. Surely brother would've mentioned it—to him if not to sister-in-law—were he so deep in debt. That he had not seemed preposterous. "The figure, if nothing else, must be erroneous."

Fugger shook his bewigged head. "There is no error in the sum. It is the precise amount requested by the borrower. If you would but allow me to explain, Master Johann—"

"It is a sizeable amount the Kapellmeister appears to have gambled away," Rahier interjected much to Johann's annoyance. Why was the Estates Director always so ready to believe the worst of brother? He leaned forward, placing his hands on his desk. "I warn you, Master Johann, the Prince must be made aware of this unsavory turn of events."

"My brother has done nothing wrong," Johann replied firmly. "I am confident of it." He gripped his armrests, recalling his father's oft-repeated words.

Trust in God, Johann. No matter what the crisis, trust in God, and it will be all right.

"Yet he has racked up debts to the tune of seventy thousand gulden. And that is the principal alone."

"There is more?" Johann's head swiveled sharply in the direction of the banker.

The banker looked suitably apologetic. "I am afraid so. But the terms of the arrangement are most generous, I assure you. We had agreed to charge no more than a year's interest, and the entire amount was payable in two years."

"Two years?" Luigi's voice rose, expressing the incredulity Johann himself felt. How was such a vast amount to be paid in two years?

The banker nodded. "Three thousand two hundred and seventy gulden, to be paid every month for a period of two years."

"I am surprised the Kapellmeister agreed to those terms," Rahier commented dryly. "It is nearly four times his annual salary," He turned to Johann. "And he had best not look to the Prince to supply the remainder of the amount."

Luigi shook his head. "I refuse to believe it," he said. "Joseph has never needed a banker to underwrite his expenses. Why should he start now?"

A look of consternation appeared on the banker's smooth features. "Am I to understand Herr Haydn has not the means to pay back the loan?"

"The man earns eight hundred gulden a year," Luigi growled. "Does it look like he can make payments of three thousand gulden a month?"

"B-but," stammered the banker, appearing utterly confused, "why then did he agree to assume liability for the loan? Surely that was a thoughtless gesture. And to do it without reference to his employer."

Why, Johann wondered, did the banker expect brother to get His Serene Highness's permission before ratcheting up an enormous amount of debt? Would it have made the situation any better to have sought and obtained the Prince's seal of approval for his supposed sins?

That could hardly be what the banker was suggesting.

"We appear to be talking at cross-purposes," he said, determined to get to the bottom of the affair. "When did you and brother meet to discuss these arrangements?"

The banker shook his head. "I regret I have not yet had the pleasure of making your brother's acquaintance. I hoped to speak with him today."

"Not met him!" Luigi erupted. "How is it possible you agreed to lend Joseph money without ever having met him?"

The banker passed a handkerchief over his brow. "I never said the loan was made to him. He has assumed responsibility for it, or so I was given to understand. His Majesty assured me Herr Haydn had taken over affairs at the Burgtheater."

"The Burgtheater!" Johann sat upright. What was it sister-in-law had said the previous evening about Affligio? "You cannot think brother has assumed the impresario's debts, can you?" Surely even brother would not have agreed to such a thing.

God in heaven, what would sister-in-law say when she heard? After her repeated warnings on the matter, too.

"Praise the Lord!" Rahier muttered. "The Kapellmeister is an even bigger fool than I imagined." He emitted a loud snort. "I suppose he has, to demonstrate the goodness of his heart, promised to take on the impresario's debts. I expect he is also wandering the town in search of the man's killer. Small wonder he hasn't shown his face at the palace in two days."

Fugger frowned, puzzled. "I believe Herr Affligio's killer has already been apprehended. My information indicates only that Herr Haydn has taken over his duties at the Burgtheater."

"And you take that to mean Joseph has taken over Affligio's debts as well?" Gripping the armrests on either side of him, Luigi thrust himself out belligerently. "Are you a fool or merely an opportunistic scoundrel?"

The banker shrank back, cowering in his chair.

Johann hastily pulled the Konzertmeister back into his seat. It would not do to give Rahier any more ammunition against them than he already had. "I beg you will forgive my colleague's outrage, Herr Fugger. He meant you no harm. But his question holds. How can brother's assumption—temporary, I might add—of the impresario's duties make him accountable for the man's arrears?"

"But that is what the agreement stipulates," Fugger protested. "Our establishment would certainly not have financed Herr Affligio had that clause not been in place."

Chapter Fifteen

"I fear there is nothing I can do, Herr Gluck." Haydn cast his eyes at the contract in his hands and lifted his shoulders in an apologetic shrug. He had no sooner returned to the Burgtheater than the composer —waiting for him on the steps of the building—had accosted him.

"Herr Haydn, the issue regarding La Renier must be resolved at once. Can she—or can she not, according to her contract—be ousted from my opera? I have been waiting this half hour for your return."

"We were to meet later this morning, were we not?" Haydn asked, taken aback to see the man. He had taken the singers' contracts home, only to discover they didn't include the specific ones he needed.

He had intended to use the brief interval before his appointment to find and peruse the necessary documents. But now here was the composer, a good forty minutes earlier than Haydn had expected to see him.

"I saw no reason to dilly-dally," Gluck announced loftily. "I am a busy man, as are you. The sooner this painful issue is decided, the better. Surely you would not have me wait until the very day of the opening to break the sad news to the poor woman. Not to mention that another singer must be assigned the part."

"Indeed!" How a wait of forty minutes could make a whit of difference to anyone involved in the production of *Alceste*, Haydn scarcely knew. But Gluck's mouth, compressed into a thin line of dissatisfaction, indicated the futility of pointing out the obvious.

"Shall we go?" Gluck gestured impatiently toward the building.

Haydn had followed him up the stairs, looking longingly after the carriage bearing his brother away. If only he had given into Michael's strident urgings to visit both Leopold and his master, the Archbishop of

Salzburg. But mindful of his duty and the pending meeting with Herr Gluck, the Kapellmeister had put Michael off.

Now, in the impresario's chambers, Haydn was aware Gluck was making a vain effort to contain his fury.

"But that is impossible!" the composer cried. He raised his hands heavenward, as tragic a figure as a character in one of his own operas.

Haydn shrugged again. "Her signature is plain to see. I wish it were otherwise." He had taken a moment to determine if Loretta Renier had signed a contract to appear in his opera. Unfortunately, she had. But he had taken the unwelcome development in his stride. Why couldn't Gluck do the same?

"There must be some mistake." Gluck's voice rose to the rafters, bringing Karl to the door. "There has to be."

Turning toward the door, Gluck caught sight of Karl and waved him in.

"You there, didn't Affligio say he wished to dismiss one of the singers?"

Karl entered slowly. "He did." His gaze swiveled from the irate Gluck to Haydn. "But I cannot say whom he wished to rid himself of. Nor whether he got around to doing it."

"It was Renier, who else could it be? She was the only person who deserved to be given the boot. The woman can't act. And as for her singing, she has not a kreutzer's worth of talent." Gluck turned bitterly to Haydn. "If you had the misfortune to hear her, you could not help but agree."

"I have heard her," Haydn commented dryly. "And I am compelled to make do with her talents—or lack thereof—as well." But raving and ranting about it would not help matters. Not that he pointed this out to the irate composer.

He was feeling a smidgeon of respect for the deceased impresario. The man must have had the patience of a saint to contend alike with temperamental singers and self-important composers. How had Affligio managed it without losing his sanity?

The Kapellmeister shuffled the papers in his hand, casting his eye down another document—a list of the singers assigned to *Alceste*.

"I see there are two prominent female roles. Cannot Donna Oliveri"—Haydn had no idea who she was—"take the role of Alceste while Loretta Renier takes her part?"

"Alceste must be a soprano. Oliveri is a contralto—her voice is so deep one might be forgiven for mistaking her for a man."

"She possesses an excellent range. Herr Affligio frequently marveled at it." Karl joined the conversation. "But the soprano notes are unfortunately too high for her."

"Can she go as high as mezzo-soprano?" Haydn asked, thinking of the need to cast a different Lesbina for his own opera now that Fräulein Renier had been persuaded to sing Eurilda.

But Gluck mistook his intention and instantly snapped, "Mezzo-soprano is not good enough. It simply will not do. I need a soprano. Why can't Matilda Bologna take La Renier's place?"

Haydn glanced at Karl, unable to answer this demand.

"She will do no more than two operas at a time," Karl informed them both.

"Good heavens!" Gluck trod a frustrated circle around the floor, his feet stamping into the carpet. "Am I to be tormented, thus? All I ask for is a decent singer!"

Returning to the desk, he reached out and plucked Loretta Renier's contract from Haydn's hands.

He stared awhile at it and then raised his head.

"There is something wrong with this signature. Look!"

"What is it?" Haydn peered forward, straining to see what error it was that Gluck had detected.

"The ink, my dear man, the ink."

Haydn inspected the signature. It was written in a flowing hand in a dark ink—no different than the kind of ink used all over the Empire. A mixture of oak gall and copperas suspended in gum Arabic. He could see nothing amiss.

He said as much.

Gluck snorted. "It is black, don't you see?"

"So it is. What of it?"

Gluck raised his eyes toward the ceiling and sighed deeply. "And what is in Affligio's inkpot?" he asked.

Haydn lowered his eyes toward the cluttered desk and located the inkpot. It was filled with a deep blue fluid. He glanced at the contract Renier had signed, promising to sing a role in his opera. That signature was blue—like the ink in Affligio's glass pot.

Karl scratched his head. "Herr Affligio made sure to keep black ink on his desk. The blue ink was reserved for the Kärntnertortheater."

"Then, no doubt, that contract was signed in the Kärntnertortheater," Haydn concluded. He could see no reason for Loretta Renier to—what? —forge her own signature?

Or was Herr Gluck insinuating that the soprano had stolen a contract and affixed her signature to it? Affligio's name was on the contract as a matter of course, but it was understood that singers and composers signed theirs in the impresario's presence.

Karl shook his head. "The contracts for the specific operas were always signed here."

"And there was no black ink here to sign it!" Gluck flung the documents on the desk. "It should be declared null and void."

Haydn was loath to take such drastic action on the basis of a reason so flimsy. He was wondering how to assert his position when something caught his eye.

"I cannot do that. Black ink or not, that contract holds. It is countersigned by the Emperor himself and contains his seal." He raised his head. "I regret, Herr Gluck, the matter is out of my hands."

The Emperor's seal with an engraved impression of His Majesty's signature was kept under lock and key in the inner chamber. Haydn had seen it the evening before. The presence of the seal meant Fräulein Renier had signed her contract in the impresario's presence. Affligio must have then impressed the Emperor's seal upon it.

"It is a binding contract," Haydn asserted firmly. "Nothing more can be done. Unless you wish to involve His Majesty in the matter." The effort would be fruitless, Gluck knew that as well as he.

"Much good that will do!" Gluck snarled, nearly gargling in outrage before storming out of the room.

Steffi was getting ready to leave when Rosalie returned to the servants' hall. Greta, who was helping Steffi into her cape, turned toward the door the moment it opened.

"What did the old stick-in-the-mud want, then?"

She must have caught the expression on Rosalie's face, for she paused in her task.

"Why, Rosalie, what is it? You look like you've seen a ghost?"

She did feel as though she'd seen a ghost, Rosalie thought, as she gripped the wall for support. Something was terribly wrong. She'd known it the moment she'd heard Herr Fugger mention the reason for his visit. And the utter stupefaction on poor Master Johann's face had confirmed her worst fears.

"Is it Gerhard?" Greta asked again. "Or your mother?"

Rosalie managed to shake her head, no. Seeing the look of consternation on her friends' faces, she forced herself to stifle her anxiety.

"It was someone asking for Herr Haydn," she explained as calmly as she could. "A banker. A gentleman by the name of Fugger." Then unable to contain herself any longer. "I think Herr Haydn must be in a terrible bind."

"Herr Fugger?" Steffi asked at the same time as Greta exclaimed: "What kind of bind?"

Greta turned to her friend. "You know the gentleman?" Would that she did, Rosalie thought, staring hopefully at their friend.

Steffi nodded. "His Grace has had occasional dealings with him." She shrugged her cape off and returned to the table. "But Herr Fugger's establishment only deals with the nobility." She turned to Rosalie, her green eyes wide with curiosity. "What could he possibly want with Herr Haydn?"

Rosalie sank into a chair. "Herr Haydn is in debt," she said, her face pale. "He owes money. To whom I know not. But the sum is enormous. Seventy thousand gulden."

"That can't be because Herr Affligio hadn't paid his men at the Burgtheater, can it?" Greta's mouth formed an 'o' of dismay. Karl had told them both that Herr Haydn had generously delved into his own pocket to pay the men the impresario had neglected to recompense.

Rosalie shook her head doubtfully. "I don't see how that could add up to seventy thousand gulden?" Besides, surely the Kapellmeister had more sense than to give away money he didn't have.

She said as much and Greta agreed.

"But what does Herr Fugger have to do with any of this?" Steffi's probing gaze shifted from Greta to Rosalie. "If Herr Haydn is in need of money, you may be sure Herr Fugger will not lend it to him."

"But he must mean to help," Greta insisted. "Otherwise, why would he come in person?"

"That is odd." Steffi's eyes narrowed as she considered Greta's surmise. "But it's not like him at all. I'm telling you, it's not. Herr Fugger never visits anyone in their home—except for the Emperor, of course. He's willing to make an exception there, I hear. But even His Grace must set out for his establishment when he wishes to meet the gentleman."

Greta turned to Rosalie. "How do we know this man really is Herr Fugger?" she demanded. "Just because he says he is means nothing. Had he a card?"

"If he had, he gave it to Herr Rahier. Even the Estates Director was appalled at the sum he mentioned." And if he managed to use this unfortunate circumstance as an excuse to get rid of Herr Haydn, then their jobs wouldn't be far behind. They could be sure of that.

The Estates Director had fought tooth and nail against the Prince granting them their new positions and salaries. Rosalie forced her mind away from the thought, turning her attention to Steffi instead.

"If you want my opinion," Steffi was saying as she shook her curls, "this visitor claiming to be Herr Fugger is an imposter. A cheat trying to swindle Herr Haydn—and no doubt His Serene Highness as well. He must know your Herr Haydn doesn't have seventy thousand gulden stashed away."

Greta nodded her agreement. "It's true. And if Herr Haydn were in trouble, His Serene Highness wouldn't hesitate to come to his aid. Everyone knows that. Did Herr Fugger even mention to whom it is that Herr Haydn owes so much money?"

Rosalie shook her head. "No, he simply said it was a matter of money. That's all he said, now that I think on it. But Herr Rahier—well, you know how he is—he kept insisting Herr Haydn was in debt."

"But Herr Fugger mentioned nothing about debt, did he?" Greta persisted.

"No. But he didn't deny it, either. He said the principal was seventy thousand gulden. Then there's the interest. So there must be something to it."

"Could Herr Fugger have loaned the Kapellmeister money?" Greta wondered.

"Impossible!" Steffi was adamant. "I'm telling you, the Fuggers never loan anybody below a Prince or a Baron money. Why, Herr Mozart was complaining about it loud and long the other day. He'd asked the banker to advance him a few hundred gulden, but apparently Herr Fugger simply looked down his nose at him and said no."

A mischievous smile spread over Steffi's features at the memory.

"Then Herr Mozart asked His Grace to speak to the banker on his behalf. Or to give him what he's owed for the months he's been traveling. But, of course, His Grace refused on both counts."

Chapter Sixteen

"Poring over those papers will not change the situation, Johann," Luigi said as he paced energetically about the Music Room.

Fugger had long since left and the two men were still digesting the unwelcome news he had brought.

"No, it will not," Johann agreed quietly. He sat on the fortepiano bench. "But there must be some solution, some way out of this predicament." He lowered his head, perusing once more the papers Fugger had left with them. "Brother is burdened enough. I can hardly present him with this."

"No, I suppose not." Luigi paused in the middle of the room and ran his hand through his thick auburn hair. "But good God, what are we to do?" He glanced despairingly at Johann. "And how long are we to keep the news from him?"

It was not a question that required a response, Johann knew. And, even if it had, he had none to make. He sifted through the documents Fugger had provided them with. There was no mistaking the clause the bankers had inserted in the loan agreement.

He read it out loud.

"The borrower guarantees he will remain in his current position as impresario until such time as his debt is paid in full." Johann glanced up. Luigi was staring aimlessly out the window. "How Affligio could guarantee any such thing I know not. Although he certainly could not have expected to lose his position in so short a period of time."

"Such promises are pro forma," the Konzertmeister replied. He turned to face Johann. "Besides, Affligio would undoubtedly need to vouch for a continued source of income for the loan to be approved."

His brow wrinkled as he continued, "But I would not have thought the proceeds from ticket sales and box subscriptions could cover the monthly payment."

"It seems not to have," Johann reminded him. Fugger had explained that for the past few months Affligio's payments had been increasingly late, and he had only paid half the stipulated amount.

"He said he was awaiting his partner's payment for the other half," Fugger had said. But the banker had professed to know no more than that. "It was a private arrangement. Nothing to do with the bank. Our terms were with Herr Affligio himself."

Luigi rammed his clenched fist into the palm of his other hand. "That smooth-faced charlatan Fugger should be chasing down Affligio's partner. But it is easier to hound the likes of us."

He began his feverish perambulation again. "What kind of partner is this, in any case, who keeps silent and stays out of sight? He must share in the profits, though. The Burgtheater must rake in a considerable amount of money when the opera is popular."

"As it often is," Johann put in.

The impresario—to give him his due—had been almost prescient in his ability to gauge the public's reaction. He had known, to an uncannily precise degree, which operas would be pleasing enough to draw the public in for more than one performance. And his talents were such, it had not been uncommon for audiences to flock to every single showing of an opera for the entire month it was presented!

But had Affligio's partner been able to share in the profits? Or had Affligio been forced to use the money to pay his workers? What if there had been a dispute?

But these were fruitless speculations. Far better to figure out how to track down the elusive individual.

"If there is a partner," Johann reflected, "Karl might know something about him." Fugger either knew nothing about the man or had no inclination to pursue him. Johann stroked the fortepiano lid, deep in thought. "If we could but identify the man and get him to assume responsibility for Affligio's debts—"

"That is an *if* I would not pin my hopes on, Johann," Luigi warned him sharply. "The man—whoever he is—should have come forward at the news of Affligio's demise. But he has stayed hidden, and I doubt he can be so easily persuaded to come forward."

He strode forward and plucked the document out of Johann's hands. "Not with a clause like that." He jabbed at the relevant section. "*Should he lose, be removed from, or voluntarily give up his position, the impresario guarantees that his liabilities will be assumed by his successor.*

"How could Affligio agree to anything so asinine? Small wonder the Emperor refuses to appoint a replacement. Who would take on the position with a stipulation like that staring him in the face?"

"Could brother have known?" Johann wondered. Or for that matter His Serene Highness who had saddled the position on his unsuspecting Kapellmeister? It seemed doubtful. Most likely His Serene Highness had, in his haste, neglected to examine the proposition more thoroughly. And now brother was forced to suffer the consequences. Johann sighed.

"Something must be done, Luigi. We cannot keep brother in the dark forever."

⸺◦◦◦⸺

Rosalie wiped her hands on her apron and hurried into the Music Room. She had been expecting the summons ever since the banker had made an appearance that morning, talking about Herr Haydn needing a vast sum of money.

For the Burgtheater, no doubt, although it seemed unlikely. Besides, why hadn't Herr Haydn turned to His Serene Highness for help, then? It was something neither she nor Greta nor Steffi could understand.

"Ah, Rosalie!" Master Johann greeted her as she entered the room. He looked paler than usual, his face pinched, his expression agitated. Master Luigi, looking equally solemn, nodded gravely at her and beckoned her forward.

"This business with the banker," Master Johann began as she stood before them in the middle of the room. His hand cradled his chin, fingers nervously gripping his thin cheeks. "We must be discreet about it."

"To be sure." Rosalie eagerly nodded her agreement. "I only mentioned it to Greta"—she felt a twinge of guilt as she said this; Steffi had been present as well—"but it will go no further, I assure you."

"It must not be mentioned to Herr Haydn," Master Luigi added. "Not immediately, that is to say."

"No?" Rosalie frowned, voicing her agreement hesitantly. How was the news to be kept from Herr Haydn? If he was in need of money—gracious Lord, what a vast sum it was!—could he really be unaware of the fact?

"He has his hands abundantly full without being bothered by this—uh—" Master Johann dithered before finally settling on a word. "This mundane matter," he said, although his face and voice suggested he considered the situation to be anything but.

"To be sure," Rosalie agreed again, but she surveyed Master Johann seated at the fortepiano and Master Luigi standing behind him with increasing curiosity. Had she been called merely to be warned against breaking the news of his debt to Herr Haydn?

It seemed a foolish way to protect the Kapellmeister from his troubles. Besides, who was to say he was unaware of the situation in which he found himself. Unless—

Enlightenment dawned on her. Unless it was to save the poor man from the embarrassment of knowing the entire world had learned of his predicament.

She smoothed her dress down, wondering how to broach the concerns she and Greta and Steffi had come up with as they discussed the matter.

"Is the banker," she began tentatively, "is this Herr Fugger truly who he says he is?" She coughed hesitantly. "That is to say, can we be sure . . . ?" Her voice trailed off, unsure how to phrase her doubts more delicately. But what if Herr Fugger was an imposter, trying to con the Kapellmeister—or more likely His Serene Highness—out of his hard-earned money?

It was easy enough to dress up in fancy clothes, although the gentleman had seemed genuine enough. Certainly, he had been discreet, unwilling to discuss private matters out in the open.

Master Johann smiled gently at her. "We have no reason to doubt his identity, I fear, Rosalie. I only wish that we did."

Master Luigi lowered himself into a nearby armchair. "What made you ask?" he enquired hopefully. "It is not just your good opinion of the Kapellmeister that makes you suspicious of the young banker, does it?"

Rosalie shook her head. How was she to explain the matter without mentioning Steffi at all? It had been Greta's friend after all who had raised the issue. And a very pertinent issue, it was, too.

She took a deep breath. "Well, when I told Greta about Herr Fugger's visit, she said—it is something she has heard from a friend, you see—that the Fuggers are most unlikely to advance money to anyone less than a Baron or a Prince."

"Is that so?" Master Luigi's hazel eyes gleamed with interest. He leaned forward. "And how reliable is Greta's friend?"

"Oh, very," Rosalie assured him. Steffi had seemed to know what she was talking about.

"It is not something I had thought of." Master Luigi turned to Master Johann. "It begs the question, does it not, of how Affligio managed the deed?"

"There must be exceptions," Master Johann replied. "Although under what mitigating conditions, I know not.

"The trouble is," he turned to Rosalie, "the money has already been lent. Although I suppose"—he turned back to Master Luigi—"a visit to the bank to verify the details may not be amiss."

The money had already been lent? Rosalie was confused. If that were the case, how could His Serene Highness be unaware of the arrangement? Who else could've introduced Herr Haydn to the Fuggers?

Unthinkingly, she blurted the question out. Master Johann and Master Luigi turned in unison toward her.

"His Serene Highness—" Master Johann's voice skidded to a halt as he frowned.

Master Luigi sprang out of his chair. "You mean to say Fugger would advance the money to a man like Haydn were he to receive an introduction from one of the nobility?"

Rosalie nodded. "And who better than His Serene Highness to effect the introduction? No one else is held in quite as high esteem."

To her surprise, Master Luigi and Master Johann gaped at each other in astonishment.

"The silent partner!" Master Luigi cried.

"Of course," Master Johann agreed—although to what exactly Rosalie had no clue.

"That narrows it down considerably, Johann." Master Luigi began treading the carpet in his excitement. He swiveled around to face Master Johann. "And do not tell me Fugger has no idea who the nobleman in question is."

Before Rosalie could ask any questions, Master Luigi spun toward her. "Greta's young man was close to Affligio was he not? A trusted individual?" He didn't wait for Rosalie's response. "Would Karl know whether Affligio had entered into any partnerships?"

He turned to face Master Johann. "It matters not whether commoner or nobleman, does it?"

Master Johann shook his head. "At this point, no. We had better question them all. Who knows what influence even a commoner might have brought to the table."

Master Luigi began pacing again, feverishly rubbing his hands together. "But on what pretext are we to send Greta and Rosalie out? Rahier will want to know why," he explained, turning to look at Johann and Rosalie, "and I am loath to reveal our reasons to him."

Rosalie, whose head had been bobbing from Master Johann toward Master Luigi as she tried to follow their conversation, now chimed in: "Do the maids at the Burgtheater need any additional help? That would be as good a reason as any to go."

"There are no—" Johann's eyes widened. "That is it! The Burgtheater has no maids. And the backstairs are badly in need of cleaning. Brother was complaining about it just yesterday."

<hr>

"We must set out for the Burgtheater at once, Greta." Rosalie swung open the door to the servants' hall. She was about to explain the errand Master Johann had charged them with when she noticed Steffi still standing by the back door.

The girl had on her cape and it looked as though she was finally ready to leave. God be thanked, they had not a moment to lose.

Realizing Greta was staring at her open-mouthed, waiting for an explanation, Rosalie hurriedly went on: "The place lacks a maid and is in need of a thorough cleaning."

"*Ach so!*" Greta nodded. She turned to Steffi. "Our Herr Haydn can't abide dust." She turned back to Rosalie, her brow puckering into a puzzled frown. "I'm surprised he didn't send word of it this morning. We'd have had the place set to rights in no time. And it's not as though Frida, Katya, and the others can't manage here on their own."

"He must've been too busy to think of it," Rosalie said. "What with the opera and having to visit Herr Mozart's family," she added hastily, seeing Greta's frown deepen. It was the first explanation that had popped into her head; she'd overheard Master Johann and Master Luigi talking about it just that morning.

And it served, thank the Lord, to squelch Greta's curiosity on the subject. She'd have been forced to tell a lie—or break her silence—if Greta had persisted in dwelling on it in Steffi's presence.

But the mere mention of Herr Mozart set Steffi off.

"I'm telling you, he's not innocent," she declared, her mouth set into a determined line. "Be sure to ask your Karl about it, Greta. His actions will bear me out. After all, he must've feared for Herr Affligio's life to come running to His Grace for help."

Steffi swept her cape forward and stubbornly jutted out her chin.

"And the sooner His Grace can be persuaded to that conclusion the better for everyone. He can take himself back to Salzburg and leave me free to join Count Kohary's household." She clutched Greta's hands. "You will help, won't you, Greta? For old times' sake?"

Greta hugged her. "Of course, I will," she promised as she showed Steffi out the door.

But the moment Steffi was gone, Greta shut the door firmly behind her and directed a knowing gaze at Rosalie.

"All right, tell me the truth," she demanded. "Why must we go to the Burgtheater?"

Dear Lord, what had she said or done to betray herself, Rosalie wondered. Not that it mattered. It was only Greta.

"Well, the Burgtheater does need a good cleaning. But that's just a ruse Master Johann came up with so Herr Rahier doesn't make a fuss about our going."

Greta smirked. "I knew you were keeping something from me. I can always tell," she gloated. "All right"—she thrust her head and chest out conspiratorially—"so what is it we need to find out? And from whom?"

Chapter Seventeen

IT took no time at all for Haydn to put Gluck's unseemly outburst out of his mind. The encounter had been sharply unpleasant, but dwelling on it would do no good. Instead, Haydn pulled out Affligio's thick account ledgers, diligently scanning the pages to see if any money was owed to the establishment.

Each entry had been scribbled in the impresario's crabbed hand, the letters running untidily into each other. *All in black*, Haydn noted with a smile. If only Herr Gluck were here to see it! It took a dint of concentrated effort to make out Affligio's hand, but Haydn was soon able to decipher it.

Count Schrattenbach had only paid half the amount he owed; Countess Herberstein owed a quarter installment; Count Podstatsky still owed close to two-thirds of his payment. The names were known to Haydn, and he knew a simple request would suffice to obtain the necessary payment.

Here was a Count Kohary who had yet to pay his subscription for the year. The name was unfamiliar to Haydn, but he jotted it down along with the rest. A request would need to be sent to him as well.

But a few entries in the ledger puzzled him. On several occasions, substantial sums had been paid to a Fugger. The banker? Surely not, Haydn thought. More than likely, it was some supplier of theatrical goods and provisions. Papa Keller might know. He would have to remember to ask his father-in-law about it later that evening.

But the sums—Haydn stroked his chin pensively as he gazed at the most recent amount—were inordinately large. If this was a supplier, he would need to find a less expensive alternative. Small wonder, the theater was, if not bleeding money, in some financial straits if Affligio contracted with such exorbitantly priced tradesmen.

He had been working steadily for about a half hour when a name caught his eye. *The Archbishop of Salzburg.* Haydn lifted his quill from the paper, tilting the nib up so it would not drip ink. He could pen a letter to His Grace, he thought. But would it not be better to go in person—and kill two birds with one stone?

The Kapellmeister had keenly felt the embarrassment of Frau Mozart's position—forced to remain in the city while her husband was incarcerated, yet with no source of income to discharge her expenses. His Grace, the poor, unfortunate woman had reiterated to him, had categorically refused to spend "another kreutzer" on his employee. "Erstwhile employee," His Grace had reminded Frau Mozart in his message to her.

But surely now that Leopold had agreed to return to Salzburg, he was entitled to his salary again. Haydn would not fight to get him paid for the months he had spent traveling—without permission, it would appear. But in agreeing to return to His Grace's service Leopold had earned his current month's salary. If nothing else, he was surely—as an erstwhile employee—entitled to a pension or severance of some sort.

"There must be some provision in your husband's contract," Haydn had assured the poor woman—all but widowed, he thought.

What if it did come to that? How was the poor woman to survive—with two young children no less? It was not to be thought of.

Shaking his head, he dipped his quill into Affligio's indigo-tinted ink. There was another thing to be remedied. The blue ink sufficed well enough for marking objects as Maria Anna did, but to be expected to write with it? And should he have a few spare moments to jot down a few motifs for a composition, would he have to do it in that annoyingly bright blue?

He had just started to add the Archbishop's name to his list when a low, melodious voice intruded upon his consciousness.

"Herr Haydn?"

He glanced up. A raven-haired, sloe-eyed woman stood at the door. She might have been attractive, were it not for the heavy cast of her features and the sturdy build of her frame, rather taller than was usual for her sex.

"My name is Donna Oliveri," she announced without waiting for him to acknowledge his name. She entered the room, her heavy silken skirts of a deep purple sweeping the carpet. "I wish to know whether the roles for *Le pescatrici* have already been assigned."

"Donna Oliveri." Haydn rose and stretched out his hand. "You have a contract with the Burgtheater, I believe." He recalled seeing it when Gluck had been present.

She inclined her head and smiled. At least, Haydn thought she did. With her kerchief covering her mouth and nose, he couldn't at all be sure of her expression.

"I recently renewed the agreement," she confirmed.

"And the contract for the opera in question?" Haydn shuffled through the papers on his desk. Had there been one? He couldn't recall.

"I was to approach you for a specific assignment," Frau Oliveri replied in her low, even voice. From what Karl had told him, the woman was widowed. Her husband, a tenor, had died on the stage when the blade of a prop knife had failed to retract into its handle.

A painful way to die. Even more painful to have to observe, Haydn thought. Frau Oliveri, Karl had said, had been the hapless individual to wield the deadly blade.

Approach him for an assignment. The woman's words eventually sank in.

"Herr Affligio had not assigned you to a role?" Why not, Haydn wondered, when he had taken it upon himself to assign Fräuleins Bologna and Renier theirs without reference to the Kapellmeister's wishes?

Besides, the contract never specified a role, thus enabling composer and impresario to re-assign roles as they saw fit.

He raised his head to meet Frau Oliveri's dark, level-headed gaze.

"He suggested I discuss with you which part would best suit my talents. My range goes as high as—"

"Mezzo-soprano," Haydn finished for her with a smile. "Yes, I know. Karl mentioned it."

She nodded gravely. "And as low as tenor." She sang a line or two assigned to Burlotto in the quartetto that ended the first act.

Haydn's eyebrows shot up. "Indeed! Your vocal range is more impressive than I was given to understand." Had she not been standing before him, he might've supposed a man had sung the lines.

"I cannot keep up the very lowest ranges for long, I fear. Even my trouser-roles, I prefer to sing in contralto." She gestured toward a chair. "May I?"

"Yes, of course." Haydn felt his cheeks burn. He should have offered her a seat instead of compelling the contralto to request one. "I beg your pardon. I know not where my mind was."

Frau Oliveri smiled graciously, carefully dusting her chair before seating herself in it. There was not as far as Haydn could tell a speck of dust on that chair. And no stench in the room that he could detect, yet Frau Oliveri still kept her kerchief pressed to her face.

She pointed her shapely palm toward his chair. "Won't you sit down as well, Herr Haydn?"

"I have read the libretto," she announced when he had lowered himself into his chair. "I think Eurilda's role would be best for me. A contralto voice would suit the part very well. She is young, but wise beyond her ears. And a deeper voice would certainly suit both members of the *parti serie*."

So, it would. Eurilda's opposite, Lindoro, was played by a bass.

"I regret the part has already been assigned to Fräulein Renier." And she was most ill-suited for it, Haydn thought.

Frau Oliveri lifted her thick, dark eyebrows. "A soprano? For the part of Eurilda?"

Haydn spread his hands out helplessly. "The vocal lines are simpler than that of the other two female roles. And the coloratura is simply beyond her."

Frau Oliveri clasped her hands together. "I wish the impresario had not died before settling the matter," she said quietly. "He impressed upon me the need to approach you—barely a day or two before he died, in fact." She raised her dark expressive eyes to him. "I had promised to do so today. Little did I know—" Her voice thickened and her eyes glistened as she hastily turned her face away.

Haydn allowed her to compose herself before continuing. "You have read the libretto. Would the role of Lesbina suit you? The part can be brought down to a mezzo-soprano, but the passagework—"

"I am well able to handle runs, trills, and other such passagework," Frau Oliveri assured him with an amused smile. "There is but the contract to sign. The impresario thought the role should be assigned to my satisfaction before I signed a contract," she explained.

"Then, let us by all means finish the business." Haydn pushed his chair back. But as he entered the inner chamber to withdraw a contract and the imperial seal, he wondered whether any of the other Burgtheater singers had been aware of the preferential treatment Affligio had granted Donna Oliveri.

Had the other singers known Frau Oliveri was allowed to choose her role rather than simply be assigned one? Matilda Bologna would've accepted the situation with good grace. But Loretta Renier, a woman with all the temperament of a spoiled diva albeit none of the talent, would undoubtedly not have taken to it so kindly.

Fräulein Renier's strenuous protestations of the morning before returned to the Kapellmeister's mind. Was Leopold Mozart paying the price for another's sins?

Returning to the other room, he wrote out the details and slid the contract across the desk to Frau Oliveri.

"The ink, I fear," he began apologetically only to be interrupted by a low trill of amused laughter.

"Matters not a whit, Herr Haydn. Black or blue, it is all the same."

Not to Herr Gluck, Haydn thought bitterly. He must have spoken aloud for Frau Oliveri's hand paused.

"Herr Gluck was here? What did he want?"

"It had to do with your colleague, Loretta Renier," Haydn replied, deliberately vague.

Frau Oliveri nodded. "She must be distraught, poor thing! I imagine she is hardly able to sing."

"Distraught!" Haydn's voice rose sharply. "Why would she be distraught?"

Donna Oliveri lifted her dark eyes and stared at him. "How could she not be? She was the last to see the impresario alive that Sunday night. The last—other than his killer, of course."

Renier had been the last to see Affligio alive? Haydn frowned, his mind churning busily as he pondered the information.

"Herr Affligio needed to see her—for some reason or other—after our rehearsal that day," Donna Oliveri went on. "It was the last time any of us saw the man. Not that we knew that, of course."

Signing her name with a flourish, she returned the contract to him. "There!"

Haydn turned the contract toward himself and pressed down the imperial seal upon it.

Still clutching her kerchief to her face, his visitor rose. "The room needs a good dusting," she remarked, rubbing her forefinger on the desk. "The maid has yet to show her face, I suppose."

"It seems clean enough," Haydn replied, puzzled. Then, unable to contain himself, he asked: "Does your nose detect some odor that I am unaware of?"

"Oh, no!" Frau Oliveri shook her head. "It is just that I cannot abide the dust in the streets."

"The streets, to be sure," Haydn agreed. But they were not in the streets.

"And to breathe in another's stale air is simply repugnant to me. Particularly in a small, confined place such as this." She cast a disparaging look around the impresario's chamber.

"I see," Haydn responded. And so, averse to breathing the general air, she breathed in her own stale, regurgitated supply. Thank heavens, fate hadn't conspired to make Donna Oliveri Empress of the Holy Roman Empire. There would be a promulgation for every citizen to cover their mouth and nose were that luckless day ever to come!

Chapter Eighteen

Laden with buckets, brooms, mops, and washcloths, Rosalie and Greta were about to set off for the Burgtheater when they heard the loud clip-clop of horses' hooves and the rattling of wooden wagon wheels on the rough cobblestones of the Haarhof.

"It is Gerhard!" Rosalie's heart leapt with a guilty start as she twisted around to see her husband's rack wagon trundling toward them. Dear God, what was she going to tell him?

She had barely time to ponder the question when Gerhard's wagon rolled to a stop, and with a broad smile, he jumped off his perch.

"Where are you two off to? It's not your day off, is it?" Then his gaze fell on the bucket dangling from Rosalie's wrist. "What do you mean to do with all that—clean the streets?"

Rosalie shook her head and turned quickly toward Greta. "You'd best be off. I'll follow you directly."

Gerhard swept her into his arms as soon as Greta's back was turned.

"Don't you look fetching this fine morning, Frau Heindl!" he said as his mouth closed upon hers.

Rosalie gave herself up to the kiss, hoping Gerhard wouldn't ask any more uncomfortable questions. She didn't want to have to lie to her husband. But telling him the truth was quite out of the question.

"Where are you off to?" he asked again, drawing back.

She smiled. It wouldn't be an utter lie to tell him they were going to clean the Burgtheater.

"To the Burgtheater—" But before she could get the rest of the words out of her mouth Gerhard's brows had gathered into a forbidding frown.

"You're not going to stick your nose where it doesn't belong, are you, lass?" His blue eyes narrowed as they roved searchingly over her features.

"O-of course not." She made a vain attempt at a laugh. "Why would you say that?"

Gerhard studied her face. "I hear the impresario is dead. Murdered from the looks of it." His eyes held hers in such a penetrating stare, Rosalie had to force herself not to blink. "And it won't be the first time you've taken it into your head to look into an affair like that."

It wouldn't, Rosalie thought ruefully. It was how they'd met—four years ago. She had suspected him of murder only to realize— She pressed her lips together, unwilling to think of the regrettable fallout of their coming together. It hadn't been his fault—or hers, for that matter. But the incident would forever taint what should've been a pleasurable memory.

Gerhard's work-roughened thumb brushed against her cheek, wiping away the tear that, God alone knew when, had begun to roll down her cheek.

"What is it, lass?" he asked, his voice warm with concern.

She shook her head. "Nothing. I was thinking of how we first met, and . . ." She knew she didn't have to finish the sentence. Gerhard would understand.

He drew her closer in response. "It's in the past, lass. And there's nothing you or I can do to change it. You know that, don't you?"

She nodded, pressing her cheek closer to the coarse fibers of his linen shirt. Then, deliberately turning her thoughts to the present, she asked: "How did you hear of Herr Affligio's demise?"

He drew back to look down at her. "How could I not hear of it, lass? I had a delivery to make at the Kärntnertortheater. The place was in shambles. No one knows whether it'll stay open or be closed down. The impresario's assistant took all the wine I'd brought, but he's canceled all future orders."

His lips pressed together in a quick flash of dismay. It was not the end of the world, Rosalie knew, but the wine orders from the Kärntnertortheater represented a good chunk of their business. Before she could utter a word, however, the wry look had vanished from his handsome features.

He smiled down at her. "But all is not lost. I hear the Burgtheater has a replacement."

Rosalie nodded. "Herr Haydn has taken charge for the moment. But who knows whether there'll be a new impresario or not." Then, in an attempt to quell any suspicions he might still have, she added, "That's why we were going there. It seems Herr Affligio never bothered with a maid, and the place is filthy."

Gerhard gazed deeply into her eyes. "And that is all there is to it?"

"Of course." Rosalie nodded her head vigorously. "His murderer has already been arrested. Hadn't you heard?"

"The assistant said nothing of it. The news can't have reached him yet. But God be praised if it is true!" Gerhard raised his eyes heavenward. "There'd be no stopping you and Greta from meddling if it weren't so."

—•—

It was not a long walk to the Burgtheater. It usually took Greta no longer than five minutes to make the short journey from the Esterházy Palace on Wallnerstrasse.

But today—laden with a heavy bucket, a broom, and a mop and having to contend with the mid-morning traffic of carriages thronging the streets—it was nearly ten minutes before she rounded the curve on Michaelerplatz and turned onto Reitschulgasse.

The summer heat was so relentless, Greta was nearly faint by the time she came in sight of the Burgtheater. A bead of perspiration had formed above her upper lip and her cheeks felt uncomfortably hot. She set her bucket down, leaned against a post, and swiped her sleeve across her face.

"Greta?" It was Karl, standing across the street. "What brings you here?" He rushed over to where she stood.

"Herr Haydn sent for us." She must look a fright, she thought. If only she could brush back her limp curls and powder her face. But Karl seemed not to notice as he drew closer to give her a quick kiss. "Well, actually it was Master Johann who suggested we come.

"Rosalie is on her way," Greta went on.

"B-but—" Karl frowned. "Why . . .?" As he spoke his gaze fell on her bucket and the broom and mop she'd brought with her. His face cleared and he smiled. "I see your Herr Haydn can't abide dust any more than our Frau Oliveri."

Greta was about to ask who Frau Oliveri was when she realized it was one of the singers. It had to be. Besides, she had more important things to discuss with Karl.

"Come, let's go in." She took his arm, knowing Karl would carry the bucket and its contents for her without having to be asked. "Steffi came by this morning."

Karl looked down at her. "The girl who works for the Archbishop of Salzburg?"

Greta nodded. "She opened the door to you on Sunday?" She wondered why Karl hadn't mentioned Herr Mozart's altercation with the impresario to her. It wasn't like him to keep things from her—even unpleasant details about his work.

But if she'd hoped mentioning his visit to the Archbishop's residence would loosen Karl's tongue, she was mistaken.

Karl's clogs scrunched to a halt. "Opened the door for me? On Sunday? Whatever are you on about, Greta?"

Greta looked up, trying hard not to be hurt by his reluctance to confide in her. "I don't suppose you remember. You must have been in quite a tizzy. Steffi said you begged His Grace to come to the Burgtheater at once."

But Karl was still looking at her as though she'd lost her mind.

"It was because the Salzburger—His Grace's employee—was threatening Herr Affligio. That's what Steffi said."

Greta's voice faltered. Had her friend made up every word of that story?

She held his gaze, determined to get to the truth. "Didn't you go to His Grace's residence on Sunday?"

Karl shook his head. "No. Why would I?"

"You didn't see the Salzburger—his name's Leopold Mozart—threatening Herr Affligio?"

Karl shook his head again. "I wasn't here to see him threaten anyone."

"Then you didn't fear for Herr Affligio's life?"

"I had no reason to. If someone ran to His Grace for help that evening, it was not me."

Greta bit her lip. "Steffi's always been one to see a mountain where there's just a molehill. But I've never known her to lie."

"It must've been someone else then." Karl tucked her arm under his and they resumed walking. "It isn't for nothing that the Salzburger lies in prison. Someone may have heard a dispute, maybe even seen him trying to strike Herr Affligio. Fortunately they had the presence of mind to send for His Grace."

"It would have to be someone who knew His Grace employs Herr Mozart," Greta mused. Would anyone other than Karl and the singers be aware of the fact? It was unlikely.

"All the singers and Herr Gluck and Herr Coltellini are well aware of who he is," Karl informed her. "Fräulein Renier was with Herr Affligio when I left that evening. If she was still here when Herr Mozart arrived an hour later, maybe it was she who went in search of help."

"But it wasn't a woman Steffi saw. It was a man." Greta bit her lip. Had one of the stagehands hurried to His Grace's residence that evening? Steffi had never met Karl, and she must've assumed the man who'd rushed to His Grace's door was the impresario's assistant.

It was impossible to believe Steffi was lying. But there was no reason for Karl to lie either, was there?

Besides, if help were so urgently needed, wouldn't it make more sense to seek it closer at hand—from one of the police guards on Habsburgerstrasse? Armed with truncheons, they'd be in a better position to restrain a violent Herr Mozart, wouldn't they?

The questions rattled around in Greta's brain, as her mind zigzagged from Steffi's certainty about what she'd seen to Karl's denials.

Karl had just pushed open the door when Greta heard a sound.

"That's Rosalie!" She spun around, relieved to see her friend.

Rosalie climbed down from the wine-laden rack wagon, reached up to give Gerhard a kiss, and then came sprinting toward them.

She looked eagerly from Greta to Karl. "Have you asked him?"

"Asked me what?" Karl asked with a smile. His hand still rested on the door.

"About Herr Affligio's partners," Greta said. "Herr Fugger, the banker, came by the palace this morning." She looked at Rosalie, hoping her friend would explain. Why Master Luigi and Master Johann had wanted to know about Herr Affligio's partners, she hadn't quite understood.

"Your master was deep in debt, Karl," Rosalie said earnestly. "Did you know that?"

Frowning, Karl pulled his hand away from the door. It drifted forward, closing with a small click. "The profits weren't what they should have been," he said. "But none of us knew he was in debt. Herr Affligio never mentioned it. I never heard him talk about any bankers either. Are you two sure of what you heard?"

Greta and Rosalie nodded vigorously. "There's no mistaking what the banker said," Greta told him. "Seventy thousand gulden. And that's the principal alone."

"And now that Herr Affligio's dead, his partners will have to discharge his debts for him," Rosalie added. "Herr Fugger wanted to know who they were."

Greta's eyes widened. She'd thought it was Herr Haydn who, for whatever reason no one could fathom, had to take on Herr Affligio's debts. She was about to blurt that out when Rosalie's warning glance quelled her.

"I doubt Herr Gluck will be happy to hear that," Karl said, tugging uncertainly on his beard. "Or Herr Coltellini for that matter. Herr Affligio asked them to be partners and to share in the profits in return for investing a certain amount in the Burgtheater. It was a way of raising money as well as getting out of paying them a fee every time they supplied him with an opera."

"A fine scheme that is," Greta said, unable to keep the opinion to herself. What if the profits weren't forthcoming—as in fact it seemed they weren't! "I hope he didn't try any such thing with you."

Karl smiled ruefully as he shook his head. "No, he didn't. I haven't the money, my dumpling. But I can't blame Herr Affligio for what he did. That was how he secured the funds to pay the rest of us. In fact, he was trying to persuade His Grace to become an investor as well."

"So, that's why he went to see His Grace," Rosalie said. She turned to Greta. "Remember, Steffi said he called on His Grace on Saturday."

Greta nodded. "I wonder if His Grace agreed to that proposition."

"He may have," Karl said. "Although God alone knows if anything came of it. Herr Affligio assured us he'd have our money for us on Monday. But he never lived to see the day. And even though we've searched high and low for it, your Herr Haydn and I, we've found not a single kreutzer.

"But I should get back to work. And you had better start cleaning, I suppose. It's down here." Karl pushed open the door again. "Be careful now, it's dusty." He was about to lead them downstairs when a coach rumbled to a stop behind them.

It was a hackney cab dropping off a passenger—a tall, thin, weasel-featured man, who quickly paid the coachman and then called out to Karl.

"You have the knife, I trust. I've brought a replacement."

Chapter Nineteen

THE coutelier—for that was who the ferret-faced newcomer was—brushed his forefinger along the dust-encrusted stair rail and then inspected his finger closely.

"A fine pair of cleaning women you've got yourself, Karl." He twisted around to pin his dark, beady eyes on Rosalie and Greta. "You two gossip more than you clean, don't you?"

Greta bristled, about to spout off at him, but Karl gripped her wrist and cut in before she could say a word. "They're not to blame, Felix. This isn't their work. Fräulein Schmitt here and her friend Frau Heindl are from the Esterházy Palace. Herr Haydn—he's taken over as you may have heard—sent for them to swab the place down."

Felix grunted. "Well, you have your work cut out for you, I see." He trod heavily down the stairs. "It's in the prop room, I take it."

"In the usual place by the weapons." Karl raced down the stairs behind the coutelier. At the bottom of the stairs, he turned and squeezed Greta's hand. "I'll see you in a while, my dumpling. Come to the prop room if you need anything. You remember where it is?"

Greta nodded and squeezed his hand back.

"Dumpling!" Felix snickered as the two men walked away. "Don't tell me you're sweet on that one, Karl!"

Seeing Greta glaring balefully after the man, Rosalie tugged on her arm. "Come, let's get started. It'll take us a month of Sundays to get this place in shape."

But Greta shook her head. "I want to see what this business with the knife is all about."

"What is there to see?" Rosalie asked impatiently. "It's just a prop knife." Greta could be so stubborn sometimes. Once she got a bee in her bonnet, there was no getting rid of it.

But her friend's plump lips were pinched together and she'd sucked in her cheeks as though she were debating within herself.

"What is it, Greta?" It was something to do with Karl, no doubt. Rosalie had seen the same irresolute expression in Greta's blue eyes when she'd arrived at the Burgtheater. Something her beau had told her had displeased Greta, Rosalie was sure of it. "Is it Karl?" she asked tentatively.

"Oh, Rosalie!" Greta turned to her, eyes wide with alarm. "I've no idea what to think."

Rosalie listened as Greta recounted Karl's denial of ever having gone to the Archbishop of Salzburg's residence.

"And only the singers or Karl himself would have known to call for the Archbishop, Rosalie," Greta finished. She didn't have to finish the thought. Rosalie knew what she was thinking. If it had been one of the singers or even Herr Gluck who had gone to the Archbishop for help, Steffi would not have mistaken the person at the door for a working man. It would have to be one of the stagehands—or Karl himself.

"Now, I'm wondering if it was this fellow Felix." Greta peered around the corner.

"He does seem to know his way about the place," Rosalie agreed. And no one in their right mind would mistake the man for either an opera singer or a composer. He dressed like an ordinary workman. His hands were rough and calloused.

"But would he have known to go to the Archbishop?" Greta asked doubtfully. "Or did someone send him there?"

Rosalie thought about that. Had someone else been here along with Felix, the coutelier, at the end of a long Sunday? "I doubt Herr Mozart would be foolish enough to threaten anyone if there were people around." Either he'd been unaware he wasn't alone with the impresario. Or—

The thought that entered her mind was so startling, Rosalie's eyes nearly popped out of their sockets.

"What is it?" Greta glanced up at her, alarmed.

"What if . . ." Rosalie took a deep breath, still unable to take in the enormity of what she was about to suggest. "What if Herr Mozart wasn't here? Not when Herr Affligio was murdered at any rate."

"You mean whoever killed him tried to lay the blame at Herr Mozart's door?"

"Why else would they go running to the Archbishop?" Greta had been right about that, Rosalie thought. It would've been easier by far to send for one of the police guards. But, no, the killer had gone straight to the Archbishop all the way on Am Glacis.

"And they would've known Herr Mozart was expected. Didn't Karl say the impresario's appointment book was open on his desk?"

Greta nodded. "But that would mean—" Her voice became little more than a whisper. "That would mean that Steffi saw the killer."

They both peered around the corner. Was it Felix, the obnoxious coutelier, who'd done the impresario in?

Greta tucked her arm into Rosalie's. "Come on. We'd better go see what he's up to."

<hr>

Greta nearly fainted at the sight that greeted her eyes when she entered the prop room. There was Felix laughingly dragging a knife along his wrist, oblivious to the trail of blood that oozed from his flesh. "Works perfectly as you can see."

And Karl looked quite indifferent to what the man was doing. It was only when he turned to her, startled, that she realized she was shrieking.

"Greta, what. . . ?" He hurried toward her, then as he followed her gaze back to Felix, the expression of alarm on his features eased. "Oh, that's just a trick. You didn't really think Felix was cutting his wrist, did you?"

"But how is he doing that?" Rosalie gasped.

"Come and see." Karl pulled Greta along and Rosalie followed. He took the knife from Felix and turned it over. "There's a bladder filled with pig's blood on the handle. See? And when you squeeze it, it squirts out a trickle of blood through this hose."

"And you can feign a stabbing as well," Felix added. "Look!" He took the knife back, raised it high, and plunged it into his breast. Blood poured out, soaking his shirt. "The blade retracts, you see." Keeping his hand on the bolster, he removed the knife from his breast to show them. "A fine design it is. Just as fine as the other one your master insisted upon replacing."

"It killed a man. On stage, Felix," Karl reminded him. "The singers won't touch it. It's good of you to take it back, though."

"Didn't have much choice, did I?" Felix grunted. "Your Herr Affligio threatened to put me out of business if I didn't fashion a replacement free of charge." He scrunched his thin features into a heavy scowl at the memory. "I told him I'd do it if I could have the original back. No reason to keep a perfectly good knife here where no one will use it. And I can prove—I can—that there's nothing wrong with it."

He glanced around him. "Where is it, then?"

"It should be here, in its sheath," Karl said. He bustled about near the weapons as Greta and Rosalie exchanged a glance. Felix had as good a reason as anyone else to get rid of Herr Affligio. A better reason than Herr Mozart, if truth be told.

After all, his very livelihood and his reputation as a coutelier had been at stake, thanks to the impresario.

—◆◆◆—

Haydn dipped his pen into Affligio's blue inkpot, about to pen his second request for the payment of box subscription fees when a resounding rat-a-tat on the door startled him. The pen jerked in his hand, flicking ink onto the clean sheet of paper before him.

"Herr Haydn?" Karl pushed open the door before the Kapellmeister could invite him in. "I fear we have trouble."

"More trouble?" Haydn probed gently, taking in Karl's somber eyes and the stricken expression on his broad features. There had been nothing but trouble since he'd returned to the Burgtheater that morning.

Karl nodded. "It is a minor issue but distressing nonetheless. A prop is missing."

"A prop? What kind of prop?" Haydn retrieved a balled-up piece of paper he had earlier tossed into the trash can and began dabbing at the mess of ink on the sheet before him. It was completely ruined, but force of habit drove him to clean it nevertheless.

"It is the knife," Karl said. "The retractable knife used for fight and stabbing scenes. Fräulein Renier insisted it be replaced. She said nothing would persuade her to use it."

118

Haydn didn't blame the soprano. The knife, from what he had heard, had been known to jam. It was the very instrument that had killed the unfortunate Donna Oliveri's husband.

The blade had hit the bolster, refusing to withdraw into the wooden handle. Why it had not been replaced sooner was a mystery?

"We have searched high and low for it," Karl went on. "It is nowhere to be found. I can't imagine where it might have gone."

"Can it not be replaced?" Haydn asked. Then he remembered. The dress rehearsal for *Giulietta e Romeo* was on the morrow. A dagger of some sort would be needed before then. "The coutelier will have no time to fashion a new one, I suppose," he went on, answering his own question.

"That isn't the problem." Karl shook his head, still looking grave. "The coutelier has already fashioned a new knife. He is here with it. The blade is made of wood, covered in silver paint and edged with velvet. But with no money in the coffers, the agreement was to give him our knife in exchange for the new one."

"*Ach so!*" And the Burgtheater's knife with its fine steel blade was missing.

Absentmindedly Haydn tossed the ink-stained crumpled ball and the stained sheet into the trash can. "Will the coutelier accept money?" It seemed hardly likely he would refuse it, given Affligio's arrangement had been made only as a result of his lack of ready cash.

Karl swallowed, his Adam's apple bobbing nervously up and down. "He wants eighteen ducats for it."

Eighteen ducats! Haydn's eyes widened. That was no less than eighty-one gulden. A good, sturdy pair of Hungarian horses could be purchased for the amount the coutelier was demanding.

But he had already paid the carpenters and painters out of his pocket. What was eighty-one gulden more? Hoping to God, Maria Anna would never find out, he reached into his coat pocket for the amount.

"Very well, then, pay the man," he said. "But be sure to get a receipt for the amount from him." The Estates Director was sure to make a fuss about reimbursing him if there was no receipt to accompany his request.

The Kapellmeister's head was bent low over his desk when Rosalie appeared at the door of the impresario's chamber. She had his money in her hands. There was no need for the Kapellmeister—strapped for cash as he appeared to be—to spend eighteen ducats on a prop knife. Made of wood, at that!

Appalled at the coutelier's demand, she and Greta had given the man a good piece of their minds and haggled him down to a more reasonable price.

Now Rosalie rapped her knuckles on the door to announce her presence, took a step inside the room, and waited.

"Rosalie!" The Kapellmeister seemed surprised to see her. "What brings you here?" His brow furrowed in concern. "All goes well with the rehearsal, I trust." Fräulein Renier was expected at the palace this morning along with one of the basses performing in the opera.

"Master Johann had no complaints." None that she knew of at least, Rosalie thought as she approached the desk. "Although he did ask Greta and me to come here and scrub the backstairs area."

"Excellent!" Haydn beamed approvingly. "I fear it's been weeks since the place was cleaned."

"We'll have it looking like new in no time at all," Rosalie assured him. The area was quite as dreadful as Master Johann had made out. But what with one thing and another, they had yet to begin cleaning it. "But that's not why I'm here."

She reached forward, poured the Kapellmeister's silver onto his desk, and explained the reason for her presence. "Karl misunderstood the price the coutelier was asking. It was four ducats. Not eighteen."

Still more than it should have been, in Rosalie's opinion. Sixteen gulden for a knife! Good grief! But the coutelier had made such an inordinate fuss about accepting a mere four gulden for his trouble that both she and Greta had caved.

Herr Haydn stared at the mound of silver she'd piled on his desk, then raised his head to stare at her. "Karl mistook four ducats for eighteen?"

The sharp edge of skepticism in his tone made Rosalie bite her lip in dismay. Oh dear! Now she'd done it. Made it seem as though Karl was a common thief. Of course, no one in their right mind would make a colossal mistake like that.

"Well," she started slowly, wishing she'd told the truth to begin with, "the coutelier was demanding eighteen ducats. But Greta and I thought that was far more than he deserved. Karl was loath to bargain with the man, but . . . " Her voice trailed off.

The truth was it had been neither her place nor Greta's to quibble about the price. They had stepped in heedless of the consequences, never considering whether it was proper or not. She inwardly cringed at the memory of their raucous argument with the coutelier. They'd sounded like a pair of shrill fisherwomen. What Herr Haydn would think of that, she didn't know.

To her relief, he smiled. "I suppose four ducats was more than the knife was worth, too."

"It was." Rosalie nodded her head emphatically. "But at least we didn't give him eighteen."

Herr Haydn smiled ruefully at her, seeming to agree. "I should've questioned the amount myself, but"—he surveyed the mess of papers on his desk—"with so much to do, it was not a task I wished to take on."

"We didn't mean to meddle, Greta and I, but—"

"I am grateful that you did," Herr Haydn interrupted her with a smile. "It was more money than I could afford to spend."

So he did know about his predicament, Rosalie thought. Poor gentleman, and yet he'd been willing to use his own money for a silly knife made of wood. Did the airheaded Fräulein Renier know how much her antics were costing the Kapellmeister? Not that she was likely to care even if she did. Women like her rarely did.

"The other prop knife must be somewhere around," Rosalie assured Herr Haydn. How could it go missing in such a small place? "Greta and I will keep an eye out for it." She was sure Fräulein Renier was making a needless fuss over it. The coutelier had said as much.

"I told Herr Affligio, I did. If there's something wrong with the knife, I said, show it to me. He was loath to do it, which tells me the entire tale. He simply wanted a new knife without having to pay for it."

"And so you returned the favor by demanding eighteen ducats!" Greta had rolled her eyes. "A fine man you are."

Rosalie grinned at the memory; Greta was sweetness itself until something got her hackles up. Then her tongue was sharper than vinegar. But Herr Haydn's head was bent over his papers once more. Seeing that, Rosalie prepared to tiptoe out of the room and leave him to his work.

She had barely reached the door when she heard a sharp intake of breath and what sounded like a softly muttered curse.

Astounded, she spun around. Dear God, whatever was the matter! She had never heard Herr Haydn so much as utter an angry word let alone swear. What had gotten into the poor gentleman now?

Her curiosity aroused, she trod back to the desk to see what the matter was. Herr Haydn leant down, impatiently pulling drawers in and out. "Did the man never keep a stock of fresh nibs?" he was grumbling under his breath. "Blue ink and no nibs! Heaven preserve me from such a shabbily run office."

He slammed another drawer shut as Rosalie peered over the mound of papers on his desk. The steel nib from the pen the Kapellmeister had been using had broken off. Small wonder! The tip was nearly rusted through and it lay now in a puddle of indigo-blue ink.

"Shall I go to the bookseller's?" Rosalie asked, seeing the growing frustration on the Kapellmeister's features. "There is one not too far on Bräunerstrasse." If she was not mistaken, it was Herr Grimm's shop that supplied the Burgtheater with its stationery.

Whether the Kapellmeister had heard her offer or not, she couldn't tell. He pulled opened yet another drawer, then grew abruptly pale and rigid as he stared down at its contents. A minute slowly ticked by before he slammed the drawer shut and stared blankly ahead.

Was he even aware she stood before him?

"Herr Haydn?"

"Y-y-es?" His eyes, wide with horror, slowly met hers. What had he seen, she wondered, to look like that?

Not daring to ask, she repeated her offer to him.

"Er-yes, of course. By all means. A supply of nibs and some black ink, if you would. *Vielen Dank!*" Still seeming shaken, he reached into his pocket, drew forth more money than anyone could possibly need to purchase a few nibs and a quantity of ink, and dropped the coins into her outstretched palm.

"I doubt Herr Grimm charges more than a few gulden," Rosalie said, handing back all but four gulden of the money Herr Haydn had given her. "Black ink and some nibs," she repeated to make sure she'd got it right. "Will you need paper as well?"

"No, just the ink and the nibs." The Kapellmeister shook his head. "And please send Karl in. Directly, if you will. It is urgent."

Chapter Twenty

MINUTES after Rosalie had left the room, Haydn remained frozen in his chair, unable to believe what he'd seen. Had he imagined its presence?

He bent down to open the lowest drawer in the desk. There it still was—the dagger that had apparently taken Affligio's life. The wooden handle was inlaid with ivory, the bolster was made of brass, and the blade of fine steel.

Haydn closed the drawer again. What precisely had killed Affligio, then? Karl had told him the impresario had been found with his own dagger buried in his chest. But the bloodstains on the carpet—the memory of them caused Haydn to thrust back his chair and stride into the inner chamber—had made the Kapellmeister doubt the fatal blow had come from a dagger at all.

And here was proof of the fact. Haydn whipped around, eyes drawn toward the desk in the outer chamber and the drawer where the dagger was concealed.

Yet the Police Inspector himself had corroborated both Karl's story and the account reported in the court newspaper. The impresario's body had been discovered with a dagger protruding out of his chest. Von Beer, it was true, had been loath to provide him any information, but Haydn thought it unlikely the Police Inspector would lie about so trivial a fact.

Clearly, whatever had killed Affligio, it was not his own dagger.

Haydn walked pensively back toward the desk. Could it have been the prop knife that had done the evil deed? That would certainly explain why it was inexplicably missing. Nowhere to be found, Karl had said.

Dear God! The weapon was undeniably dangerous—plainly not functioning as it was supposed to. Had that been the result of an unfortunate mistake on the coutelier's part? Or was it a deliberate attempt on the impresario's life?

No, no. That was impossible.

Haydn resumed his seat. Affligio had commissioned the making of the knife himself—not above a year ago, if the records were to be believed. Barely months later, it had malfunctioned for the first time, resulting in Frau Oliveri's husband meeting his demise.

Haydn shook his head gravely. He should have spoken with the coutelier, ascertained the details of the commission as well as the more recent arrangement to return the faulty weapon in exchange for a wooden one. Was it the coutelier who had demanded the knife's return or Affligio who had forced the issue?

Other questions swirled through his mind. Where were the props kept? Who had access to them? Haydn doubted Leopold would've known where to find the prop knife. But Karl most certainly would.

Karl who had refused to be paid, Haydn remembered. Karl, who knew more about the impresario's affairs than anyone else. Had he done it for the money? Haydn had no concrete evidence of it, but unless he was very much mistaken Affligio had recently acquired a sufficient quantity of money. Enough of it to promise his men they'd be paid.

But no money had been found. If it had ever existed, it was more than likely the killer had made off with it.

Haydn glanced at his timepiece. Where was Karl? There were questions he needed answered before he paid von Beer another visit.

If the prop knife had found its way into the impresario's chest, Karl was not the only one under suspicion. There was another equally likely to have done the deed. The last person to see Affligio alive; too distraught to sing; close to being dismissed, if rumor had it right. That was as strong a motive as any to get rid of the impresario.

And had she not been the only person to insist Affligio could not have been murdered? That it had all been an accident?

Was that why she'd demanded the knife be replaced? Not out of fear, but guilt.

Herr Grimm's shop was situated a short distance from the Burgtheater. Rosalie had memorized the directions Karl had given her—"Go along Reitschulgasse until you get to Habsburgergasse. Turn left there and then right onto Stallburggasse. After a short distance, turn left onto Bräunerstrasse."

But as she repeated Karl's directions under her breath, her mind burned with curiosity on another question. What exactly had Herr Haydn found in his desk drawer? The money he and Karl had been searching for?

She shook her head. That didn't seem likely. He should've been pleased to find it—pleasantly surprised, even.

But, no, there'd been an expression of utter stupefaction on Herr Haydn's face. Clearly, he'd seen something he hadn't expected to find.

Deep in thought, she nearly passed by the apothecary at the corner of Reitschulgasse and Habsburgergasse. "Egghead!" she cursed herself when she realized she'd missed her turn and needed to walk back.

She forced herself to concentrate until she found her way back to Habsburgergasse, and then her mind returned to the question that had preoccupied it.

What had Herr Haydn discovered? It had been something both unpleasant and unexpected, of that she was sure.

The prop knife? But she dismissed the idea as soon as it occurred to her. Why hadn't he said something, then? He knew they were searching for it. Of course, it was odd that it should have been in the impresario's chamber rather than in the prop room. But Herr Haydn had reacted as though he'd seen a snake coiled up in the drawer.

The next thought that entered her mind made her stop abruptly in her tracks.

Good Lord, had he found the knife—the impresario's knife? The one that was supposed to have killed him?

Oh dear! She clutched the edge of her apron, twisting it around in her agitation. But the more she considered the scenario, the more plausible it seemed.

Aware of her presence, the Kapellmeister must have chosen to keep silent. And then he'd immediately called for Karl. Why? Rosalie's violet eyes narrowed. Was it because Herr Haydn suspected the poor young man of killing his master?

And if that were the case, how long would it be before he received confirmation of the matter from Steffi? The Archbishop's maid would swear on a saint's grave that it was Karl who had hotfooted it to His Grace's residence on Sunday and begged him to hasten to the Burgtheater.

Who else but the killer would have reason to drag His Grace into the affair?

Clenching her fists, Rosalie hurried on, eager to complete her errand. She'd have to warn Greta about the danger. They'd have to find some way of proving to Herr Haydn it hadn't been Karl who'd gone to fetch His Grace on Sunday. But how?

Worried, she turned at last onto Bräunerstrasse. Ah, there was the bookshop—a dark green building with glass-fronted doors.

⸻◦◦◦⸻

"The sheath is still here." Karl gestured toward the empty scabbard hanging on a wall in the prop room. The missing prop knife should've been encased in it. "I put it back myself after the last rehearsal."

That had been on the evening of Affligio's demise, Haydn recalled. He pivoted his head, inspecting the commodious room in which they stood. It was lined with cluttered shelves and pieces of furniture.

The door behind led into the workshops for the painters and carpenters.

"Is there another way into this room?" the Kapellmeister enquired.

Who else would know the prop room could be entered through a door at the back of the painters' workshop? No one other than those who worked at the Burgtheater, he'd wager.

"Yes, through that door." Karl pointed at the corner across from where they stood. There was a faint outline of a door—dingy and grimy with age—in the wall. "But it is always kept locked. Herr Affligio had a key. As do I, of course."

"And beyond that door?" Haydn asked, wondering where it led to.

"That is the area beneath the rear stairs," Karl explained. "The door to Herr Affligio's inner chamber is directly across the hallway as is the cabinet where our rigging equipment is kept."

The sandbags and pulleys, Haydn thought, recalling the cabinet door he had passed by the previous afternoon.

"Do the singers know about this room?" It would be strange if they did not, Haydn reflected. But there was always the possibility that the performers—far too concerned about the arias that would showcase their talents and the costumes that would apparel their figures—didn't trouble themselves with the more mundane aspects of the performance.

"To be sure they do." Karl snorted and barely refrained from rolling his eyes in exasperation. "They are supposed to return any props they handle back here. Not that any one of them cares to do it. That's all left to me and the other stagehands."

"And it is through there that they enter the room?" Haydn pointed toward the door through which they had come in. At Karl's nod, he continued, "And I take it none of the singers brought their props back on that evening."

"Why would they, when the likes of us will do it for them?"

That meant that only Karl had access to the knife. Unless, of course, Loretta Renier had stolen back into the room after all the workers and singers had departed. Haydn had learned it was Affligio—always the last to leave—who locked the doors to both the workshops and the changing rooms. As long as the impresario remained in the Burgtheater both doors remained unbolted.

The Kapellmeister stroked his chin pensively as his gaze roved around the room.

"Was any visitor ever brought here?" he asked after a few minutes.

"What reason would there be for that?" A bemused frown appeared on Karl's brow.

None, Haydn supposed, but the question had to be asked.

"And the Salzburger?" he pressed on. "Did Herr Affligio ever bring him here?"

"I would be very much surprised if he did." Karl shook his head adamantly. "There was never any reason for the man to be in either workshop, much less here. I doubt the Salzburger stole the knife, if that's what you're thinking. What would he do with it?"

Other than drive it into Affligio's chest? The words drifted into Haydn's mind, but he refrained from voicing them. No need to let young Karl— a suspect himself as far as Haydn was concerned—know what he was thinking. He had not mentioned finding Affligio's dagger either.

He saw Karl tugging at the coarse, curly hairs of his red beard. "I can't think who might've taken it or where it could've gone."

Haydn followed Karl's gaze, staring at the empty sheath. His eyes rose, alighting on the line of swords and shields dangling from the wall above. "Could it have been put somewhere else?" The weapons were kept near the door, but perhaps someone had mistakenly set it down elsewhere.

Far better that than what he suspected, that the knife was at this moment in Affligio's breast. That would mean a killer roamed free in the Burgtheater. And who knew what deadly lengths the murderer would traverse to keep his—or her—awful secret safe?

"I have searched the entire room, every shelf, every drawer," Karl answered the question Haydn had almost forgotten having asked. "It is not—"

To Haydn's surprise, the young man's voice skidded to a halt as his eyes widened. "Dear God!" Karl turned to the Kapellmeister. "Could he have been killed with it?"

Haydn searched the young man's features. "Killed with the prop knife, you mean?" He spoke softly, careful to betray nothing of what he suspected. What, he wondered, had led Karl to the very conclusion he had drawn?

Karl swallowed. "It looked very much like his dagger. It could easily be mistaken . . ." He swallowed again, overcome by his thoughts. "There was a dagger on his desk," he murmured in so low a voice, Haydn could not be certain he had heard him aright.

Had Karl mistaken the prop knife for Affligio's dagger? It would account for his stupefaction at the notion that had entered his head.

"But you yourself had returned it to its sheath, had you not?" Haydn pointed out. "Who then could've transported it to his chamber?"

Karl pursed his lips. "He himself, perhaps. Fräulein Renier's acting was far from satisfactory that evening. The scene in which she thrusts her dagger into her breast most unconvincing. Both the librettist and the composer were far from pleased. What if Herr Affligio wished to rehearse it with her?"

"He asked to meet with her?" Haydn enquired, glad Karl had raised the subject himself. He had found himself at a loss to broach the issue without arousing the other man's suspicions.

"I saw Herr Affligio catch her eye and signal to her—surreptitiously it seemed to me." Karl's eyes narrowed as he attempted to recall the evening. "He would do nothing to openly humiliate her. She enjoys the Emperor's friendship."

He ran his fingers through his thick red hair. "God in heaven, what if it was the prop knife that killed him!"

"The thought troubles you," Haydn remarked quietly.

Karl turned to him, eyes wide and despairing. "How could it not? The Police Inspector is sure to think one of us is the culprit. It could hardly have been the Salzburger who removed the knife from the prop room."

Chapter Twenty-One

Deep in thought, Haydn set forth on the short walk to the police station on Habsburgergasse. Never one to dawdle, he found his steps lagging now, slowed by the troubled thoughts that churned in his mind.

He had been all but certain Leopold was guilty of Affligio's murder. Now the matter seemed not so cut and dried.

Everything he'd learned recently served only to point the finger of guilt away from Leopold—and squarely at someone within the Burgtheater. The impresario had been discovered in a chamber that few knew about, and that fewer still were permitted to enter. The dagger that had supposedly killed him—yet how could it be a dagger when the man had bled from his head?—was still in a drawer in his desk.

And to compound matters, the prop knife that looked exactly like the dagger was missing. There was no question in Haydn's mind that it was this knife that was buried in Affligio's chest. A knife, Haydn reminded himself, that only the singers and the men employed at the theater would've known where to find.

A coach hurtled wildly around the corner just then, nearly running into him. Startled, Haydn hugged the street corner, waiting for it to pass, and then walked on. The coachman yelled out what could've been either an apology or a curse for all the attention he paid to the words; his mind had already returned to the issue at hand.

It was unlikely Leopold had barged into the inner chamber. (Affligio was hardly likely to retire there in the middle of a dispute.) Even more improbable that he had armed himself with a prop knife.

No, anyone with half a brain would be forced to conclude the impresario's death had come at the hands of someone closely associated with the Burgtheater.

But then again—Haydn's steps ground to a halt—Leopold had an appointment with the impresario. And he had kept it; Frau Mozart had freely admitted to that. Worse still, someone had seen him. A pair of reliable eyes, according to von Beer. Who could it be, Haydn wondered.

Could the individual, whoever it was, have been mistaken in what he saw?

It was the only explanation, Haydn reflected, as he resumed his walk. A man engaged in a physical dispute would most likely be in a state of disarray following it. Furthermore, a man who had committed murder could certainly not hope to return home in a pristine state.

Yet Frau Mozart, when Haydn had discreetly put the question to her, had replied her husband had not a hair out of place when he returned. No blood on his clothing or scratches on his arms and hands.

"My husband returned home as clean as he was when he set out," she had replied, puzzled. "Why should it be otherwise? He merely went out to meet a man," she'd added with a faint smile of amusement, "not to wash the streets."

But surely a fellow as broad and stout as Affligio would not have meekly submitted to murder without putting up a fight. And that being so, the evidence of the struggle would be plainly seen on his attacker's person.

But neither in his person nor in the state of his mind had Leopold exhibited any signs that could suggest anything untoward had occurred during his supposedly deadly encounter with the impresario. Would a God-fearing man so easily escape the shame, fear, and self-condemnation that must surely follow upon the commission of so heinous an act as murder?

Haydn thought not.

The man would've had to be a monster to feel nothing—not so much as a twinge of guilt or remorse. No, it was impossible!

"And the dust," he said to himself. "Never forget the dust."

Von Beer's witness had claimed to have seen Leopold emerging from the backstairs. No person who had trod up or down those filthy stairs could hope to protect their clothing from the infernal dust. Not if he were in haste as the killer must have been when he attempted to make his escape.

"No, the man is innocent. It is as clear as day," Haydn declared to himself as he came in sight of the police station. His head held high and his back straight, he marched up the stairs and into the police station.

"I wish to see Herr von Beer," he announced in a voice that made it clear he would brook no opposition. Much to his relief, the police guard offered none, promptly lowering himself from his perch instead to inform the Police Inspector of his arrival.

<hr>

Cheeks flushed with anxiety and her heart pumping frantically, Rosalie pushed open the double doors into the bookseller's. The bell above jangled, loud and discordant, as she stepped in.

"Coming," called an old, creaky voice. "Be patient, I am coming."

It took Rosalie's eyes a while to adjust to the dim interior of the shop. Gradually she made out a stooped, bespectacled, white-haired man in an ink-stained apron, standing on a stepladder near the bookshelves that climbed the entire back wall of the store. He had a collection of leather-bound tomes in his arms and was engaged in meticulously finding a place for each one.

"What is it you need?" he asked, peering along one of the shelves before inserting a volume into the tightly packed row.

"Black ink," Rosalie replied, craning her neck up to look at him.

She was on the verge of asking him to hurry up but stayed her impatience. It would do no good. Besides, it was not in her nature to be so rude, no matter what the provocation.

"For the Burgtheater," she contented herself with saying.

"Ah!" The old man nodded. "Herr Affligio's ink. I ordered it for him. It has been waiting here for him since Monday. But when he did not come. . ." He shook his head sadly.

"You've not sold it, have you?" Rosalie asked, dismayed.

"Oh, no. It's still here." Herr Grimm climbed down the rungs of his ladder. "Poor gentleman! He was here just the other day. Saturday, it was."

That would have been the day before the impresario was murdered. Had Herr Grimm heard the news, she wondered.

"Of course, I have," he replied when she asked him. "How could I not? And to think he was hale and hearty just the other day! He bounded into the shop, wanting a supply of black ink."

"Black?" Rosalie repeated. "But the ink in his pot is blue."

Herr Grimm bustled about the store, poking his head into one cabinet after another under the counter. Rosalie couldn't see him; she could merely hear the creaking sound of the doors opening and the soft click of their closing.

"I'd run out of all the black," Herr Grimm's voice came from under the counter. "And there was just a single pot of blue left. I told him I'd have more for him on Monday."

Another door creaked open. "Ah, there it is. Four pots of black ink." Herr Grimm poked his head above the counter. "Do you need pens as well and paper?"

"Yes!" Rosalie said, startled. Good heavens, she'd nearly forgotten about the pens. And she couldn't remember whether Herr Haydn had asked for any paper, but it would be just as well to get a ream.

Herr Grimm reached up to set a bundle of quills, a ream of paper, and four pots of black ink on the counter. "You'd better take some blue ink as well," he said, bending down for some.

"We don't need any." Rosalie leaned over the counter and peered down at the old bookseller.

"It will be required at the Kärntnertortheater, my girl, mark my words."

"The Karntnertortheater uses blue ink?" Rosalie asked, mystified. Why would they do that?

Herr Grimm found a few pots of blue ink and set them on the counter alongside the other items. "It was Herr Affligio's way. The general contracts for the theater were signed in the Kärntnertortheater in blue. The specific ones for each opera within the Burgtheater in black. It helped him see at a glance which contract was needed."

He began calculating the cost on a scrap of paper.

"You'd better take a few pots of the blue," he continued as he carried over a digit to the next column. "I'll warrant they're in need of some by now."

"Very well," Rosalie agreed, although she didn't think Herr Haydn was inclined to use any of the blue. He seemed to be adamantly set against the color. But arguing with Herr Grimm would only prolong her errand, and she was eager to be done.

⁕

Von Beer's icy blue eyes held Haydn's gaze in a piercing stare. "A prop knife is missing from the Burgtheater, is it? And on the strength of that, I am to believe my prisoner is innocent?" He leaned back in his seat, steepling his slender fingers together. "There is no chance, I take it, that the object in question is merely missing. Misplaced, perhaps?"

Haydn sighed. He had sought to gather his thoughts into some semblance of coherence, but he had clearly failed. Drawing a deep breath, he began again.

"The knife found in the impresario's body, was it retractable?"

Von Beer's eyes rested impassively on Haydn's features. "As a matter of fact, it was. Although what difference that makes to the guilt—or lack thereof—of the man in my prison cell, I fail to see."

"The impresario's assistant saw his employer's corpse and the knife buried in it. He thought it was his master's dagger, but the dagger in question is still in the impresario's desk. And I am told the prop knife —a retractable one as weapons used in the theater usually are—looks exactly like it."

Haydn paused, then lest von Beer should remain unconvinced, he hurried on: "Affligio's dagger and its replica are unique enough that there's no mistaking them. Besides, I think we can agree that the impresario could only have been stabbed"—*if stabbed, he was*, although Haydn kept that particular thought to himself—"by his own weapon or one of those that belonged in the Burgtheater's prop room."

Von Beer's expression remained unchanged, a fact that irked Haydn no end. Was there no persuading the man?

"The man you hold is a composer. Do you really suppose he goes about with a dagger on his person? He is as likely to carry a weapon as you are to have a flute in your pocket."

The words brought the faintest of smiles to the Police Inspector's face.

"The impresario's death was not—as it happens—caused by a knife. His own or any other."

135

"No!" Haydn felt his pupils dilate as the single syllable flew out of his mouth. He had suspected all along that it was not a knife that had killed the impresario. But he hadn't expected the Police Inspector to confirm those suspicions.

"Not the knife," he repeated. "What was it then?"

"A hard blow to the head," von Beer informed him. "Caused, the medical examiner surmises, by a heavy object swinging into the skull. The back of it was completely smashed in."

"God in heaven!" Haydn shuddered at the painful images the Police Inspector's words elicited in his mind. But what kind of object? Something on Affligio's desk? Something Leopold could have obtained just as easily as anyone else?

He had been so certain Leopold could be proven innocent. But if Affligio had been killed by something other than the prop knife . . . It would explain the lack of blood on Leopold's person.

"Does the medical examiner say what the weapon could be?" he asked. "Or who could have wielded it?"

Von Beer's smile grew. "It could have been anything—a small, heavy glass or metal sculpture. And, although it could have been wielded just as easily by a woman as by a man, the matter has no bearing on our prisoner's guilt. You forget he was seen."

"By a pair of very reliable eyes," Haydn said bitterly. "Yes, I remember. But"—he straightened up as his previous doubts returned to his mind—"How can he be so sure of what he saw?"

The Police Inspector had all but admitted the witness had seen little more than a profile, shadowed by a hat pulled low over the features. Under such circumstances, might a man's own mother not have doubts? But von Beer's witness was prepared to take an oath upon the Bible that it was Leopold—and none other—outside the Burgtheater.

"It would have to be someone long familiar with him to surmise the cape-wrapped figure belonged to Leopold Mozart," Haydn pointed out.

"It was," von Beer confirmed. "A gentleman as familiar with the prisoner as his own wife."

And who, Haydn wondered, could that be? Other than the Mozarts and his brother Michael. Who else was there so familiar with Leopold as to have not a shadow of a doubt about the man he had seen?

Von Beer shuffled some papers on his desk. "I have pressing matters to attend to, Herr Haydn, and while your faith in a fellow musician does you credit, I have no doubt the man is guilty. Believe me, my conscience would not rest easy were I not assured of the fact."

He opened a folder and glanced pointedly at his timepiece.

"But the knife," Haydn pressed on, reluctant to leave the matter where it stood. "Where could Leopold have obtained it? And why would he seek to drive it into the impresario's breast? I take it he was already dead when he was stabbed."

"He was indeed. And the knife merely confirms our impression. The prisoner's disputes with the impresario were legion and well known to all. Aroused to a fury, God knows how or why, he swung a blow at the impresario and then proceeded to stab him in a rage.

"It was passion that led to this murder, Herr Haydn. A violent, uncontainable passion."

That might have been true enough, Haydn thought as he pushed his chair back. But he doubted it was Leopold's passion that had been the cause. Overly importunate he may well have been, relentlessly and annoyingly demanding. But violent?

It seemed unlikely.

"May I see the man?" he asked. His only hope was that Leopold could furnish some small clue to his own innocence. Who knew but the man may have seen or heard something that could lead them to the killer.

Chapter Twenty-Two

A long-faced prison guard, his keys jangling at his waist, led Haydn down a flagstone-paved hallway. "There it is," he said, stopping short of the third cell down the corridor.

But to Haydn's astonishment the guard did no more than lean in to bellow out his presence to Leopold—"Wake up! There is someone to see you."—before turning on his heel to make his way back to the entrance.

"Am I not to be let in?" he called after the man.

The guard turned sharply at the sound of his voice and looked pityingly at him.

"The man is a murderer, and you wish to share a cell with him?"

"It would make it easier to converse with him," Haydn explained calmly. "Besides, I am acquainted with the gentleman and feel myself in no danger from him."

The guard shook his head. "Not even his wife is allowed into his cell," he replied. "The Police Inspector forbids it. Killers are to be kept apart, he says."

Haydn pursed his lips, barely able to restrain a caustic comment from bursting out of his mouth. He was expected to feel himself safe in the presence of a ruffianly police guard and yet quake at the thought of being near an even-tempered, God-fearing gentleman!

But any argument was out of the question and would get him nowhere. Turning, he drew nearer to the bars of Leopold's prison cell. It was clean enough, God be praised. A little light entered through the dingy panes of a tiny window set high in the walls.

A broom stood near the bed, and it was clear Leopold had employed it to sweep the dust away from the rough flagstones that paved the floor. The coarse blanket had been neatly spread over the bed. A plain white jug and a washbasin stood on a table under the window, and on the chair beside it, staring disconsolately at the floor, sat the hapless prisoner.

Haydn gripped the iron bars that separated him from the composer.

"Herr Mozart," he called softly. "It is I, Joseph Haydn, Michael's brother."

"Michael sent you?" Leopold raised despairing eyes and a face dotted with stubble. He rose from his chair and came slowly to the bars, bringing with him the pungent odor of unwashed flesh. It was all Haydn could do not to recoil in disgust.

Leopold must have noticed the expression on his face, for he retreated from the bars. "I beg you will pardon my state of hygiene." He cast a glance around his cell. "I am not allowed much as you can see."

Haydn bit his lip, ashamed. All Leopold had left to him was his dignity and in one stroke Haydn had taken even that from him.

"I will ask the Inspector if a fresh set of garments can be brought in for you," he said briskly. He saw no reason why the request should be denied. "But there are some questions I wish to put to you. I have temporarily taken over Herr Affligio's duties—"

"Wolferl's opera!" Leopold's features brightened. He began to come closer to the bars, then caught himself and stood by the bed, looking eagerly at the Kapellmeister.

"I fear I am not in a position to bring it to the stage," Haydn informed him quickly, only to regret the words when he saw the crushing disappointment on Leopold's face. "It is an impressive undertaking for so young a boy," he remarked, hoping to put Leopold at ease.

"It is, indeed," Leopold replied with a smile. He sank onto the bed. "I have been graced with a son whose talent far exceeds mine or that of any man alive today, Herr Haydn. I feel obliged to nurture his gift, to bring the world to a recognition of it. Everywhere we've traveled, the boy's genius has been praised. But here in his own country, he is ignored.

"The impresario—" Leopold choked and his features darkened. "He accused me of attempting to prostitute my own child, Herr Haydn. He said he would see to it the opera failed if I insisted upon—" Leopold choked again, unable to repeat the cruel words the impresario had hurled at him.

It was an outrageous insult. Simply hearing about it had made Haydn's blood seethe. How must Leopold have felt? And this was the dispute everyone had heard! Why, any man could be forgiven for thrashing the impresario within an inch of his life.

Forcing himself to calm down, he asked gently, "What did you do?"

Leopold shook his head resignedly. "What could I do? I turned back. What choice had I but to accept the opera was not to be?"

And that had been on Friday, if Haydn remembered aright. But Affligio had been killed on Sunday. What man would wait two entire days to get his revenge?

"Affligio had long objected to having the work performed, had he not?" Haydn remarked, hoping to turn Leopold's mind away from that bitterly painful memory. "On what grounds, did he ever say?"

"Grounds?" Leopold uttered a harsh laugh. "The man had none. Someone had set his mind against the boy, I'm convinced of it. He insisted the work was untheatrical. A series of arias, he said, with little action." Leopold looked up. "I ask you, is it the composer's job to consider the action or the librettist's? The composer can only work with what he has.

"And the singers. My God!"

"Fräulein Renier?" Haydn hazarded a guess.

"Her voice is mediocre, but at least she can read music. That's more than I can say for most of that lot. Frau Oliveri, for instance, can barely read a note. She learns all her pieces by ear. The slightest change in the score necessitates a lengthy conference with her that she might hear the entire work played all over again and begin once more the process of memorizing her part!"

"A tedious process," Haydn agreed, and he was sure Wolfgang had chafed at it. "But then the impresario agreed at last to pay for the work, did he not?" Hadn't Frau Mozart said something to that effect? Had remorse caused the impresario's change of heart?

"He claimed to have had some proposition. But what it was, I was never told. He never answered his door."

"You kept your appointment?" Haydn asked. "At the usual hour?" The appointment had been for half past five, according to Affligio's appointment book. It had been shortly after that von Beer's witness had claimed to see Leopold.

Leopold fingered the blanket on his bed. "It was an hour later, to be truthful."

"An hour later?" Haydn exclaimed. "Not half past five, but half past six, instead? But his appointment book has the time down as half past five?"

"It was initially set for that time," Leopold acknowledged, "but then his assistant came to say Affligio wanted to push it back."

"Karl?" The young man had made no mention of any such thing. Why not, Haydn wondered.

Leopold nodded. He tugged at his wig, discreetly scratching his scalp. "Yes, Karl. The man with the wooden clogs. There is no mistaking him."

"And you were there at half past six?" Haydn asked. "Not a moment sooner?" Good heavens, that cleared the man, did it not? But who then had von Beer's witness seen? And why hadn't the Police Inspector considered this information in conjunction with his witness's statement?

"What did the Police Inspector say when you informed him the appointment had been changed to a later hour?"

"I—" Leopold frowned, looking puzzled. "I have not spoken to him of it. Why should I? He never asked."

<hr>

"Herr Haydn!" With a resigned air, von Beer laid down his pen. "You have returned." He waved the Kapellmeister in. "What may I do for you now? Is it the condition of the prisoner's cell that you wish to find fault with?"

"Not at all." Haydn took the seat offered to him. "The cell seems clean enough, but Herr Mozart is greatly in need of a wash and his wife must be allowed to bring him a fresh suit of clothing."

An expression of surprise and relief washed over the Police Inspector's features. Haydn was glad to see that; he had intentionally broached the lesser matter first.

"Of course," von Beer agreed readily enough. "Is there anything else?"

It was the opportunity Haydn had been waiting for, and he pounced on it.

He leaned forward. "Were you aware that the impresario had pushed back the time of his meeting with Herr Mozart? It was an hour later than the time notated in his notebook."

"It is what he tells you, I suppose." Von Beer's features hardened into a watchful wariness. "Surely, you must be aware the prisoner's word alone counts for nothing. He—"

"Affligio's assistant went himself to delay the appointment," Haydn broke in.

"He will confirm that?"

"He will swear an oath to it, if needed," Haydn replied. But he felt a qualm of misgiving. Would Karl corroborate the fact? Why he hadn't done so already was mystifying? If he was the killer, he had every reason to stay silent on the matter. Or was he the witness von Beer had mentioned?

The questions raced instantaneously through Haydn's mind as he spoke.

"If Herr Mozart was to meet the impresario at half past six rather than half past five, he could not have been seen outside the Burgtheater." Not to mention that Leopold had been completely confounded when Haydn commented on the state of the backstairs.

"It is more convenient to use the backstairs," he had said to Leopold. "But the area is filthy, is it not?"

"The backstairs?" Leopold had repeated, his brow creasing into a deep frown. "Why would I use the backstairs like a common tradesman. No, I used the staircase everyone else is accustomed to using. And they are clean enough."

Now Haydn reiterated his point. "Herr Mozart was nowhere near the theater at that hour."

"Impossible!" von Beer shook his head vehemently. "The—" Abruptly he brought himself short.

Haydn's eyes narrowed as he regarded the man. What had he been about to reveal? The name of the *reliable* witness? His mind darted through the possibilities once again. It could not have been Loretta Renier; Haydn had received the impression the individual in question was a man.

Besides, would a mere singer's statement be accepted without a single effort made to question or verify it? No, he thought not.

Von Beer had begun with a definite article before cutting himself off, Haydn recalled.

The Emperor? No, His Majesty could not claim to be as familiar with Leopold as Frau Mozart herself. Who then?

The—Good heavens!

"The Archbishop!" The words gushed out of his mouth as soon as they entered his head. He regarded the Police Inspector closely. "By God, it is the Archbishop, isn't it, who claims to have seen Herr Mozart?"

Von Beer's mouth tightened, but he said not a word. Even so his silence spoke volumes.

"It was the Archbishop, then. And you have taken His Grace's word for it that Herr Mozart is a killer and was lurking outside the theater?" Haydn continued, outraged that not a modicum of effort had been made to see if Leopold was indeed guilty of the crime.

"What would you have me do?" von Beer erupted at last, incensed. "Challenge His Grace's account of the events?"

Haydn closed his eyes and shook his head, appalled. Would it have cost the Police Inspector anything to use a few well-placed questions to draw His Grace out? What, for instance, had His Grace been doing outside the Burgtheater at that hour? And why had he even been near the backstairs?

But when he put these questions to von Beer, the Police Inspector lifted his shoulders in a frustrated shrug.

"He was adamant about what he'd seen. Besides, the assistant, whom you insist pushed back the impresario's appointment, was the one who ran to His Grace for assistance."

"Karl?" Haydn was astounded. The young man had said nothing of that either.

"I know not what his name is," von Beer replied tetchily.

"But what did Karl say when you asked him whether he had indeed rushed to the Archbishop's residence?" Why go all the way there, he wondered.

Von Beer frowned. "I saw no reason to question the man. I already had His Grace's word on the matter, after all. Why would I question his account? His Grace says he saw no sign of life within the theater that evening, and the next morning, fearing for Herr Affligio's safety, he went straightaway to the Emperor."

So that was how His Majesty had come to find the body.

"Why go to the Emperor?" he muttered to himself.

Von Beer looked at him as a slow smirk spread over his face. "I take it our prisoner didn't tell you that the Emperor was considering him for a position at court. His Grace felt obliged to let His Majesty know that the man he was thinking of hiring was entirely unworthy of the honor. An ungrateful wretch, an opportunistic snake prone to violence."

"Prone to violence?" Haydn repeated.

"As was borne out by the Emperor's subsequent investigation into the matter. Fearing for the impresario's well-being, His Grace suggested someone be sent to the Burgtheater to make sure Herr Affligio was unhurt."

"And the Emperor chose to come and see for himself," Haydn finished for the Police Inspector. That particular fact didn't surprise Haydn in the least. But why, he wondered, had His Grace not bothered to ensure Affligio was uninjured that very evening?

Why wait until morning? Why insist upon the Emperor's involvement before the truth of the matter had been determined?

To get Leopold into trouble? It certainly seemed to be the case. Moreover, hadn't Michael said His Grace had been looking for an opportunity to rid himself of Leopold? And what better chance than this?

"If the Archbishop saw anyone at all"—and that was doubtful, Haydn thought, as he pushed his chair back and rose to his feet— "it was the individual who was in actuality responsible for the crime, not Herr Mozart."

"His Grace was lying, then, was he?" von Beer demanded sarcastically.

Haydn pressed his lips together, determined not to say another word. But he was certain His Grace was lying about something—either about whom he'd seen or about being called out in the evening. One or the other—possibly both—was a falsehood.

But how could that be established?

Chapter Twenty-Three

HAYDN emerged from the police station into the bright sunlight of a Viennese summer afternoon. Recalling the advice his father had habitually given his sons—*Trust in God*—he sent a silent prayer heavenward as he quietly closed the door behind him. The task ahead was daunting.

Innocent Leopold might be—Haydn had little doubt on that count now—but he was utterly lost if the Archbishop's word was all that stood between him and the gallows. His Grace seemed to be determined to let Leopold hang.

Preoccupied, Haydn barely noticed the tall, stout individual with apple-colored cheeks and a mane of gray-black hair who began limping up the stairs with the aid of a walking stick as he himself prepared to descend them. Haydn was about to pass him by with a courteous nod and a smile when the gentleman turned to him, his face wreathed in a smile of startled pleasure.

"Herr Haydn!" Leaning upon his walking stick, he held out his other hand to the Kapellmeister. "Gregor Fischer at your service. I have long been an ardent admirer of your music. What a pleasure to meet you!" Then, evidently struck by a sudden realization of their surroundings, Fischer's face fell. "But what brings you to our police station? No trouble, I hope."

"None of my own," Haydn acknowledged with a weary smile. Prompted by God alone knew what and against his better judgment, he went on, "But I fear the Police Inspector holds an innocent man in his cells. Herr von Beer is convinced the gentleman—a composer and violinist of note—is guilty of Giuseppe Affligio's murder."

"Ah, the impresario!" Fischer nodded. "What a curious business, to be sure. I have never seen anything like it." Gripping Haydn's elbow, he propelled the Kapellmeister down the stairs to the street. "In all my years as a barber-surgeon and medical examiner—"

"Medical examiner!" Haydn repeated, stunned. The good Lord had lent a favorable ear to his petitions on many an occasion, but this was a veritable miracle! "You—you examined the body then?"

"Oh, yes. His killer must have been a very clever man—or woman."

"A woman could've done it then?" Haydn asked, his mind returning to Loretta Renier. "Clobbered the man on the back of his head with a heavy object?"

"It was swung, I believe," Fischer replied, gripping Haydn for support, and swinging his cane backward and then forward as though wielding a pendulum. "Although what it was, I still cannot fathom." He lowered his cane and let go of the Kapellmeister. "The knife itself was a theater prop—buried in his chest to throw us off gear, no doubt. Or because the killer harbored a deep hatred of the man."

"A prop knife is missing from the Burgtheater," Haydn told him, and then explained his own temporary role there.

"You will want it back, I suppose." Fischer regarded him ruefully. "Unfortunately von Beer won't let it out of his sight until—well, until the entire matter is resolved. He may consent to return it then. And perhaps not even then. Between you and me, the man is high-handed and intolerable.

"And his attitude toward evidence"—Fischer rolled his eyes—"why, it is more reverent than a priest's view of the sacrament. 'The evidence is sacred,' he says. 'It must be kept pristine.' To hear him talk, one would fancy his guards have discovered the relics of the most pious saints during their searches!"

A swinging object, Haydn thought, his mind wandering as Fischer rambled on. If it had been Karl or Loretta Renier who had wielded the deadly weapon, what object could they have laid their hands on? What was there in the Burgtheater that could be swung?

"A sandbag?" he wondered aloud.

"A sandbag?" Fischer repeated, startled. "What has that to do with anything?"

"Could a heavy bag of sand have killed the impresario?" Haydn asked. "It can be swung. It is usually attached to a rope."

Fischer considered this briefly and then shook his head. "No. The damage to the skull was considerable. A sandbag might have stunned him, causing him to fall and crack his head on the floor. But in that case, his skull would not be completely crushed in. No, it was something else. Heavier and much harder."

What could it be? Haydn racked his brains for an answer. If the weapon could be found—and if it could be established that only someone associated with the theater could have access to it—then, perhaps, despite the Archbishop's assertion to the contrary, Leopold could be saved.

"It must've been wielded by a practiced hand," Fischer commented.

"The swinging object?" Haydn asked, bewildered. What skill was needed to swing a heavy object? Fischer had just acknowledged anyone —man or woman—could have done it.

"No, no." Fischer laughed. "That would require no skill at all. I meant the knife."

Haydn gazed curiously at the other man. "I thought it was not the knife that killed Affligio," he said.

"It was not. But it was still buried in the man's chest. Only a practiced hand could do that. The blade retracts, you see. I pulled the knife out to examine the wound, and then—try as I might—I could not put the knife back in. Von Beer insists it remain in the body, in the exact state in which the corpse was found!"

Haydn frowned. "The knife does not always retract as it is supposed to. It has already killed one performer."

It was Fischer's turn to frown. "On the contrary, Herr Haydn, it re-tracts well enough. In fact, only by pressing one's thumb against the bolster can one prevent the blade from moving. It was quite by chance, I discovered that—when one attempt to drive the knife back in was suc-cessful.

"And it took several more to understand how I had succeeded this one time where previously I had failed. I am convinced the killer was familiar with its operation. I doubt the knife could've been driven in by happenstance. It would take too long. And his waistcoat would've been indented with marks where the bolster had hit it."

That would tend to rule out Leopold, then, Haydn thought. Aloud he asked, "Has the Police Inspector been made aware of your findings?"

"I was just about to hand in my report," Fischer replied. He glanced down at the leather case tucked under the arm that held the walking stick. "I sent a boy over earlier with the primary finding that it was not a knife but a heavy object that killed the poor impresario."

Swiveling Haydn around, Fischer continued as they walked back toward the police station: "Have you any evidence to exonerate the gentleman being held? I myself considered one of the performers at the Burgtheater was involved. Who else would know more about the workings of a prop knife?"

Other than the coutelier, Haydn privately thought as Fischer spoke, *although what motive could he possibly have?*

"But the Police Inspector must hold some incontrovertible evidence against Herr Mozart, mustn't he?"

"I suppose he must," Haydn said, disengaging his arm. "I must return to the Burgtheater, Herr Fischer. There are three operas in production."

Fischer beamed. "Of course. And I look forward to enjoying them all!"

⁂

Returning to the Burgtheater, Haydn made his way to the impresario's chambers and slipped quietly in. The contracts for the performers were kept in the inner chamber, and settling himself at Affligio's desk, he pored over them once more. Was there anyone among them who had loathed the impresario enough to take his life?

Von Beer had been certain the impresario had been killed by someone who had borne him an intense grudge. It was a possibility that had to be considered. The only other reason to plunge a knife into a man already dead was to intentionally throw them off the scent.

Could anyone within the Burgtheater be quite so devious? Haydn trusted not.

Von Beer, of course, would point out that the only person with reason enough to vent his rage on a corpse was already behind bars. What man, after all, could fail to be enraged by Affligio's despicable words?

But Leopold had not struck the Kapellmeister as the type of person who nursed his grudges, working himself up into a fever pitch of rage. If he hadn't lashed out the day the insults had been made, why should anyone suppose he'd waited two days before wreaking his revenge?

No, the killer was someone else. Someone within the Burgtheater.

Haydn shuffled through the pages scattered on the desk, carefully scrutinizing each one. But not a single one possessed anything untoward. The terms for each performer remained unchanged. And, as far as he could see, no one had been threatened with dismissal.

As the afternoon light faded, the Kapellmeister drew the candle stand with its three tall white candles toward himself. Lighting each one in turn, he wondered who—other than Loretta Renier—the impresario would have had any reason to dismiss. She was the only singer whose skills had elicited bitter complaints from composers and librettists alike.

But Fräulein Renier was the Emperor's favorite. Would Affligio risk His Majesty's displeasure by ridding the theater of her presence? It seemed unlikely. Moreover—Haydn drew the contracts toward himself again—she had signed contracts for all three operas in the Burgtheater's summer repertory. And try as he might, he could find nothing amiss in any of them.

Who else then? One of the stagehands? The carpenters or the painters? Karl?

Haydn pushed the contracts aside and sat back in Affligio's worn, leather-upholstered chair. Affligio would've been a fool to even consider giving Karl the boot. Without his assistant, Haydn doubted the impresario could have pulled off the stunning performances that drew both Viennese and tourists alike to the theater.

But had Karl been content to languish at the theater? Affligio, Haydn recalled, had smilingly taken credit for the theatrical effects of the operas he performed, never once mentioning Karl's efforts in the undertaking.

A heavy knot twisted in Haydn's stomach as he remembered what he had learned at the police station. It had been Karl who had pushed back Leopold's appointment, and Karl who—an hour before Leopold had even arrived—had made straight for the Archbishop's residence claiming that Leopold was threatening his master.

Or had the Archbishop been lying about that?

None of the performers may have known how to plunge a prop knife into the impresario's breast. But Karl—the man who habitually dealt with the coutelier—might have possessed the dexterous hand it required to kill with it.

Or worse still—Haydn's back stiffened as the thought occurred to him —had the Archbishop been so intent upon ridding himself of Leopold that he had thought nothing of arranging for Affligio to die?

But would a man of God so easily consent to such a thing?

Or had His Grace simply engaged Karl to beat up Affligio merely to summarily discharge Leopold? Unpaid, unacknowledged, what man might not have been tempted by a few bits of gold?

On the other hand, if the Archbishop had merely intended that Affligio be thrashed, would the impresario not have to be in on the scheme? Otherwise, what was to prevent Affligio from revealing that it was Karl, and not Leopold, who had set upon him?

No, it was more likely that the Archbishop had hatched a nefarious scheme with both Affligio and Karl. It had unfortunately gotten out of hand, and His Grace had not hesitated to capitalize on the subsequent tragedy. Karl—paid well, no doubt—had held his peace.

Sickened to the pit of his stomach, Haydn pushed down the bell on his desk.

Chapter Twenty-Four

"I fear I have troubling news," Haydn said gravely when Karl responded to his summons. "I have just returned from the police station and our worst fears have been confirmed."

"The p-prop knife . . . ?" Karl faltered.

"Appears to have found its way into Herr Affligio's chest," Haydn informed him dryly. The implications of the fact would be self-evident to the young man. He carefully lifted Affligio's ivory-handled dagger, which was resting on his lap, and laid it on the table.

Karl's robust features turned pale and he tugged nervously at his beard. "Herr Affligio's dagger." His eyes skittered toward Haydn. "But where . . . ?"

"It was here, where it always has been," Haydn said.

Karl had been leaning his weight against the chair across from Haydn. Now he drew it back and sank into it uninvited.

"It was the prop knife that killed him, then? Good God!" He stared, ashen-faced, at Haydn. "What does the Police Inspector think? Is he still convinced of the Salzburger's guilt?"

Haydn paused, uncomfortable about telling an outright lie. Yet, how else was he to discover the truth? Besides, with an innocent man's life in the balance, would his qualms about telling a small lie serve any purpose?

"As you can imagine, there is some doubt on the matter." It was not entirely a lie. Herr Fischer, the medical examiner, had quite openly expressed his doubts. Haydn fingered the sharp edge of the blade on his desk. "How the prop knife was plunged into your master's breast is a question that quite perplexes the medical examiner." He raised his eyes. "You see the blade retracts so well, there is no driving it into anyone."

Karl peered at him, as though forced to read at sight a particularly difficult piece of music. "But it does not always retract as it should. It has been known to fail. That's why my master pressed the coutelier to replace it."

Haydn studied the other man's features. Karl had a plain, honest face. Unless the man was a consummate actor, his astonishment was genuine. That surprised the Kapellmeister. He had convinced himself the man was guilty.

"Did the coutelier readily agree?" Haydn asked as he mulled over Karl's reaction.

"Not readily, no." Karl fidgeted in his seat. "But we were all a witness to the fatal consequences of its failure. What else could the man do but agree?"

And the coutelier had threatened to charge a hefty price for his cooperation. Had the price been for the knife alone—or had his silence been bought as well?

"It was Affligio who commissioned the knife?" Haydn asked. When Karl nodded, he continued, "And Affligio himself who insisted it be replaced?"

Karl nodded again, mystified by the questions.

"And did the coutelier demonstrate the knife's use when he first brought it?"

"To my master. It must have worked well enough then. Herr Affligio would hardly have taken charge of it if it hadn't."

"You were not present?" Haydn asked, eyebrows raised skeptically.

Karl shrugged. "My presence wasn't required. Herr Affligio was here in his chambers. He had a gentleman with him—"

"A gentleman?" The information caught Haydn's attention. "One of the singers?"

"A nobleman, from the looks of him," Karl said. "He was frequently here—the only person invited into the inner chamber other than—" Karl broke off with a blush.

"Other than?" Haydn pressed.

Karl averted his gaze. "Other than his paramours," he said.

"Fräulein Renier being one of them, I take it," Haydn said. Karl's gaze remained averted.

"It was not my place to know who he was involved with," the young man said quietly.

"No, I suppose not," Haydn acknowledged. Had Affligio known how to make the blade stick? Had he passed on the information to Loretta Renier? She had been the last person to see him. Had she killed him—accidentally, perhaps, or deliberately— and then sent—?

He drummed his fingers on the desk. "Herr Mozart—the Salzburger as you refer to him—insists his appointment was at six-thirty—"

"It was," Karl said before Haydn could finish. "I went myself to give him the message."

It was not an admission Haydn had been expecting, and it puzzled him even more. "Then why in the name of heaven did you go to the Archbishop of Salzburg's residence with the news that Herr Mozart was assaulting your master?"

"But I did not." Karl shook his head vehemently. "I can't understand why Steffi insists I did. She has never seen me. She must've—"

"Steffi?" The Kapellmeister exclaimed, having found his voice at last. "Who is Steffi?"

"Why, the Archbishop of Salzburg's maid. She told Greta she'd opened the door to me on the evening of Herr Affligio's demise. But it was not I."

"Not you?" Haydn stroked his chin thoughtfully.

"No," Karl said emphatically. "I delivered Herr Affligio's message to the Salzburger and went straight to the Seizerkeller. You can ask the painters. Or the stagehands. They were all there. Any one of them will tell you so."

But Haydn was barely listening. "Not you," he murmured again.

Had it been the killer, then? A wily individual bent on making Leopold a scapegoat for his crimes? Or had the Archbishop's nefarious plan been struck not with Affligio and his assistant, but with Affligio and someone else.

Loretta Renier? But she could hardly be mistaken for a man. Besides, why kill the impresario if she was his paramour? Had he threatened to reveal the affair to the Emperor? Or had Affligio's affections wandered?

And what of the mysterious gentleman in Affligio's chambers. He was the only person—other than Affligio himself—who had been privy to the workings of the prop knife.

Had one or the other of them been responsible for the crime and for laying the blame at Leopold's door? Or had Loretta Renier and the anonymous gentleman been working in concert?

And where did the Archbishop fit into the entire scheme? His Grace was involved in some way, of that Haydn was certain.

Arms laden with the packages Herr Grimm had wrapped up for her, Rosalie hastened past the painters' workshop and down the hallway. She would leave Herr Haydn's supplies on his desk for him and then find Greta. The sooner her friend was warned the Kapellmeister had his sights on Karl, the sooner they could think of a way to ward off the danger.

Approaching the impresario's chambers, her ears perked up at the sound of voices coming from within. Who was Herr Haydn talking to? Karl? She hurried forward and burst into the room.

It was just as she had feared.

Karl was sitting across the desk from the Kapellmeister. Neither man was speaking. The Kapellmeister, barely aware of her presence, sat lost in thought, muttering to himself. And, dear Lord, there was an ivory-handled weapon on the desk.

The impresario's dagger? It had to be.

Quietly she came forward and set her packages down.

"Herr Grimm foisted a few pots of blue ink on me," she said to break the strange silence that pervaded the room. She looked curiously from Karl to the Kapellmeister. "He insisted the Kärntnertortheater might be in need of some."

"They might well be by now." Karl unwrapped the packages. His face looked pale, his features flustered. "I will see to it they get these." He turned toward the Kapellmeister, repeating what Herr Grimm had already told Rosalie. The general contracts were signed in blue at the other theater; the contract for each opera the singer was to be in, in black here at the Burgtheater.

"I had no idea Affligio was a stickler for such things," Herr Haydn murmured. He seemed to be barely listening to them.

What had they been talking about, Rosalie wondered. Eager to satisfy her curiosity, she pointed to the dagger. "Is that Herr Affligio's?"

"Yes." Karl glanced up at her, attempting a smile, but not quite succeeding. "He was killed with the prop knife, it seems." The smile faded, replaced by a frown. "And your Steffi insists—"

"She has never seen you," Rosalie said in a loud, firm voice. "She is only repeating what she was told." She stared at the Kapellmeister. "And I'll wager it was the killer himself at the door. There was no need for anyone to go running to the Archbishop when the police station is just around the corner."

To her astonishment, Herr Haydn agreed. "No, there was not. It must've been to—"

"To get me into trouble," Karl cried, distraught. "Why would anyone wish to do that?"

"It was more likely to divert attention from himself," Herr Haydn said soothingly. "And to point the finger squarely at Herr Mozart." But these last words were uttered so softly, it was as though he was speaking to himself.

"Greta and I think it was the coutelier," Rosalie blurted. She hurriedly explained her suspicions before Karl, who was gaping at her as though she'd lost her mind, could say much more than "What reason had he to kill anyone!"

Reason enough, Rosalie thought, as she proceeded to lay the matter before the Kapellmeister. He heard her without interruption, stroking his chin pensively all the while.

"It is a possibility," he acknowledged when she'd finished. "But why run to the Archbishop? Why not kill the impresario and leave? Anyone would conclude it was Herr Mozart who had done the deed. His was the last name in the impresario's appointment book."

Rosalie shrugged. What the killer's reasons were, she didn't know. Maybe it was to make certain Herr Mozart would shoulder the blame? She voiced the thought, but even she had to agree the coutelier had no reason to draw Herr Mozart into the affair.

"Nor me," Karl muttered. "Why bring me in? I have never even had any dealings with His Grace. I've not so much as met him. It was Herr Affligio who went to see His Grace when he needed to."

That brought Herr Haydn out of his stupor. "Affligio had been to see His Grace? When? Whatever for?"

"On Saturday. It was in the morning."

"Saturday?" Herr Haydn's brow furrowed in thought. "The very day he seemed to have changed his mind about Wolferl's opera."

"I doubt he did any such thing." Karl shook his head vehemently. "The work was terrible—a string of beautiful arias directed at the audience with no story and no action at all to stitch the songs together. People may have come once to see it; no one would come again."

The Kapellmeister's frown deepened. "Why not simply change the libretto, then? Surely, one can hardly expect the composer—so young and inexperienced a lad at that—to make the changes himself."

"No one did," Karl shook his head again. "The Salzburger took the libretto never telling Herr Coltellini he meant for it to be brought to the stage. Then when Herr Coltellini realized what was being done, he asked repeatedly to be allowed to make the necessary changes, but the Salzburger balked at the additional work required.

"The music had already been composed, he said. The lad would not write another note until he was paid for the work already done."

"It was the boy who said that, I suppose," Herr Haydn said with a wry face.

Good Lord, Rosalie thought. The lad had some nerve.

"And so your master insulted the man?" The Kapellmeister went on. But he didn't repeat the remarks.

"Master should not have said what he did to him." Karl visibly cringed at the memory. "But I can tell you, he was provoked beyond measure."

What exactly had the impresario said, Rosalie was wondering when Herr Haydn propelled himself forward, elbows digging into the desk. "Then what proposition was he making to Herr Mozart? Your master sent a message to him on Saturday evening. The Mozarts thought he had reconsidered the matter."

Karl shrugged. "If he had, it must've been because the Archbishop twisted his arm. Herr Affligio was trying to get His Grace to become a partner. My master would've done anything to get His Grace to agree."

"Anything?" the Kapellmeister repeated softly. Even to the point of provoking Leopold to assault him? But Leopold hadn't been anywhere near the Burgtheater at the time of Affligio's murder.

"Who else knew of Affligio's efforts?" he asked Karl. "Any of the other singers?"

"I cannot tell." Karl shook his head. "He may have confided in his other partners. Herr Gluck and Herr Coltellini."

Or the mysterious man in his chambers, Haydn thought. Or his paramour, Loretta Renier.

Had someone known enough about the Archbishop's attempts to bring Leopold into disrepute to take advantage of the fact?

Or had the killer borne Leopold a grudge as well and taken the opportunity to hew two obstacles down with a single swing of an ax?

Chapter Twenty-Five

JOHANN was convinced one of Affligio's partners had done him in. Who else had reason enough to murder the man? But Affligio's only known partners were the composer Gluck and the librettist Coltellini.

Staring sightlessly out the carriage window, Johann recalled the dismay he and Luigi had felt when Rosalie and Greta had brought them the news earlier that evening.

"Neither man can have had the necessary connections to persuade Herr Fugger to lend the impresario such a vast sum of money," he'd said in despair to Luigi.

The Konzertmeister had nodded. "And the Archbishop was, as far as we know, still on the fence." He slid his bow over his violin strings, playing a phrase from the opening of brother's opera.

The carriage, with brother sitting lost in thought beside him, jolted unevenly over cobbled streets. Johann barely felt its motion as his mind turned over the paltry facts they had gleaned. He and Luigi had sifted through them with the utmost care, but to no avail. Not a single useful nugget of insight had they discovered.

"Is there any reason to suppose His Grace might have lent Affligio his good name, speaking to Herr Fugger on his behalf?" Johann had wondered.

But Luigi had shaken his head adamantly. "I doubt it. His Grace knows no Christian charity and is not the kind of person to go out of his way for anyone. There must be someone else."

"The Emperor, then?" Johann had tossed out the thought. "It was he who discovered the corpse. And it is his theater."

But Luigi had dismissed that notion as well. "It is not him either. His Majesty would have had no trouble getting Fugger to write off the debt entirely. And Fugger—toady that he is—would have done it willingly. No, we must look elsewhere."

Now Johann sighed, glancing surreptitiously at his brother. *Brother would know what to make of the facts*, he thought. *As for me, I can make neither heads nor tails of the matter.* If only he could toss the details over with his brother. But Johann was determined not to burden the man any more than he already was.

Brother seemed in a pensive mood and oddly quiet, Johann realized.

"Will you be able to help Leopold, do you think?" he asked.

Haydn turned to him, not ungrateful for the interruption.

"He is innocent, I am sure of it. But it's his word and Karl's against the Archbishop's—and that of his maid." He recounted the details. "If the girl were to see Karl, she might realize it was not him at the door that night." But how was that to be arranged?

Besides, would her recanting of her word be sufficient to convince the Police Inspector?

"There is still the matter of whom His Grace saw outside the Burgtheater that night."

"Assuming His Grace wasn't lying about that," Johann pointed out. "Do you really suppose he contrived a plan as foul as that?"

That His Grace—a man of the cloth—might have considered provoking the unsuspecting Leopold into betraying his own better judgment and assaulting Affligio had horrified Johann. Could anyone be so depraved?

And had Affligio truly been so desperate to get into His Grace's pocket that he had gone along with the outrage? If so, he had received his just desserts. Johann said as much.

Haydn nodded. He considered the question his brother had put to him. "I can see no other reason for the killer to go running to His Grace's residence. His Grace, satisfied that his plan had been put into action, wouldn't hesitate to hand over the money Affligio needed to keep the Burgtheater running." Haydn frowned his displeasure. "The man seems to have been unable to live within his means."

The payments made to the supplier Fugger—whoever he was—had been vast. What could the impresario have been thinking?

"But the money hasn't been found, I think you said," Johann noted. How had brother come to the same conclusion as he and Luigi—that Affligio had been killed by a silent partner—and still not discovered the truth about Fugger?

"Taken by whoever Affligio was in league with, I have no doubt," Haydn replied. "I'm inclined to think it was the mysterious gentleman Karl saw on several occasions within Affligio's chambers. Although, what reason could he have had to murder Affligio? It wasn't Leopold, we know. The man wasn't even there."

"Money, perhaps," Johann said, unable to resist giving his brother a hint as to the true state of Affligio's financial affairs. "Affligio may have gotten him involved in some scheme that turned out to be not as profitable as might be expected."

Haydn shook his head. "The only scheme seems to have been Affligio's propensity to get out of paying his composers and librettists by making them partners in the running of the Burgtheater." He turned to face Johann. "Would you believe it, Gluck and Coltellini both renounced their fees for a share of the Burgtheater's profits?"

But Johann seemed entirely unsurprised by the fact.

"I wonder how much of the profits Affligio was able to retain," he murmured to himself instead. "And how much there was to share with any partners he had."

"Not much, I'll warrant," Haydn replied. "What with the prodigious amounts he was paying Fugger."

He was about to continue when he saw, to his surprise, that Johann had frozen, his face as white as the winter snow.

"You know about Fugger?" his younger brother asked, his voice startlingly loud in the confined space of the carriage.

By the time the carriage drew up outside Papa Keller's home, Haydn had heard the entire tale. The size of Affligio's debt to Fugger—small wonder he had constantly attempted to draw his patrons and those who worked with him into partnerships—and his own unwitting involvement in the affair.

"Remember, not a word to Maria Anna," he warned Johann as he climbed down from the carriage. He had no doubt the matter would be resolved. He would meet with the banker on the morrow to determine the extent of his liability. Then he would apprise His Serene Highness of this unforeseen—and most disconcerting–situation.

His one saving grace was that he had signed no contracts or papers agreeing to take over Affligio's debts. But it was a knotty issue and would take time to untangle. And the less Maria Anna knew the better.

"Of course," Johann readily agreed. So much for keeping the matter from brother, he thought ruefully. Joseph had drawn the entire story out of him as skillfully as he played his violin.

"Did Rahier make a fuss about reimbursing you for your expenses?" he wanted to know as he followed brother in through the gate.

Haydn shook his head. "I was fortunate enough not to have to run into him. His Serene Highness approved the expenses and sent me straight to the paymaster." He looked over his shoulder at his brother. "I only wish you had chosen to confide in me. I could have raised this other issue with him as well. I'm sure His Serene Highness knows nothing of this ill-advised stipulation Affligio seems to have agreed to."

Johann nodded sheepishly, recalling the resentment he'd harbored against their employer. "I should have remembered his generosity," he confessed. "The Emperor seems to be content to let his employees die with their debts unpaid. His Serene Highness would never allow such a thing to happen."

They were almost at the door when he stopped his brother. "What shall we tell Papa Keller?" he whispered. "There is almost nothing he can keep to himself. The entire world—not to mention sister-in-law—will know of our predicament the moment Papa Keller so much as hears about it."

Haydn paused, his hand grasping the doorknob. They had both agreed Papa Keller might be an excellent source of information on Affligio's business arrangements. But it was true, there would be no keeping the matter from Maria Anna if they took her father into their confidence.

"The barest truth," he said at last, having carefully pondered the question. "Tell him no more than he needs to know. Affligio was in dire straits, his finances in shambles."

⊷◦◦◦◦⊶

The aroma of frying bacon and bell peppers greeted Haydn's nostrils as soon as he entered the warm kitchen. His mouth watered. Maria Anna was making the appetizing fish soup they'd first tasted at the Bürgermeister's table in Eisenstadt. It was a dish typical of the Burgenland region—part Austrian, part Hungarian, flavored with bacon, garlic, and rich cream.

Its rich aroma reminded Haydn of his empty stomach. He was about to ask his wife, who stood tending to the steaming pot, if the meal was ready when she glanced over her shoulder and frowned.

"I didn't expect you home so early, husband," she immediately exclaimed, displeased. "The soup is not yet ready."

In truth, it was not much earlier than it had been the evening before. Maria Anna had clearly started cooking later than usual, but to point that out would only provoke her further.

"It is no matter," Johann hastened to assure her. "We can stay our hunger. Besides, we had some things to discuss with Papa Keller. Where is he?"

"In the parlor." Maria Anna looked curiously over her shoulder at them again. "What is it you need him for?"

"Wigs." Haydn blurted out the first thing that came into his mind.

His wife stared at him, her blue eyes coldly appraising. "Wigs?"

Haydn found himself at a loss for words. God forbid, she should've guessed at the truth.

"We need three for brother's opera." Johann came quickly to Haydn's rescue. "And Affligio, it turns out, had failed to order them."

Maria Anna snorted. "It sounds just like him. Very well, go into the parlor. I will call you as soon as your supper is ready."

<hr>

Papa Keller was sitting by an open window, pulling on his pipe, when Haydn and Johann entered the parlor. With a guilty start, the old gentleman began to hide his pipe when he realized who it was at the threshold.

"Ah, it is only you," he said relieved. "I feared it might be Maria Anna. She is apt to create a fuss when she sees me smoking in the parlor. Why it matters, I don't understand. Your mother-in-law never minded."

Haydn shrugged. He had long given up trying to comprehend his wife's vagaries. It was best to go along with her whims.

"And neither did she until a few months ago," he reminded his father-in-law. "But there's a bee in her bonnet regarding the matter now. And what can we do but follow?"

His father-in-law nodded. He pulled on his pipe, gesturing for them to take the upholstered chairs across from him.

"What has she been berating you about, then?" he asked. "There's a sour look on both your faces," he explained, looking from Haydn to Johann.

"It is not sister-in-law," Johann said, lowering himself into one of the chairs. "It's Affligio—or the precarious state of his finances, to be more precise."

Papa Keller drew deeply on his pipe and nodded sagely. He was a stout, white-haired, apple-cheeked, bespectacled man, a little over sixty years of age.

"Fugger the banker came by to demand his pound of flesh, did he?" he asked, taking the pipe out of his mouth.

Johann's eyes slid toward Haydn's. Papa Keller was far more perspicacious than they'd given him credit for. "He came to apprise us of Affligio's mountainous debts," he said. "He had a partner apparently, whose share of the payments are in arrears."

But Papa Keller didn't appear to have heard of Affligio's anonymous partner.

"A partner?" he queried. "I doubt any partner would have agreed to take on his monumental debts. Gluck and Coltellini hoped to rake in some of the Burgtheater's profits, and their agreement saved Affligio the trouble of paying them. He had the same arrangement with a singer or two.

"And the Emperor's only concession on the matter was to allow the debt to be attached to the Burgtheater. Affligio would be free of it were he to give up his lease."

"His lease?" Haydn asked. "What lease?" Wasn't the impresario the Emperor's employee?

Papa Keller stared at them astonished. "What! Do you mean to say you were unaware of the fact? The Emperor leases the Burgtheater to the impresario."

Haydn struggled to take in the news. "So, for a yearly fee, Affligio had the privilege of running the theater?"

Papa Keller nodded. "And the rights to all the profits, the ticket sales, and box office subscriptions."

"And that is why the Emperor contributes nothing to the running of the theater." Haydn was beginning to understand the matter. "And doubtless little to say in which operas are performed." Small wonder Leopold had been unable to influence Affligio's decision when it came to Wolferl's opera.

How, he wondered, had Prince Nikolaus even managed to secure a promise to perform his own *Le pescatrici*?

Papa Keller puffed on his pipe. "It's a small price for His Majesty to pay to wash his hands off the entire venture. The theater is run for him at no cost to his coffers, and the leaseholder pays him for the privilege. It would have gone well enough had Kaunitz not persuaded Affligio to hire a troupe of French dancers."

"He must've long dismissed them," Haydn said. "I saw no contracts for any dancers."

Papa Keller's lips stretched into an amused smile. "As soon as he could. They were a colossal failure. But it mattered not. He had already agreed to pay them their enormous fee. It's what got him into debt."

Chapter Twenty-Six

"HE agreed to pay a troupe of dancers seventy thousand gulden!" Johann burst out when Papa Keller had finished recounting the facts. Haydn could hardly believe his ears either. Surely Affligio had possessed a better head for business than that.

"They were favored by the King of France, Kaunitz said. The Viennese public would storm the theater to see them perform." Papa Keller shook his head sadly. "But they failed to find any admirers, small wonder. Who wants to see a troupe of skinny men prancing and jumping about in long pink tights?"

"Pink!" Haydn exclaimed, shocked. "What could the Chancellor have been thinking to foist such a group on the public?"

"He was considering the advantage of having an Archduchess on the French throne," Papa Keller said dryly.

Ach so! The Empress's youngest daughter had just that spring married the Dauphin of France. Chancellor Kaunitz had bent over backward to ensure the marriage took place.

"Even so, I am surprised the Empress agreed to allow the troupe to perform in public," Johann commented.

The candle on the table had worn down to a stubby mound of wax. Seeing the flame wavering and flickering on the stump of wax, he took a fresh candle to it before snuffing it out.

"She had but to see them cavorting about once before putting an immediate stop to the proceedings. Affligio had no objection to letting them go, but neither Kaunitz nor the Emperor would compensate him for his loss."

Had Affligio made such a nuisance of himself, Haydn wondered, that the Chancellor had made arrangements to rid himself of the thorn in his side? But why involve the Archbishop—and Leopold?

He was vaguely aware of Johann asking a question.

"Was that when the impresario started bringing in partners to his venture?"

The old wigmaker nodded, puffing on his pipe. "Although, I fancy Gluck and Coltellini have begun to regret the arrangement. After Fugger had been paid, the profits were scarce. As anyone with half a head on his shoulders could've seen. Affligio even tried to entice me into joining in the venture."

Papa Keller waved his pipe in the air. "But I'm not taken in quite so easily. I asked a few questions and immediately saw the arrangement for what it was, thanks be to God."

Haydn, by this time, was only half listening, his mind churning with possibilities. Had the Archbishop agreed to wipe out the entirety of Affligio's debt in return for the impresario provoking Leopold to his limit? It seemed entirely possible.

Why else would Affligio complain about Leopold's Christian ways and the difficulty of diverting the man from them? Rosalie had told Haydn about the conversation her friend Steffi had overheard.

Thank heavens, for inquisitive maids, he thought gratefully. There would be no getting to the bottom of this business were it not for maids like Steffi spying on their betters.

"Will His Serene Highness be paying Papa for the wigs he makes?" Maria Anna asked Haydn as she ladled out his soup. The evening meal was finally ready, and Maria Anna had summoned them into the kitchen to partake of it.

"Wigs?" Haydn asked. Too late, he recalled the excuse he'd given his wife.

"What wigs?" Papa Keller began to say when Johann interrupted: "The wigs you promised brother for his opera, Papa Keller. Brother will present the receipt to His Serene Highness on the morrow."

He turned to Haydn. "Or I can, if you are needed at the Burgtheater."

Maria Anna, still standing beside Haydn, followed the exchange, a frown of suspicion settling between her brows. But Papa Keller had already caught the gist of the matter and was nodding his head vigorously.

"Ah, yes, the wigs. The singers' heads must be measured. Affligio always had me do that," he explained when Haydn gaped at him, befuddled. "The thickness of their hair varies, you see, depending upon whether it has been allowed to grow or has recently been cut. The wig fits better when a precise measure is taken every time."

Ach so! Haydn nodded. He never neglected to trim his own hair so that his wigs might fit well. But not everyone was inclined to take that precaution.

"There is to be a rehearsal tomorrow," he told his father-in-law. "They will all be there—Ernst and Bastian, the two tenors who play the fishermen, as well as Christian, the bass." It would be no bad thing to have the wigs made, he thought. Who knew whether the Burgtheater had any in stock?

"Why do the fishermen need wigs, husband?" Maria Anna slid his bowl carefully before him. "I thought your opera only has one nobleman, Lindoro."

"It's for the last act," Haydn said, feeling himself on firmer ground now. He lifted a spoon of the soup to his mouth, carefully blowing on it to cool it down. "Frisellino and Burlotto disguise themselves as noblemen, each to trick his beloved into accepting his advances."

"They were at the palace today," Johann said, accepting his bowl from Maria Anna. "They have good voices, all, but neither Ernst nor Bastian can read music to save their lives."

"They have excellent memories, though," Papa Keller informed him through a mouthful of soup.

"Must you speak with your mouth full?" Maria Anna admonished her father. But the old gentleman ignored her. He looked over his glasses at Johann, gesturing emphatically with his spoon as he spoke.

"You have only to play a part once and they can sing it back, note for note. It never ceases to amaze me!"

"Yes, but—" Johann was about to mention Fugger when he stopped himself just in time. "What with one thing and another, and Loretta Renier's antics to deal with all the while"—this last was no lie—"neither Luigi nor I had time to sing the entire role to either man."

"And tomorrow they are needed at the rehearsal," Haydn said. God alone knew how long that would take? Would there be time after to teach the tenors their parts?

"What of Christian?" he asked.

Leopold had warned him that many of the Burgtheater singers couldn't read music. Haydn had taken it as just so much irritable chafing from a much put-upon man. But there was unfortunately more truth to Leopold's remarks than Haydn had given him credit for.

"He's the only one who can be counted on to learn his part," Johann replied. "But having him sing with Loretta Renier is like putting a vicious cat and a belligerent dog in a confined space. They were at each others' throats today." He sighed. "It doesn't help that her singing leaves much to be desired. And Christian is little likely to tolerate fools."

"Oh, those two always bicker," Papa Keller chimed through another mouthful of soup. "I doubt they mean anything by it." He chuckled. "The only time they were in agreement was when there was talk of Leopold being put in charge of the Burgtheater."

"Leopold?" Haydn sputtered. "I thought you said Affligio leased the Burgtheater from the Emperor. How could Leopold be in charge of anything?"

Papa Keller shrugged. "The position was a sop for that opera of his coming to naught. He was to be in charge of hiring the singers for the theater and commissioning librettos—piddly stuff to keep him satisfied. His Majesty must have thought Affligio and Leopold could fight the matter out amongst themselves."

"Loretta Renier and Christian, I take it, were against the position being awarded to Leopold."

Papa Keller nodded. "They hated him with a venom. Leopold's taste in operas is completely lacking—tending toward the old-fashioned, stilted performances favored by Metastasio. No one can stand those anymore. They don't draw in the crowds. How could they when Gluck's operas have given us a taste of something far better? There'd be even less money to be made with Leopold in charge."

"Not to mention anyone unable to read music would be shown the door," Maria Anna remarked acerbically. "I'm surprised it wasn't he who was murdered."

"He might just as well be," Haydn said in a low voice. The man was languishing in prison for a crime he hadn't committed.

"But what objection could Leopold have to Christian?" Johann wanted to know. "The man sings well enough and has no trouble reading music. And why should Christian care so long as he's paid?"

"Ah, but he relies on a paying public and the profits from ticket sales for his salary. Affligio had—"

"Made him a partner," Haydn finished grimly. Was there anyone whom Affligio hadn't?

And what of Loretta Renier? Had she been made a partner as well? Leopold hadn't seemed as averse to her as to the other singers; surely her position was in no danger from the man. But Papa Keller, when Haydn put the question to him, didn't seem to know.

"I don't suppose Gluck and Coltellini were any happier than Christian with the arrangement," Haydn commented.

Could one of these three men have arranged for Leopold to be the whipping boy for another's crime? On the other hand, what reason could any of them have had to kill the impresario? Was an unproductive partnership sufficient reason to dispose of the man?

"Can you blame them?" Papa Keller demanded. "The profits were already abysmally low." He turned to his daughter. "Did I tell you that Affligio suggested I renounce my usual fee and take a percentage of the profits instead? Not content with getting himself into trouble, the man insisted upon foisting his debts onto other men."

But Haydn had ceased to listen. More and more, it seemed as though Affligio's partners had been in need of dispatching two separate birds. Had they done it by casting a single stone?

Chapter Twenty-Seven

Papa Keller stood by the wings, an inch-wide strip of paper in one hand and a pair of scissors in another. He had accompanied Haydn to the Burgtheater that morning, and they waited by the wings downstage, out of the way of the hustle and bustle surrounding them.

"Should I take their measure now, Sepperl?" he bawled into Haydn's ear. "It won't take but a moment."

Haydn winced. But he could hardly blame his father-in-law. It was so noisy here, a tavern would've seemed restful in comparison. Resisting the urge to rub his still vibrating eardrum, he looked out onto the stage. Singers milled around, stagehands dragged in props, and others busily arranged flats on chariots.

"Best do it after the rehearsal," he responded, lowering his head and straining to make himself heard over the hubbub. "When the chaos has subsided."

Nodding, Papa Keller tugged at his waistcoat. He tucked the scissors into a side pocket and draped the paper tape over his wrist. "When do they start singing?"

"Soon enough," Haydn said.

It felt strange to be standing here. In Eszterháza, it would be Herr Porta directing the action from the wings. Haydn himself would be seated at his harpsichord, below the stage with his orchestra, his only concern the music and the singers.

But Karl seemed to have the business well in hand. He said as much to Papa Keller.

Looking burlier than ever, his red bushy hair poking out in every direction like the spines on a porcupine, the assistant stood in the middle of the stage bellowing orders.

"That is not Karl," his father-in-law said adamantly.

"Of course it's Karl." The old man must be approaching senility, Haydn thought. "Who else would it be?"

Although there was something different about Karl today, Haydn reflected, his attention curiously riveted on the man's back. Not just the voice, which seemed deeper than usual. But something else.

"I know not, but it's not Karl," Papa Keller insisted.

His eyes narrowed, Haydn stared at the assistant's broad back. What was it about the man that seemed different? He wore a shabby, worn, loose-fitting jacket over his clothes as always. The leather apron was under it, presumably.

Klop. Klop. Klop.

It was not the hollow sound of wood striking the floor behind him that startled Haydn, but Karl's whispered voice in his ears—"All goes well, Herr Haydn, never fear."— that made him nearly jump out of his skin.

He turned to see the assistant close behind him. "I thought"—Haydn swiveled around to face the stage—"I thought you were out there." The burly individual—taller and stouter than Karl, he now realized—still stood in the middle of the horseshoe-shaped Burgtheater stage.

"Did I not say it wasn't him?" Papa Keller threw his head back, looking Haydn smugly in the eye.

"Who is it, then?"

"Christian Steiner, the bass," Karl informed them. "He has appointed himself director. It would normally be Herr Affligio's task."

"And he wears your jacket?" Haydn's voice rose.

Karl shrugged. "It hangs on a hook out in the hallway for anyone to take. I suppose he doesn't wish to get his costume dirty."

"And the red hair?"

"It is a wig. He plays Mercutio, Giulietta's brother in the opera. Herr Affligio thought the red wig would serve well to indicate the character's fiery nature."

"It seems to serve equally well to make him approximate you," Haydn murmured to himself.

With the jacket and the wig, the bass's resemblance to the impresario's assistant was uncanny. But as his gaze traveled down the man's thick legs encased in breeches, Haydn realized at last what was different. Christian's feet were clad in leather shoes, not the clogs Karl usually wore.

There is no mistaking him. Leopold's remark about Karl reverberated in Haydn's ears.

If one knew what to listen for, Haydn thought ruefully to himself. He himself had been led astray despite being familiar with Karl's propensity for wearing clogs. How much more likely that someone unfamiliar with the man would just as easily be misled. Had it been Christian that the Archbishop's maid had seen?

"And he was one of Affligio's partners as well, was he not?"

"Still is, if I mistake not," Papa Keller replied. Haydn had nearly forgotten his father-in-law's presence. "I doubt the contract expires just because one of its signers is deceased."

Just at that moment, Christian turned around. Good heavens, was the man intentionally trying to impersonate Karl?

"Is the beard false as well?" Haydn asked the assistant.

"It is. Herr Affligio thought it would look well on Mercutio. Herr Steiner is a clean-shaven man."

The bass had been casting his gaze over the entire length of the stage as though searching for someone when his gaze fell on the group downstage. He barreled his way through to them.

"Karl, there you are! Is Donna ready? She plays Romeo," he added, turning to Haydn and Papa Keller.

"Weren't Ernst or Bastian available for the role?" Papa Keller wondered. "Such tall, handsome men. Surely the audience would prefer to see one of them take the hero's part."

Christian laughed. "Well, for one thing, they'd be wasted on La Renier. And for another, Romeo's youth is best represented by a contralto —as is his reluctance to fight." He turned to Haydn. "Besides, Donna is the only one of us who has any patience with La Renier's antics." He held out his hand. "You must be Herr Haydn. I am pleased to make your acquaintance."

"Herr Haydn has taken on Herr Affligio's duties," Karl explained.

"Only temporarily," Haydn said with a smile as he and Christian shook hands. At an indication from the bass, Karl immediately left, in search presumably of Donna Oliveri.

Haydn watched him go, then indicated the stage with his chin. "Are you not needed on the stage, Herr Steiner?" If he was not mistaken, Mercutio came on in the very first act.

Christian shook his head. "It's Loretta's scenes that need the most work. In particular, the scene in which the lovers decide to kill themselves in order to be together in the next life if not in this one. Romeo plunges the dagger into Giulietta's breast and then into his own. La Renier's squeamishness about prop knives makes the entire scene implausible."

"I don't suppose one can blame her," Haydn replied, although if the knife retracted so well, how had it dispatched Donna Oliveri's husband? "But she has nothing to fear. Herr Affligio, God rest his soul, had taken steps to have the old prop knife replaced. The coutelier was here just yesterday with a new prop fashioned from wood. Nothing could be safer."

To Haydn's surprise, Christian snorted. "The old fool! There was no need to replace the knife. It is just more money spent on frivolities. And all to appease that airheaded nitwit of a woman." He glared at Loretta Renier who stood with her back arched, gazing up at the ceiling in what she no doubt considered to be a romantic pose.

Turning back to Haydn, the bass was about to say something when his gaze collided with Papa Keller who stood beside them, listening avidly to the conversation. Recalled to the old wigmaker's presence, the singer smiled.

"What brings you here, old man? Do we not have enough wigs in stock?"

"Haydn here wants some more for his opera," Papa Keller told him.

Christian's smile faded. "Something can be found in the costume room below, I'm sure. Karl will know. There's no need to spend more money on what we already have."

"For a mere performer, you seem unduly concerned with the cost of the production, Herr Steiner," Haydn commented coolly. He waited for a reaction, forcing himself to be as dispassionate as a scientist probing an animal on his dissection table. "More so even than any of Herr Affligio's partners."

"But—" Papa Keller began. Before he could say a word, however, Christian's gaze snapped back toward Haydn and his blue eyes flashed angrily.

"I am one of his partners, too, Herr Haydn. And if I am more concerned about money than anyone else, it's because I've expended a goodly amount of my own resources to ensure the Burgtheater is kept afloat. And I have yet to see the return that scoundrel promised me."

"It wasn't a good investment," Papa Keller said tactlessly.

"No, it wasn't," Christian agreed, his eyes still on Haydn. "But I mean to get my money's worth."

"I don't see how—" Papa Keller began to say, but Haydn nudged his father-in-law in the ribs, shutting him down. The same question had occurred to him. But this was neither the time nor the place to ask the bass how he meant to recover his loss.

"Any additional expenses my opera incurs will be paid by my employer, His Serene Highness, Prince Nikolaus Esterházy," Haydn assured Christian. "The wigs, any other little thing needed as well."

Christian swallowed, nodding tersely as the blood that had flooded into and darkened his features abated and his color recovered. "Very well."

He jerked his head behind the wings. "There are a couple of other matters I wish to discuss with you in private. And then"—he turned to Papa Keller—"and then you may measure my head, old man."

For a man of his bulk, Christian Steiner moved swiftly and gracefully. Haydn followed the bass down the stairs, past the workshops, to the concealed doorway into the private inner room of the impresario's chambers.

"The back entrance to Affligio's chambers," Christian said as he pushed a key into the tiny keyhole. "Few people know of it."

"But you do?" A troubling thought had entered the Kapellmeister's head.

Affligio's dead body had been discovered in the inner chamber. He had been struck in the head from behind. Had his killer entered from this concealed doorway that few except Affligio's paramours and Karl —and Christian as well, apparently—knew about?

The bass turned to face Haydn, his blue eyes cold and appraising. "I keep my eyes open, Herr Haydn." He returned to his task, jiggling the rusty key in his hands in the old lock. "I am not the only one who does so."

Unlocking the door, he pushed it open. The door creaked—an annoying squeak that grated on Haydn's ears—on its hinges. The carpet with its bloodstain and Affligio's form impressed into it was immediately visible. Haydn pursed his lips at the sight, recalling that he had meant to have it replaced.

He must have spoken aloud for Christian immediately turned to him. "It is an unsightly reminder of our mortality, is it not, Herr Haydn?" He grinned. "I suppose the sight of blood makes your stomach turn."

"Yes, it still does," Haydn confessed readily. "And I thank the good Lord that it is so." He raised his eyes to the other man—Christian was a head taller than he. "Murder is not a deed any God-fearing man should be accustomed to."

Christian rolled his eyes but refrained from commenting. "I will have Karl replace the offensive rug," he said. "It is likely too mundane a chore to have taken priority when there are more pressing matters at hand."

But Haydn was barely listening; his gaze had returned to the carpet. Affligio had fallen with his head facing the concealed door, he suddenly perceived. A sure sign the killer had been standing by this door when he had swung . . . Haydn frowned. What could the killer have swung at the unsuspecting Affligio?

Worse still, was the murderer in his presence at this very moment? Christian's voice, still speaking as he led the way to the impresario's cluttered desk, registered on Haydn's mind.

"Cleaning the backstairs, now that," he was saying, "is a far more important job. It was getting impossible to use the area with the way Affligio kept it.

"Failed to keep it, to be more precise," he added, lowering himself into the impresario's chair."

Haydn stared at the man, too troubled to notice the singer had taken his seat. "I was given to understand no one used the backstairs."

"Pshaw!" Christian emitted a rude sound, spraying the desk with spittle. Haydn squelched the sense of revulsion that overcame him, forcing himself to attend to the singer's words. "Affligio's paramours habitually entered through that door. How else, do you suppose they came here, unnoticed, other than by the backstairs?"

"I know not." Haydn settled himself heavily into the chair across from the desk. "What is it you wished to speak with me about, Herr Steiner?"

Christian threw a quick glance over his shoulder, then leaned forward. "You have had an opportunity to examine Affligio's papers?" When Haydn nodded, he continued. "Had the Archbishop of Salzburg paid his dues?"

"His subscription for his box?" Haydn asked. "No. That remains unpaid, but—"

"No, no, not that." Christian shook his head vehemently. "His Grace had all but agreed to buy a thirty percent share in the Burgtheater. The money was to be paid on Sunday. I assume he brought it when—"

"When he was asked to intercede in Leopold Mozart's supposed assault on the impresario?" Haydn's tone was intentionally dry.

A deep burgundy hue suffused the singer's fleshy cheeks. "His Grace was well aware the money was due. He had an appointment that very evening to convey the funds to Affligio."

"Are you certain of this?"

With a handkerchief protecting his fingers, Haydn gingerly cleared a space on the desk, stacking the sheets of papers littering the surface and pushing them to the side. He could not recall leaving the desk quite so untidy the last time he'd sat here. Unable to find the appointment book, he dabbed unthinkingly at the droplets of spit.

Dear God, he thought becoming aware of the action, now his handkerchief was ruined. It would have to be discarded. He dropped the kerchief.

"There was nothing noted in Affligio's appointment book," he continued. Haydn could see the page as clearly in his mind as though it lay before him. "Surely he was not expecting His Grace to come here?"

"Of course His Grace was expected here. How else—?" Christian's voice skidded to a halt.

"How else would he have proof that Leopold had been provoked beyond measure?" Haydn asked. His mind churned as bits and pieces of information settled into place. "Was that the arrangement with His Grace?"

Christian rose, stone-faced. "I know not what you speak of."

Haydn got to his feet as well. "Was Affligio still alive when you left to fetch His Grace?"

"It was Karl who fetched His Grace." Christian snarled. "Everyone knows that. Why not ask him?"

Chapter Twenty-Eight

ROSALIE stood on tiptoe and stretched her arms up, trying to direct the rag tied at the end of the heavy pole into a particularly dusty corner of the ceiling. Try as she might she couldn't reach. And her slender arms were beginning to weary of the long, cumbersome piece of wood.

With a grunt, she lowered her arms. "It's no use," she complained, turning to Greta. "It's too high for me to get to it."

They had decided to tackle the backstairs area of the Burgtheater that morning. There were cobwebs high in the ceiling, clinging to the rafters, and a layer of dust seemed to be permanently engrained into the walls and the stairs.

Greta, who was on her knees scrubbing the steps with a soapy washcloth and a sturdy brush, glanced up. It had been Karl's idea to tie their cleaning rags to a pole. Clearly it wasn't working.

"We'll have to ask Karl for a ladder, then." Greta swiped her hand across her perspiring face, leaving a trail of soapsuds and dust across her fair skin. "Or find one ourselves if he's still busy upstairs."

"If this place even has any," Rosalie grumbled as she leaned her pole against the wall and sank down onto the top step. "I've yet to see one." And Karl hadn't been too happy at the prospect of them standing a ladder on the stairs either.

"What if you were to fall?" he'd said, a worried frown appearing between his brows. "The steps are narrow and rickety. God alone knows if they'd support the weight of a ladder, never mind you two."

Or was it the thought of having to procure a ladder that had bothered him?

"Although I don't see how a theater couldn't have one?" Rosalie went on. How else was anyone to sweep cobwebs and dust from the ceilings?

"There should be one in the prop room," Greta said, busily scrubbing away. "Come to think of it"—she glanced up, her cheeks rosy from her exertions and her blue eyes sparkling—"the carpenters were building one for Herr Haydn's opera. Karl told me that. It's going to be used to climb up a mountain or a hill. I don't think anyone will mind us taking it.

"Let me finish this step and we'll go find it."

Rosalie nodded, although Greta, with her head bent over her work, wouldn't be able to see the gesture. She'd considered telling her friend about Herr Haydn's suspicions regarding Karl, but then had dismissed the thought.

The Kapellmeister's misgivings seemed to have abated on their own; there was no need to worry her friend. Still, she'd wondered about the prop knife.

"Did I tell you that Herr Haydn found out at the police station that it was the prop knife that killed Herr Affligio?"

Greta looked up at her sharply. "So that's where it was?" She dipped her washcloth into the bucket of soapy water on the step below her and wrung it out. "Small wonder the coutelier was demanding a prince's ransom for it. He must've known we'd never find it!"

"Herr Haydn doesn't think he had anything to do with it," Rosalie blurted out without thinking.

"Oh!" Greta looked sharply up again. Her eyes narrowed as she regarded her friend. "How do you know that?"

Oh dear! Rosalie bit her lower lip guiltily. In her reluctance to reveal that Karl had been under suspicion—if only briefly—she'd neglected to tell Greta anything at all about what she'd learned.

"When I returned with the ink and paper Herr Haydn wanted, I shared our fears about the coutelier." Quickly she recounted the details.

Greta sat up on her haunches. "So, he agrees Steffi may have seen the killer," she said with a thoughtful frown after Rosalie had finished.

"Yes, and he thinks the killer must be someone very familiar with the prop knife. The medical examiner told Herr Haydn only someone skilled in its use could have stabbed someone with it. It retracts too well." This last she'd heard from Karl, but she kept that fact to herself.

She had a feeling Karl hadn't mentioned any of this to her friend. How could he, when it would mean admitting that Herr Haydn had for a brief time held him guilty? And for her to say anything now would only drive a wedge between him and Greta.

Greta's forehead scrunched into a deeper frown. "That's not what we've heard."

"No, and other than Herr Affligio himself and one other man—Herr Haydn said Karl didn't know his name—no one had seen the coutelier demonstrate the knife." She kept to herself the fact that Karl had been the source of this tidbit as well.

She'd questioned Karl after they'd both left Herr Haydn's presence. Distressed at being thought capable of murder, Karl had opened up to her.

"Another man?" Greta said. "Could it be another partner? Herr Affligio seems to have had quite a few. And Karl would've recognized the singers, I'm sure, if it was one of them." When Rosalie acknowledged the observation with a nod, she continued, "We'll have to find out who it is, then. Master Johann and Master Luigi will want to know."

"Besides, who knows"—Rosalie leaned forward—"this man, whoever he is, may even be the killer. Herr Affligio couldn't have stabbed himself. And Herr Haydn is convinced it isn't Herr Mozart."

"Or the coutelier." Greta made a face as she wiped the soap off her hands. "Too bad. He seems just the kind of weasel who'd do such a thing." Then, apparently struck by a thought, she looked up. "*He* might have some idea who the other man in Herr Affligio's chambers was."

"He might at that," Rosalie agreed. Who knew, but the impresario might have addressed the other man by name. And if it had been in the coutelier's hearing, God willing he'd kept his ears open.

"If only we knew where to find him . . ." She left the thought unfinished, but her eyes twinkled. She and Greta both knew Karl would be able to tell them where the coutelier's shop was.

Greta grinned. "Well, let's find that ladder and finish up here. And then we can go see about hunting down that ferret-faced good-for-nothing."

Giulietta and Romeo were singing a duet when Haydn returned up-stairs. Loretta Renier's singing was, for once, tuneful and Donna Oliveri made a convincing, if rather imposing, Romeo.

Frau Oliver possessed a considerable flair for acting, Haydn thought as he cast his gaze around in search of Papa Keller.

The contralto's mannerisms and gestures were entirely those of a man. She clearly had an observant eye and a gift for mimicry. Were it not for her dark, heavy features and her deep voice, she might have gone far.

These thoughts were running through Haydn's mind when he found Papa Keller at last—sitting eagerly forward in a front-row seat, his eyes riveted to the spectacle playing before him.

"It goes well, I think," Karl said, coming up to stand beside Haydn in the wings.

Haydn nodded, but he was too preoccupied to enjoy either the music or the poignant love song being performed. Christian, he noticed, had positioned himself in the wings across from them. The singer glowered at the action onstage, his legs wide apart, his hands on his hips.

Recalling their conversation, Haydn pursed his lips. The discussion had been fruitless, and he had only succeeded in provoking the man. Romeo swaggered jauntily off the stage, and a scene followed with Giulietta and her nurse.

Haydn leaned over to Karl.

"Were you aware Herr Steiner had formed a partnership with your master?" The bass had a twenty percent interest in the Burgtheater —smaller only than the thirty percent the Archbishop had supposedly procured for himself.

Karl turned sharply to face the Kapellmeister.

"No. I can't say I did. But"—Karl's eyes drifted diagonally across the stage to where Christian now stood—at the edge of the forestage—directing the action—"it doesn't surprise me. Herr Steiner is reputed to be the son of a wealthy Baron. His father can't—or won't—acknowledge him, but the Baron has never denied him his purse."

"A man of means, then?" That would account for Affligio pursuing the fellow. But had the money dried up? Or had Christian invested more than he could afford?

Karl shrugged. "As long as his father lives, Herr Steiner will want for nothing. But the Baron is on his deathbed, and his heirs may not feel so kindly toward a half-brother. One fathered upon a lowly mistress at that."

"No, I imagine they would not," Haydn agreed. Small wonder Christian was concerned about the lack of return on his investment. Loretta Renier and Donna Oliveri were back onstage with a priest. "Did Herr Affligio seek a partnership with any of the other singers?" Haydn asked as he watched the scene.

Karl shrugged. "Not that I know of. Master may have considered approaching Fräulein Renier. She enjoys the Emperor's favor—and his purse, no doubt." After a brief pause, he continued. "That must've been why master pursued her."

For the resources at her command? Haydn glanced at Loretta Renier singing on the stage. She was a beautiful woman, but had the impresario's pursuit of her—solely for what she could bring him—offended her? Why—if she had the Emperor's attention—Haydn wondered.

His wandering mind snagged on Karl's voice mentioning Frau Oliveri.

"Her husband had a substantial fortune. Master hoped to convince him to invest in the Burgtheater, but the poor man died before he could agree to anything—killed, as you may have heard."

Haydn nodded. "With a prop knife. I have hear—"

An ear-piercing squeal interrupted his words. He staggered back in alarm. Dear God, what was that?

"No!" Loretta Renier shrieked again. She darted away from Donna Oliveri, who held the prop knife over her head ready to plunge it into the soprano's breast.

"Oh, for God's sake!" Christian roared. "Calm your fears, Loretta. It is but a prop knife. A new one, Karl assures me. Made of wood. It can do you no harm."

"Made of wood?" Donna Oliveri ceased her pursuit of Renier. She glanced down at the knife. "Who would believe it? It looks just like the other. Where is it?" She twisted around to look questioningly at Karl and Haydn.

"That one, madam," Haydn informed her dryly, "is with the Police Commissioner. It was found plunged into the impresario's breast."

"He was killed with it?" Christian looked aghast. "A prop knife? Not his own?"

"B-but how can that be?" Renier stammered, her breast still heaving. "I d—" Whatever she was about to say remained unsaid, swallowed in the sudden awareness of several avidly interested eyes upon her.

"You have some doubts on the subject, Fräulein?" Haydn called.

Loretta Renier, pale as the satin gown she wore, shook her head. "N-no, of course not." She recovered her equanimity and her eyes blazed. "Have I not said all along the knife was dangerous? No one would believe me!"

"Yes, but this knife"—Christian tore it out of Oliveri's hands—"is not it. For God's sake, play the scene as it should be played, Loretta. Giulietta wishes to die with her lover. It is their only hope of being together. She should be eager to sacrifice her life, not flee the knife like a hunted deer."

He raised his arms despairingly toward the ceiling. "Dear God, at this rate, we might as well give up."

"No, no. There's no need for that," Papa Keller called cheerfully. "The work is sound and has considerable merit, the acting excellent, the songs beautifully done. Why not rest awhile and let me measure your heads? A short respite will do us all good."

"It's not a bad notion," Karl whispered to Haydn. "It will allow their frayed tempers to cool."

"So it will," Haydn said, stepping forward to call for a lull in the proceedings.

Chapter Twenty-Nine

GRETA fished a large, rusty key out of her apron pocket. "There's a door here," she said as she jiggled the key into the lock. "It leads directly into the prop room." She glanced over her shoulder at Rosalie. "There's no need to walk through the workshops and have the painters and carpenters tell on us."

Rosalie nodded. There was no telling how Karl would react to their borrowing a prop.

The sound of the key grating against the lock was replaced by a small click.

"There, now, it's unlocked!" Greta twisted the handle and pushed against the door. It creaked noisily open making Rosalie wince. She glanced surreptitiously around to make sure no one had spied them. But few people passed by this section of corridor near the backstairs. Then she followed Greta in.

"We should remember to oil the hinges," she whispered to her friend. "That creaking is so loud, I'm surprised it's not brought anyone out to see what the matter is."

"Oh, I'm sure no one's heard us." Greta sounded more confident than Rosalie felt. "The painters and carpenters make far too much noise to heed anything out here."

They let the door close, which creaked to a halt just short of the threshold. Rosalie was about to close it, but Greta shook her head impatiently.

"Never mind that." She tugged Rosalie's arm, pulling her farther into the room. A few steps later, Greta's feet ground to a halt as she surveyed her surroundings.

Rolls of carpets, pillars, basins, and grottoes were crowded at one end of the large room. Shelves with vases and other knickknacks were stacked on the countless rows of shelves arranged within rectangular wooden frames.

"Nothing here," Greta whispered. "It's probably along that way." She pointed deeper into the vast room.

As they tiptoed past the aisles formed by row upon row of the gigantic wooden cabinets, Rosalie caught sight of stacks of paintings, pots, pestles, candlesticks of varying sizes, fishing nets, hooks, tools, and books.

"We must be getting closer," she said, pointing to a set of doors and windows stacked against a wall. Chairs of various types and steps were placed next to it.

"I see them!" Greta suddenly grabbed her arm.

"Dear God, Greta!" Rosalie cried. "You nearly made me bite my lip."

"Shhh!" Greta squeezed her arm again. "Look! There they are."

Rosalie's eyes followed Greta's pointing arm. There under a dingy window were several ladders—some small, small tall.

"Now if only we could tell which ones are practical and which ones are not," Greta said, creeping forward.

"Practical?" Rosalie had no idea what her friend was talking about.

"Made to bear weight," Greta explained, as she drew out a ladder and gingerly stepped on it. She wobbled slightly. "Maybe not this one," she said, stepping hastily down. She was about to drag another ladder out from behind it when Karl's annoyed "Greta!" brought her to a halt.

How had they not heard his footsteps, Rosalie wondered as she and Greta turned guiltily toward where Karl stood, his face flushed with vexation.

"God help me, Greta, you're no better than a child sometimes. Haven't I told you not to touch the props?"

But Greta, much to Rosalie's amusement, remained unfazed. Her friend waved a plump hand airily behind her. "I thought you said some of these were practical. Besides, we needed a ladder. I thought we should try to find one ourselves rather than bother you."

Karl sighed, tugging on his beard in exasperation. "There's a ladder or two in the closet by Herr Affligio's back door. I thought you knew that."

"Well . . ." Greta pouted. "I'd forgotten. Anyway, what are you doing here? Shouldn't you be upstairs helping with the rehearsal?"

Karl hesitated, his eyes shifting anxiously toward the door as though checking to see no one was within earshot. Then he came closer to them.

"Herr Haydn is convinced some kind of swinging object killed Herr Affligio," he said in a low voice.

"A swinging object?" Rosalie repeated. "Like a sword or dagger?" Someone must have swung the prop knife, she supposed.

"No, no. He doesn't think it was the prop knife that did him in at all. He has it on good authority it was some heavy object—a prop most likely—that was used to strike master in the back of his head."

"And he wants you to find out what it could be?" Greta guessed.

"I'm glad he trusts you enough . . ." Rosalie began before biting her lip. Dear God, now she'd let the cat out of the bag. Greta turned sharply toward her.

"What do you mean, trusts him enough? Why shouldn't Herr Haydn trust Karl? What's he done?" She looked from Rosalie to Karl, eyes narrowed.

A sheepish expression had descended upon Karl's heavy features. "Herr Haydn was convinced for a while I'd killed master—thanks to your Steffi's tale that I'd gone there insisting the Salzburger was assaulting master."

"What!" Greta's eyes grew round. "Why didn't you tell me?" She turned to Rosalie. "Did you know about this? Oh, you did, didn't you?"

Rosalie quickly put her arms around Greta. "Oh, Greta, we didn't tell you because we didn't want you to worry."

"But, Herr Haydn doesn't suspect you anymore, does he?" Greta turned anxiously to Karl. "Oh, what can we do to convince him Steffi was mistaken? She must've been, we know that!"

"He is already convinced of it," Rosalie assured her. But it would be nice to have evidence that couldn't be denied, she thought. The painters and the carpenters would certainly bear out Karl's story that he was at the Seizerkeller.

Yet she doubted that would be enough to convince the Police Inspector. The other Burgtheater employees were Karl's friends after all; they'd say nothing to harm him. Her musings were interrupted by something Karl said.

She turned to him. "Herr Haydn suspects Herr Steiner now?"

Karl nodded. "He was master's partner, it so happens. One of many, it seems, and not happy with the arrangement he had. Besides, with the red wig and beard he wears to play Mercutio and in my coat, it's easy to mistake him for me. Herr Haydn quizzed me about it so closely this morning, he must be convinced Herr Steiner deliberately set out to look like me."

"Well, he might have," Greta said, her brow furrowing as she considered this possibility.

Rosalie was considering it too when her gaze fell on Karl's feet. Her eyes widened. Dear God, how could she not have considered it sooner?

"Those clogs," she said, pointing to his feet. "Do you always wear them?"

Karl looked down, baffled by her question. "Yes. But what have they to do with anything?"

But Greta had understood. She caught hold of Rosalie's elbow. "That's it. The killer could get a red wig and beard and even his coat. But Karl never goes anywhere without his clogs. All we have to do is ask Steffi if she remembers what kind of shoes this man claiming to be Karl was wearing."

Karl smiled. "It still won't tell us who it was."

"No," Greta agreed. "But it will tell us who it wasn't."

———

Haydn sat on one of the benches in the parterre watching as Papa Keller deftly measured the tenor Ernst. Bastian, the other tenor, stood nearby waiting his turn. Where was Christian, the Kapellmeister wondered, as his gaze wandered around the auditorium.

Behind him on the parterre were four boxes. The enormous court box reserved for the Emperor rose from the first tier surrounded by several other boxes. Two more tiers with boxes and benches ringed the theater.

Haydn twisted back around. In front of him, behind a low partition, sat the orchestra tuning their instruments and playing snatches of phrases from the opera they were rehearsing. His own musicians would be sitting there when it was time to rehearse *Le pescatrici*, with either Johann or Luigi at the harpsichord. He himself would need to be available to address any technical difficulties that arose.

The stage rose above the orchestra. The forestage—where most of the action took place—was empty of actors. But the scenic stage bustled with activity. Stagehands were arranging wing flats on their grooved chariots; backdrops and other scenes and flats were being secured to battens above in preparation for being flown onstage when needed; and moveable sections—a massive fountain and a grotto—were being placed on chariots that would then be wheeled onstage.

Preoccupied with his own part composing the music and training the singers, Haydn had never paid much attention to the myriad actions that brought an opera to life. Now he looked on fascinated. But his enjoyment of the spectacle was marred by a niggling question that plagued his mind.

Who had killed Affligio? Loretta Renier? Or Christian? Or had they been working in concert? Had Haydn not been convinced of Leopold's innocence, the question would not have bothered him.

But Leopold was innocent. And the impresario—a maddeningly annoying man to deal with in life—still awaited justice in death. The thought that his murderer continued to walk free caused Haydn to purse his lips and shake his head.

"A word with you, if you please." The deep, low voice uttered near him startled Haydn. He glanced up to see Christian at his side. The bass took a seat beside him on the bench.

"Have you been able to discover who it was Affligio wished to dismiss?" The singer was nothing if not blunt. Turning to where Papa Keller wrapped his paper strip around Ernst's head—measuring from temple to temple, then from forehead to nape—Christian continued. "One of the singers was to be shown the door. A way of cutting down on costs and stretching our meager profits."

"One of the men?" Haydn asked. "Or the women?"

"I know not." Christian turned to face him, his expression grave. "I was hoping you would."

Why, Haydn wondered, scrutinizing the man's features but detecting nothing. Why pose the question now? Had Christian himself been about to be shown the door? That would have been a cruel blow—after the enormous sum he had invested in the Burgtheater. A man could be forgiven for taking matters into his own hands after a blow like that.

Out loud, he merely repeated what he had heard.

"Herr Gluck seems to think it might have been Loretta Renier. The complaints against her are numerous."

Christian's lips hardened into a bitter line. "That may be so. But I doubt Affligio had any desire to offend her."

"Because of the Emperor?" Haydn asked.

A few rows ahead of them, Papa Keller dismissed Ernst and began to measure Bastian. The old wigmaker draped his paper strip from the middle of the young tenor's ear, over his head, to the other ear. Then unwrapping the tape, he cut a few snips into it, marking the measurement.

"More likely because he wished to interest the woman in his godforsaken venture." Christian sat hunched forward, his large, pale hands clasped despairingly together between his knees. "God knows he spent enough time closeted with her in his chambers."

"I am told they were paramours," Haydn said, mystified by Christian's interpretation of the situation. From the painters to Karl, everyone seemed to think Affligio was carrying on an affair with the soprano. Whether for her beauty or her connections had been unclear.

"Pshaw!" Christian twisted around to gaze up at the Kapellmeister, his mouth stretching into a wry grin. "Loretta Renier is a woman of the world, Herr Haydn. Make no mistake about that. Do you really suppose she would jeopardize her relationship with the Emperor to pursue a dalliance with Affligio?"

"I suppose not," Haydn conceded, his brow furrowing. "Yet everyone seems to think . . ." He broke off, perplexed.

Christian straightened up. "They met too openly to be carrying on an intrigue. Why the Sunday Affligio met his Maker, I saw him instruct her to meet him in his chambers."

Karl had as well, Haydn recalled. But the signal, according to the assistant, had been surreptitious. Perhaps not, if Christian had perceived it as well.

"He worked hard, did our Affligio, to coach La Renier for her roles. Roles she was supremely unfit for, I might add. Not that it mattered to our impresario."

"And she was with him on Sunday?" Haydn asked.

Christian nodded. "She must have been the last to see him alive."

"Other than his killer," Haydn softly reminded him.

He wondered again whether Loretta Renier and Christian had joined together to rid themselves of a debt-ridden impresario as well as Leopold. Although if Loretta had hopes of a partnership—one that she hoped might be profitable—would she have been so ready to raise a hand against the impresario?

Chapter Thirty

CAREFULLY, the maids dragged a large ladder out of the small room next to the impresario's chambers. Sandbags piled one on top of the other and thick coils of rope stood in their way.

"I wish we'd let Karl help," Greta grunted as she set the ladder down to take a breath. "It's a good deal heavier than I thought it would be."

"It is," Rosalie agreed. She glanced regretfully down at the long, uneven drag-marks scraped into the wood floor. "We should've laid down some sacking or old canvas. There's no smoothing out those scratches."

Karl had warned them to be careful.

But Greta tossed her head defiantly. "Oh, it's an old wood floor. Who cares?" She glanced curiously around the room. "What do you think Herr Steiner could've swung at Herr Affligio to kill him? Some of these sandbags?"

Rosalie looked doubtfully at the items in question. Going up to the stack near the door, she prodded the topmost bag. The sand within shifted under her touch.

"I don't see how that could kill anyone. It must've been something harder."

"Like what?" Greta regarded her, head tilted, hand on her hip. "A vase? There were several heavy urns in the prop room."

Before Rosalie could respond, a deep voice behind them asked: "Does Karl know that you're dragging that ladder out?"

Startled, Rosalie and Greta swung around in unison. Frau Oliveri stood leaning by the door. But there was a twinkle in her eye and her lips twitched in amusement.

"Yes, madam," Rosalie said quickly. "It's to clean the backstairs." She hoped the singer hadn't heard them gossiping. If word of that reached Herr Rahier's ears, that would be the end of both their jobs!

But Frau Oliveri smiled. "Well, I'm glad to see someone has taken on that task. Our last maid must've taken great effort to keep the area filthy. There were cobwebs all the way up to the ceiling the last—" Shuddering, she pressed a handkerchief to her nose. "The dust bothers me excessively." She glanced around the room, wiping specks of dust and sand from a nearby table with her gloved finger. "Sand too."

Then with another smile, she reached into her purse and drew out five coins. "Here!" She stretched out her hand. "A small token for your troubles."

Greta looked amazed as Rosalie reached out to take the money. Seeing her friend was too stunned to say a word, Rosalie thanked Frau Oliveri for them both.

"Five gulden!" Greta gasped when the contralto had left. She stared at the coins in Rosalie's palm. "No one's ever given us an extra five gulden just for doing our work. She must be rich."

"And generous," Rosalie admonished her friend. She dropped the money into her apron pocket. "Come, let's finish cleaning. We can give ourselves a treat on the way to the Kärntnerthortheater."

It was on a street near the theater that the coutelier had his establishment.

Karl had fortunately been too intent on discovering the prop that Herr Affligio's killer could've used to murder him to ask any questions about what they wanted with the man.

⋯⋯⋯

Realizing Christian had been speaking to him and was waiting for a response, Haydn turned toward him apologetically. "I beg your pardon."

"Leopold," Christian repeated himself. "It is he who murdered Affligio. It is most fortunate he's in prison. Did you know His Majesty was thinking of appointing the prissy old fool director of the opera? We'd be bleeding money with him in charge. And anyone lacking the ability to read at sight would be shown the door."

"He seemed favorably impressed with Loretta Renier," Haydn couldn't help saying with a smile. "For that very reason."

Christian swiveled around, swinging his leg onto the other side of the bench so that now he sat astride it as though straddling a horse. He jabbed a finger into Haydn's arm.

"And that tells you how much he knows. Loretta showers his son with praise and graciously hopes the boy's opera can be brought to the stage, so he considers her favorably. But Donna was more forthright and properly enumerated the many flaws in his son's work, so Leopold disparaged her as lacking in both beauty and talent.

"I will grant you Donna is no beauty. But no one can fault either her singing or her acting. She is unable to read music. So what? Neither can many other gifted performers. It hardly detracts from her strengths."

That was true enough as it went, although Haydn privately sympathized with Leopold's perspective. It was far easier to work with a performer who could read music than to work with one who could not.

"He did not make himself easy to like, did he?" Poor Leopold seemed to possess a singular gift for offending the very people he needed on his side.

Christian eyed him. "No, he did not. I have heard your brother is a friend and colleague to him. You may not believe it, but the opera was not fit for the stage. It had considerable promise, but it was not ready."

"I have yet to examine the work," Haydn informed him, hoping to deflect any further aspersions about the Mozarts.

Christian looked at him skeptically. "Do not be tempted to bring it to the stage. Not here, at any rate. I can assure you neither the singers nor the stagehands will participate in such a travesty."

The bass rose to his feet. "Not even the Emperor—who is inclined to toss casual compliments to all and sundry when it suits him—would pretend to enjoy an opera where a beloved serenades her lover only to have him slouch on his chair, staring at the ground, rather than respond to her. Or where a man expresses his displeasure by pouting and making the most dreadful faces at the audience while others importune him toward a course of action he disapproves of."

"I had heard about the stultifying lack of action," Haydn confessed, "but this . . ." He found himself unable to continue. Dear God, the work must have been truly terrible.

He was rising to his feet when Papa Keller's boisterous tones assailed his ears.

"Herr Steiner!" Papa Keller boomed out to Christian, even though he stood but a few paces away. "I am ready to take your measure."

"There!" Rosalie stepped off the ladder and, standing with her hands on her hips, gave the ceiling one last satisfied look. Every last cobweb was gone. Not one speck of dust remained. It was so clean, she could even detect an indistinct outline of the ornate carvings wrought into the edge of the ceiling.

Time had eroded their clean, sharp lines and for a while dust and cobwebs had completely obliterated them. But now they were faintly visible.

"It must have been pretty when it was first done," Greta observed, taking in the yellowing plaster surface above them.

"It must have." Rosalie nodded emphatically. She turned to her friend. "Do you think Karl could get one of the painters to touch up the area? It seems such a shame to let it gather dust and dirt like this."

Greta shrugged, carefully brushing off her apron into the small bucket they were using to dispose of the cobwebs, bits of plaster, chipped wood, and other detritus that had accumulated in the area. "We can ask, but who knows if they'll have the time."

"We've done a good job, haven't we?" Rosalie was still gazing at their handiwork. The stair rail was positively gleaming and even the steps seemed to have regained their old luster.

Too busy untying her apron, Greta didn't bother to look up. "Yes, we have. But hurry up and get yourself clean," she urged when she realized Rosalie was still staring at their handiwork. "I'm starving. Besides, after we've given ourselves a treat we have to go find that coutelier."

The reminder sobered Rosalie instantly. She hastily scrubbed the dirt off her apron and untied it. "I hope he can tell us who it was he saw with Herr Affligio. I'll wager it was the same man who killed the impresario." Other than Herr Affligio himself, the mysterious stranger had been the only other person familiar with the workings of the prop knife.

Besides, if the knife retracted as well as the medical examiner insisted it did, it likely had a mechanism that caused the blade to remain out when the person wielding it needed it to. But Karl had dismissed the idea when Rosalie suggested it to him.

"Master would've mentioned it to me if that were so." He'd shaken his head stubbornly.

But what other explanation was there? And the longer Rosalie pondered the matter, the more she was inclined to believe that the impresario might have had his own foul reasons for concealing the truth from Karl.

From the little she'd gleaned of him, the impresario was desperate for money and would've done anything to obtain it. And hadn't Karl himself said Frau Oliveri's husband was wealthy—and adamantly opposed to investing in the impresario's crackbrained scheme?

She was wondering how much of this to share with Greta—who was always inclined to take Karl's view of things—when her friend interrupted her thoughts.

"What if it was no stranger?" Greta's eyes had widened. "What if it was Herr Steiner in disguise?"

"I suppose it could've been," Rosalie conceded. That Herr Steiner had made himself look like Karl had caused Greta no amount of consternation.

Although, Rosalie mused, the singer had worn the beard and wig at the impresario's suggestion—not on his own initiative. Had the bass murdered Herr Affligio?

"It certainly wasn't Herr Mozart," she continued aloud. "Herr Haydn is convinced he's innocent. And that someone at the Burgtheater is responsible instead."

"No one at the Burgtheater is responsible for Herr Affligio's death." Loretta Renier's voice—strident with barely concealed fury—fell on them like a thunderbolt.

The soprano stood behind them, fists balled up, knuckles an ashen white, and blue eyes blazing. "Have you nothing better to do than to stand around gossiping?" An expression of disgust twisted her features. "If you spent more time cleaning, and less time discussing your betters, this area wouldn't be covered in filth."

Rosalie was about to apologize, but Greta jutted her chin out determinedly. "We have been cleaning, madam. We've been on our hands and knees since the morning. Not that it's our job. We only did it because Herr Haydn asked us to. If you'll look around you, you'll notice no filth remains."

Unused to being corrected, Loretta Renier bristled. "Be that as it may. Bestir yourself some more. My changing room has not been cleaned in a while. The wastebasket is full and needs to be emptied."

She swung around ready to march away, but a sudden thought made her glance over her shoulder. "And while you're at it, clean the other changing rooms as well. I can't imagine your Kapellmeister would wish you not to."

So she had recognized them as maids belonging to the Esterházy Palace, Rosalie thought. But that hadn't stopped her from shouting orders at them.

"The nerve of that woman!" Greta fumed. She would've said more had not Frau Oliveri peeked her head from behind the wall, a rueful expression on her face. "Do not take her words to heart. She's highly strung and Herr Affligio's death has taken a greater toll on her than on the rest of us, I fear."

"Does that mean we don't have to clean the changing rooms?" Greta asked far more bluntly than Rosalie considered appropriate. But her friend frequently blurted out her thoughts heedlessly.

Frau Oliveri fortunately took no umbrage. "I'm afraid ignoring her request will only annoy her further. Besides, the rooms do need cleaning. Would it help if I paid you for the trouble?" She gazed eagerly from Rosalie to Greta. "And there's no need to do mine. I keep it clean enough."

Greta bit her lip. Rosalie knew her friend was ashamed of her outburst. They were paid well enough, and it wasn't as though their work here would go unrewarded. Herr Haydn would make sure that didn't happen.

"That won't be necessary, madam," Rosalie spoke on their behalf. "Herr Haydn will see to it that we're paid. And you've rewarded us handsomely as it is."

The smile that lit up Frau Oliveri's heavy-featured face made her appear almost beautiful.

"Honest as well as diligent, I see. I trust His Serene Highness appreciates your worth."

When she'd left, Greta sighed and tied her apron back on. "I suppose we'd better get to it, then. Her Bossiness will be finished with her rehearsal soon enough. God forbid her room should be left soiled and grimy."

Chapter Thirty-One

Wʜɪʟᴇ Fräulein Renier had been assailing them with her demands, Rosalie's sharp ears had heard a click indicating that the door at the top of the stairs had been opened. She'd turned her head at the sound, but the door had just as quickly closed shut.

Now that both singers had departed, she was eager to see who it was that had opened the door only to beat a hasty retreat.

"Don't just stand there—" Greta, just as eager to get on with their tasks, began to grumble, but Rosalie shushed her, putting a finger to her lips and then pointing silently at the door above them.

"I heard someone up there," she whispered to her friend. "I think they were trying to come in. And I've a feeling whoever it is might still be up there."

She wasn't sure Greta believed her, but there was no time to explain. Rosalie tiptoed up the stairs, quietly put her hand on the door handle, and then with a quick, sudden movement pulled the door open.

A young woman with a freckled face and frizzy red hair pulled back into an untidy bun tumbled onto the landing.

"Hey!" she yelped, clutching at the wall to steady herself. She cast an angry glance at Rosalie. "That was a nasty thing to do! What'd you do it for?"

Rosalie ignored the question. "Who are you?" she demanded. "You had your ear pressed to the door, didn't you? Who sent you? What do you want?"

The woman folded her scrawny arms defiantly over her thin breast. "I wasn't listening in on your talk, if that's what you're insinuating."

Greta had by now galloped up the stairs. "Oh, you weren't, were you? What were you doing, then? Resting your back against the door?" With her hands on her hips, she leaned belligerently forward and scowled at the newcomer. "You heard her: Who are you?"

"Never you mind who I am!" The woman's pale blue eyes held Greta's gaze firmly. "I want my money. You've stolen my job, I see; I don't care about that. But I'm not leaving without being paid for the weeks I slaved here."

"Good heavens!" Rosalie gasped. "You're the maid Herr Affligio employed?"

The woman pressed her lips together and said not a word.

"Petra, isn't it?" Greta asked, her eyes narrowed in suspicion. Karl had mentioned that was the former maid's name.

"So what if I am?" Petra stared at her, her voice harsh. "I am owed money. I demand it be paid. I've waited long enough."

"You want your money?" Greta repeated. It had been a week or more since Petra had shown her face. "You have some nerve."

Rosalie stepped adroitly aside as Greta swung her arm around the area, her voice getting louder and shriller.

"Do you know how many hours we've spent on our hands and knees? Doing your work? And you want your money! That's rich."

A bewildered frown appeared on Petra's brow as she shrank back against Greta's onslaught. "I don't understand. Why would you have to spend hours doing anything? I didn't shirk my duties."

"Didn't shirk your duties?" Greta repeated, her voice shrill with indignation.

"You should've seen the state the backstairs was in!" Rosalie chimed in simultaneously.

"That's hardly my fault." Petra looked sullen. "Herr Affligio himself told me to leave it alone. What was I to do? Go against his orders? There's no need to come here, he says, no need at all. So I didn't."

"To be sure, he did!" Rosalie rolled her eyes. "Do you take us for fools?

But even as she spoke, she realized Petra had a point. This was the only part of the theater that had seemed long neglected. It was clean enough everywhere else. Could Petra be telling the truth?

Haydn drew his gold timepiece out and glanced at it. The rehearsal had resumed and he had once more taken his position within the wings. It had gone on longer than he'd expected.

Would there be time enough afterward to pay Herr Fugger, the banker, a visit?

With Romeo and Giulietta opening in a week, Christian—who seemed to have appointed himself director—was determined that every scene should be perfect. Normally, Haydn would have appreciated such diligence. But this morning, eager to be off, his entire being chafed at the prospect of being detained.

Stifling his impatience, he tucked his timepiece away. Would to God, they could continue with no further mishaps.

Onstage, Donna Oliveri leaned amorously over a balcony and gazed deeply into Giulietta's eyes.

"Grant me but a token of your love, my lady," she sang in her beautiful deep contralto. The melodic line of the recitative was rich and sweetly pleasant. The composer, Sacchini, had clearly sat at Gluck's feet, learning to dissolve the abrupt and sometimes harsh distinction between recitative and aria.

"The work is sure to be a success," Haydn said to himself with a smile.

"If Fräulein Renier's performance doesn't mar it," Karl said beside him. Haydn turned to see the young man gazing worriedly out at the scene. "When she doesn't forget her lines, she forgets her props," he explained to the Kapellmeister.

Haydn turned back to the stage. "She appears to have her reticule with her," he said, as Fräulein Renier smilingly agreed to gift Romeo a scented handkerchief embroidered with her name.

"Here it is! Here it is!" Singing the line again, Loretta Renier reached into her pink satin reticule. She fumbled within it, her smile replaced by a frown of bewilderment and frustration, her voice fading into a confused mumble.

"Where could the wretched thing be?" Loretta gave up all pretense at singing and bending her head low dug deeper into the satin drawstring bag.

Had the impresario really insisted the backstairs be left untended? But why, Rosalie wondered.

"He said he couldn't afford it." Petra gave Greta and her a knowing look. "But that wasn't the reason, mark my words."

"What was, then?" Rosalie's gaze slid toward Greta. But her friend seemed just as mystified.

Petra's lips spread into a sly smile. "It may be he didn't want it found out which skirt he was chasing at the time. He never chased the same one for too long." She pointed down the stairs. "Down below is a door that leads into his inner chamber. Not many know about it."

Rosalie and Greta's gaze involuntarily followed Petra's pointing finger.

"That's where he took them when he was feeling frisky. But he wasn't always careful about closing the door tightly enough."

"And you had no qualms about listening to their doings." Greta turned to her in disgust.

Petra shrugged, indifferent.

"Who was he chasing?" Rosalie wanted to know, although she suspected she knew the answer to that question.

"Who else?" Petra tipped her chin toward where Fräulein Renier had been standing. "Miss High-and-Mighty herself. It was probably the only way she could keep her job. Although I doubt even her caresses changed Herr Affligio's mind."

"He wanted to dismiss her?" Greta's voice rose. "But she is the Emperor's favorite!"

"That she may be." Petra leaned in closer. "But mark my words, she's a dangerous woman to cross." She quickly crossed herself. "And whatever you do, don't mention my name to her. I can't tell if she saw me or not that night. But if she did"—Petra shuddered and turned pale —"I'm done for."

"God grant me patience!" Christian—standing across from Haydn— bawled, clapping his hand to his forehead. "Don't tell me you've lost the dratted thing again, Loretta!"

"Of course, I've not lost it!" Loretta Renier was deeply indignant.

"God willing, she has not." Karl leaned closer to Haydn to whisper. "If she has, it will be the third time so far."

They watched as Loretta Renier's fingers agitatedly probed her reticule.

"It simply isn't here." She turned the bag upside down, shaking it over the stage floor.

Haydn's heart sank. Here was yet another setback. And he doubted Christian could be persuaded to let it go.

As though he'd read the Kapellmeister's mind, the bass strode angrily onto the stage.

"How hard is it to keep track of a simple handkerchief?" he roared. "Can you be that addle-brained that the task is beyond you?"

"There's no need to bawl at the poor thing," Donna admonished him, but Christian ignored her.

He snatched the bag from Loretta's fingers and looked inside it himself. "Where can the godforsaken thing be?"

"Think, Loretta," Donna urged her colleague. "Can you not remember what you did with it? You had it with you on Sunday."

"I-I" Loretta's flustered gaze searched the theater, coming to rest upon Karl. "Karl will know where it is, won't you? I'm sure I gave it to you."

If Karl was dismayed by the accusation, he didn't allow it to show. He shook his head. "I would not have taken it. It was to be kept, along with your reticule and costume, in your changing room, madam."

"Could it not be there?" Donna asked hopefully. "You asked the maids to clean your room, did you not?"

Haydn had heard enough. "Can we not run through the scene without a handkerchief?" he asked, stepping forward. "Or if we must have one"—he drew a large white kerchief out of his pocket—"mine should suffice for the moment."

But Loretta pouted. "That will hardly do. It's not pretty enough."

Haydn gritted his teeth and glanced at Christian, who plucked the fabric from his fingers and nodded.

"It will do for the time being. The seamstress can fashion a new one for the opening."

But the words were no sooner out of his mouth than Karl strenuously objected.

"There's not time enough for that, Herr Steiner. The seamstress has yet to finish the costumes for Herr Haydn's opera. Besides, she has replaced the handkerchief twice already. She will not do it a third time. She's already threatened to leave more than once. If we overburden her, it'll be the last straw. We can't afford to lose her."

The words spewed out of Karl's mouth in a torrent of frustration that left his listeners speechless. Most likely, Haydn thought, no one had seen the young man lose his calm. Karl's cheeks were flushed red and he was very nearly breathless after his speech.

Eager to have the matter resolved, Haydn turned to Loretta Renier.

"Do you not have handkerchiefs of your own?" he asked the soprano. "If you could but remember to put a few into your reticule, it may solve the problem." It would save everyone the bother of searching for the items, he thought.

Christian seemed to think so as well, for he nodded.

"Just make sure they are the same color," he grunted. "The audience will notice if you give Romeo a pink handkerchief on one day and a blue one on another."

Loretta Renier still looked doubtful, her features set into a mulish expression.

"It may be in your room," Donna Oliveri suggested again. "Shall we call the maids to ask them? They will have found it if you left it there."

"There's no need for that," Haydn decided the matter firmly. Calling the maids would only result in further delay.

Besides, given Loretta Renier's proclivities, the handkerchief was more likely to be in Affligio's chambers than in her room, although he chose not to embarrass the soprano by mentioning that possibility. And as for the woman freely ordering Rosalie and Greta about, Haydn forced himself not to dwell on that issue either.

"Let us carry on.

"I wish to meet Herr Fugger before the day is over," he explained, seeing Donna Oliveri's eyebrows rise in surprise. But his remarks were as much for Christian and Loretta's benefit.

If Loretta had been a partner in the impresario's venture, the banker would no doubt know. And if Christian were in straitened circumstances or had employed his father's connections to persuade Fugger to lend money to a commoner like Affligio, that might be ascertained as well.

The Kapellmeister held each singer's gaze firmly as he went on:

"There are far too many irregularities in Herr Affligio's finances—and his partnerships—than can be ignored. I trust the banker can provide some aid in sorting them out."

Chapter Thirty-Two

Rosalie and Greta exchanged a glance. What had Petra seen? What had Fräulein Renier done?

Greta tucked her arm into the other woman's. "Come sit with us for a while. You'll get your money. Rosalie and I will see to it you do. But you must be honest with us. Why didn't you want Miss High-and-Mighty to see you?"

But Petra shook her head, shrugging Greta's plump arm off. "How do I know if I can trust you?" She regarded them, her eyes darkening with suspicion. "I don't want any trouble. I have a sick mother and three younger sisters to take care of. They can't afford to lose me."

Hearing this, Greta hesitated, but Rosalie wasn't about to be put off so easily. "You've already told us more than enough. And if a little bird were to tell Fräulein Renier what you said . . ." She left the threat unfinished.

The red freckles stood out against Petra's pale skin like tiny specks of fear. She looked from Rosalie to Greta, her features harried. "If you tell anyone what I said, I'll just deny it," she said firmly.

"I thought you said you saw Fräulein Renier. Maybe she caught sight of you as well. What will your denials serve you then?"

"All I saw was her hurrying out of the impresario's outer chamber," Petra said. "If she went in to see him, what business was it of mine? I just wanted my money."

Oh! Things were beginning to make sense at last.

"And you went in," Rosalie guessed, "after she'd left. And that's when you found Herr Affligio—dead? Stabbed in the chest?"

"He hadn't been stabbed!" Petra immediately contradicted her. "He was dead, even I could see that—lying flat on the floor, his vacant eyes staring up at the ceiling. I felt his wrist; it was still warm to the touch. There was blood on the floor beneath his head. But no dagger. She must have poisoned him or struck him so hard he fell backward and hit his head on the floor."

"There was no dagger? Are you certain?" Rosalie's eyes sought Greta's. How could that be?

"Wouldn't I remember seeing one if there was?" Petra sounded impatient. "Why do you want to know, in any case?" She drew back, suspicious again. "You're—you're not spies for the Police Inspector, are you? I've heard he employs all kinds of people as spies."

She scrutinized their faces.

"Doesn't matter if you are. I'm telling you, if you say a word of this to anyone, I'll deny it. I only saw Fräulein Renier leaving the impresario's chambers. And when I went in, he wasn't there, so I left." She jutted her chin out defiantly. "There's no one can say that's not the truth."

Greta grinned at her. "And is that when you decided not to return? Even though you were owed two weeks' wages and Herr Affligio had still not paid you?"

Petra's eyes began to fill with tears. "Please, you don't understand. If she could take the impresario's life, she could easily take mine.

"Or"—her eyes widened in fear—"what if she says it was I who must've killed him? That I had reason to do so because I was owed two weeks' worth of wages? It'll be her word against mine. And who'd believe the likes of me?

Petra sniffed, swiping her fist angrily across her nose.

"I can't understand what Herr Affligio saw in that shrew. If only he'd taken up with Frau Oliveri. I thought he intended to. She's a funny one with her disdain for dirt. And she's certainly no beauty, but she always has a kind word for everyone, she does. "

⸺•••⸺

On stage, the singers returned to their positions.

"Now, once more from the top of the scene," Christian commanded, gesturing imperiously at the orchestra with one arm and at the singers with the other.

At Karl's direction, the stagehands began lowering the backdrop that obscured Giulietta's chamber and her nurse bustling about within it.

Only the balcony on which Loretta Renier in the character of Giulietta stood was to be visible.

A heavy bank of clouds obscuring the full moon was simultaneously being flown out of view. They would be lowered toward the end of the scene—a vivid foreshadowing of the young couple's doomed love.

"Slowly, now, slowly," Karl called, using a variety of hand signals to orchestrate the intricate movement of the various pieces.

Haydn was marveling at the various scenic details Affligio had constructed to enhance the opera and subtly accentuate its central theme. Romeo could just as easily have serenaded his love under a slim crescent moon on a cloudless night.

Yet the brightness of the full moon brilliantly evoked the fullness of the young couple's rapidly swelling love. And the clouds obscuring it —just as her nurse calls out to Giulietta—effectively suggested the darkness that would prevent the lovers from ever coming together. The music swelling to a crescendo at the beginning and growing more hushed toward the end underscored the themes suggested by the visual effects.

Small wonder Affligio attracted crowds. The impresario had prided himself on putting on operas so well-favored, the Viennese public was never content to enjoy a single showing, but found itself compelled to attend several performances of each work during the season.

Just then a faint creaking sound as of metal straining caught Haydn's ears, interrupting his thoughts. He stepped forward, craning his neck up in the direction of the sound in time to see a dark object hurtling down toward him. He had barely time to step aside when the object crashed into the floor at his side, denting the wooden floor.

At the same moment Fräulein Renier shrieked. The clouds that were being raised up had come plunging down toward her, barely grazing her head.

Too shaken to react, Haydn stood frozen to the spot. Had the metal object, whatever it was, landed on his head, his wig would've been no protection from it. He would have met his Maker in an instant.

Loretta Renier's shrieks still reverberated in his head until Christian barked at her and her screams abruptly subsided.

"This swinging thing, whatever it is, that killed Herr Affligio," Greta said in a low voice to Rosalie as they hurried down the hallway toward the performers' changing rooms. "It's bound to be in Miss High-and-Mighty's room. We ought to have a good look around when we clean it."

"It'll be wherever she dropped it," Rosalie agreed. "She doesn't seem the type to put anything back in its place."

The door leading to the performers' changing rooms was next to the painters' and carpenters' workshop. It swung open easily when Rosalie pushed it, revealing a narrow hallway lined with a row of green doors, each marked with the name of the performer it was assigned to.

"She can't even be bothered to close her door properly," Greta sniffed, pointing to the one marked with Fräulein Renier's name. It was the only door that stood ajar. The embroidered sleeve of a gown spilled out from under the bottom rail of the door panel, and its silken skirts lay in an untidy heap across the threshold.

Greta lifted up the gown, careful not to let its lacy edges snag on the hinges attaching the door panel to the jamb.

"It looks clean enough," Rosalie observed, casting an experienced eye over it. "Let's just hang it up in her closet." She opened the door wide and held it open, letting Greta enter before she stepped in after her with the bucket, mop, and broom.

Utter chaos reigned within the mid-sized room with its cream-colored walls. Pots and jars of various creams and powders had been left open on the dresser and surrounded a floral arrangement in front of the mirror in no particular order. Another gown was stacked on top of the bench at the dresser, its flouncy sleeves sweeping the none-too-clean floor.

"That one will have to be laundered," Greta said as she opened the closet doors. "Can't she be bothered to put anything away? I've never seen such a mess."

Rosalie approached the dresser and was dismayed to see small pools of water on the wooden surface radiating outward from the crystal vase. The vase itself was crammed with damask pink roses; a few long-stemmed flowers and stray leaves littered the area behind the vase.

"What a thoughtless woman!" she cried, hastily pulling out a wash-cloth from her bucket and dropping it in the puddle to soak the water in. "That's going to leave water stains."

And they'd be lucky if that was the extent of it. If any of the moisture had seeped in, it would make the wood swell up and form unsightly bubbles on the dresser.

"How bad is the closet?" she asked, pulling out another washcloth. She could hear the rustle of silks and satins as Greta rummaged around behind her.

"There are more gowns on the floor than hanging on their pegs," Greta told her. "She must drop her garments where she sheds them."

There was a moment's silence, then Greta went on, "After what Petra told us, I'm surprised we haven't found any of her skirts and petticoats in the impresario's chambers."

Rosalie giggled at that. "Herr Affligio must've made sure she put all her clothes back on before she left him." She was on her third washcloth now. It would no doubt take a fourth before she was done drying the mess of water on the dresser.

While she'd been wiping the surface, she'd also busied herself putting lids back on jars. One of them contained paper-wrapped packets of sleeping powder. There was some dried chamomile in another. Why Fräulein Renier should've kept her stock of medicaments in her chang-ing room, Rosalie didn't know.

She wrung the wet rags into the washbasin and then tossed them back into the bucket. The dresser was equipped with four drawers. Each one was messier than the last. But other than soiled handkerchiefs, ribbons, and other odds and ends there was nothing that looked like it could've been used as a weapon.

"There's nothing here," she said, turning to where Greta knelt before the open closet.

"I can feel something hard under here." Greta's fingers were patiently untangling the sleeves of one gown from a second one under it. "And the other sleeve of this one is tangled up with a third," she sighed.

"Here let me help." Rosalie hurried forward. Working together, they untangled the sleeves and lifted the gowns carefully out of the way.

Greta was busy hanging the gowns up when Rosalie saw what lay on the closet floor underneath. Her eyes widened.

It was a teardrop-shaped iron object with a large ring attached to it. Bending down, Rosalie gingerly picked it up. It was heavier than it looked, the metal weighing down her palm. Within the outer teardrop-shaped covering were three circular wheels, each with some rope coiled around it.

"What is this thing?" she asked Greta, still staring down at the object. She gently probed the metal underneath and the sides with her fingers.

Greta turned just as Rosalie's fingers registered the stickiness on the object. "It's a sheave," Greta said. "It's used for the rigging." She reached out for it. But she must've felt the sticky substance on it as well, for she let go almost immediately.

"Dear God, what is that!"

"Careful!" Rosalie caught the sheave before it dropped to the floor. Then she stared at her fingers. Bits of dried blood and matted hair caked the tips.

"This must be it." Greta looked round-eyed at Rosalie, her face white as a sheet. "The swinging object used to kill Herr Affligio. And now we know who did him in."

❦

"Herr Haydn!" Karl grabbed his arm; Haydn hadn't even heard the man run up to him. "You are not hurt, are you?" When Haydn mutely shook his head, the young man stretched forward to pick up the round metal wheel.

"What could this be doing here?" Karl gazed up at the ceiling, puzzled.

"What is it?" Haydn asked, finding his tongue at last.

"Part of the rigging." Karl's eyes were still trained on the ceiling. "A pulley. But we should have a sheave here."

"A sheave?" Haydn was unfamiliar with the term.

"A system of pulleys," Karl explained. "Three, to be exact." He tugged on the pulley and for the first time Haydn noticed the thick rope wrapped around his finger. The pulley dangled from it.

"Hey, du, Ludwig!" Karl called over his shoulder to one of the stage-hands. A young blond man appeared at their side. "Where is the sheave that should be affixed here?" But the young man merely shrugged and shook his head.

Karl began to issue some instructions to Ludwig, but his words were lost in the deep, overpowering rumble of Christian's voice.

"Karl!" The bass strode over to them, irate. "Don't just stare at the rigging, my good man. Fix it!"

Haydn's gaze meanwhile was caught on the pulley swinging from the rope clutched in Karl's fist. Had it been a pulley that had taken the impresario's life? The thing had so nearly taken his own.

Oblivious to the conversation between Christian and Karl, he turned to where Loretta Renier stood shivering on the balcony, Donna Oliveri's arm around her. The soprano seemed unhurt, but a severed rope dangled above her head. It had been attached to the bank of clouds that had dropped upon her.

Had the entire mishap been a chance occurrence? The Kapellmeister was unable to answer the question with any degree of certainty.

Troubled, he turned to Karl. "The pulley that was supposed to be up there," he said, "where is it?"

"It is a sheave," Karl corrected him; his features seemed haggard and miserable. "I-I know not where it can be. It's not in the closet. Although it should not be there." He cast a despairing glance upward. "I hadn't bothered to take anything down last Sunday. But if it's not up there, it should be in the closet. Where else could it be?"

"What does it matter where it is?" Christian demanded, his voice brusque with ill-concealed impatience. "Can you not find another one?"

"I-I know not." Karl looked bewildered; too stunned to be capable of thought. "This has never happened before," he muttered. "In all my years here, such a thing has never happened."

Fearing another outburst from Christian, Haydn hastily took the matter into his own hands.

"Will there be one in the Kärntnertortheater?" he asked. How could there not, he thought. The two theaters were likely to have the same equipment. At Karl's nod, he continued, "Have Rosalie and Greta take my carriage there. It will be much faster."

Chapter Thirty-Three

"A sheave is missing?" Greta's voice was tinged with a barely suppressed excitement. She turned to Rosalie, and the two exchanged a knowing look.

The reaction didn't escape Haydn's notice, and it filled him with foreboding. He glanced at Karl, hoping for an explanation. But the young man, standing stolidly beside his desk in Affligio's chambers, seemed as mystified as he.

Haydn turned back to the maids. "You have found it, I take it?"

It was Rosalie who nodded. She shuffled aside the soiled garments in her laundry basket. Carefully lifting out a paper-wrapped object, she laid it on his desk.

"It was in Fräulein Renier's room. She asked us to clean it," she added hastily.

Haydn nodded. He knew that already. Gingerly, he reached for the sheave. Why had they thought to cover it, he wondered. But his confusion was momentary, replaced by the awful truth even before Greta blurted it out.

"She used it to kill Herr Affligio! His hair and blood are on it."

"So I see," Haydn managed calmly as the paper fell away, revealing a heavy metal object covered in sticky blood and matted hair. His stomach heaved and churned uncomfortably at the sight. Beside him, Karl hastily crossed himself and muttered, "God rest his soul, poor gentleman."

Like an automaton, Haydn pulled the ends of the paper over the sheave, his mind in upheaval. He had long suspected Loretta Renier. But until this moment, the thought had been nothing more than a nagging misgiving that slithered uneasily through his mind. Now, here lay incontrovertible proof of her barbaric act.

Dear God, he whispered to himself. *Dear God!* What lengths would she not go to in order to achieve her ends?

"She cannot have remembered that she'd left the sheave in her room," Rosalie was saying. "Or she wouldn't have sent us there."

"And you should've seen how she swelled up in rage when she overheard us saying Herr Haydn considered the Salzburger innocent of the crime," Greta chimed in. "We knew it was her. Petra the maid said she saw Fräulein Renier come out of Herr Affligio's chambers. And then when Petra went in to ask for her money, there he lay on the floor dead."

Affligio had omitted to pay the maid as well. The thought ran idly through Haydn's mind. How fortuitous for him, then, that his negligence should have resulted in the discovery of his killer's identity.

"But why would she kill master?" Karl asked in despair. "What wrong had he ever done her?"

The same question was buzzing incessantly in Haydn's mind.

"She had not agreed to enter into his business venture, had she?" he asked.

"Not that I know of. Master may have been pursuing her for that reason, but . . ." Karl's voice trailed off and he shook his head in confusion.

Was it possible Loretta Renier had already contracted to become a partner? And had Affligio then—with her silver safely in his hands— taken steps to dismiss her? Where then did Christian fit into the entire scheme?

Loretta Renier may have wielded the sheave that killed the impresario, but it was not she who had summoned the Archbishop. His Grace's maid had spoken with a man. Besides, why would the soprano deliberately cast suspicion on Leopold? He was the only person to praise her mediocre talents.

"How was it that the rigging failed today?" he asked Karl. "Was it simply because the single pulley was unable to take the load that a sheave could withstand?" He hoped it was nothing more than that.

But Karl shook his head. "The rope was severed—deliberately so, it would seem."

The corners of his mouth turned down in despair.

"And someone seems to be making an effort to lay the blame squarely on my shoulders. The stagehands say they saw me up by the rigging while Herr Keller was taking his measurements. They thought I was making adjustments to the ropes that attach to the bank of clouds that fell on Fräulein Renier. But I was nowhere near the rigging."

"They saw your jacket, I take it," Haydn surmised, instantly divining the truth. "And assumed it was you."

"Herr Steiner was wearing your jacket, wasn't he?" Greta demanded, her eyes wide.

Karl nodded. "He was this morning. But he'd taken it off by then."

That was true enough, Haydn thought as he cast his mind back. Christian had hurled the jacket off himself when Loretta Renier had shied away from the knife in Donna Oliveri's hands. Haydn had barely regarded the gesture at the time. But he recalled it now.

Having tossed the garment, Christian had not bothered to either pick it up or put it back on. He had certainly not been wearing it when he'd taken a seat beside Haydn while Papa Keller measured the two tenors.

"No, it couldn't have been him they saw," Haydn acknowledged. But who had it been? One of the stagehands? Or Loretta Renier herself?

The rigging had been contrived so that the sheave would descend upon him just as the bank of clouds plunged down toward her. She'd been left unscathed.

He, on the other hand, had nearly died.

Had the soprano descended so low she would murder anyone who stood in her way?

The question had no sooner entered his mind than Haydn turned toward the maids.

"Tell no one about this," he instructed them sternly. God forbid their lives should be endangered as his already had been. "I will take the sheave to the Police Inspector myself. I regret I will need the carriage." He would go to the Esterházy Palace to summon Johann, he decided. He was in dire need of his brother's calm wisdom.

"But this"—he withdrew his purse and shook out a few coins onto his palm—"should suffice to hire a fiacre to take you to the Kärntnertortheater. I trust they will have a sheave we can borrow for the time being."

⸻◈⸻

Rosalie and Greta hurried up the now clean backstairs. Rosalie had carefully tucked away the money the Kapellmeister had given them into her apron pocket.

"The coutelier is not far from the Kärntnertortheater," Greta gasped breathlessly. "Isn't that fortunate?" She folded the letter Karl had given her and thrust it down her bodice.

The note directed the aged assistant in charge of the Kärntnertortheater to hand them one of the spare sheaves stored in that theater's supply cabinets.

Rosalie nodded. "It's a blessing, to be sure. We can go see the man as soon as Herr Mueller gives us the sheave." It was far better than sneaking off on their own. And if they were a little late coming back, who would be any the wiser?

She pushed open the door and emerged out into the afternoon sun. People and carriages thronged the street, but there were no fiacres to be seen. They would have to walk a short distance to hire a carriage.

Rosalie was about to tell Greta that when she heard her friend stumble behind her. She turned in time to see Greta stub her foot against the top step. It was barely a quarter inch higher than the steps below it, yet that discrepancy was enough to make the unwary trip.

Greta's momentum propelled her, cursing loudly all the while, out onto the street. Her foot kicked a balled-up piece of linen out as well.

"Oh, Greta!" Rosalie cried, grabbing her friend's arm to steady her, while at the same time bending down to pick up the fabric on the ground. "That's not your kerchief, is it?" Although even as she asked the question, Rosalie could see that the linen was far too fine and at the same time far too grimy to belong to either of them.

"What a grimy piece of cloth!" Greta wrinkled her nose in disgust as Rosalie unrolled the fabric. Dark splotches of dirt covered the fine rose-colored linen and darkened the embroidered flowers on it. "And it even has cobwebs. *Pfui Teufel!*"

"It's a kerchief," Rosalie said wonderingly, taking care not to let more than the tips of her fingers touch the fabric.

"Whose could it be?"

Greta had no sooner asked the question than a gust of wind unfurling the embroidered name on the edge of the handkerchief revealed the answer to them.

"Giulietta?" Rosalie's voice rose and she raised her eyes in surprise to Greta.

"Good God, so it is. It's the handkerchief Miss High-and-Mighty was careless enough to lose!" Greta frowned. "But what's it doing here?" She tilted her head down to examine the fabric. "*Mein Gott*, however did she manage to get it so dirty? It can't just have been from lying around."

"No, it wasn't." Rosalie's voice was quiet. "She must have come up those stairs on Sunday and used her handkerchief to clean the cobwebs and dust from the stair rail and the walls."

"You mean it was her dressed in Karl's jacket pretending to be him?" Greta gaped at Rosalie, her mouth wide.

"It must've been her." Although how anyone could've mistaken Fräulein Renier for a man, Rosalie didn't know. She had a clear, high-pitched voice that emotion tended to make squeaky. "Unless, of course, she was accompanying the man who was disguised as Karl."

"Herr Steiner," Greta surmised. "It would have to be him. Although from what Karl says, it wasn't Herr Steiner that messed up the rigging earlier today."

"No, it wasn't." Rosalie shook her head slowly, still staring at the dirty handkerchief. "She may have bribed one of the stagehands."

"What about the man Karl saw in Herr Affligio's chambers when the coutelier came over with the faulty prop knife? Miss High-and-Mighty and he may have been working together."

"So they might," Rosalie agreed. But the gentleman Karl had seen hadn't been anywhere near the theater that morning. That left Fräulein Renier—but did she even have the ability to sabotage the rigging? It wasn't Herr Steiner; he'd discarded Karl's jacket long before the incident took place. Who else, then? One of the stagehands?

The suspicion, unwelcome in its implications, made her shudder. Could one of Karl's colleagues—the men he trusted—be instrumental in killing their master and pointing the finger unerringly at the impresario's assistant?

Greta's voice intruded upon her bleak musings.

"I doubt Miss High-and-Mighty would've trusted more than one person with her wicked plans. And I can't imagine any of the stagehands being willing to go along with the evil she'd planned. It must've been the stranger Karl saw—yet another of Herr Affligio's partners whom he'd most likely cheated." She shook her head disapprovingly.

"I'm sure you're right," Rosalie agreed, although she had her doubts. "Come, let's get ourselves a carriage. This"—she thrust the dirty handkerchief into her other pocket—"is just more proof of Fräulein Renier's guilt. We'll have to let Herr Haydn know about it when we get back."

Chapter Thirty-Four

Haydn was waiting impatiently in his carriage when Johann hurried out from the Esterházy Palace.

"What is it, brother? What troubles you?" Johann's brow was wreathed in concern as he climbed into the carriage. "Nothing untoward has occurred at the rehearsal, I trust."

He took a seat across from Haydn and searched the Kapellmeister's face.

Haydn felt a twinge of guilt. He had not meant to cause his brother alarm, but his urgent summons had given rise to it nevertheless.

"I fear my urgency has misled you," he apologized as the carriage pulled forward. He unwrapped the bloodied sheave from its paper wrapping and explained the situation to his brother. "Bad as it is, in and of itself, I am hopeful it can be a means of releasing Leopold from prison."

"If the Police Inspector can be persuaded of the facts," Johann replied, crossing himself. His face, as he stared at the sheave, was as white as a sheet. Recovering himself with difficulty, he turned his gaze toward Haydn. "Have you told Michael?"

Haydn shook his head. "It all depends upon the Police Inspector's willingness to pursue the truth. If I fail to persuade him . . ." He did not have to complete the thought. They both knew whom Michael would blame in that eventuality.

Johann nodded. "Better not to give rise to any false hope," he agreed. His eyes were drawn to the sheave again, wrapped again in its paper covering. "She is a small-minded, vain woman, full of her own beauty. And yet I find it hard to believe she could be so depraved. To so readily take a life, who would believe a woman could be capable of such a thing?"

Haydn forbore to point out the many women they'd encountered who had been all too ready to dispense with any moral outrage on the subject. But Johann was right, few would be willing to believe a beautiful young woman capable of such a heinous crime.

"And why do it?" Johann continued, his face still pale. Haydn was beginning to regret showing him the sheave. The blood and what could only be clots of flesh was a bloodcurdling sight, enough to turn anyone's stomach. "Have you fathomed her reasons?"

Haydn sighed. His brother's question was a distressing reminder of the flaw in the entire case. Yet the sheave, undeniably the weapon that had felled Affligio, had been found in Loretta Renier's room. Moreover, the maid had seen her emerge from Affligio's chambers *after*—not before—his demise. That she'd been summoned to his chambers was in no doubt.

Immediately after the rehearsal, at that. It was for that very reason Leopold's appointment with the impresario had been pushed back.

Besides, Loretta Renier had very nearly orchestrated his own demise, although Haydn decided against confiding that fact to his brother. The incident had shaken him at the time. But it was over; he had recovered his equanimity. What reason was there to recall it again and unduly perturb his brother with the distressing details?

None that he could think of.

His eyes, narrowed in thought, remained fixed on the window. The familiar street scenes passed by unremarked as the carriage jostled its way to their destination.

"All I have are rumors," he confessed finally. "By all accounts, Affligio wished to dismiss one of the singers. Although no one knows who was to be shown the door. Yet how could it be anyone other than Loretta Renier?"

"On the other hand, she has the Emperor's favor," Johann reminded him. "And you've said yourself Affligio was pursuing her—either romantically or to entice her into a business relationship."

"What if she'd agreed—and found herself with no hold on him?" Haydn leaned back in his seat with another sigh. "The trouble is it is all speculation at this point. There seems to be no evidence one way or another."

There was nothing to say to this, so Johann remained silent. A heavy quiet followed, broken only by the clip-clop of horses' hooves, the rumble of carriage wheels, and the murmur of voices from the streets. Haydn had nearly fallen into a stupor when his brother's soft voice revived him with a start.

"There may yet be a way. Affligio's partnerships were with two sorts of people," Johann was musing. "His patrons—whom he could not then trouble for future subscriptions. And his suppliers—who, as a result, renounced payment for their services in exchange for a percentage of the profit."

Haydn said nothing, watching his brother eagerly, waiting for him to reveal his design.

Johann turned toward him. "Surely, he devised some method to record these arrangements. You've examined the books, brother? Were the names of any of his suppliers or patrons marked in any way?"

Haydn scratched his chin thoughtfully. "Not that I recall. But I can look over them again." If Affligio had named his partners—and why should he not have?—there might even be a way of discovering the identity of the mysterious man Karl had seen with his master.

Had the stranger been working in concert with Loretta Renier? That she could not have carried out her nefarious plan alone was plainly evident.

Deep in thought Rosalie walked along Reitschulgasse toward Michaelerplatz, Greta trotting behind her. A fiacre or two was usually to be found near St. Michael's Church where people came frequently to worship.

"There's one!" Greta cried breathlessly just as they arrived at the point where the road widened into the vast cobblestone space that formed the Michaelerplatz. Looking up, Rosalie saw a four-wheeled black vehicle with fine gold lines outlining its doors and side panels. A young woman was stepping down from it.

"Isn't that Steffi?" she asked Greta. What a bit of luck if it was! They could confirm what they already suspected—that it was not Karl who had sought the Archbishop's help on that fateful Sunday.

Greta craned her neck, her blue eyes squinting against the sun's glare to make out the features of the slender woman who was climbing down from the carriage.

"So it is!" Hurrying forward, Greta called out loudly, "Steffi? Hey, Steffi!"

Steffi spun around. "Greta!" She came forward and seeing Rosalie behind her friend greeted her as well. "What are you two doing here?" She gave Greta a sly grin. "Have you come to light a candle so Karl can be yours?"

Greta's plump cheeks turned a flaming red. "Don't be silly!" she admonished her friend. "We've been working at the Burgtheater, Rosalie and I. And"—her eyes slid toward Rosalie as she simultaneously lowered her voice—"we've been helping to track down a murderer as well."

"Oh!" Steffi's eyes widened. Her mouth fell open as she gaped first at Greta and then at Rosalie. "You can't mean the impresario's murder, can you? His killer is already in prison. Didn't you tell your Herr Haydn that?"

Rosalie wasn't too happy that Greta had confided as much as she had to Steffi. But she reluctantly conceded that they'd have to reveal some of what they'd discovered to Steffi in order to get at the truth.

"Herr Mozart wasn't at the Burgtheater when the impresario was killed," she informed Steffi. "He did have an appointment to see Herr Affligio, but Karl himself says he was sent to him to put it back an hour."

Steffi's brow furrowed into a skeptical frown. "But that can't be true. Herr Mozart must have ventured out earlier than he was expected to. I told you Karl was at our door, knocking loud enough to wake the dead."

Greta and Rosalie exchanged a glance. Then Greta turned back to Steffi.

"You've never seen him. How can you be so sure who it was?"

Steffi looked at them both as though they'd lost their minds. "He told me who he was," she responded patiently. "Tell His Grace, it's the impresario's assistant, he says. Who else would it be?"

Greta ignored that question. "What was he wearing?"

"Karl?" Steffi looked confused. "What does it matter what he was wearing? An old, faded, baggy jacket and he had a hat pulled low over his face. I wondered why he never took it off. But I suppose he was too agitated to—"

"Was he wearing clogs?" Rosalie interrupted this voluble stream of words.

"Clogs? No, of course not. Why would he be wearing clogs? Who wears such things?"

Greta faced her friend. "Karl does. Always. He never takes them off. The person who came to your door wasn't Karl, Steffi. It was Herr Affligio's killer."

Steffi's eyes bulged, looking as though they'd pop out of their sockets. "That can't be so!" she gasped. "Good heavens! You mean we could've been killed."

"I don't think the killer meant to kill anyone other than Herr Affligio," Rosalie assured her. "But it was him all right." It must've been the man working in concert with Fräulein Renier, although she saw no reason to go into that. "You can depend upon it."

Rosalie hesitated a moment. There was something she needed Steffi to do, but would the young girl do it? It would mean contradicting the Archbishop's word. Clutching her apron in her clammy palm, she worked up her courage to ask. "Steffi, will you tell Herr Haydn—and better still, the Police Inspector—what you've told us? It's not just the life of an innocent man hanging in the balance."

Greta's head bobbed in vigorous agreement. "The killer is trying to implicate Karl as well, stealing his jacket, pretending to be him. Oh, Steffi, say you'll do it!" she pleaded, taking hold of her friend's hands.

A flurry of conflicting emotions—disbelief, confusion, and dismay—flitted across Steffi's beautiful features. She glanced over her shoulder at the cathedral towering behind them. "It's not that I want an innocent man to suffer in prison. But"—she turned back to them—"I wish the matter were settled quickly. I have only a few days more to accept that position in Count Kohary's household."

"And it will be settled," Rosalie said boldly with far more confidence than she felt. "If we make known the truth."

Steffi glanced over her shoulder again. "I was about to light a candle —for that position with Count Kohary."

"It is more likely to be yours if you can help bring an innocent man out of prison," Rosalie urged her. "Herr Haydn will speak for you, I'm sure."

"Besides," Greta added, "the maid Petra saw who it was leaving the impresario's chambers. And I can tell you it wasn't Herr Mozart."

Steffi bit her lip. "Well, it's true the man wasn't wearing clogs. And if you say Karl never takes his off, then . . . then, I suppose, it can't have been he who came by." She twisted her apron nervously. "I don't want to go to the police station myself. I'll talk to Herr Haydn and I'll—"

Just at that moment a notion struck Rosalie. "Karl's cousin is a police guard." She turned to Greta. "Maybe Karl could call him and have Steffi speak to the guard in Herr Haydn's presence."

The solution seemed to appeal to Steffi, and she looked relieved when Greta nodded.

"Light your candle. We'll walk you back to the Burgtheater."

Steffi smiled; a mischievous glint appeared in her eyes. "I'll do it on one condition. Tell me, why does your Karl wear clogs?"

Rosalie had wondered the same thing herself, but had been afraid of offending either Karl or Greta by asking about what seemed like such an odd quirk.

But Greta took the question in her stride. "It's a precaution," she explained, "suggested by his master in Naples. You see, while they were working there, a heavy sheave—bigger than the one we found today, Rosalie—smashed to the floor, making mincemeat of one of the stagehand's feet. Since then, Karl's master insisted upon all his workers wearing heavy wooden clogs."

She shrugged. "I'm not sure they're any better protection than ordinary shoes. But Karl is so used to them, he'll never wear anything else."

Chapter Thirty-Five

A tall, stout gentleman was limping up the steps to the police station with the aid of a cane when Haydn and Johann arrived at their destination.

"How fortuitous! It is Gregor Fischer, the medical examiner," Haydn whispered to Johann. "With him on our side, we may yet persuade von Beer to let Leopold go."

Leaning forward, he hailed the gentleman. "Herr Fischer!"

Gregor Fischer turned around, his full cheeks flushing with pleasure when he saw who it was calling his name. He limped down.

"Herr Haydn! We meet again. What brings you here?" His eyes, bright with curiosity, turned to regard Johann.

"My younger brother," Haydn said, proceeding to acquaint the two men with each other. That task over, he held out the sheave. "Could this be the swinging object that killed the impresario? It was discovered just this morning at the Burgtheater."

Tucking his cane under his arm, the medical examiner reached for the paper-wrapped object, slowly uncovered it, and scrutinized it as carefully as a lawyer examining a contract. Haydn watched him, hardly daring to breathe.

"Ingenious!" The old gentleman shook his mane of thick hair wonderingly. "Most ingenious! A most novel means of committing a murder." He raised his eyes toward Haydn. "In all my years as a medical examiner, I have never come across anything like it."

"It is the weapon then?" Haydn wished to be sure on the point.

"There's no doubt about it. God in heaven, who would think of using a sheave?"

Fischer shook his head again as he regarded Haydn and Johann, and then proceeded to answer his own question.

"Only a person involved with the theater—someone with an abundance of imagination."

"I doubt even his fiercest enemies could accuse Leopold Mozart of having too much imagination," Johann remarked. "His mind is sober, little likely to wander."

"One could write an opera on the subject—the sheave as a murder weapon, I mean. Not Herr Mozart's mind." Seeing Fischer about to develop on this theme, Haydn quickly interrupted him.

"Could a woman have wielded the weapon?"

Von Beer would no doubt argue it was impossible, and so dismiss anything he had to say against Loretta Renier. Haydn wanted the opinion of an expert before he confronted the Police Inspector with his evidence.

"Most certainly," Fischer declared without hesitation. "It requires little effort to swing it hard enough to fell even the stoutest man. The weapon is more deadly than David's sling. And it must've caught the poor impresario unguarded. Where was it found?"

Haydn found himself wavering. The medical examiner seemed like an extremely garrulous individual, given, Haydn feared, to gushing out the most confidential facts as easily as an uncorked bottle of champagne. Could his discretion be relied upon?

His eyes sought Johann's gaze. At his brother's imperceptible nod of encouragement, he turned back to Fischer.

"It was found among the things of a soprano by the name of Loretta Renier." He made a wry face. "She enjoys the Emperor's favor, and . . ." He found himself at a loss for words.

"And we fear the Police Inspector may be loath to take our word for it that she committed the deed," Johann finished for him. "If you were to accompany us . . . ?"

"Of course, of course," the elderly gentleman heartily agreed. "It would be my pleasure. Von Beer can be hardheaded at times, but, nevertheless, he is a man of reason. And the facts can hardly be disputed in this case.

"The Emperor's mistress did away with the impresario, did she?" Fischer continued loudly much to Haydn's dismay as they made their way up the stairs. "God in heaven! Whatever will the Empress, his mother, say when she finds out?"

Greta settled herself against the soft leather seat of the fiacre they'd hired. "It was a bit of luck running into Steffi like that, wasn't it?" she exclaimed happily over the noisy rattle of the coach wheels.

Rosalie had to strain her ears to hear her friend's remark. When she'd caught the gist of it, she nodded and gave Greta a broad smile. "That it was!" It really couldn't have worked out much better.

They had accompanied Steffi back to the Burgtheater, and the sight of Karl had done more to convince her of the truth than Greta's urgings. Steffi had no sooner seen him than she'd drawn back surprised. "You're Karl?"

Turning to Greta, she'd immediately shaken her head. "It was certainly not him that came calling for His Grace on Sunday." Even without the clogs, the differences between the two men had been so great that Steffi had needed no more persuading to report the matter to Karl's cousin and Herr Haydn.

"He wasn't quite so tall," Steffi had said, casting an appraising eye over Karl's person. "Or quite so burly. Even his voice was different."

She wrinkled her nose. "I wasn't going to say anything, Greta, but I was wondering why you'd taken up with such an effeminate fellow."

Greta must've been thinking back to the conversation, for she sniffed. "Karl effeminate indeed! I only wish Steffi had said something. I'd have set her straight immediately."

"I wonder who it was, though?" Rosalie said, holding tightly onto her seat. The rocking motion of the coach had more than once threatened to pitch her onto her friend. Fortunately, she had a strong stomach or it would've made her feel queasy as well.

"It can't have been Herr Steiner." Greta's voice came out in staccato bursts as the motion of the coach bumped her up and down. "No one could call him effeminate." Clutching Rosalie's arm, she pulled herself back against the leather-covered panel behind them. "It's almost like riding a horse," she muttered. "I've never had such a rough ride."

"Fräulein Renier dressed as a man, then?" Rosalie asked.

"I suppose so." Greta was still preoccupied with keeping herself steady.

"Or the stranger Karl saw in Herr Affligio's chambers," Rosalie mused on. The man had been slender and slightly built. Womanly, Karl had supposed, but he hadn't heard the gentleman speak. "And he hasn't been here since," Karl had informed them regretfully.

Her mind wandered on, turning over this idea and that notion. Was it possible that the man—the mysterious gentleman Karl had seen in the impresario's chambers—was Fräulein Renier in disguise? The thought made Rosalie utter a loud gasp.

"That's it!" Greta said, misunderstanding the reason for her consternation. She rapped on the glass pane in front of them and stuck her head out the window. "*Hey, du*! Drive carefully, won't you? You've nearly broken our bones. I'm warning you, any more of this, and you shan't get paid."

She stuck her head back in, satisfied. "There! That should do it. I've a good mind to break a stick over the man's head. Driving the way he is!"

But Rosalie wasn't listening. Her mind returned to something Petra had said. The impresario had insisted she stop cleaning the backstairs.

Had he wanted to make sure the area remained dirty and unused? Why? So that no one would see the soprano putting on male garb to impersonate a man?

But what earthly reason could there have been for her to do so? And for them both to keep the matter secret?

Von Beer was not overly pleased to see Haydn. He had raised his eyebrows in surprise when Gregor Fischer barged into his chambers. But the sight of the Kapellmeister and his younger brother had caused him to purse his lips in displeasure.

"The prisoner is being extremely well-treated, Herr Haydn," he said with some asperity. "He has been allowed a bath and a change of clothing—as you asked. I did pledge myself to heed your request. There was no need for you to return to confirm it."

The medical examiner spoke before Haydn could explain his presence at the police station.

"Never mind the prisoner!" Fischer declared in a loud, hearty tone. "Although"—struck by a thought, his gaze shot toward Haydn and Johann—"given the new evidence you've brought in, the man should be released."

"New evidence?" Von Beer frowned, looking more displeased than ever. "What evidence?" His eyes fell on the partially covered sheave in Fischer's hands. "It is that, I suppose?" He wrinkled his fine nose in disgust.

"It is the sheave that killed Herr Affligio," Haydn informed him. "It is covered in blood and hair and Herr Fischer here has confirmed it is the weapon that killed the impresario. Herr Mozart would know nothing of a sheave or its use or even where to find one in the Burgtheater."

"And you will scarcely credit where it was found." Fischer drew out a chair and plonked himself into it. He gestured expansively toward the two other chairs in the room, inviting the Kapellmeister and his brother to be seated as well. "Do sit down, Herr Haydn, Master Johann. There's no need to stand on ceremony among friends. Is there, von Beer?"

He turned to the Police Inspector who forbore to reply.

Seeing no reason to remain standing like a servant, Haydn sat down and Johann followed suit.

"Where was it found?" Von Beer could not have looked upon them with more disfavor had they been maggots crawling in his fruit.

"In Loretta Renier's changing room," Haydn said.

"She is one of the sopranos at the Burgtheater," Johann explained.

"And the Emperor's mistress," Fischer added, eagerly divulging the news.

"It is the murder weapon, von Beer," he asserted. "There's no doubt about it. And that being the case, La Renier must be the murderer—her singing is atrocious," the medical examiner added, turning to Haydn. "It's a blessing the impresario wasn't done in by any of the other performers. At least, La Renier will not be missed."

The medical examiner turned to face von Beer. "The question is, what will you do about it? The Emperor must be informed. It is a delicate matter, but we can hardly ignore it. The facts must be placed before His Majesty."

The Police Inspector glanced down at the sheave sitting on his desk, then averted his gaze from it. "I will add a note to my report that the weapon that killed the impresario has been found. I see no reason to do anything more. I certainly see no reason to bring up outrageous speculations against Fräulein Renier to His Majesty."

Haydn found himself speechless at this utter disregard of the evidence. What more did the Police Inspector need? Would even an admission of guilt from the soprano's own mouth help?

Fortunately, his brother was not so impaired.

"Outrageous?" Johann lifted an eyebrow quizzically and stared at the Police Inspector. "The weapon was found in her room. She was seen by the maid leaving the impresario's chambers and he was discovered lying dead on the floor shortly after that. These are hardly speculations, Herr von Beer. They are facts. They speak for themselves and must be examined further."

"We have only the maid's word for it that Fräulein Renier was seen leaving the impresario's chambers. And from all accounts, the maid is unreliable. And had reason enough to murder her employer." At Haydn's stunned expression, he went on somewhat irritably, "Do you suppose the police guards are unaware that the impresario was delinquent in his payments?

"What possible reason could Fräulein Renier have for murdering the impresario? A well-respected singer, one who'd found favor in the Emperor's eyes?"

Haydn found his eyes driven toward his brother. Certain as he was of Loretta Renier's guilt, even he had to admit the motives he had come up with were feeble at best.

Taking a deep breath, he returned his gaze to von Beer. "The Burgtheater composers and her colleagues were deeply dissatisfied with her. Her performance leaves much to be desired, and there is every indication Affligio meant to dismiss her."

Best not to mention that Affligio was pursuing her—and to what purpose. There was even less evidence for that assertion. But that Affligio meant to dismiss a performer—most likely Loretta Renier—could be easily ascertained.

Von Beer was unconvinced. His eyebrows rose skeptically.

"The impresario intended to dismiss the Emperor's favorite, did he? And what evidence do you have of this? Or are you merely skilled in reading dead men's minds, Herr Haydn?"

"He did mean to dismiss one of the performers," Johann quietly asserted. "No other performer caused as much trouble as Loretta Renier. The impresario was a shrewd, hardheaded man of business—not one to meekly sit by and take a financial loss. Do you really suppose he would not take steps to remove an impediment to his profits?"

"Only a fool would do nothing under the circumstances," Fischer agreed, nodding his head vigorously.

The argument caused the Police Inspector to waver. Haydn closely watched the changing expressions on his face, the skepticism warring with a realization of the undeniable good sense in Johann's words.

"But you have nothing more than rumors," von Beer finally said. "I cannot risk provoking the Emperor's displeasure on so flimsy a ground."

"Surely you can question her?" Haydn leaned forward to press his point. "The sheave was discovered in her room. Surely an explanation must be provided for that?"

An indulgent smile spread over von Beer's lips. "Fräulein Renier is a beautiful woman—an intimate friend of His Majesty. Do you suppose she is without her detractors? Someone envious of her could've placed the sheave in her room, hoping to implicate her. Who knows, but the maid herself might've been the one to do it. Or one of the other performers. I am aware she is not well-liked."

"Then why," Haydn asked, exasperated beyond measure now, "did she try to kill me?"

Chapter Thirty-Six

"WHAT? When?" Johann started out of his chair like a timid horse at the sound of a gunshot.

Even Fischer who had been quietly following their conversation looked startled. "God in heaven, whatever next!"

"You never mentioned it to me, brother?" Johann turned accusingly toward Haydn.

"I survived the attempt," Haydn said, spreading his hands apologetically. "I saw no reason to disquiet you."

Johann nodded to indicate he understood. "Praise the Lord that you survived," he said fervently before turning toward the Police Inspector. "What further proof do you require, Herr von Beer? Is this not enough?"

Von Beer's frown deepened. "It is a grave accusation, Herr Haydn," he said sternly. "I will need to know more. What precisely did Fräulein Renier do?"

But when Haydn had recounted the details, the Police Inspector was no closer to being persuaded.

"Am I to believe that a woman dressed in all her finery climbed up to the rigging to manipulate it? That she might even possess the knowledge, let alone the ability, to tamper with it is beyond belief."

"She must've been working with someone," Haydn persisted. "A stagehand taken in by her beauty or paid to help." Or possibly the mysterious man seen in Affligio's chambers, but he could hardly mention this without going into Affligio's business affairs and their speculations about Loretta Renier in that regard.

"Am I to question all the stagehands, then?" von Beer demanded irritably.

Was it not his job in the pursuit of justice, Haydn wondered, although he refrained from voicing the question.

He rose. "You will do nothing, then?"

Von Beer got to his feet as well. "My hands are tied, Herr Haydn. The sheave in and of itself is no proof of Fräulein Renier's guilt. That it was found among her things means nothing other than that someone wished to implicate her in the impresario's murder."

How it could mean any such thing, Haydn was at a loss to understand. But it was von Beer's last words that he found excessively galling.

"Find me incontrovertible proof of her guilt, and I will arrest her. But I cannot allow speculation and rumor to be reason enough to persecute the innocent."

"In other words, I am to do his job for him," Haydn complained bitterly to Johann once they were back in their carriage.

Fischer had deeply regretted not being able to do more to help and had shaken his head ruefully at the Police Inspector's parting words. "Von Beer is being unduly stubborn. How could anyone expect you to do more than you already have, Herr Haydn? Find proof indeed! The man has taken leave of his senses."

"On the other hand," Johann pointed out as the carriage rolled away from the police station, "one could say he has granted you the liberty to pursue the matter yourself. I would wager you are far better equipped to do it than he. I only wish he had agreed to release Leopold. Any person of sense could see the poor man had nothing to do with the impresario's murder."

<hr>

Herr Mueller, a gray-haired individual with a gently protruding belly, greeted Rosalie and Greta with much grumbling. "Karl should be more careful." He bustled ahead of them into the Kärntnertortheater. "Losing a good sheave like that! What was he thinking? Not thinking, more likely, as is the case with most young people these days."

Following close upon his heels, Greta twisted her features into a rude grimace and stuck her tongue out at Herr Mueller's broad waistcoat-clad back. Seeing that made Rosalie want to giggle, but she choked back her mirth.

But for all his complaining, Herr Mueller found the spare sheave readily enough, wrapped it in sturdy brown paper and tied it with a stout piece of string, and accompanied them out to the waiting fiacre.

"Now be careful, you hear!" He set the sheave gently on the leather seat of the carriage. "Be sure not to let it fall. It'll put a dent in the floor —and your feet."

He stood anxiously by as the coach rolled slowly forward—as though his watchful gaze might prevent any damage to his precious sheave. Greta waited until he finally went inside the Kärntnertortheater before rapping on the glass pane and thrusting her head out the window.

"Stop at the corner of Walfischgasse, won't you? And wait for us. We have some business to attend to."

"It'll cost you," the grizzled coachman warned. "Are you sure you have the money for it? Don't waste my time if you don't."

Greta looked down her nose at the man. "We have money aplenty, don't you worry." She pulled her head back in. "The nerve of some people!" she muttered to Rosalie.

———◦◦◦———

The coutelier's shop was a few paces from the corner. The dusty wood door stood ajar and the gold lettering on the shop window was faded. Felix, the coutelier, stood behind the counter, whetting the sharp edge of a dagger.

He raised his eyes as soon as they stepped in, and his features soured.

"What is it now? Don't tell me! The wooden blade has killed some-one, has it?"

"Of course not!" Rosalie said.

"Then why are you here?" Felix thrust his thin cheeks out. Gray-brown stubble dotted his chin and surrounded his mouth. "It's always one thing or another with Affligio's folks."

Rosalie's eyes sought Greta's. Why were they here? They'd been so eager to come here, they hadn't thought things through. They could hardly burst in and bombard the man with questions. Greta lifted her shoulders in a tiny shrug.

"We wanted to as—" Greta began only to be interrupted by Rosalie.

"We wanted to apologize," Rosalie hastily said. "Karl and Herr Haydn sent us to apologize."

Felix's beady eyes narrowed. "Whatever for?" he demanded suspiciously.

"For doubting you about that old prop knife."

"You've found it, then?" Felix stared at her from under lowered brows.

Rosalie shook her head. "It was discovered on Herr Affligio's person." No need to mention it had been buried in his chest. "And the Police Inspector said it retracted so well, it couldn't have killed anyone."

"Of course, it couldn't!" Felix's thin mouth tightened. "Haven't I been saying that this whole time? But no one will listen. *It killed my husband, it killed my husband*, the woman Oliveri cried. *We must have a new knife made.* And Affligio, fool that he is, was only too happy to listen."

"You can't blame him," Greta began apologetically. "She's been with the theater a long time. And she is one of the better singers. Most likely, he couldn't afford to lose her."

Felix rolled his eyes. "I wouldn't know about that. I've never heard her sing. But I can tell you, it wasn't for the sake of her singing that he was so ready to comply."

"Why then?" Rosalie and Greta exchanged a glance. Felix wasn't suggesting the impresario had been in love with Frau Oliveri, was he? Gracious and pleasant though she might be, she was no beauty.

"Why do you think? He was sniffing up her skirt." Felix grinned. "Don't believe me, do you? She's no vision, but she does have her charms, if you know what you're looking for. And Affligio, God rest his soul, was no stallion himself."

"That's rubbish!" Greta looked him straight in the eyes. "Everyone says Herr Affligio was after Fräulein Renier."

Felix shrugged. "Not then, he wasn't. He was after Dame Oliveri. I'll warrant she knew it—and wasn't too displeased about it either." He tapped his nose. "I can sniff out a dalliance, I can." He leered at Greta. "Didn't I see at once that Karl was sweet on you?"

Greta made a wry face, but she couldn't deny his claim. Rosalie shook her head impatiently; she didn't want Greta arguing with the man. It wasn't the coutelier's abilities to detect dalliances that they were after. She turned to Felix

"How do you suppose Frau Oliveri's husband was killed, then?" she asked. "She had the prop knife in her hand. Everyone saw that. And rather than retract, it plunged straight into his breast. Isn't that odd?"

But Felix, to Rosalie's surprise, remained unfazed.

"Not if the slider under the handle was pushed up. Could be the Oliveri woman's thumb accidentally pushed it forward. But if you ask me, someone most likely put the lever up, and then forgot to put it back down. I warned Affligio, several times I did. Check the slider every time, I said. But—

"Wait, what slider?" Rosalie and Greta were gaping at each other aghast. No one had said anything about a slider. Karl, most certainly, hadn't known a thing about it.

Felix seemed puzzled by their reaction.

"What do you mean, what slider? The one under the handle, of course. To prevent the blade from retracting."

"B-but why?" Greta burst out. "Why would you have such a thing?"

"Why?" Felix mimicked Greta's rising tone. "Because Affligio asked for it, that's why. And that partner of his—Count Kohary."

"Count Kohary?" Rosalie and Greta turned to each other again.

"Yes, Count Kohary. That's what Affligio called him. Why would I doubt his word? Not that I cared about his name. I was there to deliver the knife and show them how it worked. They seemed happy enough with it. Although how well His Lordship understood the mechanism, I can't say. It should've been Karl in there. But"—he shrugged—"I suppose it was His Lordship's coin paying for the knife."

The mysterious man in the impresario's chambers had been Count Kohary? Rosalie couldn't believe it. She turned to Felix.

"What did he look like?"

———❖———

The visit to Fugger's establishment had been long overdue. But now that he was here, Haydn wished he'd stayed away. Extricating himself from the financial morass Affligio had sunk into would be no easy task.

"No papers were signed?" A frown marred Jakob Fugger's smooth brow as he gazed at his visitors. "But His Majesty gave me to understand . . ." He left the sentence unfinished, his lips pursing into a thin line of displeasure.

Haydn sighed. Fugger seemed loath to be persuaded that he hadn't assumed the impresario's debts as well as his duties.

The banker's chambers were as opulently furnished as he himself. Haydn sat before the man, unable—despite his concern—to keep his eyes away from the enormous painting that covered the entire wall behind Fugger.

An early work by Johann Baptist von Lampi, it portrayed the Messiah within the temple overturning the money changer's tables. What had caught Haydn's eye, however, was that it was Fugger's features on the face of the Lord.

That the banker, a man whose family relentlessly pursued money, should view himself as Christ opposing mammon, struck Haydn as especially ironic. A subtle nudge from his younger brother, seated beside him, forced him to tear his gaze away from the painting.

"It is a temporary assignment, nothing more. You may confirm the matter with my employer," Haydn informed Fugger, recalled by Johann's prodding to the purpose of their meeting. "How could I lease the theater? I can undertake no commission without His Serene Highness's express consent. My contract forbids it."

"And as far as we know," Johann added with a gentle smile, "the Prince has no desire to run the Burgtheater. It would necessitate living in Vienna, a city he detests."

Fugger twirled the quill clenched between his thumb and forefinger. "Very well." His lips were still pursed. "But there is still the matter of the impresario's arrears. Herr Affligio assured me he would have the money here to me on Monday."

Haydn glanced at his brother. "I fear the impresario was full of such assurances. He left his employees unpaid—for weeks. Manipulated his suppliers into receiving a share of the profits rather than a set fee."

"He left no money?" Fugger's face wore an expression of outrage that rivaled that of the Messiah on the painting behind him. "But he assured me the Archbishop of Salzburg had—"

"Purchased a share in the Burgtheater?" Haydn leaned forward, unable to keep from interrupting the banker in his eagerness.

"Yes." Fugger nodded. "A thirty percent interest. You were aware of this?"

It had been a mere supposition until the banker had confirmed it, but Haydn had no intention of revealing this to him. He looked at his brother, indicating with an imperceptible shake of his head that Johann should ignore the question as well.

"I imagine His Grace has yet to pay the amount," he responded lightly as he turned back toward Fugger.

"But Herr Affligio expected to have the money on Sunday," Fugger objected with a frown.

"The day of his demise," Johann murmured, causing the banker to look instantly contrite and to cross himself devoutly.

The Archbishop had certainly been at the Burgtheater that evening, Haydn recalled, urgently summoned to Affligio's aid. Had His Grace remembered to take his purse with him? Surely the prospect of ousting Leopold from his employ had not been so thrilling as to cause him to forget to reward those who had helped him orchestrate it.

That Affligio and some other person had deliberately conspired with the Archbishop to goad Leopold into violence—or, failing that, to maliciously implicate him in some trouble—was in no question.

The other person was not Karl. It could not have been Fräulein Renier. She had hurled a sheave at Affligio. But she had certainly not stabbed him as well. After all, the maid who'd seen Loretta Renier leave the impresario's chambers had not seen a knife anywhere near his dead body.

Who else but the mysterious gentleman in Affligio's chambers could it have been? A man who, according to Karl, looked like a nobleman. It must have been he—this unknown gentleman—who had taken advantage of a desperate situation to ensure the Archbishop kept his side of the bargain. The workings of the prop knife, after all, had been known only to Affligio and the gentleman with him.

Had Fräulein Renier sought the gentleman's help in covering up her heinous act? Had he—in a keen desire to please the Emperor and his current favorite—agreed? It would be killing two birds with a single stone if he had. And if he were one of the nobility—

Struck by sudden insight, Haydn turned to Fugger.

"On whose recommendation was it that you agreed to loan the impresario such a vast sum? I doubt he could've interested your establishment to do business with him on his own merits."

Fugger leaned back in his enormous leather-padded chair, clearly hesitant to reveal the name.

"It may be that the gentleman can be asked to serve as a guarantor for the man's debts," Johann said, hoping Haydn knew to prod Fugger into revealing the name.

The tactic unfortunately failed to work.

"That was not the arrangement we had," the banker replied tersely. "Besides, it was his partner who had obtained the letter of introduction."

"His partner?" Haydn's eyebrows shot up. "Which one? The impresario had several."

"A minor member of the Hungarian nobility," Fugger replied. "Count Kohary."

The name was familiar to Haydn from Affligio's account ledgers.

"And it was the Count who had obtained a letter of introduction?" Haydn's voice rose. He glanced at his brother. "On Affligio's behalf?" The matter seemed most confusing.

Fugger spread his hands wide, finally letting go of the quill he had been clutching the entire time. "He wished to purchase an interest in the Burgtheater, but had no wish to invest in a debt-ridden venture."

Ach so! "Then it must have been Chancellor Kaunitz who provided the letter of introduction," Haydn exclaimed. Who else could it be? Papa Keller had said it was at the Chancellor's insistence that Affligio had hired a French dance troupe.

The Chancellor had no doubt sought to repair the damage by providing Affligio with the means—however convoluted—of obtaining a loan to stay afloat.

Fugger made no reply, but his crestfallen features confirmed Haydn's suspicions.

"It was Chancellor Kaunitz, was it not?" he pressed the point.

"You seem to be as well acquainted with the facts as I, Herr Haydn," Fugger replied. "That is all I can say."

But surely it was not the Chancellor that Karl had seen in his master's chambers. Karl would have had no trouble recognizing His Excellency. Was it the Count? Surely not.

"This Count Kohary—?" Haydn began only to be interrupted.

"Rents an apartment for the summer on Naglergasse. It is not too far from the Esterházy Palace. You can meet him for yourself."

Haydn had been about to ask for a description of the gentleman, but he realized Fugger would be loath to provide any more details than he needed to.

"I believe we have met the gentleman," he said instead. Johann looked at him surprised, but Haydn forged ahead. "He is a slender man of slight stature, is he not? With a swarthy complexion?"

It was the only way to wrest the information from Fugger's reluctant lips. The banker would be sure to contradict him if he was wrong. And Haydn had no doubt that he was.

But to his eternal astonishment, Fugger nodded eagerly and smiled.

"Yes, that is he. You know him, then?"

Haydn's eyes opened wide. Dear God! He had been describing the mysterious individual Karl had noticed in Affligio's chambers. *That had been Kohary?*

Fugger continued to speak, but Haydn was barely listening.

"I recall he had trouble with his voice that day. It sounded hoarse— and light enough, I thought, to be mistaken for a woman's. Herr Affligio did most of the talking that day."

Fugger leaned forward expectantly. "But if you are acquainted with the gentleman, perchance you can persuade him to assume Herr Affligio's debts. Until such time, of course, as a new impresario can be found to take over his duties," he added hopefully.

Chapter Thirty-Seven

"ROSALIE?" Greta stole a hesitant glance at her friend. Judging by her attitude, Rosalie had come to the same conclusion Greta had. She sat unnaturally pale and still, huddled in the corner, her fingers clenched tightly together.

Dear God, it was true then! In the excitement of learning the name of the stranger in Herr Affligio's chambers, they'd initially missed an important tidbit Felix the coutelier had let fall. The mechanism to ensure the prop knife failed to retract had been deliberately installed.

Herr Affligio himself had insisted upon it.

The past five minutes had been spent in silence, broken only by the muted street sounds that penetrated the fiacre's windows and the steady rhythm of the horses' hooves beating upon the cobblestones. There had been plenty of time to consider the implications of the coutelier's information.

There could be only one reason for the impresario's insistence. And it was too foul to contemplate.

Rosalie turned at the sound of her name but said nothing.

"You don't suppose—" Greta swallowed, hesitant to voice the question that had invaded their minds ever since they'd left the coutelier's establishment. "You don't suppose Frau Oliveri's husband was deliberately killed, do you?"

"I very much fear he was," Rosalie said gravely.

Greta chewed on her lip. She'd suspected as much but had fervently hoped she was wrong. She had hoped Rosalie with her quick mind could provide a happier explanation for the facts than she herself had.

"But what could Count Kohary have had against Frau Oliveri and her husband?" Greta cried. It was even harder to believe that Herr

Affligio—a man who had so favored Karl and been so gracious to him —could've had anything to do with the deed.

Why would the impresario harbor such murderous feelings against his own singers? Surely he'd been hoodwinked into complying with the Count.

But she was arguing against her own conviction, and Rosalie must have known it, too.

Her violet eyes flashed fiercely as they bore into Greta's desperate blue ones. "You do realize nothing could've been done without Herr Affligio's knowledge, don't you? He is just as culpable as the Count."

"But why kill her husband? Because he was in love with her—as that weasel-faced wretch Felix claims?"

"No, I don't think it was for love that the impresario committed murder. I think it was for money." Rosalie turned to face Greta. "Frau Oliveri and her husband are wealthy. Isn't that what Karl said? And Herr Affligio wanted to get Herr Oliveri to invest in his venture and so rescue him from his debts."

Greta nodded. "And Herr Oliveri declined. But to kill the man? To have blood upon his hands for such a feeble reason?"

"Seventy thousand gulden is a vast sum of money. He must've been lost to all good sense, thanks to his debt." Rosalie shuddered. "God save us from selling our souls so easily to the devil."

Greta clasped her hands together. God forbid, Frau Oliveri should ever find out the truth. It would bring her no peace to realize that the impresario—a man she trusted—had caused her husband's death.

"Poor Frau Oliveri!" She turned to Rosalie. "She must blame herself every time she recalls the incident. But how much worse would the truth be."

"I only hope she refused to give him any of her husband's money," Rosalie said. "Or that the money was so tied up, she could do nothing with it. It would serve the impresario right if all his evil had been for nothing."

⁕

Steffi had already left the Burgtheater by the time Rosalie and Greta returned. When Greta found out, she was beside herself.

"Where is she?" she demanded, craning her neck around Karl's broad back and standing on tiptoe to peer over his shoulders. "Why did you let her go? Did I not tell you—"

"I did not let her go anywhere, my dumpling." Karl reached out to Greta, setting his large, work-coarsened hands on her shoulders. "Franz"—that was his cousin the police guard, Rosalie remembered— "took her to the police station. He thinks her word might be sufficient to secure the Salzburger's release."

"Well, that at least is something." Greta's agitation subsided and she allowed Karl to draw her into his arms.

"Yes, it is," Karl agreed. "What's more, Franz is even willing to tell a small lie and say it was the Archbishop himself who urged Steffi to come forward. Herr von Beer is hardly likely to go asking His Grace any questions about it when he hears that."

He looked over her shoulder at Rosalie and smiled.

"Did Herr Mueller have a sheave to spare?"

"He did. And he let us have it, but not without much complaining."

Rosalie stretched out her hands to show Karl the carefully packaged sheave the elderly assistant at the Kärntnertortheater had given them.

She wondered when Greta would get around to telling Karl about the unpardonable deed his master had committed. Should she mention it herself, she wondered.

"We happened to pass by the coutelier's shop," she began.

"Oh!" Karl, still holding Greta close to his chest, raised his eyebrows.

Rosalie nodded. "We weren't very nice to him, Greta and I, when he was here. So we thought we should go in and apologize."

"And let him know where the prop knife was," Greta added, nodding her head. She drew back from Karl and gazed up into his eyes. "Do you know what he told us?"

Gazing fondly down at her, Karl shook his head. "No, my dumpling. What did he say?"

"It turns out Herr Affligio had asked for a prop knife that could be made to not retract."

"Nonsense! Why would Herr Affligio do such a thing?"

"It's true." Rosalie bobbed her head emphatically. "The knife had a lever under the handle. If it was pushed forward, the blade would fail to retract."

"But I never saw anything like it," Karl protested. "God knows, there's been many an occasion when I've had to handle that knife. There was no lever."

"It was cleverly placed, he said," Greta informed him. "You wouldn't be able to tell it was there unless you knew what to look for."

"And Herr Affligio as well as his partner would've known what to look for," Rosalie reminded them both.

"His partner?" Karl frowned. "Which partner? You don't mean the man I saw in his chamber, do you?"

Rosalie and Greta nodded. But Karl still looked skeptical, more inclined, Rosalie felt sure, to doubt the coutelier's word—or their own understanding of it—than his dead master.

"There was no reason for him to lie, Karl," Greta persisted. "We told him where the knife was. The truth of his tale could easily be put to the test."

"But what would this partner of his—if it indeed was his partner—have wanted with such a prop. Why, it could've killed one of the performers. In fact, it did. You don't mean to say . . .?"

Karl's eyes widened and his jaw fell open in horror. His gaze veered wildly from Rosalie to Greta and back again.

Rosalie wished they could reassure Karl he was mistaken. But he was not, and all she and Greta could do was to mutely nod.

"Who was this man? What hold must he have had on master to make him kill a man? Did Felix know his name?"

"Count Kohary," Greta told him. "That's what he heard Herr Affligio call him."

"Count Kohary?" The skeptical expression had returned to Karl's features. "Is that who Felix told you he was? Now I know he was lying, although I wish I knew why. That slender, womanly-looking man, whoever he may have been, wasn't Count Kohary. His Lordship has a box at the theater. He doesn't often come here, but I'd know him anywhere."

<hr>

Naglergasse 7, the building in which Count Kohary kept an apartment for the summer was but ten paces from His Serene Highness Prince

Nikolaus's wine cellar on the Haarhof. Leaving the carriage at the Esterházy Palace, Haydn and Johann walked the short distance to Naglergasse, climbing up a short flight of steps to the Count's apartment.

A much harried steward admitted them into the apartment and led them into a lavishly furnished parlor to await the Count's presence. Large six-paned windows overlooked what was essentially a narrow alley.

"How shall we broach the subject, brother?" Johann leaned over to whisper into Haydn's ear when the steward had left the room. "We can hardly ask His Lordship if he plunged a prop knife into his partner's breast."

"No, certainly not," Haydn agreed, shaking his head. "We must first get His Lordship to acknowledge the partnership. He has a box at the Burgtheater and his subscription, I noticed, has not been renewed."

"Herr Haydn!" A stout, red-featured individual with a rotund belly, a brown mustache, and a wig that nearly covered his ears stood at the parlor door. "It is a pleasure to make your acquaintance." He stepped into the room, his hands outstretched.

Haydn rose, along with Johann, and allowed the gentleman to grasp his palm in both of his hands.

"What may I do for you?" the gentleman asked, beaming genially at both men.

Puzzled, Haydn turned to Johann and then back again to the gentleman. "We were here to meet Count Kohary. Is His Lordship—?" He was interrupted before he could utter the word, *unavailable.*

"Yes, my steward informed me." The stout gentleman gestured toward the couch the brothers had been seated in and sank into a capacious armchair in front of them.

Haydn exchanged another glance with his brother. *This was Count Kohary?* He looked nothing like the man Herr Fugger had described. Still mystified, Haydn resumed his seat.

"Your Lordship has a box at the Burgtheater," he began tentatively.

The Count nodded, the flesh beneath his chin sagging to form a second chin every time he lowered his head. "Yes, indeed! And I eagerly await the season's offerings." He smiled. "I hear you have assumed Affligio's duties." At Haydn's astonished stare, he continued, "The news is all over Vienna. How could it not be when the matter involves a musician of your stature?"

Haydn lowered his head, made momentarily uncomfortable by this reference to his fame. It was something he would never get used to—that he, the son of a mere wheelwright from Rohrau, now dealt with kings and emperors.

Fortunately, Johann took up the thread of their conversation. "Brother has had occasion to examine Herr Affligio's accounts, Your Lordship. And it appears—unless the impresario was mistaken in his accounting—that the fee for Your Lordship's box at the theater has yet to be paid."

His Lordship's brow furrowed, seeming bewildered. But much to Haydn's surprise he did not contradict the charge; a partner would have owed no subscription fees.

"I thought I had asked Anton—that is my steward—to pay the fee," His Lordship said instead. Reaching over to a bell pull hanging by his armchair, he tugged on it.

Minutes later, the steward, a lean, worried-looking man, appeared at the door. "Your Lordship rang for me?"

"The fee for my box at the Burgtheater, Anton. Did I not give it to you, asking you to make sure the subscription was paid?" Count Kohary demanded.

Anton's face fell. "You did indeed, Your Lordship, but"—he chewed uncertainly on his lip, his gaze drifting from the Count to his visitors—"what with one thing and another, and having to hire a new maid—"

"It escaped your mind, did it?" His Lordship gave an understanding nod. "Well, no matter. Bring the money here and give it to these gentlemen."

It was clear to Haydn that Count Kohary was not the man Fugger had met. Nor was he Affligio's elusive partner. Who, then, had Fugger seen? A relative, perhaps?

"Forgive me for asking, but does Your Lordship have a son?"

"A son?" The Count guffawed heartily. "No woman has ever seen fit to give me her hand, Herr Haydn. And I am too old now to entertain such hopes."

"A nephew, then?" Haydn persisted, determined to get to the bottom of the mystery.

"I am at a loss to understand these questions." The Count frowned, his geniality apparently exhausted at last. "Why should you wish to know such details?"

At a loss himself to provide a response without revealing more than he cared to, Haydn looked to his brother. Johann, as always, had a ready reply.

"My brother means no impertinence by these questions, Your Lordship. Herr Fugger, the banker, mentioned meeting you with Herr Affligio."—Haydn was glad his brother had chosen to omit the specifics.—"But the man the banker described as Count Kohary bears no resemblance to you."

"*Ach so!*" The Count's brow cleared. "He must've been mistaken. I have never met the banker. Although I did suggest to Affligio that he should request a letter of introduction to Fugger from Chancellor Kaunitz."

He had been right in his surmise, then, Haydn thought.

"Did the impresario ever approach you, seeking an investment in the theater?" he asked, wanting to satisfy himself on the point. "I am to ascertain whether any payments need to be paid out to his partners." It was a lie, but a small one, Haydn consoled himself. And in the service of the truth.

The Count's smile broadened. "I had no wish to take on his debts, Herr Haydn. I understand he had persuaded his singers to invest in his venture."

"His singers?" Haydn raised his eyebrows. "We have only heard of one." He looked at Johann and then turned back to the Count. "There were more?"

"He had persuaded Christian to invest," the Count replied.

"The bass, yes." Haydn nodded.

"That was later, of course. His very first partner was the singer who accompanied him when he approached me. I cannot recall her name, but she was a most striking woman."

"A woman," Haydn repeated. A striking one at that.

Who else could it be but Loretta Renier?

Chapter Thirty-Eight

MICHAEL was climbing down from a hired carriage when Haydn and Johann returned to the Esterházy Palace. The sight of his middle brother made Haydn's stomach clench up. He was tempted to hurry into the safety of the palace, but was loath to act the coward.

"I suppose he is here to fault me for leaving Leopold in prison," he muttered to Johann, bracing himself for the recriminations that were sure to follow.

But Michael's fleshy face, when he turned toward them, was wreathed in smiles, and the sight of his brothers seemed—oddly enough—to add to his joy.

"Brother!" He hastened toward them, hands outstretched. "I cannot thank you enough for what you have done. I will admit there were moments when I had my doubts. But you have proven me wrong."

"Wh-wh—?" Haydn was stumbling to bring out the word when Johann gracefully interjected.

"It is good to see you so joyous, Michael. But what is it our brother has done to so earn your gratitude?"

His eyes widening in astonishment, Michael looked from Haydn to Johann. "You have not heard the good news?"

"What good news?" Haydn asked cautiously. The only thing that could please Michael was not to be—made impossible by von Beer's intractability.

"Leopold has been returned to his family, Joseph. I am surprised you have not heard the news. He was let go not above an hour ago. I was so sure it was your doing, I came to thank you." The smile faded from Michael's face to be replaced by a suspicious frown. "Had you nothing to do with it?"

Haydn winced, experiencing a moment of unease. He could not in all honesty say that he had. Yet Michael would take that to mean that he had entirely neglected to do anything at all about the situation.

But before he could say anything, one way or the other, Johann once again intervened.

"Brother has been hard at work trying to persuade the Police Inspector to let Leopold go. He was able to convince the medical examiner of Leopold's innocence. But Herr von Beer was another matter altogether. When we left the police station, he was still reluctant to do the right thing."

Michael nodded, sagely. "God worked on him, then, I am sure of it. Joseph planted the seed, and the Lord did the rest. That is the only explanation for it, Johann."

"To be sure," Johann and Haydn agreed in unison, albeit not without exchanging puzzled glances. How had the mule-headed Police Inspector been brought to his senses?

"Herr Haydn! I am glad to see you." Von Beer raised his eyes from the papers on his desk to greet Haydn. But the glacial expression in his eyes and the stony cast of his lean features belied his assertion.

Haydn took a seat, surprised. The Police Inspector had never felt the need to confess any kind of joy at his presence.

Von Beer went on: "I have let the prisoner go, Leopold . . ." His frown suggested he was having trouble recalling the name.

"Mozart," Haydn supplied. "Yes, so I heard. I wished to thank you."

Von Beer's lips stretched into what was no doubt intended to be a smile; although in Haydn's opinion, the Police Inspector only managed to look even more like a wolf about to devour its prey.

"There's no need to thank me, Herr Haydn. Thank the Archbishop instead since you have managed to procure his favor."

What that meant, Haydn knew not, but von Beer gave him no opportunity to speak.

"I have let the Emperor know that it is thanks to you that our prisoner had to be released. That you know who the killer is and have sworn to bring him to justice."

"But I said no such thing!" Haydn protested. All the evidence pointed to one person, but the Police Inspector had still to stitch the facts together. It was clear he was refusing to do so.

And now His Majesty would hold Haydn accountable for not bringing the impresario's murderer to justice. "I merely established Herr Mozart's innocence."

What Leopold's employer had to do with the matter, Haydn did not understand at all. Nor did he care to ask. Von Beer seemed in no mood to supply him with answers.

"If you are so sure who it is not, it can only be because you know who it is," the Police Inspector countered, his steely gaze boring into Haydn's. "Is that not so?"

Haydn chose not to respond. It was going to be left to him, he understood, to break the bitter news to the Emperor that his own paramour, Loretta Renier, was involved in the impresario's heinous murder. Fräulein Renier and someone else, that much was clear.

With a light shrug and an easy smile, Haydn rose to his feet and took his leave. But as he walked slowly back to the Burgtheater, his mind was troubled.

The clatter of carriage wheels on the cobblestones, the clip-clop of horses' hooves, and the muffled rhythm of his shoes beating the street rang distantly in his ears. He walked, barely aware of the world around him.

Loretta Renier had swung the sheave at Affligio, but she had not stabbed him with the prop knife. That could only have been the mysterious gentleman Karl had seen in Affligio's chambers. The man who had impersonated Count Kohary and accompanied the impresario to Herr Fugger's bank.

Who could that man be? Loretta Renier, Affligio's first partner, dressed as a man?

A woman laden with a basket pushed past him. Haydn barely noticed, his mind still on the soprano.

Loretta Renier would make a most unlikely man, he thought. Besides, it would mean she had returned to Affligio's chambers after the maid had left in order to plunge the prop knife into his breast. Could she be quite so cold-blooded?

She *had* orchestrated his own demise not more than a few hours ago he reminded himself.

Still, Haydn could not help thinking it was some other singer, yet another partner Affligio had acquired—a man in disguise, which would explain why Karl had failed to recognize him.

From what Count Kohary had said, Loretta Renier had been Affligio's first partner. Could he have acquired another between the time he approached the Count and then sought out Herr Fugger for a loan? He did not think Loretta Renier had planned the entire affair alone.

Could a woman as frivolous as she—concerned solely with her appearance—have the intelligence to make the murder look like a stabbing and then pin the entire thing on someone else? The knife buried in Affligio's chest had made it seem quite plausible Leopold had done the deed.

The sheave, on the other hand, made it clear it was someone closely involved with the theater instead.

Still pondering the issue, Haydn strode into the Burgtheater, his head bowed.

<hr>

"Herr Haydn!" The greeting was made in a light tenor that caught Haydn's ears. His head rose sharply.

"Bastian?" He had not noticed before how slender the tenor was, almost like a woman in a trouser role. And was it his imagination or did Bastian's voice sound hoarse?

"You do not mean to keep us here, rehearsing, do you, Herr Haydn?" Bastian asked, straightening the lacy edges of his silk coat. His lean features were dark, as though he spent too much time in the sun.

"You do not mean to walk off in your costume, do you?" Haydn countered. The costumes were meant to be kept in the theater. But dressed as he was, Bastian could be mistaken for a nobleman, a minor count, even.

Bastian glanced down at his garb and smiled ruefully. "I was in such a hurry to leave, I had not realized I was still dressed in all my finery."

"It is no matter." Haydn was about to walk past him when Bastian stopped him again. "But I may leave after I have changed out of my costume, may I not?" he pleaded. "You were gone so long, Christian said we could rehearse another time."

Haydn nodded. "Yes, of course." He stepped forward, but then glanced over his shoulder. "I apologize for the delay. I was summoned to the police station. Leopold Mozart has been allowed to go."

"Indeed?" Bastian's eyes widened for a fraction of a second before regaining their normal size. "Then the Police Inspector is convinced he is innocent?"

"It would seem so."

But as he walked away, Haydn realized he had failed to clarify anything. Had it been a flash of dismay he'd seen in the tenor's eyes when he had mentioned Leopold's release?

He had barely reached the impresario's chambers when he was accosted by Karl, Greta, and Rosalie, all speaking in unison. Stepping inside the room, he held up his hand.

"One at a time, I beg of you. I can hardly understand a word."

It was Rosalie who poured out the account to him, helped sometimes by a word or two from Greta and a grunt or a nod from Karl.

"The handkerchief was found near the backstairs door?" Haydn frowned as he gingerly took the fabric. It was grubby.

"She must've used it to wipe the stair railing as she walked up that evening," Greta explained to him.

"That's why it looked as it did," Rosalie agreed, "splotchily cleaned."

"She or whoever else went up the stairs." Haydn nodded, dropping the fabric onto his desk. He was thinking of Bastian. Was it the tenor who had raced to His Grace's residence? The tenor who, dressed in an overcoat, had been mistaken for Leopold on a dark evening?

Yet why would Bastian have Loretta Renier's kerchief?

But now the maids were talking about the knife.

"It had a lever to prevent it from retracting?" Haydn's voice rose. "And you say the impresario himself had ordered it so?"

"That's what Felix says," Karl said with a roll of his eyes.

"Why would he lie?" Greta tossed her curls. "And it was Count Kohary—the man in Herr Affligio's chambers—who paid for the knife?"

"That was not Count Kohary," Haydn informed her absently.

"Did I not tell you?" Karl turned to the maids. But Haydn was barely listening.

He was still trying to absorb the implications of what he'd learned. What had Affligio and his mysterious partner wanted with a prop knife that would act like a regular one?

"They meant to get rid of Herr Oliveri," Rosalie's voice broke into his musings. "Herr Affligio was desperate for his money. Desperate to acquire a partner."

But had he not already acquired one in Loretta Renier? She was his first partner, according to Count Kohary. And the man with Affligio—the man who was more woman than man? Had that been Bastian?

How was it possible that after all these days he had more questions than answers? Haydn was about to drag his fingers through his locks when he realized he would only succeed in dragging his wig off his head. He stopped himself, hand awkwardly raised, elbow bent.

"Has Loretta Renier left?" He gazed sternly at Karl and the two maids. "I wish to speak with her."

⬥

As soon as he was alone, Haydn pulled out Affligio's account ledgers. If Johann was right, there would be some indication of which of his suppliers, patrons, and singers, the impresario had duped into joining his venture. Licking his thumb and forefinger, Haydn paged through the thick sheets of the ledger.

Ah, here was Coltellini's name. Was that a mark of some sort? He bent his head and peered closely at it, detecting the small symbol—almost like a tiny crucifix—scrawled next to the librettist's name. Most fitting, Haydn thought wryly, considering the nature of the venture.

He turned the pages over until he came to Gluck's name. It too had a similar mark next to it. In black ink, Haydn noted with a smile, recalling Gluck's objection to Loretta Renier's contract.

If the crucifix were an indication of a partnership forged with the impresario, Christian Steiner's name would be so marked as well. It was.

Haydn set down the ledger and leaned back in his chair. How had he not seen the notations in his earlier perusal? What of Count Kohary, he wondered. He sat forward, picked up the ledger, and leafed through its pages until he found the Count's name. He read the hastily jotted note about the missing subscription fee and—recalling the money His Lordship had given him—put a line through it.

"Paid in full," he wrote out in his neatest hand next to the entry he'd crossed out. The Count had not been lying. He was clearly not a partner. The tiny mark Affligio used to stipulate who his partners were was nowhere to be seen on the page.

As he flicked through the pages in search of Loretta Renier's name, another marked name caught his eye. But he was too preoccupied to pay much attention to it. But when he came to the page with the soprano's name, he saw nothing to indicate she had been a partner.

But how could that be? Haydn pushed the ledger away from him and sat back again. Had he been mistaken in his assumption that it was her Count Kohary had seen? But who else could it be? Matilda Bologna was beautiful enough, but only Loretta Renier could be described as striking.

Even so, he turned to Matilda's name. It was not marked in any way either.

Would the contracts serve to illuminate the matter? He pushed back his chair, went into the inner chamber, and pulled out the singers' contracts from the desk there. Bringing the stack back to the desk in the outer chamber, he sifted through it until he found Christian Steiner's name.

It was one of the general contracts—written and signed in blue—with a note at the end specifying that the bass was entitled to a share of the profits only. Christian had put his name to the additional clause as well.

The same clause had been entered into the contract the bass had signed for Haydn's opera. Christian agreed to forfeit his regular fee for a share of the profits garnered from ticket sales for each performance.

He searched for Loretta Renier's contract. Here was the general contract. He quickly perused it but could find no clause stipulating that she would only receive a share of the profits from each performance. That was strange. He read through the contract again more closely, and then a third time.

Had the soprano insisted on being paid a fee rather than sharing in the uncertain profits? If she was his first partner and knew the precarious situation the impresario found himself in, she may well have insisted on an arrangement like that to protect herself.

To make sure of the matter, he searched for the contract she had signed for his opera. It would be the most recent one each singer had signed and would, no doubt, have the most current information.

His eyes scanned the stilted language that the impresario used in his contracts, searching for the one clause that should've been there. But it wasn't. That was puzzling.

But there was also something not quite right with the document. Haydn set the paper down and stared at it. If only he could put his finger on what it was that seemed out of place.

His eyes roved over the sheet, inspecting each word and going over the large rounded hand in which Loretta Renier had signed her name. It was not as neatly done as her signature in the general contract, Haydn thought as he compared the two signatures. But it was the same hand, written in the same blue ink—

Blue ink. Haydn found his gaze ensnared by the blue letters sprawled across the page. The contracts for specific contracts were signed in black were they not? He shuffled through the untidy stack on his desk until he found the contract Christian had signed for *Le pescatrici.* The signature was in black.

What had Karl and Rosalie said? The contracts for the operas were signed at the Burgtheater—always in black ink. But the evening before he'd died, Affligio had run out of black ink and Herr Grimm at the bookstore had only been able to supply him with a pot of blue ink.

A chill ran through Haydn's being. Loretta Renier had signed her contract either a day before Affligio's murder or on the day itself. His eyes flickered from Christian's contract to the soprano's.

It was then that he saw it. Yet another difference between the two contracts. A small omission—one he had failed to catch earlier. But there it was, as plain as day—a mute testament to the truth.

The impresario had not been alive to see Loretta Renier put her name on this contract.

Chapter Thirty-Nine

LORETTA Renier's pretty pink lips were twisted into a displeased pout when she flounced into Haydn's presence.

"I was about to leave, Herr Kapellmeister." She stood before his desk, her hands on her hips. "What is it you want with me now? Christian said we could go."

"It will not take more than a moment of your time," Haydn responded firmly as he gestured for her to take a seat.

Reluctantly, Loretta lowered herself into the chair, but not before searching within her reticule for a handkerchief to brush the non-existent specks of dust off it. She was unable to find it, and used her hand instead.

"Dust bothers you, does it, Fräulein Renier?" Haydn couldn't help remarking.

"It bothers every person of sense, Herr Kapellmeister," she snapped. "I cannot abide dirt or disorder. What of it?"

"Your changing room does not, unfortunately, appear to bear witness to your distaste," Haydn parried. At the startled expression in her wide blue eyes, he went on: "The palace maids were complaining of it."

Loretta's nostrils flared. "It is hardly their place to complain, is it?"

Haydn leaned forward, his palms flat on his desk. "It is hardly your place to order the servants of His Serene Highness, Prince Nikolaus Esterházy. I doubt even the Emperor's favor would spare you the Prince's displeasure."

An expression of uncertainty mingled with apprehension flickered over Loretta's beautiful features. "There's no reason to tell His Serene Highness anything, is there? I meant no harm.

"But"—she bent her head toward him, her voice hushed—"you ought to know those girls behaved most cheekily toward Donna Oliveri. She merely asked them to go through the changing rooms, and they categorically refused. Even though she offered them a reward. I thought someone should teach them how to treat their betters."

Haydn pursed his lips. That was not what had occurred. The maids had already told him the entire tale.

"I doubt it is a lesson they need, Fräulein. They are trusted servants. And they bear Frau Oliveri—who appears to have treated them very graciously—the utmost gratitude."

Loretta seemed confused. "But Donna w—"

Haydn waved her objections away, fingering her contract. "That is not what I wished to discuss with you." He pushed the document toward Loretta.

She gave it the merest glance. "That is my signature, yes." Then she raised her large blue eyes and stared challengingly into his dark ones. "What of it?"

Haydn felt his anger growing. How brazen could the woman be? He had yet to see anything like it.

Jabbing his finger at the bottom, he said in a tightly contained tone, "It is missing, as I am sure you cannot fail to have noticed, both the impresario's countersignature and the Emperor's seal."

He raised his head and allowed his eyes to bore into her. "The contract was signed in this very room, and had it been signed on any day other than the day of Herr Affligio's demise, it would've been in black ink. But the impresario only had blue that Sunday. He was dead when you put your name to the contract, or he would surely have affixed the Emperor's seal to the document and added his own signature."

Loretta Renier drew back. "What are you suggesting?" she hissed. "That I killed him. His Majesty—"

Haydn was in no mood to hear her threats. "The Police Inspector is so convinced the Salzburger Leopold Mozart is not the killer, he has let the man go." He paused to let that sink in.

Loretta appeared to have trouble assimilating the news.

"He is convinced it is someone in the Burgtheater. And I must say I agree." Another pause. "He has asked me to look into the matter." That was certainly not an untruth. Von Beer had all but left the affair in his hands.

Loretta was stuttering, struggling to frame a response.

Haydn continued relentlessly on: "More than one person at the Burgtheater has attested to the fact that you were the last person to see the impresario that evening."

Loretta shook her head. "No, it was the Salzburger. The man had an appointment with Herr Affligio."

"You knew about that, did you?"

"Why shouldn't I? He told me about it himself. And he sent Karl—"

"To delay the time of their meeting. Herr Affligio was already dead by the time Herr Mozart arrived and knocked on the door, only to receive no answer."

Loretta started to say something, but Haydn held up his hand.

"Stay your lies, Fräulein. You were seen leaving the impresario's chambers by a reliable witness. The witness came into the room and was horror-struck to see the impresario lying senseless on the floor."

Haydn thrust his torso forward. "What is it that you are hiding, Fräulein Renier? Would it not be best to tell the truth? The evidence against you is such that the Police Inspector would have no choice but to arrest you."

He held up the grubby handkerchief the maids had found.

"Giulietta's handkerchief was found at the exact spot where His Grace, the Archbishop of Salzburg, caught sight of a figure he mistook for Leopold Mozart. It was you."

Loretta was shaking her head vehemently. "I didn't have the handkerchief with me. I remember now. It was after the rehearsal. Besides, I thought the killer left the Burgtheater by the backstairs."

He was about to ask her how she knew that when he recalled the details had been included in an article printed in the court newspaper.

"I would never use those stairs." Loretta held herself up stiffly. "They hadn't been cleaned in weeks. At Affligio's orders, if you must know."

Haydn frowned. The maids had said the same thing. Besides that, Loretta's statement seemed to contain the ring of truth. He tapped the contract sitting on the desk between them.

"This contract—clearly illegal—tells a different tale. Not to mention that the sheave that killed the impresario was found concealed in your changing room." He spread his hands wide. "I wished to give you the opportunity to tell the truth before approaching the Police Inspector." He paused meaningfully. "But you give me no choice."

Haydn glanced at the door, about to tell Loretta that Karl had at this very moment set out for the police station when Loretta finally broke her silence.

"I didn't kill him," she said in a small voice. "At least, I didn't mean to." She tilted her chin up defiantly. "And it was certainly not with a sheave."

⚬

"What did Loretta Renier tell you when you approached her, brother?" Johann lightly fingered the fork in front of him. Maria Anna had set the cutlery out, but the *Tafelspitz*—too hot to serve—was still cooling on a plate by the stove.

On the carriage ride back to Papa Keller's house, Haydn had recounted much of the day's events since he had parted from his brother earlier that afternoon. But he had not said very much more about his encounter with the soprano.

It was not only that the carriage had just then rolled to a stop before their destination, interrupting the conversation. Loretta Renier's confession had been so startling, Haydn was still mulling over its details.

That she had not killed the impresario was plainly evident. Herr Fischer, the medical examiner, had conducted a thorough examination of the dead body. It had been the sheave and not a dangerous concoction of valerian or any other sleeping potions that had killed the impresario.

But Loretta Renier had labored under the mistaken impression that she was responsible for poor Affligio's demise, and she had carried the heavy weight of guilt like a millstone around her neck.

Neither was it Loretta who had plunged the prop knife into the impresario's body, making it look like a stabbing. And just as Haydn had suspected, it was not the soprano who had rushed posthaste to the Archbishop's residence. She'd been too distraught to do much more than flee.

Haydn had also deduced that it was not the soprano who had allowed herself to be mistaken for Leopold in the evening gloom that Sunday. Although why—and how—her handkerchief had found its way to the top of the backstairs, he could not fathom.

Unable to face the appalling result of her act, Loretta had confided in someone—an individual who had promised to cover up both the crime and its cause for her and to throw the scent of suspicion elsewhere. It was the identity of that confidante that had stunned Haydn.

It made so little sense, he had at first suspected the singer of lying. Shards of information shifted within his brain. A different pattern was beginning to emerge, but it was so startling he could not allow himself to accept it.

"Of course, it could still have been someone else who committed the murder," he murmured, unaware he was speaking loud enough to be overheard.

"Brother?" Johann's astonished voice broke into his musings.

Haydn stared blankly into his brother's eyes. Johann repeated his original question, forming the words twice before the sense of them penetrated Haydn's befogged brain.

Aware of Maria Anna glancing suspiciously at him as she deftly placed thin slices of boiled beef, carrots, and parsnips on a plate, Haydn collected his thoughts.

He gripped his fork. "Apparently, Affligio wished to marry her," he said at last.

Papa Keller was at the table, too, and he had no desire to add to the gentleman's store of gossip. Not before he had delved to the root of the matter, in any event.

"That was why he called her into his office that Sunday. To beg her to call it off with the Emperor and accept his hand instead."

Maria Anna brought his plate over and snorted. "Why in the name of heaven would she do that, a beautiful young woman like that? The impresario was fifty if he was a day and stout to boot." She set the plate laden with beef, vegetables, fried potato slices, and horseradish sauce before Haydn.

"I expect he hoped she would, like our Lord, look at his heart and not his outward appearance," Haydn said mildly as he pierced a wedge of beef and brought it to his mouth.

Maria Anna's only response was another snort, and even Papa Keller laughed heartily.

"Being the Emperor's mistress is a lucrative business. And La Renier is no fool. Not even the handsomest man could tempt her away."

"What did she tell him?" Johann asked, gazing curiously at Haydn.

"She steadfastly refused. He, of course, was most persistent. At that point, she poured a large tincture of her sleeping potion into his wine. It was merely to make him drowsy, but it knocked him unconscious instantly."

"And thus he fell to the ground like a heavy log and cracked his skull," Papa Keller surmised through a mouthful of beef and horseradish sauce. Maria Anna admonished her father, but he was not to be kept silent. He continued to speak as he chewed. "Poor woman! Imagine having to live with the guilt of that."

"And that is all there is to it?" Johann's voice barely rose, but his eyebrows were raised high above his wide gray eyes, and there was an expression of deep skepticism in them. Haydn sighed. His brother knew him all too well.

He tightened his lips, giving an imperceptible shake of the head. "That is her story. It may still have been a deliberate act." Loretta had also said the impresario had intentionally withheld the contract for Haydn's opera from her to force her hand. Seeing him dead, she had taken the opportunity to sign her name on it.

"Husband is right. It could just be a tall tale," Maria Anna said, bringing a plateful of buttered bread to the table. "Besides, the impresario was not the marrying kind. Isn't that right, Papa?"

Papa Keller nodded so vigorously, his glasses slipped down his nose, and the thick curls covering his head quivered. "Definitely not. Why, there was some talk of him pursuing the other woman. She's no beauty, but she's quite remarkable in her own way."

"Donna Oliveri?" Maria Anna supplied.

Papa Keller nodded again. "Most likely it was because her husband possessed money, and Affligio wished to interest him in an investment."

"And when he did, I suppose Affligio stopped his pursuit, instantly," Haydn surmised.

"Oh no, not at all."

"No?" Haydn looked up startled. Surprised that his father-in-law could be so mistaken.

Gregorio Oliveri was no fool. He was adamantly against the venture."

Haydn remained silent. Affligio's ledgers were proof his father-in-law was mistaken. The tiny crucifix that marked Affligio's partners had been next to Gregorio's name as well. He saw no reason to correct the old gentleman, though. It mattered not—one way or the other—whether Affligio had succeeded in persuading the dead performer or not?

"Then he died—a tragic accident." Papa Keller shook his head. "Although I've had my doubts about that."

"The timing of it was suspicious," Maria Anna agreed. She looked at Haydn. "Don't you think so, husband?"

Seeing no other way but to concur, Haydn mutely inclined his head. "But appearances can be deceptive," he cautioned, although the more he considered the matter, the more it made sense. But that coupled with what he had learned from Renier that afternoon only made things so much worse.

His stomach churned. The depth of evil in the world was to be wondered at, he thought gravely.

"Anyway," Papa Keller continued, "no sooner was Gregorio dead than Affligio's pursuit of Donna ceased. Or talk of it ceased. Who can tell what really happened? And it's true she's hardly beautiful—or young, for that matter."

Chapter Forty

UNABLE to sleep, Haydn threw the covers off himself and quietly eased himself out of his bed. He reached for the tall unlit taper on his nightstand, lit it by the fire burning in the porcelain stove, set it carefully on a candle stand, and let himself out into the hallway.

He hesitated by the door. Should he sit in the parlor where Papa Keller kept a bottle of good cherry brandy? Or should he make his way to the kitchen? Maria Anna, he recalled, had forgotten to throw away the previous day's coffee. He could heat it up, sit at the kitchen table, and ponder the questions that troubled his mind.

His mind made up, he walked noiselessly toward the kitchen and set about heating up the stale coffee. His thoughts rattled uneasily in his mind as he shook the handle of the saucepan, agitating the brown liquid within it.

When Loretta Renier had told him about her confidante's promise to cover up the crime, he had instantly assumed it was the confidante who had driven the prop knife into Affligio's breast.

But no one other than Affligio's mysterious and yet to be identified partner knew that the knife had a lever to prevent it from retracting.

As he agitated the coffee, he noticed tiny bubbles breaking the surface of the dark brew. It would soon be hot enough to drink. He shook the pan again just as he had seen Maria Anna do.

Had the lever been in position at the time the prop knife had been used? Or had it been mere chance that Loretta's abettor had succeeded in plunging it into the impresario's chest?

And who had gone straight to the Archbishop? Only Affligio's partner would have known of the arrangement with His Grace. But surely the theater could not have contained Renier, her confidante, Affligio's partner . . . as well as the killer?

Larger bubbles broke the surface of the coffee. Haydn took the saucepan off the fire and set it on the green tiles lining the countertop. He brought a mug down, carefully poured the hot brew into it, found some milk, and added a spoonful of sugar. Then, bringing the cup to his lips, he took a cautious sip.

Dear God, it was vile! He should have settled for the cherry brandy instead. But it was too late for that. Sighing, he took the awful brew to the table.

Then again there was the matter of the sheave? What had made the killer place it in Loretta Renier's room? Was it because she alone of all the singers was known for keeping her changing room unkempt? Or was it because the killer had known she might plausibly be considered the murderer?

But there was only one person Loretta had confided in. And it would seem her confidante had meant to put Loretta in the crosshairs of the Police Inspector—or anyone investigating the crime. But what could have provoked such a malicious attack?

Setting the coffee down, he pulled out a chair and lowered himself into it. He doubted there were quite so many individuals roaming the Burgtheater that evening. That meant either Affligio's partner had killed him. Or Loretta's confidante.

He took a second sip of his coffee and grimaced. How had he managed to make a mess of such a simple task?

But if it was Loretta's confidante who had also fetched His Grace, then the same individual was Affligio's mysterious partner as well. But Affligio's ledgers—

His eyes widened as a possibility occurred to him. Then he shook his head. Even so, why kill Affligio? Was there any truth to the rumors he'd heard that day? More than one person had mentioned it. Even the maid who had discovered Affligio's corpse had let drop a comment or two on the matter.

She might have been mistaken, but Haydn knew that was unlikely. No one knew more about what went on anywhere than the maids who went from room to room with their pails and mops.

But the handkerchief—Giulietta's handkerchief. How had the killer managed to get hold of it?

Making a wry face, Haydn gulped down the rest of his coffee, rinsed out the cup, and walked back to the bedroom. Was he dealing with three separate individuals? Or just one? He couldn't be sure.

By the morning, Haydn had come to the disquieting conclusion that Loretta Renier's confidante was both the elusive partner they had been seeking as well as the impresario's killer.

As the carriage sped through the streets, bearing Johann and himself to the Esterházy Palace, Haydn weighed the facts again. Would the impresario's partner have been as eager to dispatch Gregorio Oliveri as Affligio himself? Most certainly. It was the only way to gain access to Gregorio's money.

To blame Leopold for Affligio's murder made equally good sense. The impresario's partner had been privy to the arrangement with the Archbishop and had certainly taken advantage of it.

Moreover, what better way to completely eliminate the possibility of Leopold ever being put in charge of the Burgtheater? The prospect could've pleased no one, Leopold had so successfully alienated everyone at the theater.

But why kill Affligio? A light breeze wafted through the open carriage window as Haydn considered the question, causing the ringlets on his wig to flutter.

If the rumors he had heard were correct, there had been a betrayal of the deepest kind. Or was it the threat of dismissal? His breath caught as he examined this possibility. Dear God, it couldn't have been Loretta Renier who was in danger of being dismissed. Affligio may have withheld the contract for *Le pescatrici*, but would he have had her sign the general contract if he'd meant to let her go? Of course not!

But it might well have been Affligio's partner—and Loretta Renier's confidante—about to be shown the door. Haydn gripped the leather seat, stunned by his surmise. The contracts would tell the tale. And now that he knew what to look for, it would be a simple enough matter to verify.

He pursed his lips. Poor Loretta had suffered the singular misfortune of entrusting her secrets to the killer. Small wonder she had been so skillfully set up. And he, fool that he was, had nearly fallen for the ruse!

The carriage rolled to a stop in front of Wallnerstrasse 4.

"The singers are to rehearse here," Johann informed him as they climbed down from the carriage and entered the palace. "I have undertaken to work with Bastian and Ernst while Luigi rehearses with Frau Oliveri."

Haydn nodded. All three of the singers needed to memorize their melodic lines, he recalled.

Johann must've read his mind, for he replied as though Haydn had spoken his thoughts out loud. "Bastian and Ernst can read some music, but I fear Donna Oliveri is completely deficient in the skill. Her voice and range more than make up for it, however. Affligio must have considered her quite the asset. He was fortunate to have her."

"I suppose he was," Haydn quietly agreed. They had just stepped through the palace door, and a figure hovering by the staircase caught his eye. A nobleman? A visitor, no doubt. He stared curiously, wondering where the footmen were, when the figure turned.

Good heavens, it was—

"Frau Oliveri?" Johann turned to his brother, astonished. "Whatever is she doing down here? And dressed like that, too! She is supposed to be working with Luigi."

Before Haydn could respond, Donna Oliveri—a slim figure clothed in the costume designed for Romeo—saw them and stepped forward.

"Herr Kapellmeister, Master Johann! I have been waiting a good fifteen minutes for you both. I regret to inform you I cannot rehearse today. None of us can."

"Any why not?" Haydn could not prevent a frown of intense displeasure from creasing his brow.

"Christian wishes us to rehearse *Romeo e Giulietta*—from the scene in which Giulietta hands her handkerchief to Romeo."

"Giulietta hands her handkerchief to Romeo?" Haydn repeated the words uncomprehendingly, as though they had been uttered in a foreign tongue. He had been struck by a sudden thought. And now he stared wide-eyed at Donna Oliveri, considering the implications of the startling revelation he had just received.

"Herr Kapellmeister?" Donna Oliveri, looking puzzled, turned from Haydn to Johann.

Haydn repeated himself, much to the confusion and consternation of his listeners. He could hardly do any more.

"It is in the script, brother," Johann reminded him. "Do you not recall?"

"Yes, yes, I do," he stammered. "I cannot believe I did not consider it sooner."

"Consider what?" Donna Oliveri wanted to know.

Quickly, Haydn recovered himself. "That Herr Steiner might wish to rehearse the scene again. It certainly needs to be gone over." He managed a smile. "It is perfectly all right, Frau Oliveri. *Le pescatrici* can wait for another day."

"It was good of you to let us know," Johann added. "But there was no need to trouble yourself. You could simply have sent Karl."

They were about to take their leave of the singer when a footman wearing an agitated expression hurried up.

"Herr Haydn! There you are. His Serene Highness must see you at once. It is the Archbishop of Salzburg."

"What about the Archbishop of Salzburg?" Haydn had all but forgotten Donna Oliveri's presence.

"His Grace arrived this morning demanding to see you. He will hear no excuse nor leave until he has confronted you."

"Take us to him," Haydn ordered. "This will be about Leopold, mark my words," he said in a low voice to his brother. Out of the corner of his eye, he caught the amused smile that crept over Donna Oliveri's face.

"His Grace cannot be overly happy the Salzburger has been released," the singer lightly remarked as she took her leave.

⸻ ❖ ⸻

Hieronymus von Colloredo, Archbishop of Salzburg, was a man who clearly brooked no opposition. His eyes as he glared at Haydn blazed with barely contained fury. His nose swooped down the length of his face, forming an imperious hook over the contemptuous curl of his large, mobile lips.

Were it not for his employer's presence, Haydn might well have felt intimidated.

His Grace leaned forward, his fists planted on his knees. "By what authority, may I ask, Herr Haydn, did you compel the Police Inspector to release Leopold Mozart?"

Prince Nikolaus, Haydn's employer, released an audibly irritated breath. "The Archbishop is under the impression that you used his name to force the Police Inspector's hand, Haydn. It is in vain that I have explained you would do no such thing."

"I am afraid there has been a misunderstanding." Haydn chose his words carefully. He was well aware of the lie Karl's cousin had perpetrated and all too conscious that a single misplaced word or phrase from him would cause both Steffi, His Grace's maid, and Karl's young cousin to be dismissed from their positions.

"You did not mean to have the man released?" the Prince asked.

"No, that is not it. But I did not suggest I was acting on His Grace's authority. Nor did anyone else, for that matter."

He turned to the Archbishop who was still fuming. "That is not what I heard," His Grace hissed through tightly clenched lips.

Haydn spread his hands wide in a gesture of supplication. "When your maid realized she had—albeit inadvertently—made a false statement, she immediately stepped forward. Being under your authority, she feared the Almighty might hold Your Grace responsible for her mistake.

"She was so agitated on that point, Herr von Beer or one of the police guards no doubt misunderstood her, thinking Your Grace had commanded her to come forward."

Succinctly, he recounted the facts. "Your Grace had not, I take it, met the man who called for your assistance that day?"

"No." An annoyed, aggrieved expression descended upon the Archbishop's features. "The thickheaded dimwit Affligio was pleased to call an assistant had already fled, leaving me to find my way to the theater on my own."

"And that is when Your Grace saw the figure on the backstairs?"

"It was Leopold. The wig, the hat, I would recognize them anywhere."

"But Your Grace did not see the individual's features."

"Of course not." The Archbishop pursed his lips, his tone testy as though he were dealing with a numbskull. "Dusk had set in. Besides, his face was turned away from me."

"Then you were duped, my dear Archbishop," Prince Nikolaus concluded. He reclined lazily in his seat with his hands clasped together on his protruding belly. "Anyone can see that."

Before the Archbishop could respond, Haydn leaned forward with a question. "Was Your Grace not surprised to hear that a man you knew so well—one of your own employees—was assaulting another?"

"No," the Archbishop replied crisply. "Affligio had already complained of his behavior to me. At that point, it came as no surprise."

"Indeed." His Grace was lying. Haydn knew it, but how was he to expose the truth?

"The impresario was unfortunately not a man who could keep much to himself," he began. "He boasted of the connection he had with Your Grace and of your desire to support him in his endeavor."

"I agreed to a partnership. What of it?" His Grace eyed Haydn coldly.

"Affligio was heard to lament," Johann quietly intruded upon the conversation, "that Herr Mozart could not be easily diverted from his Christian ways." The Archbishop's face turned white at the words, but he remained silent as Johann continued to speak. "He feared that unhappy fact might jeopardize his partnership with Your Grace."

"God in heaven!" Prince Nikolaus's ears had perked up at this bit of information. "Why would it do any such thing?" He turned in avid curiosity to the Archbishop. "What kind of arrangement did you have with the fellow, Colloredo?"

"The impresario might of course have been exaggerating the details," Haydn said, looking meaningfully at the Archbishop. "What he thought he was expected to do is too vile to repeat. And it was out of a sense of delicacy that I kept those details from the Police Inspector."

It pleased him to see the Archbishop's lips tighten and his eyes widen.

"But that fact," Haydn went on, "and some others that have since been brought to my attention have convinced me Leopold was not the killer."

"Who is, then?" the Prince asked.

"Someone else associated with the Burgtheater," Haydn replied. "And there may be a way of exposing the individual."

"There may?" Johann looked at him, astonished. Haydn nodded. There had been no time to share his revelations with his younger brother.

Turning to the Archbishop, Haydn continued, "May I ask who it was who alerted you to Herr Mozart's release from prison?"

"A person claiming to be Affligio's partner. A Count Kohary."

"Count Kohary?" Johann repeated, astounded. He would've said more but Haydn interrupted him.

"This Count Kohary, is he a short, stout, elderly gentleman?"

The Archbishop frowned. "Quite the contrary. He is slender, swarthy, of middling height, and no older than yourself."

"Ah, that Count Kohary," Johann breathed much to the surprise of both Prince Nikolaus and the Archbishop.

"It is someone within the Burgtheater who has assumed the Count's identity," Haydn explained. "I have yet another question, Your Grace. Had you paid Affligio the initial investment to become his partner?"

"I left the silver on his desk that night. He did not respond to my knock and when he failed to confirm the receipt of the money the next morning, I was naturally anxious and immediately set out to alert the Emperor."

Haydn nodded. It was all as he had suspected. "We can use the silver to entrap the killer. But I shall need Your Grace's influence with the Police Inspector. He is loath to listen to anything I have to say."

Chapter Forty-One

THE rehearsal was already underway when Haydn arrived at the Burgtheater. He entered the auditorium—as though he were a spectator—and strode down to the stage. But how he was to set his plan into motion, he knew not.

Still, he crossed his fingers at his side, trusting to the impulse of the moment.

The seats in the second parterre were empty, but a bulky figure—Christian, no doubt—occupied a seat in the parterre noble. It was the section directly in front of the stage, reserved for the nobility and with the best view of the proceedings.

Haydn was aware of Christian's head jerking up with a single, sharp movement as he strode past, but he ignored the bass, coming to a halt behind the partition that separated the parterre noble from the orchestra.

He brought his hands together in a loud, startling clap. Giulietta, about to give her handkerchief to Romeo, leapt back with a shriek. Then her hand rose to press itself over her mouth. Romeo spun around, his hand on his sword. In the scenic stage, the tenors Ernst and Bastian, standing with their heads together behind a flat shaped like a bush, immediately drew apart.

"What is the matter, Herr Kapellmeister?" Donna Oliveri, garbed as Romeo, asked. "Is the scene not to your liking?"

"It was being played just as it ought to be, I thought," Karl said from the wings. He peered out at Haydn, astonished. The Kapellmeister had never interrupted a rehearsal so rudely.

Behind Haydn, Christian covered his face and groaned. "The production is doomed, I tell you. Doomed." He released his head and raised despairing eyes toward Haydn. "What possessed you to barge in like that? It has taken us all morning to get to this point. And for once, Loretta had neither forgotten her lines nor her kerchief."

"I apologize." Haydn swiveled around, taking in the performers. "But I have received most disturbing news."

"If it's about Leopold Mozart's release," Christian informed him, "you may save your breath. We have already heard the news. Donna told us just this morning."

"It is not that." Haydn surveyed the company, deliberately looking as grave as he possibly could. "The Archbishop of Salzburg called upon me this morning." He paused again. "His Grace wished to find out why no one had bothered to acknowledge receiving the silver he had left for Herr Affligio on Sunday."

Christian's eyes narrowed. "The Archbishop was here that day? And with silver?"

Even the tenors came forward at that revelation. The killer would not have expected anyone to discover the existence of the money.

"Summoned by someone claiming to be from the theater," Haydn said. "The Police Inspector is convinced it was the impresario's killer —an attempt to blame Herr Mozart for his own deed. The person left before His Grace could meet him.

"Then when His Grace arrived with the money he intended to invest in the Burgtheater, Herr Affligio was nowhere to be seen. He departed, leaving his purse on the impresario's desk. But the money is nowhere to be found. No one has seen it."

"It was stolen?" It was Karl who spoke. Ernst and Bastian exchanged perplexed glances.

"By the killer," Haydn replied. "The police guards are quite convinced of it."

Loretta Renier looked as white as a sheet, he was pleased to notice. He had not bothered to reassure her the previous evening that she was no longer under suspicion.

It will be all the better to convince the killer that it was she who did the vile deed, Haydn thought to himself.

"Why do you bother telling us this?" Donna Oliveri asked. "You cannot think one of us would stoop to do such a thing, can you?"

Haydn turned to her. "No, of course not, madam. But I merely wish you all"—he swiveled around to survey each of them in turn—"to stay alert to its appearance. Whoever has it is surely a killer."

A small smile lit up Donna Oliveri's dark features. "To be sure."

Haydn was about to turn away when Loretta Renier clutched at his sleeve, preventing him from leaving. He glanced down at her. Her blue eyes were wide with consternation and her lower lip trembled.

"May I have a word with you, Herr Kapellmeister?" she asked. "In private, if you please?"

"Can it not wait until after the rehearsal?" Christian brusquely demanded before Haydn could respond.

"It is Fräulein Renier's contract," Haydn explained, turning to the bass. "It needs to be finalized."

It was most fortunate the soprano had approached him herself. It granted him the opportunity he'd been seeking to give Loretta the instructions she would need to bring the situation to a head.

"And it had better be done sooner rather than later."

***

In the vast area beneath the Burgtheater auditorium, Rosalie and Greta waited breathlessly to play their roles in the spectacle Herr Haydn had designed.

"Is Herr Haydn sure of his facts?" Greta whispered into Rosalie's ear as they desultorily swept the section immediately behind the broad, crimson-carpeted staircase.

Rosalie nodded. Greta had already left for the Burgtheater when Herr Haydn had sent for them to explain the details of the ruse he'd devised to draw out the killer. It had come as no small surprise to her that the Kapellmeister believed Miss High-and-Mighty to be innocent of the crime of murder.

And Greta was having an even harder time believing it.

Still bent over her broom, Rosalie swiveled her head around to look at her. "Fräulein Renier's contract was not the only one with a problem. There was another without either the impresario's signature or the Emperor's seal. Meaning it was signed after Herr Affligio had met his Maker."

"Dear God!" Greta gasped as both her eyebrows simultaneously rose.

"It was one of the general contracts, signed in blue. Or else Herr Haydn would've caught it sooner. That it wasn't signed well before his death can only mean the impresario intended to dismiss the performer."

"And for that he was killed?" Greta stared at Rosalie, aghast.

"It was but one of many reasons." She'd barely finished speaking when she heard the sound she'd been instructed to wait for—a resounding rap on the newel post above. Muffled steps sounded on the stairs and a few minutes later, Herr Haydn swept into view followed by Fräulein Renier.

The Kapellmeister had managed to bring the rehearsal to a halt. The moment they had been waiting for had arrived.

"I still can't believe it's not her," Greta hissed into her ear. "Such an obnoxious woman. I wouldn't put anything past her—not even murder!"

"Shh!" Rosalie admonished her friend. "At any minute now, they'll be coming down."

A murmur of voices floated down the stairs to their perked-up ears. It was followed by the heavy sound of several footsteps.

Rosalie signaled to her friend. Energetically running the broom over the floor, she began in a loud whisper, "Did the police guard really say that?"

"Oh, yes!" Greta was striving to inject some emotion into her lines. "The Police Inspector is certain she murdered the impresario, and equally sure she stole the money left on his desk. It's just a question of finding it, and then Fräulein Renier will be arrested. Serves her right, too!" Greta couldn't help adding.

Rosalie smiled. Greta's spontaneity had made her speech all the more believable. "But they have searched her apartment, haven't they, and not found a thing?"

The footsteps were coming closer, and she pumped her palm up, indicating that Greta should speak in a louder voice.

Greta obediently allowed her voice to rise. "Mark my words," she said, "she's hidden the money somewhere within the Burgtheater. Karl's cousin says the Police Inspector will be here before long, demanding to search the place. The prop room, the workshops, even the changing rooms."

Their words must have carried, for the tramping of footsteps slowed. Out of the corner of her eyes, Rosalie caught sight of three figures trooping down the stairs, heads shaking gravely as they looked at each other.

"Fräulein Renier—" Greta was going on when Rosalie deliberately made a loud shushing sound.

"Be quiet!" she hissed loud enough to be heard by the performers. "I hear footsteps. We could be overheard."

She pulled Greta's hand and quietly moved aside, sweeping all the while. Heads bent low, they pretended not to notice the three male figures that strode past them and in through the door that led to the changing rooms. Herr Steiner hesitated by the door, half-turning as though he wished to question them further, but he changed his mind.

Rosalie released the breath she'd been holding as he opened the door and followed his companions in.

When the door to the changing rooms had clanged shut, Greta bent closer to Rosalie and whispered, "Do you think they heard?"

Rosalie nodded. "The trap's been set. It only remains for one of them to take the bait."

Loretta Renier waited until Haydn had unlocked the door to the impresario's chambers before confronting him.

"I must know," she began, her features white, her lips trembling, "does the Police Inspector consider me guilty of Herr Affligio's murder?"

Still standing by the door, Haydn gazed down at the soprano, debating whether to tell her the truth. But Herr Gluck had disparaged her acting abilities, and Haydn had seen nothing to dispute the composer's judgment.

"I fear all the evidence points to you, Fräulein Renier," he said gently. *God forgive me this small lie,* he thought. *But without it, the plan has no chance of success.*

Loretta's eyes widened in dismay. "But I am no thief, Herr Kapellmeister," she protested. "I did not take any money, I swear it." She twisted her fingers around the brass door handle.

"It is not just the money, Fräulein. You were—as far as anyone knows —the last person to see the impresario. There is the matter of the handkerchief, the bloodied sheave found in your room. And the contract you illegally signed gives you a strong motive."

"But Giuseppe—Herr Affligio—withheld it from me, as I have already explained." She swallowed convulsively, then raised her blue eyes to him in a strong plea. "Can you not speak with the Police Inspector?"

Haydn shrugged ruefully. "He is disinclined to hear anything I have to say. The discovery of the stolen money is our only hope. The Police Inspector is convinced whoever has it must be the killer. If we could only find it . . ." He left the thought unfinished.

"Then there is no hope for me." Loretta glanced away, shaken. "I know not where the money is. Nor how to find it. What can I do? I am not liked, I am well aware of it. There is no one here who will take my part, and I certainly cannot approach the Emperor."

It was the opportunity Haydn had been waiting for. "You have at least one friend, Fräulein Renier. Your confidante may perchance bestir the others to action. If the money is found, it will be proof of your innocence."

Something like hope shone in the singer's eyes and she turned to leave. Confident the trap had been sprung, Haydn watched her go. The money would find its way to her changing room, he was sure of it. All Herr von Beer had to do was lie in wait for it.

———

The atmosphere within Loretta Renier's closet was oppressive. It was a confined space, made more so by the numerous satin and silk skirts that encompassed Haydn and his two companions—von Beer the Police Inspector and Fugger the banker.

"How long must we stand here in the dark, Herr Haydn?" Von Beer's voice echoed eerily in the stillness. Haydn had insisted upon snuffing out the single taper they had brought in. "It has been an hour or more, and your killer has yet to make an appearance."

Haydn sighed. The Police Inspector had made no bones about his skepticism regarding Haydn's surmise.

"I have seen operas with plots more believable, Herr Haydn. Besides, was it not yesterday that you were convinced Fräulein Renier should be arrested for the murder?"

Fortunately, the Emperor—egged on by the Archbishop, who was eager to have his money back—had forced von Beer's hand. But how long could he persuade the Police Inspector to stay and to retain the police guards he had brought with him?

"Patience, Herr von Beer!" Haydn whispered, forcing himself to stay calm. "It has been no more than twenty minutes. The bait has been set, the fish hooked. It is but a matter of time now."

Von Beer shifted, his elbow jabbing painfully into Haydn's ribs in the crowded closet.

"It is a fool's errand, mark my words," he grumbled in a low undertone. "All these men brought out for nothing."

That was the Emperor's doing. His Majesty had insisted upon placing police guards in every changing room, by the backstairs as well as the front entrance of the theater.

There were men concealed in the tiny closet where the ropes, sandbags, and sheaves were stored as well. His Majesty had wished to accompany them but had been easily dissuaded from that course of action. But it had not prevented him from sending Fugger along with them.

"The man has an interest in the matter," His Majesty had insisted. "He should be there!"

Now as von Beer grumbled on, Haydn was grateful for the banker's presence. It made the whole operation more bearable. After a while, even Fugger felt compelled to whisper: "Would it not be best to stay quiet, Herr von Beer? We risk alerting the killer to our presence."

Von Beer snorted, but—unable to refute the good sense of Fugger's remarks—subsided at last into silence.

It was utterly quiet now. Only the ticking of the clock could be heard in the inky stillness. Haydn waited, hardly daring to breathe. Johann and Luigi were nearby, he knew. God forbid, any harm should befall them. He had not been able to dissuade them from coming.

At last a quiet creak penetrated the silence, followed by a slow, careful scrape, then a muffled footstep, and the tiny click of the door closing.

Beside him, Haydn felt von Beer grow alert. The closet door was slightly ajar, and all three men strained to see who had entered the room.

The changing room was clothed in darkness, but through the gloom, Haydn made out a slender figure. A match flared, and the flickering flame of the candle revealed the intruder's face.

Haydn heard a sharp inhalation of breath beside him.

"It is Count Kohary!" Fugger hissed. "I recognize the man—it is the same wig and the garment is very nearly the same as well."

"Taken from the Burgtheater's stock of costumes," Haydn said in a low voice. "And that, if I mistake not"—he tipped his chin at the large leather pouch in the intruder's hands—"is the Archbishop's money."

Von Beer was about to open the closet door to confront the man, but Haydn put out his hand to restrain him. "Allow me."

He stepped out of the closet.

"Frau Oliveri!"

The intruder spun around. Accustomed to seeing her in male garb, Haydn had recognized the singer despite her disguise and despite the wig she had hastily thrown over her dark curls.

"I have been expecting you." Haydn held out his palm. "It was good of you to return the Archbishop's money. It was not yours to take."

The startled expression on the singer's swarthy features was replaced by a sneer.

"I will not ask how you found me out, you are a clever man. But it was not wise of you to come alone."

She drew out a dagger from her sleeve and held it out.

"It is over. Turn yourself in, Frau Oliveri." Haydn took a cautious step toward her.

"Take but one more step, and I will not hesitate to plunge the blade into your breast. I have done it twice."

"Do it a third," von Beer boomed, coming out from the closet, "and you will be a dead woman."

Haydn kept his eye on Frau Oliveri, whose eyes darted wildly from him to the Police Inspector and to Fugger.

Luigi had by now appeared at the door, his own pistol held out. "Drop your knife, Frau Oliveri. The Police Inspector may spare your life. But I will not."

Donna Oliveri stood frozen, staring at the men before her. Then after what seemed like an eternity, her knife clattered to the floor. The leather pouch followed suit, falling with a muffled thud on the wooden floorboards.

"He deserved to die!" she shrieked with her head thrown back and her fists clasped angrily at her side. "That cheating swine deserved to die!"

Chapter Forty-Two

HAYDN dipped his pen into the pot of black ink on Affligio's desk. Eager to begin work, he had arrived at the Burgtheater early that morning. Now he shook the ink off the tip of his nib and pulled a sheet of paper with its neatly lined staves toward himself.

The opening phrases of the overture he was composing needed to be notated while they were still fresh in his mind. How exquisitely wonderful it was, he thought, to return to the day-to-day business of being a Kapellmeister.

The pages of Karl's libretto—an especially well executed *dramma giocoso*—lay open on his right, and he glanced down at the work from time to time as he quickly jotted down the musical notes.

Judging by the libretto, the impresario's assistant was a skilled storyteller with a flair for the dramatic. Haydn had asked for and started reading the work as soon as he'd arrived that morning. The opera had pleased him so greatly, musical phrases had effortlessly presented themselves to his mind.

The daily running of the Burgtheater—and Affligio's murder—had left him little time for anything else. But now, with the murder resolved, he could once more turn his mind to music. It would not be until later in the day that the singers would come in to rehearse. Moreover, the Prince had assured Haydn he would soon be relieved of his duties as impresario.

"His Serene Highness will not regret hiring Karl," Haydn told himself as he worked. He had already broached the subject of hiring a librettist for the theater in Eszterháza. The Prince—delighted at the prospect of putting on original works in his theater—had authorized Haydn to make an offer.

"As long as the man possesses talent, Haydn—it goes without saying," His Serene Highness had said.

The offer was contingent upon the quality of the libretto, and Haydn had yet to make it. He was about to send for the young man when there was a knock on the door.

He raised his eyes.

"Ah, Karl!" Haydn gestured the young man in. "I was about to send for you." He was going to say more when he saw a familiar figure following Karl into the room.

"Papa Keller? What brings you here?"

"Your wigs, Sepperl!" Papa Keller staggered into the room, bearing three large black Chinese lacquer boxes. "They are ready. I would've given them to you this morning, but you had already left."

Haydn thrust his chair back, striding around his desk to relieve his father-in-law of his burden.

"Have you the receipt? His Serene Highness will need to sign it before Herr Geld, the paymaster, can issue the sum."

"There is no need for that!" Christian Steiner's deep bass sounded at the door. He strode into the room and plucked the receipt from Papa Keller's outstretched hand. "The Burgtheater is quite capable of making its own payments."

⚫

"Indeed!" Haydn was too stunned to protest. He set the stack of boxes down on a table by the wall. Where the money was to come from, he knew not. The Archbishop's purse had, as far as he knew, been returned to him. He was still struggling to frame his question when Christian with a smile provided the explanation he had been seeking.

"The Archbishop has graciously allowed us the use of his purse."

"In return for—?" Karl asked the question in Haydn's mind. He cast a worried glance at Haydn.

"In return for nothing. He does not wish to invest in the theater any longer." Christian pivoted his bulky frame toward Haydn. "Thanks to your employer, the Emperor has undertaken to pardon Affligio's unpaid debt."

Haydn inwardly cringed. That meant poor Fugger had been induced by His Majesty to take a loss on the entire amount. No doubt, he had received property or mining rights somewhere within the Empire to compensate him for his troubles.

"And the existing partners?" he asked.

"Have been recompensed—or will be shortly, His Majesty promises." Smiling broadly, Christian perched himself beside the wig boxes on the table by the wall. "And I am to take charge as impresario. And Karl—" He turned to the young assistant, who had turned a warm shade of red as his gaze drifted toward Haydn.

"Will be returning to Eszterháza with us as His Serene Highness Prince Nikolaus's librettist," Haydn informed them. He turned to Karl. "The position is yours if you wish to have it. I have no hesitation in making the offer. And you will be richly rewarded if you take it."

Taken aback by this good news, Karl could do no more than mutely nod.

"I see I am about to lose a valuable assistant," Christian said, but the bass had a good-natured grin on his face.

The smile faded, replaced by a rueful expression, as he turned to the Kapellmeister.

"I wish to thank you, Herr Haydn." He clasped his hands together. "Truthfully, I did not think any good would come either of your taking over Affligio's duties or of your meddling—at least that's how I regarded it. But were it not for you, bitterness and strife would've reigned among us. And the Burgtheater would have been forced to close down."

Haydn acknowledged the singer's thanks with a deprecating smile and shrug. He had done no more than any other God-fearing individual would have.

The bass was not done speaking, however. He shook his head gravely. "I still cannot believe Donna killed her husband and Affligio. I don't say Affligio didn't get what was coming to him. But whatever did Gregorio do to deserve such evil?"

Papa Keller who had made himself comfortable upon one of the chairs in the room leaned forward. "How came you to suspect her, Sepperl? She has always seemed such a gracious woman. Far easier to believe that Loretta Renier might dispose of another than to believe Donna Oliveri would do such a thing."

"Yes." Christian turned his curious gaze toward the Kapellmeister. "What made you suspect her?"

"Well." Haydn walked back around the desk and took his seat, marshaling his thoughts as he did so. "I had not considered her to be involved in the matter at all until I learned that it was she whom Fräulein Renier had confided in."

He succinctly recounted the details.

"It was Frau Oliveri who had made Affligio's murder look like a stabbing. It seemed only reasonable to suppose that it was she who ensured the Archbishop was here to see a mysterious man leaving by the back-stairs. Expecting to see Leopold Mozart, that is exactly whom His Grace saw."

"She pretended to be me." Karl was understandably outraged. "I cannot believe she would do something like that."

Haydn turned to the man. "I doubt her intention was to cast suspicion upon you. It was a convenient disguise, nothing more." He took a deep breath, attempting to find the words to discreetly explain the rest.

"His Grace was not happy about an employee of his taking on a position at court—without his permission at that. Affligio was to persuade Leopold—by word and deed—that returning to Salzburg would be the better option. The only person other than Affligio who knew of the arrangement was his partner."

"And it was his partner as well," Karl chimed in, "who knew about the prop knife and its working."

"Indeed!" Haydn nodded. "And that was another thing. Everyone had said, Gregorio had categorically refused to join in Affligio's venture. Yet, Affligio's ledgers showed him to be a partner."

"A clear indication he was falsifying the books," Christian immediately responded. "Gregorio had too much sense—God rest his soul—to give Affligio any money. I suppose that was why Affligio pursued Donna."

Haydn nodded. "Duped into thinking he loved her, she was willing to kill her husband. But once she had given Affligio her money, he lost all interest in her."

"And began pursuing Loretta Renier," Papa Keller said. "Small wonder, Frau Oliveri was incensed."

"Once I began considering her to be the mysterious partner," Haydn said, "everything else fell into place. Her acting skills are tremendous, and she is able to impersonate a man—albeit not for long. Everyone who met her 'Count Kohary' considered him a womanly individual and commented on the quality of his voice."

He absently fingered the pages of Karl's libretto. "Had Affligio's ledgers been truthful, one would have to count Gregorio Oliveri his first partner. But the actual Count Kohary had told us Affligio's first partner was a woman. If it was not Gregorio, it would have to be Donna."

Comprehension dawned on Christian's heavy features. "And then you noticed her contract?" When Haydn nodded, he continued, "I can hardly believe Affligio meant to get rid of her rather than Loretta Renier."

"A fool's move," Papa Keller declared. "I thought the man had more sense than that!"

Haydn smiled. "He was duped by Fräulein Renier just as he himself had deceived Frau Oliveri. She was merely toying with him to keep her position." He forbore to mention that it was the Emperor himself who had counseled Loretta Renier in that plan. Or so the soprano had said.

"We should've known it was Frau Oliveri from the moment Giulietta's handkerchief appeared where it did," Karl said, grimacing wryly. "The rehearsal broke that Sunday right after Giulietta hands her kerchief to Romeo."

"True enough," Haydn agreed. "Fräulein Renier had no opportunity to retrieve the fabric. I myself had wondered how it had found its way outside the back entrance."

With a grunt, Christian hoisted himself off his perch.

"I feel bad about yelling at the poor woman. But she would try the patience of a saint! I shall have to find a way to rid myself of her once the season is over."

He turned to Papa Keller. "Come with me, old man. The new impresario has no intentions of keeping his suppliers waiting for their money. You will be paid immediately."

Papa Keller was about to follow the bass when Karl stopped them. "There is one other matter, however. We need another singer." He looked from Christian to Haydn. "To take Frau Oliveri's place, of course."

"Dear Lord, I had not thought of that." Christian's features were wreathed in dismay as he looked helplessly at Haydn. "Can the Prince spare one of his singers?"

"I doubt it." Haydn shook his head. "But never fear. My brother Michael's wife is an excellent soprano."

"She will do it? She will join us for a short time?"

"I imagine she might," Haydn responded dryly. "Michael owes me a favor."

The men were about to leave when there was yet another interruption. A portly individual entered the room followed by a taller man and a young boy.

<hr>

"Joseph!" Michael barely acknowledged the other men in the room. "I have brought Leopold and Wolferl. They wish to convey their thanks to you. Had you not found Affligio's killer, Leopold would've been forced to live the rest of his life under the weight of suspicion."

Leopold—his face shaved, dressed in a fresh suit of clothes and a new wig—came forward with both hands outstretched. "I hardly know what to say, Herr Haydn. You have done more than save my life. You have restored my reputation to me. Neither word nor gesture can sufficiently express my gratitude."

"I am grateful as well." Wolferl swaggered in and greeted the men with an insolent grin. "And we would ask one favor more."

"It is his opera," Leopold said, his hands clasped together as though he were praying. "The boy is so eager to have it performed in Vienna, Herr Haydn. If something can be done . . ."

"It is not Herr Haydn's decision anymore," Christian informed the Mozarts brusquely before Haydn could reply. "I am the new impresario, and I will not under any circumstances have the work performed."

He lowered his head to regard Wolferl and continued in a gentler tone. "Your music is incomparable, my boy. But the work lacks dramatic interest. And without drama, it will surely fail. You will be the laughing stock of the entire city. And your career—such as it is—will be over."

The words seemed to deflate Wolferl, and his dismayed blue eyes sought Haydn's gaze. "What would you advise, Herr Haydn?"

Haydn smiled. "I would advise listening to those more experienced in the matter than you. Work with singers, learn from men such as Herr Steiner, and if it is your ambition to be the greatest composer of opera the world has ever seen, I have no doubt you will achieve it. You have the potential, but you are not ready yet."

He swiveled around to face Michael. "And Michael, should you still wish to thank me, there is one kindness I would greatly appreciate."

THE END

Want more **Haydn Mysteries**? Visit NTUSTIN.COM/BOOKS. Sign up to **get two complimentary Mystery Anthologies**—one featuring your favorite eighteenth-century sleuth and the other set in California.

And, while you're waiting for the next Haydn Mystery, why not try the **Celine Skye Psychic Mysteries**? If you enjoy **art heists laced with psychic detection and suspense**, you'll love this series as well.

Read an Excerpt Or Grab Your Copy From NTUSTIN.COM/BOOKS!

Author's Note

How much of this story is based in historical fact? Quite a bit, as it happens. Giuseppe Affligio (1719-87) was impresario of the two opera theaters in Vienna from 1767 to 1770. Affligio leased the properties from the Emperor, which meant that it was the impresario rather than the court that took care of all expenses pertaining to opera production. This entitled the impresario to all the profits. The court, however, attended performances free of cost.

Now, Prince Kaunitz, State Chancellor of the Habsburg Empire, had persuaded Affligio to invite some French performers to Vienna. Believe it or not, these performers set Affligio back a mind-boggling 70,000 gulden a year. Unfortunately for Affligio, the performers weren't quite the draw he'd been led to believe they'd be. The poor impresario found himself in debt and in desperate need of productions that would be a sure thing.

It was under these circumstances in January 1768 that Leopold first conceived the idea of having his prodigiously gifted son write and conduct an opera. Convinced that a cabal of jealous musicians in Vienna was determined not to recognize his son's gifts, Leopold decided an opera would be just the thing to make believers of every doubting Thomas in the city.

It was Emperor Joseph who unwittingly gave Leopold the idea. His Majesty had asked the young Wolfgang Mozart whether he wouldn't like to write and conduct an opera. What boy would've replied in the negative? Certainly, not Wolferl!

So Wolfgang wrote an opera—not an *opera seria*; his father disparagingly said that only *opera buffa* was appreciated in Vienna. But an opera is an opera, and the Mozarts were quite content with Affligio's offer of a hundred ducats for the work.

But despite Leopold's urgent proddings, Affligio never seemed able to commit to a date for the performance. Affligio, according to Leopold's letters, blamed the singers, "they were both unwilling and unable to perform it," while the singers blamed the impresario, "he had said [to them that] he would not perform it. . ."

Meanwhile—and herein lay the rub as far as Leopold was concerned—the promised 100 ducats was still not forthcoming. A heated confrontation ensued, in the course of which, Affligio made the "most scandalously unkind remark" to Leopold:

If I wanted to see the boy prostituted, he would ensure that the opera was booed and laughed off the stage.

Accusing a father of prostituting his child is a serious charge. One that I—as a mystery writer—could certainly see as a very plausible incitement to murder. What if Affligio was found murdered? Wouldn't anyone aware of the dispute—and there were few at the Burgtheater who weren't—assume Leopold was the culprit?

The opera in question was *La finta semplice*. It was never performed—at least not on the Burgtheater stage. And I fear Affligio was right in its estimation—it is terrible. I have watched it.